Friday Calls

A Southern Novel

By E. Vernon F. Glenn

Friday Calls
Copyright © 2018 by E. Vernon F. Glenn

All rights reserved. No part of this publication may be reproduced, distributed, or transmitted in any form or by any means, including photocopying, recording, or other electronic or mechanical methods, without the prior written permission of the publisher, except in the case of brief quotations embodied in critical reviews and certain other noncommercial uses permitted by copyright law.

This work is dedicated to:
M.A.C.—for so much and so much more
Mark and Sam and C.L.G.—for the gift of time
All my parents and family—for the gift of constancy

The legendary sports writer Red Smith was once asked if it was difficult writing four, sometimes five, columns a week. He replied drily, "Why, no. You simply sit down at the typewriter, open your veins and bleed."

A renowned writer of precise history once asked a renowned editor of contemporary fiction, "Fiction writers never have to leave their desks, do they?"

The editor without looking up answered, "Well, no. Except for one thing."

"What's that?"

"They have to get up to vomit."

Acknowledgements

I have dedicated this book to some folks, all of whom provided persistent, kind encouragement and who have all been very patient with me.

But there are a couple of others to whom I need to take a bow towards.

My editor Alice Osborn in Raleigh has gently pushed and prodded me along and she has culled my mishmash until it really does look and read like a book. She is so talented and I appreciate her help so much.

Of course, were it not for Formatter Par Excellence Deborah Bradseth, whatever work I and Alice have thus far accomplished would still be flopping uselessly incomplete.

I have had the excitement and pleasure of having experienced an amazing life in the bonds of a very remarkable family and they and their stories resonate with me forever.

As the old Armenian merchant's saying goes, "You cannot sell off an empty cart." Happily, my cart overflows with a never-ending cornucopia. And will.

A special tribute to my late daddy, The Big Yum Yum, Douglas Dillard. He gave me my first grown-up books to read. They were Cornelius Ryan's *The Longest Day* and Richard McKenna's *The Sand Pebbles*. He threw me into the deep end of the word pool when I was but ten years old and we swam together there for fifty-five fascinating years.

Along the way, I have been able to do so much and experience so much and to all of those people and characters I have met and dealt with through these years, I am in an eternal debt.

Lastly, as of this day, I have dear and close friends, so many lovely ladies and good gentlemen, who have said enthusiastically and sincerely, "Hurry up and get it done! I want to read it!" That's as good a spur as any for book writing. A big tip of the hat is in order to my good friend Amanda Kyser who helped drag me across the finish line.

So, here it is and there will be more to come. I am beyond grateful for everyone and everything.

As we lawyers often say, we are now adjourned sine die. I promise it won't be long.

Contents

Prologue		xi
Chapter One	Sporting	1
Chapter Two	Service	14
Chapter Three	Rise	18
Chapter Four	Kenny and PeeWee	24
Chapter Five	Beginnings	39
Chapter Six	Culture	45
Chapter Seven	Arm Candy	48
Chapter Eight	Milk Run	55
Chapter Nine	Vice	59
Chapter Ten	Pleasure	66
Chapter Eleven	The Boiling	70
Chapter Twelve	Over the Edge	80
Chapter Thirteen	Deeds Done	89
Chapter Fourteen	Lost and Found	97
Chapter Fifteen	Trails	105
Chapter Sixteen	Deliveries	119
Chapter Seventeen	Cleaning Up	126
Chapter Eighteen	Finishings	136
Chapter Nineteen	New News and Old	142
Chapter Twenty	Comings and Goings	155
Chapter Twenty-One	Plantings	183
Chapter Twenty-Two	Lawyering	202
Chapter Twenty-Three	Court Room	218
Chapter Twenty-Four	On Go	258
Chapter Twenty-Five	Showtime	268
Epilogue		285
Author's Note		287

Prologue

"Southern Serves the South." And it did that night.

It was the regular Friday to Saturday run down to Georgia and back.

Engineer H.E. Knight sat high in the right seat of Southern Railroad's double diesel large pull passenger, rolling out of the nation's capital. The weather was mild; dark had fallen, and as he crooked his elbow on the sill opening, he could see the moon rise and feel the wind push by.

His fireman, Jenkins Gordon, sat to his right, quiet, jostling, and swaying as the big train moved powerfully along. Knight gently held his control throttle, his hand lightly shaking as the giant horsepowers surged through the steel of the lead engine into his palms and fingers.

Every plate, seal, bolt, and screw hummed and vibrated, and the beer in their bottles sloshed and bubbled. The extras in the crate at their feet clinked and tapped.

Gordon asked, "Knight, you all right?"

Knight replied, "Just fine, thank you; and you?"

Gordon smiled in the dark dim of the platform and nodded slightly.

And on they went.

They pulled 14 passenger cars, Pullmans, and a caboose. The whole stick, including engines, weighed many, many tons. Running down through Virginia and the Carolinas, they curved their way first south and then west. They had made stops in Richmond, Petersburg, Raleigh, and Durham, and were now headed into Greensboro, Charlotte, Spartanburg, Greenville, and on into the original Terminus, then Marthasville, and now Atlanta. Their conductor was Mr. A.P. Kevin, and he too was an old-timer on this coveted milk run.

Mr. Kevin had come up earlier from his ticket taking and sat silently on a jump seat behind the engineer's seat, pulling quickly on a couple of bottles until they were emptied. He never spoke much—just hummed and sighed and grunted.

These were senior railroad company men on a schedule and their time was tight, but there is still an opportunity or two for some quick and satisfying leisure within their ordering clocks.

One of those is a quick stop at the legendary Green's Supper Club out on the far eastern fringe of Greensboro, in the county north of the city. The club sits 50 yards from the tracks and thus makes itself nicely available for off-the-books pickups and deliveries from the great trains that pass through.

Green's is no ordinary place. Legendary entertainers raucously regaled its high-toned clientele—from Moms Mabley to Redd Foxx to Brother Dave Gardner—while all drank the best whiskey, ate the best Kansas City steaks and gulf oysters, smoked Cuban cigars, and often availed themselves between the Egyptian sheets of the cozy motor court cabins that arched in a semi-circle just off from the club, bar, and restaurant. Of course, Green's paid protection to the Guilford County Sheriff's Department and the local district North Carolina Highway Patrol—and she was frequented by local officials and constabulary of all stripes. A lot of things happened at Green's.

About 45 minutes before, they had slipped a stop in there, dropped off a few passengers—some couples, some not yet—whom they would pick up on the return trip to hand off some turtle soup and steaks sent down from D.C. A couple of club porters came out, took the crates of provisions, and directed the new guests in the right direction. As the big engine idled, they handed up some fine wax paper-wrapped ham sandwiches and a half-case of Miller Hi-Life to the men in the engine. The levers were pushed slowly forward, and the wheels turned again, steam screeching and hissing as the cars lurched into synchronization. They were ten minutes off schedule, but they would make that up neatly and nicely in the good, clear night.

Chapter One

Sporting

Archer Glenn is a good-looking man in an angelic, cherubic sort of way. Dark-haired, medium build, and charming—people like him. He is a businessman, and it was often said in great approbation of him, "Hell! He could sell snowballs to Eskimos!"

He works hard and effectively. He helped grow the family company in Winston-Salem, North Carolina, and had become quite a fine expert on transportation and logistics and the intricacies of bulk hauling since leaving the university early at the behest of his two older brothers.

He has a lovely, cheerful wife from a family of high status. They have two daughters living in a home of classic, understated Georgian elegance. They have servants. He has friends who are his peers. He plays a fine game of golf.

He is finishing a good week of work and is straightening his desk for Monday's renewals. He put a few papers and files and folders in his briefcase for some Sunday afternoon reading after church and a brisk 18 holes. He is, as always, running just a little bit late.

Carolina is playing Georgia tomorrow afternoon, and the outlook is exciting and promising. The Tar Heels had pasted the detested Wolfpack of N.C. State just last weekend and while Georgia had rolled over the sacrificial lamb of George Washington in their season opener, the game is in Kenan Stadium, a sellout is expected, and the weather expects to be beautiful. And later tonight, there is a house party of a few like-minded fellows and Heel fans at Charlie May's farm, out in the country near Chapel Hill, where good liquor will be drunk, bawdy stories and tales will be told, business will be discussed, fine food will be served, and the music will play and play.

Just before leaving the office, Archer asks his secretary, Miss Sue Simpson, to get Harry down at City Beverage on the phone.

She buzzes him in a few seconds, telling him through the intercom that Harry is on the line. Archer picks up.

"Hey, Harry."

"Hey, Archer, how you doin'?"

"Fine, Harry. Thank you for asking. I need to be quick here. What kind of line you got on Carolina-Georgia tomorrow?'

"Arch, lemme see here—yep—Dawgs giving seven and a half."

"Damn, Harry, can't you push that half-point again to eight?"

"Arch, can't—all you Tar Heels ain't pushing that thing on along the way the UGA crowd is."

Archer pauses, laughs, sighs, and says, "Okay, I'll take the Heels for a small stack and get the seven and a half."

"Got it. Please make sure you write it down now."

"Done. Harry, I'll call tomorrow evening about the Redskins-Lions."

Archer cradles the receiver, grabs his briefcase, looks his neat office over, goes out the door, down the hall, and tells Miss Simpson to have a good evening.

She looks up over her horn-rimmed glasses and smiles, her eternal burning Camel hanging from her bright red lips, and says, "You too. Go Heels!"

* * *

Bo Diddley shrugs his shoulders, slides them into his sleek, black, silk jacket with the red piping, glancing rapidly once, and then twice, at his set of gold chains and juju roots in the cheap, full-length mirror hung on the back of the door. He pauses, then hisses through his perfectly straight white false teeth, "Bo! You good-looking son of a bitch!" He is well-pleased. Bo smiles again at the mirror, snapping his lapels. He opens the door and steps out toward the coming night.

* * *

Friday Calls

Kenny's head is fighting the battle of alcohol, Mary Jane, errands to be run, the need for quick hands, keeping track, and staying smart. It is like going to a meeting. He knows he needs saving, but is hoping the plate will be passed to him this time around. He shakes at the blur and keeps moving toward the lights. Pee Wee keeps hissing, "C'mon. C'mon, man."

* * *

Friday is hot.

Harry Davis's desk is a trash pile surrounded by papers. The telephone on it begins to ring, while Harry looks at it, squints, and wrinkles his nose as though something smells rotten. He picks up the receiver and cradles it between his neck and hunched shoulder, almost far enough away from his mouth and mind so as to keep the stench at bay, but knows that won't work, not in his line of cheap business. He opens his mouth and inhales a gasp.

"Ahhh...City Beverage. Uhm...hey, Frank. Where you been? You got an order for me?"

Harry fishes a pencil out from the mess, rolls his sagging and squeaking chair across the warped linoleum, leans forward, and clears a path with his elbow, finding a clearing and a pad. He begins to write deliberately and neatly. Harry has always had beautiful handwriting. It had been struck into him early. He quietly repeats the received order.

"Six cases of Miller High-Life. One case of Coca-Cola. One case of Canada Dry ginger ale, eight-fifths of Jim Beam, and four-fifths of Haig & Haig."

He reads it back. "Anything else?"

Then, "I'll have Big Rise's boy bring it over by three o'clock."

He hangs up.

Big Rise trundles by, a mammoth woman. She is damp-sweeping dust and their offspring bunnies with a mop that's tiny in her hands.

"You want me to be calling him, Mr. Harry?"

"Naw, Bing'll do it. He's gotta put the orders together."

"Uh-huh." And around the stacks of boxes, crates, and cartons she goes, rattling, banging and bumping, all while humming and singing low snatches of Etta James and the Sunday hymnal, interspersed with her unintelligible mumbles.

Harry's knees are jammed tight in the keyhole of his desk, surrounded and encased in his dusty work sarcophagus of cardboard boxes and wooden crates stacked well above the level of his bald, mottled, and moldy head. He looks out the big, plate glass window, beyond the yellowed and half-cocked venetian blinds and the bigger, peeling CITY BEVERAGE lettering, spreading its crescent shadow across the room with the high sun of the early autumn afternoon. The sun is still too bright to look at. It hurts the eyes. He is a long, knotty, taciturn man—unpleasant and sour. He is a man of many low talents and skills that are sought by others, and he is an equal-opportunity provider, as long as the money, safety, and the profit margins of both maintain their three-legged stool equilibrium.

He calls out flatly, "Bing. Bing. Get in here."

Harry's youngest son, a human cross between a gnome and a cantaloupe, appears in the doorway leading from the office to the front counter. Always anxious, he says, "Yessir?"

Harry hands him the order sheet and tells him to get Mr. Archer Glenn's order together and to have Homer make the delivery a little after three o'clock.

Bing says, "Yessir," and wanders back into the storage spaces to huff and pull the order together, placing the boxes behind the counter shelves which also holds a sawed-off 12-gauge and a small revolver secured in place under the cash register with electrician's tape.

With the Glenn order prepared, Bing dials the counter phone and says, "Hey. It's Bing. Tell Homer he needs to come on by here now and get an order for delivery."

There is a small pause. Bing continues, "Fine, but he ought to be through mowing that yard soon. Get him on over here. Okay? What...aw, hell. I'll just call the booth over there."

Bing hangs up and speaks toward the office where Harry still sits, staring out the window. "I'm on it, Daddy. He'll be here in a little bit."

Harry grunts.

The phone on Harry's desk rings again. He answers it.

"Hey. What do you need for the weekend?"

He writes again. The order is a large batch of cheap vodka, some good corn and lots of cheap wine. It is exactly 15 cases.

He asks, "Who is picking up? Who is bringing the money?"

The receiver garbles. Harry nods, says okay, and hangs up.

"Bing. Bing."

"Yessir?"

"That was Bo. Here's his order for the weekend. Get it together. Homer is picking it up. He'll have cash. Bring him in here to see me when he gets here."

"Well, I guess he can pick up both."

"Yes." He winces as he speaks to his boy.

Bing goes about his tasks.

The door opens in the front, its tinny bell ringing.

A man steps in, taking off his hat and wiping sweat off his face with his hand.

"Harry? Harry? Bing?"

Bing comes back out to the counter, passing Harry as he's slowly starting to stand.

"Oh, hey, Mr. Siddon. Daddy, Mr. Syd is here."

"Send him back."

Syd Siddon lifts the counter door and walks through and back to Harry's desk. He sits down in a ladder kitchen chair and the two men grunt to each other in greeting. Syd is a tall, nondescript, sallow fellow, lanky with a big Adam's apple and an eternal stubble. His hands are large with fingernails thicker and harder than diamonds. He smokes all the time. He carries a small pistol, just enough not to show but always just enough to be good to go. He and Harry have known each other a long time. Their grunts and nods are expansive in meaning and import.

"You got the lines?" asks Harry.

"Yes."

Syd further gangles into his seat, folding his lankiness into the confines of the sagging webbing. He raises one haunch and reaches to his elevated butt pocket to pull a folded notebook out with his left hand. With his right, he produces a short, yellow pencil. He says, "Harry, you ready?" Harry nods and picks up his pencil too.

And the weekly liturgy begins.

It is no different than church in its solemnity and single-mindedness.

It is quiet in the room.
Lord have mercy.
Christ have mercy.
Lord have mercy.

Syd, in monotone, begins the readings. "Game 68 West Virginia giving Furman 13."

Harry intones his echo.

"Game 70 Auburn giving Vanderbilt 7."

Harry repeats everything precisely each time.

Game 75 Clemson giving Rice 10
Game 79 Virginia Tech giving Davidson 13
Game 81 Duke giving Pittsburgh 7 ½
Game 83 Georgia giving North Carolina 8
Game 84 Georgia Tech giving Florida 14
Game 90 Alabama giving Louisiana State 3
Game 91 Maryland giving Washington & Lee 45
Game 92 Michigan State giving Michigan 10 ½
Game 93 Mississippi giving Kentucky 7
Game 98 Notre Dame giving Indiana 28
Game 108 South Carolina giving The Citadel 17
Game 112 Tennessee giving Mississippi State 13
Game 113 Texas giving Purdue 7
Game 114 Texas A&M giving Texas Tech 14
Game 117 Tulane giving Miami Florida 6 and a half
Game 119 Virginia giving George Washington 21
Game 120 Virginia Military Institute giving Richmond 24
Game 121 Wake Forest giving North Carolina State 10

Here endeth the lesson. A nice, solid, early season 20-game smorgasbord of college gridiron offerings.

They are selective with their offerings. Always keeping things pretty "in the South-centric" along with always a few big, national names. Their clients are that way and it doesn't make sense, especially early in the season, to be floating some obscure Montana-New Mexico sort of thing out there. For something like that to show up in a line request call smacks hard of a tipster service for sure, and there is no good way to adjust a line to create a money balance. Usually such an ask was a one-shot call. They shy away from that. Sometimes the fellow—there were never any ladies calling...never—doing the asking has obviously been drinking more than a little and is taking a flier on something that he doesn't really have any idea about. Now, usually wagers made under the influence are easy money for the house, but they are gentlemanly about the entirety of the business and that includes not taking advantage of a pigeon begging to be broke-necked and plucked. They know who their savvy customers are and they also know which ones are not exactly smart about it all too. They play it straight down the line with everyone.

The rule is whenever one side of the equation or the other got up or down $250, payment is made. A new customer has to establish his bona fides over a period of a few months and that includes introductions, understanding of the procedure, regularity, and constancy and only then is credit established. Harry's computations are The Word, and he is meticulous with them.

Failure to pay up in a timely manner is just a cut off until square. There is a three-strike rule too. If someone fails to make good on time three times, that is it, but it rarely happens. These gentlemen enjoy playing and to be excluded is a badge of shame.

Every new customer is a referral from an established client because otherwise a random call could be from a fisher or an unfriendly. Everyone passed down the ever-lengthening vetting line, the virtual incantation of Harry's reputation and that which is expected of his customers in the business.

There had been a long-time client, a fine businessman and a solid customer, who had died suddenly after a long illness. Harry knew about the illness which incapacitated the fellow, so Harry would, from time to time, call on him and make exchanges when necessary. Harry had been away on business for a week when the fellow passed and did not know about the death.

His son Bing had been taking calls and keeping books. Upon his return, Harry reviewed the books and saw that he needed to go see the gentleman to settle things, which he did.

Arriving at yet another handsome home surrounded by the regular paint of English boxwoods and dogwoods, he rang the doorbell.

A uniformed maid answered, and Harry asked to see Mr. So-and-So.

The servant looking confused and flustered. "Let me get the Missus."

In a few minutes, the lady of the house came to the door.

"Hey, Harry. How are you? She says you want to see Joe." Joe's wife cast her eyes to the floor and then suddenly straighten her back. "Harry, Joe died last week. I guess you didn't hear..." Her voice trailed off.

It was Harry's turn to be flustered. His hat came off his head and was held by his side in respect and deference.

"Oh, oh my. I didn't know. I am so sorry. Please pardon my interruption. I'll be going now. Again, I am so sorry."

A bemused smile came across the widow's face and her eyes sparkled just enough to show.

"Harry, did you come to collect from Joe?" There was no animosity in the question, just pleasantness.

Harry had stepped down the walk a few steps and paused.

"Well...yes, but...never mind. It's not that important. You have much more to deal with. I'll be on my way."

"Harry, please come back here. Don't you know that if you had owed Joe, I'd have known about it and would have been down to see you in a few days?"

"Well, I expect that's so."

"How much did he owe?"

"Well, $290."

"I'll be right back."

And she came back with the cash in just a few minutes.

"It was time to clear out that cigar box under the bed anyway. We square now?"

He smiled and bowed slowly, "Yes, ma'am."

She said, "You know, Harry, Joe always loved his business with you, enjoyed it so much. And y'all have always brought the Coca Colas, ginger ale, beer, and all like clockwork. I know we don't see much of one another, but I am glad I got to tend to that. Thank you. Thank you so much."

Harry said, "No, ma'am, thank you. I'm glad it worked out."

He turned to go and as he went down the walk, she called to him one last time with just a little laughter in her voice.

"Besides, Harry, it wouldn't do for Daddy and Brother to ever know that Joe stiffed you at the end!"

Harry chuckled, waved, and walked on to his car.

Harry never told the story. The lady did, over and over and over again. It became a part of the community, embedded in honor and good humor.

Harry and Syd are bookmakers, always on duty when games are to be played. Syd had been a farmer and still messed with it some. He had a tobacco allotment that he worked a bit—the government paid good money for that—and a truck garden with pole beans, cukes, tomatoes, and corn that he took down to market to make a little cash in the growing months. He also quietly trafficked in small quantities of stolen goods—usually TV sets and record players, maybe a loose pistol every now and then. But his cash crop is college and professional sports with their betting lines and folks' general, consistent, and hot need to gamble.

Syd had gotten into the business when he met a friend of his daddy's, also a farmer, who was in the children's blankets and pajama business. The fellow was an ex-Marine; a tough guy, loud and boisterous and very successful with a couple of big mills that loomed the stuff out and sent it all over the country and the world.

Syd had taken some fresh vegetables out to Mr. Crossingham's big house in the country late one afternoon and as Mr. Crossingham had just returned from a successful visit to Las Vegas. He was half-drunk, and he greeted Syd with the happy crowing of a strutting victor, gleefully cooing over his good fortune at the tables and in the sports book. He showed, no waved, at young Syd, a neatly held stack of one hundred dollar bills.

"Goddamn, son! How's your daddy and mamma? Quite a few days! Come home with $2200 clean, got drunk, had a ball, got laid, fed, comped, and flown. Can't beat it with a stick! Ha! Ha! And picked up a thousand of this on those sorry-ass Redskins! They covered for once! How you doin'? Those are some pretty 'maters! Come over here—do you want a drink? Sure you do!"

Now in these days, Syd, like almost all boys and men with a pulse in the South worshipped at the altar of the gridiron and in the transepts of North

Carolina, Duke, and the Washington Redskins. They were the Holy Grail of their days and while basketball was all right in the cold country gyms and baseball was perfect for the slow heat of the growing summer, football was King.

The Redskins were perpetually awful—slow afoot, basically minimally skilled, and not very strong. But they were the only game televised on Sundays, unless they were on the road west of the Mississippi, and then you got the hated Eagles or the snotty Giants. Syd and his family and friends watched the Redskins—the team was always featured in the local newspaper with articles about this player and that. It was also more than fair to say that the Redskins' owner, a towering racist, George Preston Marshall, despised the coloreds, the nigras, and would not for one moment countenance drafting such a player of color or having one on the team. Perhaps because of his goal to maintain a self-pleasing team of racial purity the Skins were always in a talent deficit.

The idea that one could make money off the sorry-assed, sad-sacked, nonetheless beloved Washington Redskins glimmered in Syd's mind. Being opportunistic, albeit provincial, he took the proffered glass from Mr. Ed Crossingham. "Mr. Crossy, how do you gamble on the Redskins and make money?" It had already occurred to him that one could lose money, too. That gave him pause.

And thus, began the education. "Take a seat, son, and I'll give you the *Reader's Digest* version."

"First off, it's not just the 'Skins. It's everything—Chapel Hill, Duke, Wake Forest, Tennessee, 'Skins, Eagles, Giants, Colts, basketball, college, pro, baseball—plenty of action for plenty of people." He grinned and continued, "Let's say you have a hundred dollars." The amount waffled Syd's mind. "You want to bet a game. Okay, let's say the Eagles are six-and-a-half point favorites over the Redskins. Which side do you take? If you bet your money on the Eagles, that means to win, the Eagles gotta win by seven. No such thing as a half-point in a final score. If you take the 'Skins, they gotta either win outright or lose by six or less. And if, let's say the betting line was seven with no half point hanging around on either side of it, and the game ended with the Eagles winning by exactly seven, that's what we call a push and nobody wins or loses. The bet is evened and thus canceled."

Syd's mind wrestled with this.

"If you bet a hundred and win, you win a hundred. If you lose, you lose a hundred and ten."

Syd's mind torqued a bit.

Crossy saw his perplexed frown and then its double-down.

"Son, the extra ten dollars is the price paid to the bookmaker for the loss. It is the price of losing. It's called the commission or juice or vig or vigorish. Sometimes it's called the steam."

Syd nodded deliberately. Mr. Crossingham took note of Syd's sponge-like interest. "Syd, I'm not great at it but I ain't bad either. Want to learn a little from me? I think I can teach you some and even maybe stake you some to start. We need a good bookmaker around here so we don't have to do so much long distance telephone business with Charlotte and more faraway places. I ain't much interested in making a gambler. I'm way more interested in building a bookmaker. More money, more safety there— 'cept for the law and we'll talk about that later—he tossed it off like a penny candy wrapper. What do you say?"

Syd sat still for a few seconds, took a big swallow from his sweating glass, looked up and nodded.

"Yessir, this farming thing gets right tiresome."

They shook hands and another dawn came.

Syd would get the betting lines over the telephone—in an almost always different telephone booth—safer—from a fellow in Charlotte who in turn would get them from a fellow in Richmond or Atlanta and so on. Syd would disseminate them to his customers up in the Mount Airy part of the world and then either call them over to Harry or drive them down if he needed to go to the bank, do some shopping or make other visits.

Syd had gone into the city one day years and years ago to do a little business. He needed to go to the big bank and cash a few checks to round up enough smaller bills—fifties and hundreds—for the expected traffic of the coming month. By simple chance, while in one of the teller lines in the cavernous main lobby, his name was called by a fellow in the next line. The guy was one of his clients from the mountains.

"Syd, hey, how you doin'? What brings you to town?" the man asked quietly.

The man was a good customer, regular and faithful to paying up and getting paid. He always paid attention when the lines were read out, never tipped his hand as to which team or school he was interested in (those that did always got a higher price—their beloved and obvious leanings often helped pad the weekend's take...it was a hard enough business without betting with your heart instead of your head.)

He was a businessman, had a nice tie and suit on and a newspaper rolled up under his arm. He said he was there to get a check cashed.

Syd explained he was getting ready for the weeks ahead. The fellow nodded and Syd asked, "By the way, do you know your way around here? Is there a good beer and liquor store around here where I can do a little discount business, if you know what I mean...?"

"Yeah, sure. Sure is. Go back down 5th Street out here and hook left down little hill onto Burke Street. In the first block on right, you'll see a sign sayin' 'City Beverage'." That's the place. Ask for Harry Davis. Tell him Graham Scott suggested you drop in."

He did. A younger boy was at the counter by the name of Bing. Syd introduced himself. Bing went to the back. Harry Davis came forth and asked Syd to come back to his desk. Proper introductions were made and contacts established. Mr. Scott's name was solid barter. They smoked. Syd wanted to know about picking up some "discount" alcohol from time to time.

Davis allowed that that was something that could probably be worked out and such could include beer, whiskey, even some wine and 'shine. Of course, pricing depended on quantity and quality and from time to time, there might be other "items" that could be had.

It appeared that the two men, one country and the other small town, were immediately comfortable and even pointedly casual and at a quiet, to-the-point ease with one another.

Syd paused and then further explained that he was a farmer by trade but that he had well evolved into someone who helped those who had an interest in athletic contests. He thought if he could provide his customers with some refreshment when they came by to settle accounts, it would be a pleasant bonus when they collected and a comforting balm when they paid.

Davis, always fine and accurate with numbers and ciphering, both with pencil in hand and within the cavernous labyrinth of his roiling mind, felt his eyes open just a tad more for a few seconds, his curiosity and instincts aroused.

"Are you speaking of betting on games, sporting events and the like, Mr. Siddon?"

"Please call me Syd. Yes, I am."

"Thank you. Please call me Harry." He paused, looked down, looked up. "I am interested in learning more about that. My late father who started this place a long time ago loved to bet the ponies. I was always curious but never quite got around to learning much about it. There is a demand for gambling, betting, wagering—however you'd like to put it, I think, in this town. It's growing. It's a good cash town and the people with some extra money are getting larger and folks want to recreate more now than they even recently did."

Syd nodded.

Harry continued, "It occurs to me that you need to come this way, come down the mountain from time to time, that I have something that I can help you with and you...well, you have something that you might be able to help me with...I have a lot of customers who are business and banking people, men who belong to golf and downtown clubs...I think more than a few would be interested..."

Syd realized quickly that Harry's pool of potential customers and clients was of much greater size than his small hill pool. He also realized that Harry was smart, as easily furtive as he was, taciturn and willing to engage in illegal work which helped blanket the tasks.

Syd asked, "So, you'd like to see if we could scratch each other's backs a little?"

Harry looked over the top of his glasses. "Yes, that's one way to put it."

And thus, a small collaboration of vices was birthed.

Chapter Two

Service

Frank Cuthrell is the Major Domo who keeps this place moving. The manager, Frank Johnston, is sweet and gracious and constantly fumbles, but Frank Cuthrell is sweet and gracious and effective. He runs the joint.

Frank stands next to the telephone box in the employees' locker room at Old Town Club. Because it is a fine country club, there was no need for any signage so terse as to say "Colored."

It is a darkened room with two small light bulbs laced overhead. Rows of wooden lockers, cubbies with two hooks each, line each side with a common bench running down the center. In the corner is a table with a radio on it, the phone box slotted underneath.

Beyond the main room is a side toilet room with a door, an open sink and mirror for shaving, a small gang shower, a good-sized space with a large ironing table for both uniforms and linens and a shoe shine stand.

The locker room is reached by the back stairs running down from the back of the kitchen, then down a short hall past the members' liquor lockers and club storage.

The radio is eternally set on WAAA, 980 AM, proudly and affectionately known by the coloreds and the whites as, "Triple-A, The Black Spot of Your Dial."

Frank is the maître d', the fixer, the runner, the gang boss, the go-to man, the liaison, the Black Bug, the confidant, the Man. He is fit and of moderate height, always lightly self-effacing with a sweet grin and honeyed laugh, all organized and memorized, dark eyes always scanning, never darting. He keeps a pad and two little golf pencils in his jacket pocket. He makes constant notes just as others breathe, never looking away from his thought or subject.

No one can ever remember seeing him in any other clothing save for his white or black dinner jacket (depending on the season and the time of day), black striped trousers, board-starched white shirt and black bow tie. No one can ever remember seeing him drive to the club or leave the club. It seems he had been there forever, the classiest and most permanent and effective of the regal plastered lions that always stand watch at the entrance to the club's driveway.

Frank had earlier been making the rounds of the men's card room, checking to see if the emerging weekend necessitated extra staff or provisions. Friday's lunches brought forth larger numbers of members and often requests for this and that not offered on the club menu.

The room is a haven of male conviviality with a long bar, maple paneled walls, bookcases, sofas, television sets and plenty of four and six top tables for card games and conversation. All upholstery is red and green leather or similarly colored Scottish tartan wool. Ashtrays, coasters, decks of cards, pencils, pads and stacks of counter checks were everywhere.

Overlooking both the first and the tenth tees and the golf shop and caddy yard tucked in just beyond and between them, the view is back draped with high hardwood forest and the tightly marked fairways running away from the clubhouse.

Today's guests have been large in number, among them captains of industry and banking and law and trucking, to include the local chief of police, an undertaker, the Mayor and a few ne'er do wells who some time ago bounced out of varying levels of schools and jobs and found the men's card room to be their "work" and their "office."

There are always quick card games, some bridge, more often gin rummy or tonk. Some folks eat or munch peanuts. Just about everyone drinks. It is Friday, after all.

Frank is watching; looking over, checking, calibrating needs and wants. These are his people, his charges.

He will exchange nods and looks with his two senior card room lieutenants, Bratcher and Haywood. They know the habits of these people, know their moods and ways.

Mr. Archer Glenn has been playing cards with Mr. J.T. Barnes, Chief Justice Tucker, and Mayor Marshall Kurfees.

The Mayor likes to juice it along slowly as the day passed—just a little bourbon in a sweet iced tea would do on a hot day like today—no reason to rush. He is simple and canny, enjoys the perks and access of elected office, is a yellow-dog Democrat and does as he was told. He thinks being mayor is fun.

The Chief likes cold beer and an egg salad sandwich, two of each, please. He had been a star high school four letter athlete, had gone to seed after walking a beat and then rising to desks.

Glenn and Barnes are peas in a pod, beer and tomato sandwiches, have been lifelong like that and in so many things.

"Hey, Frank, how you? Same pour, same ice topped, please!" Lawyer Phil Whiting, rattles his short glass pleasantly, three successive lemon slices pulped, awaiting one more and always more vodka. Frank nods at Haywood who moves for the pickup and pour like a fine halfback hitting the hole on his way to open field. Whiting has a bassoon voice, always wears a wool suit, even if it's hotter than a well digger's butt in the desert, carries a brilliant mind, a huge capacity for alcohol and is hung like a Madrid stud bull.

Purvis "Never Nervous" Farrior wanders in from the tennis courts with Jimmy "Ray Don" Holt up from the golf shop. Farrior is always fidgety and jumpy in a sweet way. Holt drawls so matter-of-factly, it is said he can freeze time. They sit on a couch, shell peanuts, and drink beer.

Ralph Hanes asks Bratcher for a hamburger, medium, and a Bloody Mary. The most patrician man in the room, his dignity is Olympian as is his ability to make money. He is not imperious, but actually quite funny as are they all. Certainly a cast of characters.

Vernon Ferrell comes in from the locker room with Bobby S.D. Freunde.

Ferrell is old line top to bottom real estate, had started as a kid collecting rents for his daddy from ramshackle rent houses in the worst parts of town, moved up the line to construction and mill town projects, commercial development, residential, land deals, timber, you name it.

He is a fastidious dandy of a dresser and a close observer of his and other's shoes.

S.D.'s family had been properly and expensively burying people in the town from the beginnings of the settlement in the mid-1700s. His by blood Prusso-Germanic work ethic had long ago found the pleasures of skirts and booze, but he is charming, empathetic, sympathetic and deadly good-looking.

Frank sees them, says with a kind smile, "Good afternoon, gents. What may we get for you this fine day?"

They answer and are attended to promptly along with menus.

Tag Montague is sitting with Jigs Willis. Montague is a stockbroker and Willis the head barber at the Hotel Robert E. Lee; the two are close friends. Tag loves to play with money, especially that of other people, and Jigs always liked to cut hair. That's just the way it is. They both enjoy watching the Friday afternoon reel unspool.

They are asked for a drink order, but both demur. Jigs quips, he regularly does, that he has a few more heads to do later that afternoon and would prefer not to nick early before nipping later. Tag snorts in the appreciation of the familiar and says to no one in particular, "No, thanks. I'm driving..."

And there are others of course, walking in and out, some playing golf or tennis, some leaving work early, some going back to their offices, some off for the weekend. They are all so different and yet so homogenous. Everyone brings something to the party but they are all always—or almost always—on script, singing from the same page of the hymnal.

Frank Cuthrell looks over his crowded room, winks at his old retainers, short bows to all and to none and goes back up the stairs.

Archer Glenn gives Frank a piece of paper with an order on it for delivery later in the day. Frank knows this drill, and he then passes Mr. Archer Glenn's order to Harry. Frank and Harry have known each other for a very long time. Mr. Glenn is going to some sort of get-together over the weekend and is taking an important part of the picnic. Frank now needs to line up the evening's preparations for the Friday night cocktail party and buffet dinner-dance.

He turns the radio back up. Daddy-Oh On The Patio is pattering away. He walks down to the sink and turns on the hot water and shaves.

Chapter Three

Rise

Her Christian name is Evelina Starlight Peak, but to everyone, she is known as Big Rise. The name came onto her early as she did not just grow as a child; she rose large like biscuits in a skillet. She was big before everybody else was just straining to get to small.

A massive slab of a woman in her mid-thirties, not just fat but big and tall, she has a backside that would put the trunk of a four-holer Buick to shame and a back that could do as an aircraft carrier landing deck in a pinch. She does not walk—she lumbers and at nimble speed too, her head topped by a sprout-topped Afro and her ever-present African scarf. Her forearms are roped, her fists bricks, her legs channel a Steinway. She is a formidable thing.

A smart and sly woman, she speaks in a constant staccato soft voice that has always implored, always explored and always flattered and sought favor.

She had earlier been a line whore for a pimp named Ben—this was before the weight overtook her. She was the poster child for "the bigger the cushion, the better the pushin'" and she was often sought for her "charms" and efficiencies...as she grew larger, Ben put her in charge of a small stick of others. She kept them in line, made the appointments, collected the money and parceled it properly. Ben never found any need to ever punish, chastise or strike her. She was a pro. She was his pro.

Ben William is simply put a bad-ass, mean-ass strong as an ox glowering frightful very smart cat. He can look the bark out of a mean dog. Tall and built like a V, he takes it all in all the time. His hands are enormous and one of his squeezes on a smart-ass's collar bone is always a painful teaching moment. It is said he had beaten the hell out of more than a few and that he has killed a few along the way. No one questions such.

He has his own drink house but it was way away from Bo's flash pit, a quiet little house up behind Happy Hill Gardens in some deep kudzu and thickets. He speaks but a little, communicates more in nods and grunts and gestures, but from time to time, he breaks into a smile and his customers like him as they know he runs a quiet, pleasant, no-nonsense kind of juke-joint, more joint than juke.

Ben had met Rise by way of an introduction from Curt Minor. They were at the bar leaning and drinking and smoking and watching at Gore's Gay 90 club up on Patterson Avenue behind the tobacco factories. Rise and some other more rounded, supple ladies had come in and were quietly giggling and fanning themselves at the other end of the counter, glancing about with the eyes that beckoned.

Ben had known Minor for years and their manner mirrored one another. Both were crooked and tough in solid ways and there was a trust that came from being fair competitors and respecters of turf. Both are good business people.

Minor knew Rise through her little brother Kenny who had pulled many odd and wiggly jobs for Curt and Bo Diddley. Rise worked from time to time over at Curt's place. She could keep an eye out for Kenny whom she knew Bo fucked and messed too hard with from time to time, could make some decent extra scratch, and she also could keep an eye on that strutting fool Bo Diddley. Ben had always cautioned Rise to be careful with Bo because he was flashy and stupid, a threatening combination, and he would sooner rather than later fuck it all up.

Ben knew and Curt Minor shared his knowledge that Bo was at the front of the house, was good for business with his gandy-dancer, clown-act ways and though Ben does not care for Bo any more than a pig would care for a book, he really did not-care either. He liked Minor and he stayed out of it.

Minor saw Rise's eyes in the mirror behind the bottles. He said sideways to Ben, "You want to meet a gal?" Ben nodded.

Curt called, "Hey, Rise, wanna meet my friend Ben?"

Rise said, cut staring down the line at them, "Yes, I would."

She strolled to the men, held out her hand to Ben and as she looked at Curt, laughed and said, "Now that's a man that wears my size."

They hit it off, learned to be helpful to one another in the world of nature's business and in the process, became close companions with one another, moving in and out of the various worlds they chose to dig in.

She was intuitively bright, a realist, and also was a fine street runner, deliverer of stolen goods, small packages and weapons, and a good street banker, but she truly excelled as a check booster.

Ben wanted to become more deeply expansive in this graft. Single shot, random hit and runs were haphazard and sloppy. So he had Rise watch such workings and after a few passes, she suggested a more complete and sophisticated approach. It meant adding a couple of extra people, but all of them were crooked any way so their complicity and felicity were more rather than less assured.

One of their lead runners was a grasshopper of a man by the name of Pete Miller. Miller's handle was "Kaboom" because he was smart, reckless, and one never knew when he might go off. He carried a small pistol and all times was jangling about, twitching and humming and often all in a world unbeknownst to others around him. But he played close attention, was a good soldier and had that innate ability to be seen and then not be seen like that rabbit in that Harvey movie. Miller loved Ben like a slobbering dog. If Ben had said to Miller, "Shit." Miller would have replied with a grin, "How much and how high!" He liked what Ben liked and he did not like what Ben did not like.

Social Security checks always arrived on the first couple of business days of the month. The elderly recipients would slowly fish them from their mailboxes, take them inside and usually wait for a neighbor or family member to take them to the bank for deposit, almost always over the next number of days. There was no urgency to this.

The city was awash in these poor folks in rattletrap houses and clustered public housing mailboxes.

Big Rise implemented a blitzkrieg approach. The mail trucks would be watched as they were loaded at the main post office. The uniformity and color and shape of the Social Security checks stacked in neat rows in the delivery cartons would tell this was the day.

Scouts would follow the trucks and determine the precise routes. Checks were placed in mailboxes, and often times in large groups or in clusters. The driver would sometimes dismount and walk a portion of the route and then drive on.

Diversions were always set up just ahead to distract and divert attention. Fights, bicycle accidents, shouting matches, stumbling drunks, flat tires…the possibilities were endless. Most of the postmen were older, too, and riveted in their ways and routines.

So as all this was going on, the boosters would swiftly tail the prey and boost the Social Security checks from the mailboxes, often times within but a few square blocks sweep up a few hundred at a time. Then Ben and Rise would drive to any number of small loan offices in smaller towns and cities in the area, forge them, hand them to the "ask-me-no-questions-I'll-tell-you-no-lies" clerks and tellers and slip a $20 here and there so no one was then the wiser. Many times, old people didn't report, forgot or if they complained or asked, the postal service's waterlogged response was slow and clumsy.

Rise's scheme worked beautifully for almost a year and was a transferable, portable operation with low, compromised manpower that could work in many areas. Furthermore, it was hugely profitable with fantastic margins and did not involve violence.

And Rise was really good at it. She worked it like a rented mule, plowing and plowing. And, too, it was a federal crime.

Rise's boosting finally got boosted by the Feds, not once but twice.

The first time out, she had a sincere young shave-tail of a court-appointed attorney with true morals the local citizens admired. Since she had no previous bad behaviors, the succor of motherhood and family also elegiacally elevated her to but two notches below a lesser saint. It was also pointed out that she was in a calamitous place in her life and was but a tool of men and forces that overwhelmed and virtually enslaved her in servitude for filthy lucre.

The prosecutor, an apathetic, career drowned, eternal in his Assistant United States Attorney sinecure had nothing very negative to say other than she was the taker of things that did not belong to her and that it had been going on for a while. The deal had been cut so that in return for the guilty plea to one count of invading the province of more than one mailbox—there was no one who had ever seen her do such a thing—and one count of the thievery and misappropriation of Social Security funds—after all, everyone had been made square, a probationary sentence of three years and a small fine representative of mild restitution would be recommended.

The sweet-natured, soft spoken almost to a whisper federal judge, not inclined to put a woman—even one so immense as this one—into a prison on a first offense and with the day's lunch moment imminent, took the legal powder. Rise graciously thanked the judge with a ponderous bow and walked out of the courthouse with her brilliant lawyer.

Predictably, the second busting and go-round about a year later did not have such a gentle end as the first. The facts were incontrovertible; the matter was docketed for first thing in the morning when matters moved with slicing briskness, there was little the same lawyer could say in mitigation. The Assistant United States Attorney was alert to the kill, and thus a quick pelt on his monthly summary chart. There was also a different judge, this one being the stern, cold and severe one who was the local yang to his judicial compatriot's ying down the high-ceiling hallways behind the courtroom.

Thus, Big Rise surgically and efficiently was the recipient of three years in the Federal Correctional Institute for Women in Kentucky and was rendered unto the United States Marshall's office for transport and delivery.

She pulled two-thirds of her time, caused no problems, was given an early release and returned to her hometown. Her parole officer gave her a list of prospective places of employment. One of them was a box and packaging place down near the hospital. She made the obligatory visit, was as bored and disinterested in the prospect of the place as the wan woman she briefly spoke with, but did glean from her that a man who bought supplies from them was looking for someone to do some cleaning and such. She was told it was a place called City Beverage up the hill and the man's name was Harry Davis.

She went up there. A younger man at the counter named Bing got his daddy—after whispering to him that the visitor was the biggest damn woman he had ever seen— who came out to meet her. She told him she was looking for work, had pulled time for boosting in the federal pen and that she knew how to work hard and was generally a pretty nice person. Harry Davis was amazed at her size, appreciated her straightforwardness, and amused simply by the ridiculousness of it all.

He hired her on the spot.

There was a baby girl from an unlovable tryst a few years ago whose support was helped by a man whose blood test made him grudgingly amenable to making more or less regular payments into the clerk's office. The child was tended to by Rise's momma. Rise did not see much of her but when she did, the visit was dotingly brief. Rise's primary interests were Ben, boosting, and beer, and lots of all three.

And too, Rise has a little brother who is also big. Named Homer Kenny Peak, he is tall and very strong, yet all over gently round like the rolled, smooth top of an artillery shell. His voice is soft like a curve, too. He is not bright—more like a dim bulb—and he is sensitive. Kenny does not carry the threat of great big physical violence that so many great big men do.

Rise dotes on him. But he takes instruction well and is very good at raking and lawn mowing and weeding and heavy manual chores. He lives with his sister in a small rental property owned by Ben, over behind some slummy projects, locally called JumpJack Squares in spite of the municipal signage labeling the place Hunting Hills Gardens. No one really expects to see the fox and hounds and the horses and pinks come flying through anytime soon.

Kenny is the fellow who is there if anyone needs anything—The Master of the Job, the Errand, the Task. He works for many people, does many things, knows more than they think he does and keeps his mouth shut.

Chapter Four

Kenny and PeeWee

The screen door to Kenny's wretched doorframe clatters with the slaps-napping knocks.

"Yo, Kenny. Hey, Kenny—Booth be holding a call for you. It's for a delivery. He says hurry up."

Kenny Peak drapes his country ham of an arm off his eyes and slowly torques his slab of a body toward the voice and away from the shabby couch. It is pretty much the same as seeing a building fall in except the opposite. With concentration, he stands and blinks and absentmindedly slips into his shoes.

He walks toward the door where PeeWee wiggles with inquisitive nonchalance. "Can I go? Can I?"

Kenny grunts and gives a "maybe" to walk onto the hot sidewalk, down past the stinking, fly-ridden garbage racks, past the dirt tracked pathed coursings in what was once grass, past the filthy, old scattered toys and rusted swing set, walks about 50 yards passing dead-eyed red brick rotten buildings and the same and the same and walks into the telephone booth not so very well-maintained by the good people at Southern Bell (Why would they? This was dangerous territory where white folk were not welcome and when they were "in country" those same white folk were skittish and scared.).

The receiver swings slowly in the booth. Kenny takes it and puts it to his face. "Uh-huh."

Friday Calls

"Homer, this is Bing. How ya doin'? Got an order for you. Actually, got two."

Kenny has long ago given up on wondering why everyone in the world calls him Kenny except the guy from the beer store. He figures his full, Christian name had been read off some old warrant by someone feeding Bo, and Bo had given it to the beer people. Homer Kenny is reliable. Can be trusted with small jobs and errands. He does not think himself smart and he acts accordingly. He keeps his mouth shut. He does not complain.

"Hey, Mr. Bing. How you be doin'?"

"Fine, sir, thank you, Homer. Homer, need you to come by the store and make two grabs and deliveries, please if you would. Daddy would be grateful. "

"Yessir, what time you want me?"

"Three o'clock would work best. And, Homer, the second one is for Bo. He says for you to pay us for it and he'll pay you back tonight."

"Yessir. I'll be there."

Kenny hangs up the phone.

He shuffles back down the sidewalk. There is always the little spoken dance that he and the Davis son lightly waltz. Lots of "sir" and "grateful" and "Daddy" and "please." The well-mannered formality of dishonesty grafts onto the prospect of money.

The sun is higher and glaring now. PeeWee waits at the apartment door, hot-boxing a Camel, clicking open and snapping closed again and again his worn Zippo and glancing in every direction all at the same time, smoke flaring from his little head and wide nostrils.

PeeWee has earned his moniker honestly. Not only is his head little, his body is too and his facial features spread across his head take almost more space than is there. He always seems to be studying his interest from the underside, always looking up at the subject from beneath its neck and jaw, his eyes cut to the angle.

Long ago it had been forgotten that his Christian name was Thomas Ravenel, just as it had been forgotten too that he was named for Doubting Thomas. He had parents and family, he had attended school, and had been a decent and curious student. He's a joker of trades, master of but a few, they being the arts of thievery, deception and temptation.

He is a quick study and limits all such analysis to whatever fun could be had in the vulnerability of the here and now. His movements are often akin to the flicks of a serpent's tongue.

PeeWee also has his clientele, his coteries of those who use him. Kenny does. Drink house owners do. He only helps himself rarely. A little boosting from the boost is to be expected from time to time.

At 13, his father had beaten his momma too hard for the last time and she had up and left, taking his three youngsters with her. PeeWee had been at school when all this happened and when he returned to their slummy dump of an apartment late that afternoon, where his daddy made him keep coal in the bathtub, and the dish towels were sodden yellow from decay, his drunken old man had explained the new and deep absences with a flailing hand and a package of slurred excuses and had then stumbled out in an unsteady, feigned dignity to find solace elsewhere. PeeWee did not expect any imminent returns.

Big eyed, heavy browed, large flat nose, long sideways mouth and jug ears all jammed together to make him look like an oversized Mardi Gras Parade Float Head, he was never puzzled or perplexed by this fast turn of events. He had always sensed the violence and despair would find an apex sooner rather than later. He sat down in an old kitchen chair and thought a bit, staring out the window. He was on his own now.

That was more than two years ago now. In the interim, he had left his book bag on the floor of the hall, left home for good, went down the street, and asked for and got a part-time job running errands and sweeping up and such at the repair and chop shop on the corner and then gone to see his older friends, Rise and Ben and Kenny, over in the gardens. He had also gone to see Curt Minor. They all took him in and he ended up living with Kenny. He knew everyone from the drink house.

He knew his momma and all had gone home to be with family in the country, he knew that was a better, much better place for her and them and also knew he didn't want to be there. He would see them all later, when time and hurt had passed some.

He knew his daddy was doomed to be a drunk and worse and was quickly destined for a long walk out the end of a glass and trash-strewn short alley where the last steps were just straight over the edge. He was right. His daddy ended up a babbling, drooling fool living in a box and drinking paint thinner and hair tonic and rotting away. PeeWee passed him from time to time, but they never spoke again and it would be highly questionable if the man ever even recognized his boy. He died a while back of exposure one hard January night.

Kenny then began studious graduate courses in shoplifting, thievery, keeping watch, grifting, lying, gambling, con games, stolen goods transportation and holding his hand out for a little more. He took up smoking, posturing, drinking, dope, smack and whores and turning his nights and days upside down.

He was adept and becoming more so.

"Where we goin', Kenny?"

Kenny starts to brush PeeWee off because PeeWee is always a pain in the ass, buzzing about as the fat tiny fly that ever seems won't land. Kenny says the basic, "Oh, what the hell" to himself and keeps walking toward the parking lot telling PeeWee to come.

"We going down to City B. Mr. Bing has some pickups and deliveries. Let's go get some beer first. It's hot. Need to be there at three. I'll give you some juice to help."

PeeWee is again, as always, validated. He's excited. He's going to meet some more folks with lots more money than him who break the law easily and for a nice profit. He loves connecting the dots. The ability to know these people by name, the ability to see them work and get a feel for all the little high-wire acts and net-webbing that goes on mostly unseen beneath the surface of the white and just right world.

They walk around the building, past the stringy clotheslines with hanging limp wrung out underpants and work clothes cast out into the hot breeze of that dying summer and even more trash cans and trash. There is the pitted parking lot, once blacktop, now skinned and everywhere pimpled with its cheap gravel now rising from beneath it. Like everything else, it is hot.

No one would ever mistake this place for an auto showroom floor. Rusting cars. Bondo cars. Cars up on blocks. Cars missing bumpers and quarter panels. Cars hard-taped together. Cars with faded, burnt out paint.

Mismatched doors, big and little dents. It is a place where the poor park their shabby, seamed-up rides, their mechanical miasma.

Kenny has an old broke-ass Ford panel truck with creaking doors, shot shocks, a worn down to the yellowed foam bench seat, latticed in tape, time and sun clouded windows, but it has a radio.

The two get in, Kenny turning the key as PeeWee settles into his pose of shotgun.

The engine catches strong, Kenny gasses it hard, blue exhaust plumes up, throws it into drive and they pull out...

Kenny thumbs the radio volume to real loud real fast. There is only one station—Triple-A...W-A-A-A 980 The Black Spot On Your Dial...ringleader one half-crazy, usually half-drunk Daddy-Oh! On The Patio, Shaking Down Some Stacks of Wax For You and Your Brown Skin Momma. His Christian name was Oscar Alexander. He is Legend.

Garnett Mimms and The Enchanters are caught in mid-wail of "Cry, Cry Baby." Daddy-Oh rattles in *sotto* with the "So Come On So Come On," PeeWee gets into wah-wah mode, a skinny trumpet with a filter.

Kenny completes the chorus with an emphatic, "Shut the fuck up, PeeWee—you're fuckin' the song up."

They drive down West Fifth Street, out of the flaking dinginess of East Winston, under the interstate overpasses filled with pigeons and back up the rolling hills where the banks and tobacco factories and tall office buildings stand. Past the fine churches—The First Baptist Church domed like a Constantinople mosque, the Methodist church a great giant rock pile chasing Buck Duke's iconic chapel—past the public library, all with lush, green lawns and shrubbery.

Triple-A plays on; Daddy-Oh patters. The Ford steadies on.

Heading back downhill toward the sprawling Baptist Hospital, they slow onto Burke Street at the base of West End, and as they swing off the street into a narrow alley and around back to a triple padlocked corrugated steel door. Kenny palms the horn twice, quick.

Bing comes around the corner, moving far more efficiently than his body would seem to allow. He grips a good-sized key ring. He bends to the unlocking and then rolls the heavy wrinkled door open. He carefully looks around, then at Kenny and PeeWee, who are opening the car doors and stepping out.

"Good afternoon, sir; and you are...Homer, right?"

"Right. Uh...yessir."

Kenny nods slightly in approval.

"Hey, Mr. Bing. How are you and what are we doing today?"

"Good, sir. Couple of deliveries. Daddy really appreciates your help."

"Sure. What we got?"

"Let's go get them. Put this one in the back. It's the smaller. Take it over to Frank C. at Old Town. He'll finish the delivery later this afternoon. It's on account."

They walk into the garage storage area. Cases of whatever could be thought of as drinkable, save for water, are stacked high with aisles here and there, making for selection and organization. Bing Davis begins to scan about and then starts handing boxes and cases to both men, who in turn walk them to the truck.

Bing asks Kenny, "Homer, you carrying?"

Kenny shrugs, "No, it's just a quiet liquor run. No need."

Bing nods.

"Okay, that's the first one. Now, this one, I bet you can guess, is for...?"

Kenny laughs. And as his mouth began to answer, PeeWee squirts, "The One and Only Bo D. Diddley!"

Kenny glares slightly. "Little man, don't be knowin' too much..."

PeeWee glances at Kenny in a combination of "I know I have just been too familiar" and "Damn, man why are you putting a call out on me for something like that in front of this man."

PeeWee mouths, "Right."

There is a wooden pallet with many cardboard cases: Canada Dry vodka, gin, and bourbon. Black Bull and Scorsby's scotch. Four Roses Blended whiskey. Some kind of rum. All of it the cheapest, crummiest rot-gut. There are cases of Miller High-Life and Pabst Blue Ribbon and Schlitz and Ripple wine.

This is the alter-ego soul of a properly run drink house, the other being reefer, and from time to time, the "white demon," cocaine. Add a juke box, red and green and blue Christmas lights, folding church-circle chairs, card tables and playing cards, dice and the other accoutrements of licentious living, so once the sun got good and down on Friday nights, the action begins.

Bing says, "Like I said, Daddy says that first one to Frank C. out at OTC is on an account out there. This one is, as you know, cash and carry. It's $500 square."

Kenny nods and reaches way down into a back hip pocket for his billfold. He creases it carefully open, takes a thumb and finger and carefully feels the edges of greasy bills five times twice, then slowly pulls them out in a fold and hands them to Bing.

Bing does not count or even look at them. He just puts them in his shirt pocket and says, "Thank you. See y'all later. PeeWee. Nice to meet you, Kenny. Y'all be safe out there."

Bing walks back into the building, the gate rattling down behind him. The locks and chains can be heard snapping down.

The shadows in the alley are getting a little longer now as the sun begins its arc to the west. It is still hot in the shade, no air moving.

As they pull back down and out of the alley to the sidewalk and the front of the building, Kenny waves at a girl with a broom at the front of the store.

The truck stops.

"Hey."

"Hey, whatcha doin'?"

"Picking up. Making some for the weekend deliveries."

"Oh." She leans down and looks in. "Who you got with you? Do I know you?"

Kenny says, "That's PeeWee. He helps me out from time to time. Lives over in the Gardens on the back side."

PeeWee says, "Hi, I'm PeeWee." And smiles sweetly at her.

Kenny says, "This here is my big sister, Rise. She works for Mr. Davis now."

"Oh. Nice to meet you."

"Un-huh."

Kenny says, "Well, we gotta go."

Rise says, "Yeah, take it easy out there. Gonna see you tonight?"

"Oh, yeah. Bye."

"Later."

And the truck moves on out into the street.

As the truck bumps over the curve, PeeWee says, "Your sister, she seems nice."

Friday Calls

Kenny allows, "Yeah, but she can go tough too..."

PeeWee replies, "Well, I'm sure not getting sideways with a lady that size..."

Kenny grunts, "Watch it."

"Yessir. No disrespect meant. Mr. Bing seems pretty nice too."

Kenny looks far off and says, "As long as there ain't no trouble. He does dirty work for his daddy sometimes..."

Kenny says, "As long as there ain't trouble..." and leaves it there. He thinks, *I am goddamn sick and tired of being Bo's bank. By time we get delivered and get back to Curt Minor's tonight, Bo will be high and drunk, and I'll have to work and beg like hell to get my money back—just like damn always...*

PeeWee wiggles the radio knob, the music comes warbling up. He asks Kenny, "Something on your mind?"

Kenny says, "Naw—let's get to the house."

They drive back across town, back into the projects and scraped paths of clothesline-webbed public housing, and crummy rent houses and more and more hand-painted side-crossed sag-assed churches and scraggly weeds. The random dust and gravel stick everywhere. The streets get narrower once they cross under the interstate and head back up the hill. There is less uniformity in the buildings that don't have that planned and laid out feel. It is slap-dash.

They turn here, then there. There are no traffic lights, just random stop signs. Kenny rolls the truck through each of them. No one is watching. It is shimmering end-of-day hot now.

They pull up a hill and park on the curb, facing the opposite lane down. There are three dilapidated, ramshackle, virtually identical frame houses, rent houses in a tilted row going up the hill, and then there's a bowed out wooden church with a huge ragged purple cross painted on its side with the obligatory "Jesus Saves" hand painting with drips and smears above it. Above the failing eave, an off-balance spear of a steeple with a small cross stands watch above, a sparse sentry for a sparse people.

Kenny and PeeWee get out of the truck, open the back doors and start walking the cases into the house. The house belongs to Curt Minor, a tall good-looking man with skin the color of burnt okra. Curt is trim and carries a perpetually menacing air about him. As they walk through the worn yard up to the front porch, Curt meets them door open eyeing them closely.

A well-run drink house lays out in such a way that it is recognized as nothing more than a home in the poor section of town. There is a front porch which is covered and usually there are worn and ratty swings and chairs on it with one light next to the door. There is a front room which is modestly put together with a small television set, some air chairs, a sofa, religious icons, plastic flowers, overwhelming potpourri, and photographs and pictures of beloved presidents and Jesus Christ. Through a small doorway there is a larger-than-one-might-imagine kitchen with plenty of countertops and from there are bedrooms down the side with a large room and another porch on the back. This is where the drink house is established on Friday afternoon and where it exists until early Sunday morning when it goes back to repose.

Kenny and PeeWee make repeated trips and stack the cases in the kitchen. Curt Minor simply nods at them and then says, "Kenny, you know you're supposed to be on duty at eight tonight. It's hot and we expect a big crowd."

Kenny says, "Yes." PeeWee stands there for a moment, taking it all in and trying to learn the business to which he aspires. This is a cash business. No one pays taxes. It all comes in small bills which are easily moved about and distributable. They all know that Bo Diddley will be there later in the evening and that he will be the carrier of the marijuana and cocaine and will also be the bank.

Curt asks, "Where are you fellows going next?"

Kenny replies, "We're going over to see Frank C. at Old Town and make a delivery for one of the members." Minor nods and the delivery boys leave.

Kenny gets in back of the truck. PeeWee stands outside for just a moment. Kenny says, "Come on. Let's go. We got to move." PeeWee goes back to check the doors to make sure they're secured and he eyes the cases that remain to be delivered.

He then comes around to the driver's side and leans in the window and says, "Kenny, when are you gonna get paid back for that money you paid over there to Mr. Bing?"

Kenny says, "I guess tonight, but I supposed you know that it'll take some doin' to get it pried loose from Bo."

PeeWee says, "Why?"

Kenny replies, "Bo loves to be the boss. Bo loves to be the man and Bo loves to lord power over everybody and everything. You've seen him before but tonight you come with me and we'll see him up close. He is a hard man. I have been his errand boy for so long. To tell the truth sometimes I don't like it but it's a way to make enough of a living."

PeeWee stares at Kenny and then brightens. "Hey, let's make this a little better than maybe it usually is. You know, we're taking this other load over here to Mr. Cuthrell at the club and he's gonna deliver it to some nice white gentlemen over there and they'll go off and do whatever they do with it, but no one's gonna be countin' or lookin' because that's not the way white folks are. Let's get these boxes sealed and marked with something that says C.B. and a checkmark, but only after we've taken a few bottles for ourselves. Then we can have a little party and sorta get in the mood for tonight and we can be mellow."

Kenny looks at PeeWee up and down quietly then he says, "Little man, that ain't such a bad idea. We might as well be havin' a little fun too. Go back there and pull two bottles of Ancient Age and we'll take care of the rest real quick."

PeeWee goes back and removes two bottles of bourbon from the crates, brings them to the front seat. Kenny cranks up the truck and they drive quickly back to Kenny's place. They go in, Kenny rummages around, finds some duct tape and a great big black crayon and they seal all the crates uniformly and mark each one with a big C.B. and a checkmark, thus illustrating that the boxes have been inspected and certified.

Quickly, they drive back across town to Old Town Club, come down the driveway, swing around to the back of the club where the service entrance sign is. Kenny gets out and rings the bell.

A woman comes to the door and Kenny says, "How do you do, ma'am. I'm here to see Frank C. I'm Kenny."

The woman leaves and in a few minutes Mr. Frank Cuthrell appears. "What do you have for me, Kenny?"

"Mr. C., I have the delivery from City Beverage I was told to bring to you. It's in the back of my truck.

Mr. Cuthrell says, "Drive around to the employee's servants' parking lot next to my car."

Kenny does so and pulls in next to a turquoise Indianhead two-tone blue Chevrolet. Mr. Cuthrell walks out behind them, unlocks the trunk and the cases are transferred from Kenny's truck to Mr. Cuthrell's car.

Nothing is checked, everything is looked over, all is fine.

Frank Cuthrell thanks them and they all part company.

Kenny and PeeWee are now mildly amused at the trickery they are perpetrating and they are on their way back to Kenny's place. Before they cross under the interstate they have cracked the seal on one of the bottles and have both taken long and satisfying pulls of high quality bourbon whiskey.

Frank Cuthrell walks back into the servants' locker room at Old Town Club, takes off his maître d' dinner jacket. Puts on another jacket, another coat and reflectively pulls the collar up and walks quietly back to his car. He drives west for about 15 minutes past the hospital and out and into the growing sprawl of this small southern city and pulls into a large parking lot where a gentleman in a suit and tie awaits him. They nod at each other and the gentleman says, "Hello, Frank," and Frank says, "Hello, Mr. Glenn," and with nothing further, the trunk of the black Ford company car is opened and the two of them put the cases in. The trunk is closed. Frank Cuthrell is handed a $20 bill and Frank Cuthrell then says, "Thank you," nods and drives back to Old Town Club for the evening's activities.

Kenny and PeeWee shuffle back into Kenny's thin shit crib. There are old newspapers and magazines and drink and beer cans and a couple of bongs and empty whiskey bottles and dirty, food dried paper plates and tin foil wrappers scattered on the table in front of the plastic covered faded floral-themed couch.

A few strap shredding plastic seated, aluminum framed lawn chairs complete the home theatre that surrounds a large television set crowned with a big set of rabbit ears. The screen door slaps shut behind them. They put their bottles on the counter. The place is an unsolvable puzzle of mess and no one is reaching to figure of which pieces ought to be moved. Kenny goes into the kitchenette, opens the refrigerator door, and rummages around in its cold dark, the bulb having burned out a year ago.

His bulk rises up and back out with a large bottle of Coke and he then dives straight into the top shelf freezer encrusted with permafrost for an ice tray.

Friday Calls

He snorts, "Check this shit out. We gonna have a fuckin' party."

PeeWee giggles, "I'm down with that."

It's about 5 p.m.

Kenny gets out some big jelly jar glasses, Fred Flintstone for him and Davy Crockett for PeeWee. Ice clinking, whiskey guggling, Co-Cola slow fizz on top.

He hands one to PeeWee and they both drink big first swallows followed by the obligatory "Ahhh..."

Kenny tops each off with some more Kentucky Jump Juice.

"It's hot as hell out there. That helps. Now, little man, what sort of Mary Jane are you in touch with?"

Kenny walks over and clicks the television on, jangles and wiggles the rabbit ears and looks at his helper.

PeeWee reaches into his pocket and produces a small, smashed up brown bag, and lays it out of the small kitchen counter.

They search through the debris of the place and find enough tin foil to make a nicely formed pipe. PeeWee gives it a good, competent blow through to clear it, loads it and produces his Zippo, gives it one rolling click and fires up the load. He jams it first, hands it Kenny who sucks it like the Goodyear Blimp filling up.

The air is fogged with exhale.

And they sit down on the nasty couch to let the poverty and vague sadness and the dirt and the basic, grinding shit nastiness of their day wash into a temporary place of happy numbness. It ain't so bad.

The television is blaring. There appears to be some sort of local production western-themed Southern kid cartoon show on, a sort of Howdy Doody and Buffalo Bob knock-off for some of the lucky rug rats of the region. The children are young and loud and boisterous and giggling and laughing and shrieking—making a lot of near-hysteric noise. One child is tight-lipped as he holds his crotch. It appears he will pee in his pants at any moment. There are no children of color on the screen. It is shown in color, but is unfaithful in its green and purple tinting.

Kenny looks blankly toward the set and notes, "Look at all those loud-ass whitey kids. You know, they sometimes show Mighty Mouse cartoons, Popeye too."

PeeWee slowly responds, "Uh-huh, that's cool."

The bulk and charge of the proceedings appeared to be one bespectacled, avuncular fellow dressed as a cowboy with a top hat and string tie and a fellow dressed as his sidekick, in Mr. Green Jeans bib overalls and a raggedy straw hat. They are interviewing these screaming children who have clearly had too much ice cream and sugar. The questions are pretty much "name, rank and serial number" and the answers are idiotic and unintelligible and the television simply floods the room with sound.

The show goes mindlessly on and on—they do get one really good Mighty Mouse cartoon—the one where Mighty knocks the shit out of some jerkoff Nazis—they giggle—and then there is more kid yelling and screaming and then it mercifully finally goes off and the local news comes on and there is something lengthy about the ongoing heat wave. People on the street are being interviewed.

"Lordy, it's warm, isn't it?" the reporter rhetorically asks an elderly interviewee and she mops her sagging chins.

"I've done lived here a good while and I can't ever remember nuttin' like this," wetly muses a sweat-soaked fellow who appears to work at a tire place.

"Well, these fine Kenmore air conditioners (he gestures to racks that are only spottily populated) are just jumping off the shelves!" exclaims a man with Vitalis hair and a large Sears nametag.

The weather lady has pointy tits that look to be formed out of large Dixie cups and crisply lacquered tightly coiffed hair. She reports with a glued-on look of amazement that it is SO HOT.

The rayon suited anchor agrees sagaciously.

It all drones on with a finish of sports, afternoon baseball scores, a quick report on the morrow's Dawgs at Heels gridiron tilt and the city swim meet.

Kenny's mellow is interrupted by a growling.

"Do any coloreds ever get asked anything or play anything?"

PeeWee glances at him.

Kenny's look loses its edge and resumes its blankness.

At this point, Kenny and PeeWee really don't care. It is all background noise and light which now accompanies the surging drunk and dope-fueled high they are both on and that satisfies them greatly. It almost contains them.

Friday Calls

The sun is just beginning its next few hours of going down and they know that it is almost time to go to work. PeeWee looks at Kenny and says, "What time is it?"

Kenny says, "I don't know, but I guess it's close to time to go."

PeeWee says, "I'm pretty fucked up; how about you?"

Kenny says, "Yes, I am too, but I'm good to go so if you're ready I'm ready." They have one more top-off and smoke one more pipe.

They left some of the bourbon in the two bottles and set it aside in the kitchenette area. They smoked enough dope to make them feel carefree.

They are both now very hungry. They are, for sure, plenty fucked up.

They drive down to the Rail Line Avenue to the Bennett's Chicken and Rib place. The counter lady is a sweet old thing who bats her eyes and smiles hopefully at Kenny. Her name is Ruby and has known him and Rise and their people a long time.

"Hey, honey. How you been? Y'all hungry for anything?"

It is a mildly salacious ask. She has been around the block. A quick blink and she can tell immediately that both the man and the boy are working very hard on looking and acting normal and rapidly flunking both sides of the quiz. She chuckles.

"What kind of shit have y'all jumped into?" She laughs.

They look at her sheepishly.

"Boys. Boys. Boys. My my..."

Her flat-line smile is back, giving up nothing that she doesn't already know.

"All right then, what'll it be? Kenny, ain't you working tonight over at Bo's? Damn, we need to load that belly up!" Ruby turns and looks back into the kitchen.

The line cook in the back looks at her over the warmer and silently mouths, "Those niggers are fucked up."

She nods.

"Kenny, how's Rise? Who's your friend? I've seen him over in the Gardens, haven't I?"

Kenny steadies and says, "Rise pretty good. She gotta job with man that runs City Beverage, Mr. Davis, down on Burke near the hospital. Miss Ruby, this is my friend, PeeWee. He helps me at Bo's."

PeeWee steps forward and stiffly extends his hand and says, "I'm PeeWee, ma'am. Hello."

Ruby takes his hand with a brief shake and observes him up and down. "Hello, PeeWee, I'm thinking we need to work on building you full too." She grins.

They know they are safe.

Bennett's is on the close perimeter of the railroad and railyard. Before they order, all stop while the roar of an express blowing through grinds over them, shaking the food shed.

"Those damn trains"..." Ruby mumbles to herself. "Okay, boys, what y'all wants? Or maybe why don't I just put some plates together?"

The two nod their grateful assent. Their thinking is dicey right now.

They sit and in a few minutes Ruby brings them fried chicken, ribs, corn bread, beans and cherry pie along with two large, sweating plastic tumblers of sweet tea. They are thrilled and pleased and lay into the devouring of the food. In a few minutes, it is done. They are filled.

"Miss Ruby, thank you! We gots to be going. How much do we owe?"

"Call it five a piece."

"Yessum." Kenny and PeeWee each hand her an Honest Abe and then remembering, Kenny fishes some crumpled ones out and puts them on the counter before her, saying, "Sorry!"

Ruby nods and smiles and says, "Thank you for remembering your manners. I know today just might have taken a little longer." She winks.

After eating their meals, the two grin and go out the door and into the truck.

As the engine is gunned and the truck backs away from the shack, the line cook says to Ruby, "Good appetites, but too late, you know. They both hard stoned and drunk. The juice and the smoke beat that meat and beans to the finish line waaay before you tried to catch 'em up. They gonna be messed up for hours, just bluffin'..."

Resignedly, Ruby says, "Uh-huh..." sighs and throws the empty, smeared plates in the trash and rag wipes the counter down.

Chapter Five

Beginnings

Over cross town, Archer Glenn drives home. Large, old trees line his street and fine houses line up one by one behind the screen of summer leaves. His is a lovely home, white brick, guarded by sentries and sentries of dogwood.

Pulling up part-way into the garage, he goes in through the back door off the back porch, through a small pantry and into the kitchen where two women are standing at the sink, one with an apron on, peeling tomatoes, the other clutching a brown paper bag into which she is catching the tomato peels.

"Hello, ladies!" Archer says brightly. "How is your day?"

The woman at the sink turns the splashing water off. She is Retha, short, of course, for Aretha.

"Hey, Mr. Archer. Fine. Fine. You?" She has a casual way and is obviously amused by many things, not the least of which is the weekend bounce her employer has in his step and way. She is a broad shouldered woman with a wide face and searching, always searching eyes. There is a deep, burnished voice from within her which matches her skin. Her peeling knife is held with light touch. One look at her says, "Old Pro."

"Good. Fine, thank you, ma'am. How 'bout you, Mamie?" Mamie is the much smaller and slighter of the two women, very bird-like with finer features and a lighter skin tone. She is more carefully watchful and more withdrawn, more courtly reserved than her counterpart.

"Oh, fine, Mr. G. Thank you."

Both women have been Glenn family retainers for years and years. Both wear uniforms and solid shoes. They know this family. They are their people, part of their people.

Retha asks, "What you doing home? Aren't you going to Mr. May's country place for the evening with that sorry bunch from the club and then y'all going over to Chapel Hill for the ballgame tomorrow afternoon?" She winks and grins big as she interrogates with the slightest of pricks from her ever-ready pin cushion of accumulated knowledge.

Mamie allows a tiny pursing smirk of a smile and looks down to the black and white tile of the kitchen floor.

Archer laughs and says, "You know it all, don't you! Yes! Gonna have a big time and be back by about sunset tomorrow evening. Came home to throw some stuff in a bag. Where are the girls? Miss Louise?"

Mamie ripostes, "Don't you know it! Miss Louise is upstairs. Mamie, where are the ladies?"

"A few minutes ago, they were in the den watching the television."

"Well, thank you, ladies. I've got to get myself together. Mamie, are you coming back this weekend?" he pushed the door to the dining room open to make his rounds.

"Yessir, I'll be here at noon tomorrow. Retha's making everyone's supper. She'll be back Monday."

"Thank y'all! Make some extra and I'll work on it tomorrow night!"

He found his young daughters, seated in the den, eyes entranced by the glowing tube and moving shapes before them. It was a sort of hypnotism. They were each sitting cross-legged in matching yellow dresses, a bottle of Coca-Cola in their resting hands.

"Hey, girls!" He bent and kissed each on the head. They looked at him quickly and kindly, then just as quickly resumed their primary focus.

"Girls, I just wanted to give you a kiss. I'm going to see the game tomorrow. I'm late. I love you."

"We love you, too, Daddy," they murmur in only slightly off-key unison.

He walks briskly up the stairs, looking down onto them into the den above the rising bannister, admiring how pretty and nice they are.

Archer walks into their master bedroom. His wife Louise sits at her dressing table, a lit Camel in one hand, an Old Fashioned glass mostly full of brown liquor and a few ice cubes in the other. Archer winced slightly, but this isn't the time to start all that up.

She is a handsome woman, not necessarily beautiful or even good-looking, but she has a wonderful slightly off-kilter smile, a grand figure, an ironic and perceptive sense of humor and she is nobody's fool. She had smiling eyes, but those were not seen so much these last few years. She is, as is he, discreet and has presence.

She takes a long swallow, then a sharp pull on the cigarette.

"Hey, honey." He goes to touch and kiss her. She first turns imperceptibly away from him as the gray cloud flows round her head, then to him and they brush cheeks.

"I've got to throw a few things into a bag and get going. I'm late."

"Oh, I'm sure. I know. I know..." Her voice trails off.

Again, he knows the larger match is there to be struck but he desists.

Quickly and efficiently, he pulls a small bag from the closet to pack his clothes and shaving kit in. He takes off his suit and tie and changes into some khaki pants and a short-sleeved sports shirt. He dons on a light blue blazer and pats a starched white handkerchief into his breast pocket as he turns toward her.

Louise eyes him carefully. He calmly smiles at her. She takes another swallow and carefully notches the cigarette into a large crystal ashtray. He has seen this all this many times before.

She is very still for a moment and then quickly says, "Well, you look nice. How many of y'all are going? How do you think the Tar Heels will do? When will you be home?" Her eyes have softened.

His careful constructing wall of departing defensiveness evaporates and he is grateful.

"Thank you," and with a slight bow further answers, "I think they're eight of us. Me, Purvis, J.T. and Tag and, of course, Tim and some of his Beta buddies from Burlington."

He pauses. "Georgia's always pretty good—they got a lot of people back but we did play real well against State so...we'll see...and I should be home in time for dinner late tomorrow afternoon."

She nods. "Well, y'all behave and have a good time. The girls and I will hold down the fort till then."

He bows more deeply, "Yessum!" and busses her again and heads down the stairs.

A few blocks from the Glenns, in not any particular direction, the others from the city are in various stages of departure as well. The evening promises a good time and there is the ball game as well.

Purvis Farrior was the wrinkled tennis pro at the club. Patient, a natural teacher, funny, self-effacing and gnome-like, he loved to gamble and play cards as they all did. He was far smarter than he first appeared. His tennis whites always looked as though they had just been freshly laundered for a man two sizes larger than he, but that was a full deception. He could whistle the ball hard from either side and moved quickly and surely on the court. Off the court, he ambled pleasantly.

He had been around so long; he was another of their brotherhood, not one of those one slot down on the pecking order of members. He drove a big blue boat of a Cadillac, the vast trunk of which carried at all times many cases of whiskey as there was no telling the need for such that might arise. A widower, he enjoyed winking here and there.

J.T. Barnes was a trucking company executive, the second in command of a growing fleet of small and medium haul tractors and trailers that were being shepherded at the top by a logistics wizard. He had the head of a glorious Roman, a man of silvering hair that always looked to be brushed back with the help of a slide rule. He was fit, trim and strong, blue-eyed and decisive. He was a fine golfer. Gruff and determined, he could often be brusque, then quickly alternate to sweet and kind. His wife Bookie was known for her ability to handle him as easy as he could be hard. She laughed at him and with him and it leavened him. Even as smoking was ingrained in them all, he was on the far right side of the bell-shaped curve with rarely a moment in the day when he was without something going into his lips.

Tag Montague was something out of the school of the British Officer Corps from the movie *The Bridge on the River Kwai* and he knew it and loved it and played to it with both gravitas and wit. Until he opened his mouth, most were certain he was English. He was in truth a drawling Southerner and his twang made his appearance all the more intriguing. Naturally, he owned a small clothing store and let others run the business while he fashioned the front of the house.

Tall and angularly thin, with close cropped thinning hair and brush moustache, Tag favored tweed and plaid suits, double-breasted blazers and whenever possible, even in cooler weather, Bermuda shorts and dark over-the-calf socks. He carried a long walking stick at all times. He did not walk—he strode—and was in perpetual good humor. He was married to a perfectly nice, but rather mousy woman who was as introverted as he was extroverted. He was chipper, he was a sport and he was always game, clapping his hands enthusiastically whenever any next proposal was made. He was but moderately bright and knew it so he never overplayed his mind.

They were all graduates of the University and had all known each other for a very long time. They belonged to exactly two clubs each: one country, one town. They all drank and gambled in those places and each other's homes. Harry Davis was their bookmaker of choice just as he was their bank, their tobacco, even their funeral home that would eventually carry them to ground.

At more or less the same times, they point their cars to the east. The end of day shadows are longer now. They have a few things left to do, errands to run.

They have all already touched in with Harry. Their bets are in and the money is down.

* * *

Kenny one-hand wheels his truck around the tight-mazed turns and corners that lead to 12th Street and the drink house. Every curling swing he takes is a little too wide and sloppy and PeeWee sways back and forth as Kenny grips hard. They are going too fast. The radio is turned up too loud. From time to time, the tires squeal. Neither speaks. They both know they are going to work drunk and stoned. There is no reason to talk of it. And too, they are both full of greasy food which made them sleepy and full. It has not been the magic antidote to their settling highs. They are both in moods other than pleasant. And now they are here in front, getting out, going up the slight rise to the porch of the drink house.

The bare yellow bulb porch light is on. There are a few chairs and an old, beat-up sofa on the porch. Next to the base of the front door is a blue candle shrouded by a milked glass lantern. The blue almost blends with the scratchy paint on the house, but if you are looking for it, you'll spy the "Open For Business" lamp. The sun is moving on down.

Curt Minor stands again on the top step.

He eyes the pair. He knows. He shrugs his shoulders.

"You two better get your shit together and quick. We gonna be busy tonight and don't need you two fucking things up. Gonna need to be paying attention and moving product."

Kenny looks up at Minor and nods. PeeWee stares straight ahead.

Kenny asks, "Bo here yet?"

Minor says, "Oh, you bet."

Kenny sighs. PeeWee stares ahead a little longer.

Kenny burps, blossoming heartburn coupling with his headache.

Up the wooden steps they go, Curt holding the door open for them.

Chapter Six

Culture

The South was always set up for the under-culture sale of booze, and Winston-Salem was a good drink house town. Drugs got into the mix later as the commerce of it all simply unfolded as supply met demand. The North and Midwest and West, and the rest had a bar/saloon/speakeasy culture. The South did not. The Southern well-to-do went to "the club" or to each other's' homes.

The rest scrapped around in places where the word got out. There was always music. A radio, a guitar player or a guy on a stand-up piano.

The South was religious, so piety trumped reality and the consumption of alcohol was an automatic "bad thing." The South bought into Prohibition early and with the passage of the 18th Amendment, the pursuit of a jug of juice became cloudier and not only morally reprehensible but illegal to boot. And so the underground-bred underbelly culture was born.

These juke joint operators bought their rotgut whiskey and beer in bulk from illegal, out-the-back-door suppliers who in turn had gotten the hooch from warehouse and truckload pilferers. Money changed hands, folks looked the other way.

There were no permits, no licenses, no sales taxes. There were no hours of operation. They just operated as and when they wished. Blue laws? What blue laws?

Most of the time the police welcomed the drink houses. In the less than well-to-do parts of town, there was one every few blocks. They were local. People were in one place. They were not roaming the streets. It was all self-contained and most always peaceable. Drink houses countenanced a good time, even rowdiness and dancing, but fighting was abhorred and quickly quelled and heavier violence was absolutely verboten. If a place got marked as dangerous, it instantly was known as a "bucket of blood" and people stayed away with the end game predictable result.

And as marijuana came into play, the attendees were usually even more soothed and calmed.

A drink might be two or three bucks, usually a darker whiskey cut by half with water.

If there was a call for a straight shot, the price went up. Places usually kept the offerings pretty lean. Canada Dry bourbon, a blended whiskey, cheap vodka, one kind of beer—lower-shelf Blatz or some such. Moonshine was often available. Some folks like to call shine "chicken" because it made you real limber. Some folks called it "Joe Louis" because it had the knockout punch.

In a tobacco town like this one, they had a couple of brands of cigarettes—even those came from workers lightly lifting off production lines, no taxes on those either. It was an all-cash business and highly profitable. Some might offer food, usually a ham or fish sandwich would be the top-of-the-line fare.

Most of their patrons and visitors were steadily employed. Folks got their checks every or every other Friday afternoon. They went to their banks or the credit unions—those all stayed open till six and beyond as was necessary on Fridays—and stood in long lines to shuffle toward the ladies behind the high counters with the small bars rising to their foreheads with their fast hands flashing in and out of their full cash drawers.

Those ladies were like machines, their fingers and thumbs counting it all out twice and then handing it over as quick as you could draw a breath. "Next."

Sometimes some of the take went into a savings or a Christmas Club fund. The rest came with a few small bank envelopes for parceling. There was always going to be some "cut loose and have fun money." It was a rite. It had been, depending on the depth of one's party the weekend before, five or six hard-working, nose down to the grindstone days and there was a hunger, a need for the respite of play.

Some of the older people could remember that moment of chaos when many years before, some damn fool of a kid decided he would try to rob the First Tobacco National Bank late one Friday afternoon. While his thinking about his goal may have had more money-meat-on-the-bone than usual, his timing was perfectly stupid.

When he got to the head of his line and pushed a note across to the teller while pointing his lumped up coat pocket at the gal, customers immediately recognized the threat to their soon-to-be enjoyed weekend and just fast-jumped him, beat him up, pushed him out the revolving doors into the arms of the old mannequin of a security guard. They did not brook such interruptions. They were looking forward to getting on with it.

And they did.

Chapter Seven

Arm Candy

Bo is standing next to the kitchen counter when they walk in. He loved himself as well as any man ever could love himself and it glowed and radiated off him like glimmering sunlight. He is in a perpetual pose, as though stage lit.

His born name was Benjamin Franklin Winphrie. He was born a country boy raising corn and chopping tobacco west of town out in Davis Bottom, but he got out of there quickly. He met some boys picking up hogsheads of cured leaf to take to the auction houses in town. To him, they were sophisticated and worldly, unlike his dirt-poor and shambling family and he wanted instantly to be like them, just more so.

He was chainsmoking and drinking liquor by 14, running whores and moving stolen goods by 15, joined the army at 17, was kicked out by 19 and went right back to his real work then, adding drink houses and drugs along the way.

By then, he had changed his name from Ben to Bo because of Bo Diddley, the famous blues and rock and roll guitar strong man. He featured himself as an impresario, a maker of good times, almost a conductor, director of things and always a hard-ass, shit-kicking son-of-a-bitch. He was mean and tough as a constantly swung leather strop and he meant for everyone to know it. God knows he could weasel and make nice with the cops when it was the time for that, but most of the time, he was the Man.

I walk 47 miles of barbed wire,
I use a cobra snake for a necktie,
I got a brand new house on the roadside,
Made from rattlesnake hide,
I got a brand new chimney made on top,
Made out of a human skull,
Now come on take a walk with me, Arlene,
And tell me, who do you love?
Who do you love?
Who do you love?
Who do you love?
Who do you love?

The answer was easy. Bo loved Bo.

And God also knew the real Bo Diddley got played on Triple-A every day and in drink houses and juke joints every weekend. And on and on and on.

Bo was a successful small-time hood who stayed away from violence. He just liked to threaten it and he had that "not sure" look too. Nonetheless, he had a menacing presence and was known to bring muscle along. He pulled a couple of short-time stays in the state prison system, but was also a subtle but willing informant and thus cultivated some cops. Even those who were not crazy about him gave him good buffer as they knew he was consistently "helpful" to their brethren from time to time. He was careful in the doling out of his favors. As he got older, he became always prideful, sometimes arrogant and often dismissive of those who helped him. He fascinated people. He had that way about him.

He dressed to impress and on weekends, his finest faux finery would come out as would Felicia, his 17-year-old recent crib-bitch and arm candy.

This night he wears his straight leg pants with two-tone brogans, softly shined, and his red shiny vest, white shirt and skinny black necktie beneath. He is built to wear such molded, fitted attire. Of medium height and very slender build, Bo is wiry, the human equivalent of a walking pine nut, hard and pull-twisted.

His head is too large for his pipe-cleaner body and it has a permanent forward thrust as though seeking anything and anyone that could be challenged and controlled. With big teeth and big eyes, he gleams with the hunger of a predatory gingerbread man.

Bo leans slightly across the counter, just next to where Rise is putting plates of food together. He reaches out to Felicia whom he calls Catty like in "Catty. Come here, Catty." When she leans toward him, he draws his hand and slender fingers lined with rings back in a slow teasing wave and says, "Just not yet..." and she sways back and pouts. He likes to say, "Catty in my Caddy." And laugh that knowing, owning laugh.

Felicia Diane Lineberger is a cut above Bo's usual, but not too much so. She draws the distinction with dead-eyed insouciance and pronounces accordingly whenever any question, direct or implied, arises as to her relationship with Bo.

"Yes, I do fuck him for money, but I am not a ho. I am his lady. He gives me good shit and money and so." She sometimes introduces herself as "Felicia" and sometimes as "Felicia Diane."

Sometimes folks out of her earshot note that her first initial "F" simply stands for "Fucked" and the first two for "Fucked Dat." The Lineberger last name rarely comes up as everyone was beyond dubious as to how a stuck up, trashy black as coal ash nigger girl could be fired out of an at least partial Germanic parentage.

It's fair to say Felicia is affected by Bo and had her eyes on the prize, despite his low bar status in the great scope of things. It would be worthy of debate as to what Bo's description of their alliance might be, but no one wants to mess with the evocation of his assessment.

She was an early-on high school dropout with a young kid who stayed with her mother. Born with the intellect and curiosity of a gnat and thus virtually illiterate, she had no dreams, no hopes, nothing except the moments when there was going to be a party, and thus she could get high in style.

She is not slight of build, but simply all-over skinny with nothing remarkable about her save her being a prideful poseur. She likes the "fake" part but she can't describe why. She is just good at it. Like the white shift she is wearing, there is a practiced formless droop to her.

She had met Bo at this juke joint some months ago. He knew he could use her and he was at that age when he needed the plugging-in.

He had looked her over a couple of times across the room. She saw him looking and held her gaze on his. She had big eyes that could go and stay flat, thus creating that sense of detached uncertainty. That of course intrigued and excited him for it made him unsure when he was always supposed to be sure.

She had come here a few times before with a cousin. She didn't really know if the girl was really a cousin but so she had been introduced. She stood off by the side and watched the men mostly. Women were but bit players in this room. She knew by the look of him that he was at the top or very near the top of whatever hierarchy that existed in this small but rowdy busy fiefdom. There was a crowd as usual. It was as though they could curve their lookings around all those swaying and laughing and gesturing people. He walked slowly over to her, extended his ringed hand and said with both politeness and a certain leer, "Hello, miss. And your name is...?"

She received his proffered hand in the fashion of dead-fish and as she did, softly said,

"Felicia, Felicia Diane...what's yours?" And she looked up resignedly, steel dead-eyed into his cratered face.

"Why, honey, I am The Bo Diddley, King and Master of All You See." It was as though someone had put a school ruler in his mouth and thrown the light switch.

"You got a last name?"

"Why, yes. It's Lineberger."

He snorted, "Really...?"

"Why, yes, really. And is your last name really Diddley?"

"Yeah, as in I don't know diddly squat." He winked to make sure nothing could be further from the truth.

He leaned forward. "Let me get you something to drink." She nodded her assent.

He sauntered off, gracefully navigating the folks gathering and soon returned with two strong bourbon and ginger ales in the finest of Dixie cups.

Handing one to her, he said, "Drink up, to us!" He short bowed in her direction, nearly touching her forehead with his pomaded coif. He was enjoying leaning into the interesting girl.

She was on automatic, near robotic and too, she knew that she had found her sugar daddy. She swallowed it all hard and fast, watching him do the same out of the side of her eye. It wasn't bad and there was no gag.

He looked at her, smiled wanly and said, "I'll see you in a little while. I needs to be seeing my people, all my people."

And the music was playing and on came Bo Diddley's "She's Fine, She's Mine."

Ooh
Ooh-ooh-oh
Ooh-ooh-ooh
Ooh-ooh-oooh
Tell you don't love me baby
You don't love me, I know
You been takin'
Takin' all my money and all my clothes
You been takin'
All my money and my clothes
Well, you told some-a your friends
That you was gon'to send me outdoors
(Tell us about it!)
You been takin'
Takin' all my money and all my clothes
You been takin'
Takin' all my money and all my clothes
Please don't leave me
Please don't never, never go
Please don't leave me
Please don't never, never go
Well, I'll lose my mind
Go stone crazy, yes, I know

He swayed and went a little moon-eyed, then focused back into the crowded room with the white-sheathed waif in front of him.

She nodded. That's how it got started.

And that's how it is just about every weekend. Hot, cold, rain, storm, snow, whatever. And that's how it is this hot Friday night.

There have been a few people hanging around the place, off and on all day. It is a random coming and going. Neighborhood old folks sipping on something—most of them bring their own glasses—mailmen and garbage men having a shot or a beer and a cup of cold water on their way to going back out into the heat, young kids just playing and goofing and watching what the neighborhood grown-ups are up to—there was kind of a badge of thrill to that—to be privy to some of the grown-up stuff, running around the scraped-to-red-dirt yard and around the back of the house, chasing each other, the radio always on, always playing.

The few trees on the lots are listless in the heat, dried green leaves rasping in the few breezes that wander across the small hill where it all sits.

Rise comes over after work at City Beverage. She took a city bus over and then walked heavily up the hill that was to the dead end of East 15th Street. No reason to rush in this heat. Her feet hurt, she is tired and she knows she has some work ahead, but she also knows there's some fun in the coming dark as well.

She speaks with Curt, tells him Ben is coming with some friends later on and goes to the back of the kitchen and begins doing a little sandwich and food prep. There is a big salt cured country ham from Down East, a couple of baked chickens, and fish filets to be dredged and fried. Some good tomatoes, loaves of white bread and jars of Dukes. Bags of peanuts for shelling. They have some good stuff to wash it all down.

There was always some bitching about Dukes versus Hellmann's just like the same bitching about Coca-Cola versus Pepsi-Cola. "Well, fuck it..." she thinks. "This ain't the damn Stork Club."

Curt starts setting up the bar, putting bottles out, mixing a lot of the whiskey with tap water, putting cans of beer into coolers that awaited ice, unwrapping new decks of cards and sets of dice. Never let anyone bring their own. To do so was to beg for a rigged game and then a fight or worse. Curt had gone out earlier to his car in the back and gotten a small case out of the trunk. He casually walks back in and slides it under the counter. He had learned long ago that in order to offer the complete Likka House experience, you always had to have some boom bud to offer, to sell, to soothe and mellow out a few or more.

He turns the radio up a little louder. Later it will go much louder still. He makes sure his 12 gauge over and under is loaded and leaned up in the door of the broom closet in the kitchen. It is just standard operating procedure. You never know. He sets forth a huge box of red, white and blue poker chips. He looks up at the Christmas lights strung zig-zag back and forth across the cheap punched-tin ceiling and as he does, he can see through the front of the house, and to the top of Kenny's big head. He heads to the front.

Chapter Eight

Milk Run

The train sits still, wheezing in a low soft rumble, under the not-so-distant green and white neon glow of the tall Supper Club signboard. The train soon starts forward again, lurching and shuddering as the yank of its forward pull gathers the passenger cars toward the engine. The brake steam hoses hiss hot white fog; the couplers and chains clunk and clang as the great steel slinky accordion finds its roll.

Before the move, the conductor had walked back down the line of cars, inspecting and glancing at the equipment, up and down, a taking in accompanied by a long, powerful flashlight in one hand, a lantern in the other. He had quickly drunk in a few large swallows of one more beer before stepping off the ladder step onto the track grade for the stroll back. He tossed the empty into the weeds of the far bank.

He is comfortable, sees nothing that troubles him. In truth sees nothing at all as he gets to the caboose where he turns and perfunctorily waves the lantern for the "go-ahead" at H.E. Knight's head which curls out of the cab in the high distance before him. He carefully climbs up into the caboose, pulls one more beer out of his pocket, sits down on the cushion bench, takes off his hat, flips off the dome light, making sure the rear red warning light switches are flipped up and on, opens the beer with his pocket knife. He leans back and rests his eyes.

In the engine, Knight reaches down for another bottle and hands it to Gordon. The bottles, as the engines began to regain energy, are gently rattling again, almost calling attention to themselves and are beginning to sweat, the warmth of the cabin condensing their cold. The trainmen want to enjoy them now.

Knight takes another one for himself.

Gordon looks over at him and says, "You know, I suppose we've earned this, don't you think?" He takes a pull.

"How so?"

"Well, you remember when we were kids and just about died to get our hands on a real, honest-to-God Lionel train set?"

"Yes."

"And then we got it and we just about died to put it together and play with it? And we played with them and played with them and added to them and added to them? You remember all that?"

"Oh, yeah." Knight drinks and slightly pushes the throttle forward. The train begins to move. They sway a little.

"And we loved those trains and it set into our brains that we wanted to be train men and we hung around train stations and watched it all and finally applied and got jobs, you and me separate from one another."

"Yeah...?"

"And we found out that the money was good and the benefits were good, but you couldn't have a family life and you couldn't keep a wife and we were on call all the time and driving these giant beautiful bastards also included hitting crazy suiciders on the tracks and deer and splattering shit all over the place and derailments and trying to figure out how and when to sleep and some such shit as all that...?"

Gordon is speaking in a monotone, looking straight ahead, gently rocking.

"And...all that is so...and still here we are...so what have we earned?" He looks over at Gordon as the train travels a little faster.

Gordon turns to him, suddenly grinning in the dark, and laughs, "Hell, H.E., these fine cold beers!"

Gordon then lopes his empty bottle out the window and they can hear it smash up as it pops against a signal board.

Knight reaches down, gets out an empty and gives it a toss shot as well and misses. The air carries it too far. He needs to get his Kentucky windage down. He tries again and this time makes a strike. He is well pleased.

They are running about 35 miles per hour now, smoothing along, about 30 minutes from Greensboro Center. They are still behind, but will start picking the time up once they head for Charlotte.

The signal lights are showing green all down the line.

Knight takes up a sandwich and asks Gordon if he wants one. Gordon shakes his head and says, "No, I'm right satisfied right now." Knight takes a big bite and munches it slowly, enjoying the salty chew of the ham and the tang of the mayonnaise all mashed in with the soft white bread. He swallows.

The wind comes through the tops of the open windows. They rock and sway and the big engine hums them along. The moon is rounding up and is beginning to curve away from them as they begin to nose a bit more to the west. They are quiet.

Knight breaks the silence with a grin. "Hey, Gordon, do you remember that time a few years ago when old Gordo, God rest his soul, was high, fumbling around with his big bag of dope and dropped it out of the engine in the fucking middle of Greensboro, going down over near the Coliseum?"

Gordon laughs and nods yes. It was one of the wonderful stories told by the old-timers over and over again and it was always worth a retelling.

"Jesus, it took two miles to stop the train. Was Gordo gonna just let it go? Hell, no! Old Gordo just put it in reverse, rolled back looking and looking, stopped the train and got out and went up and down the track. I think he was southbound and hell, even an inbound express passed while he's out there spying for his dope. He was oblivious and damn, that was dangerous. And damned if he didn't find it—lucky it was wrapped up in tin foil and was shiny under the track lights and that's how he found it. Damn crazy son of a bitch. Damn lucky...." His voice trails off into a thoughtful smile.

"You know the company found out about it, some civilian watched the thing, saw him grab that ball of grass and crow like a fool and they called the company. They brought him in the next morning, started drug testing him, he kept flunking them, they took him off the line and said, 'Rehab or you're gone,' the union couldn't do much with that much fucking up, so into 'dry out' he went."

"What happened? He died, didn't he?"

"Yeah, he got cleaned up, was pretty unhappy after that, was like he'd lost the funny part of him, got to be real serious all the time, the Company put him back on random shit rides after that, lot of just local stuff and then he just up and had a really big heart attack after that. Graveyard dead. He was a funny son-of-a-bitch and could drive a train just fine."

The quiet comes on back in. Nothing further needs to be said then. It was just one of those stories.

They are moving along, still and becalmed and lost in many thoughts as they go. They'd been at it now for a long time. There were lots of memories. The track is clear and they blink and scan the signals and the sky and the crossings as they pass on. They can pretty much do it in their sleep.

Chapter Nine

Vice

It is what they call the "Doctor's Car," a long four-holer Buick with a great big trunk and spacious, almost Pullman-car deep seating. J.T. Barnes loves wheeling its black enormity on the streets and open roads. It fits and suits him and because he was a trucking company man, its size in his personal life parallels all the big rigs he worked with all week long.

J.T. is an expansive man, at his desk, at the dinner table, at the card table and at the bar and on the golf course. He is handsome with a cigarette always burning in his hand or in his lips. J.T. takes up more space than his physical build would seem to allow; he reaches out and across to his listeners, enveloping them with his big arms and hands, quick wit and gestures. It always seems he is halfway across whatever space he's in. His low timbered voice amplifies his presence.

He was once asked by a visitor to his company how many people worked there. He answered, "Oh, about sixty percent..."

J.T. loves making situations work and he loves doing favors. Because he was in the business of moving things around and making connections so things could get moved from here to there, he knows how to be efficient and he likes connecting dots. He knows how to fix things so there is always accommodation, if such is possible. If there is whiskey and cigarettes and pretty girls and some social to it, then all the better.

He enjoys hosting weekly poker games at his home that often went well into the night. One evening, the phone rang after midnight as a level banked fog of smoke hung over the room. The bottles and glasses crowded the cards, and the tossed chips clicked on the baize. There really were honest-to-God pictures hanging on the walls of dogs playing poker.

J.T. answered it quickly, with a snatch and a big hello.

It was a lady whose husband was supposed to have been home no later than twelve sharp.

She had known J.T. all her life and she wanted her fellow told in no uncertain terms to get his fanny back down the street home.

J.T. promised her soothingly he would make sure those instructions were given with specificity right away and said goodnight.

The fellow and J.T. kept right on playing. Fifteen minutes passed and the phone rang again.

"Hello!"

"No, he hadn't quite finished the game...well, I'll explain your intentions. Yes. Yes, indeed. Goodnight."

"Joe, she's sending the police for you and I guess for us all too. Says this is an illegal gambling den."

"That's nice."

They all continued to play.

A few minutes later the doorbell rang deeply.

J.T. went to the door, looked out the little glazed window and smiled. He swung it wide open.

There on the curb under the street light dimmed by the huge oaks and maples was a police squad car and standing in his doorway was Chief of Police Justice Tucker.

"Hello, Chief! Please come in!"

Tucker laughed and said, "Do you know why I am here?"

J.T. said absolutely he did. "Hell, you just left a few hours ago. I'm glad to see you again and so soon at that!"

J.T. asked if he wanted to search the place.

Chief walked to the back and greeted his friends. They were in high spirits.

"Make a place for me? May I have a bourbon, please?"

"J.T., would you please call Joe's wife and explain I have her husband in my personal custody and that it's going to take a while for us to examine the scene and gather evidence, and that I will in a little while make sure he is released directly to her without further difficulty."

"With pleasure, Chief. Have a drink."

And J.T. called the lady and mollified her just enough and then sat back down at the table for a few more convivial hands.

He just enjoyed working things out.

And so it is on this darkening Friday night, J.T. is running a few errands, doing a few favors and getting things gathered up on his way to the May farm.

He drives downtown and picks up some old friends, Nickels and Morgan, and another one of their friends and then they swing to the east and stop at a small, white house out in the country to pick up C. J. The car is comfortably full and the radio plays music and everyone smokes and the windows are half rolled down with the breeze blowing through. The sun is setting behind them, purples and golds and lavenders and pinks spreading into azure in their trail. J.T. has one stop left and in about thirty minutes, his tires crunch into the gravel parking lot of Green's Supper Club.

They all get out and while the rest head to the bar for a quick drink, J.T. walks around to the office behind the bar and knocks on its door. The place is about half-full, the lights are down and the jukebox is on roll play. Soft colors flit in the mirror behind the bar where the glasses tinkle and hum awaiting Friday night.

A big black man in a bigger white coat and blossoming butterfly black bowtie opens the door. With a big smile he says, "Good evening, Mr. J.T. We, of course, have been expecting you."

"Hello, Bozo. How are things?"

"Excellent, excellent. In France where we landed! Yessir!"

That was Bozo's code for, "Everything's gonna be all right—we are ashore and moving up and on." If he didn't say it, there would be cause for one's spirits to sag. Bozo was the Head Man at Green's, Mr. Spero Green's Black Greek. Bozo loved his place and always wore a good-sized Greek flag pin on his lapel.

"Mr. Spero said to be looking out for you. The Atlanta train just made the delivery. Got some nice steaks and things for you."

"Good!"

"You want a drink while I get Tommy to put things together for you and get them in your trunk for your ride up to Mr. May's place? That's a pretty spot up there."

"Yes, it sure is. A drink? Yes. That would be nice, Bozo. Yes, please. A bourbon. Could you bring it back here to me in the office? Feel like I've got a long evening in front of me." He grins as he sits down.

"Why, yes, of course."

"And make sure my friends out at the bar have what they need please, Bozo. They ain't hard to miss."

"Already being tended to, Mr. J.T. And you right about that," Bozo winks pleasantly as he quietly pulls the door closed.

* * *

It is growing dark now and the street lights mix with the blue, red, and yellow neon signs up and down Burke Street. City Beverage has been closed for a few hours, but inside, some business is still being attended to. It is a little past seven o'clock.

Everyone knows that Harry closes the phones down on Friday night at 8 p.m. sharp, no exceptions. The window of opportunity will open again Saturday morning at 9 a.m. and run until 11:30. Many of the college games would start at noon. Harry and Syd did not like to run everything close up to the starting tape. He knew other books that did and it just invariably caused trouble. People in a hurry to get in just under the wire to scratch their itch would rush, get the side they thought they wanted wrong, get their amount played wrong, and then want to argue about it later and welch on the play too. It didn't always happen like that on a late play but enough to make the availability of such messes repugnant.

The truth was that what they offered was a kind of drug, the drug of involvement, excitement and maybe even some money too. And the idea of all that mixed in with something as culturally tangible and vivid as football on an early fall afternoon was the absolute definition of "money burning a hole in his pocket." There were no casual players, no matter how soft and reserved their voices might be on the telephone, no matter whether they bet the minimum play accepted of $25 or went in for hundreds or even $1,000, the top allowed for Harry's clients.

Friday Calls

The deals took place over the telephone as Harry did not allow walk-in traffic for betting on games. People coming into the business for betting just called attention to the irregular foot traffic and caused confusion within the basic conducting the front of the house sale of beer, wine and booze. There was no reason for too many balls to be juggled at the same time by the same people. Harry and Syd offered the palliative numbers. It was their ballgame. They made the rules.

Their callers wanted to play, needed to play and it was a rite, no less so than getting to their offices on time, buying children and wives birthday presents, saying please and thank you.

It was as the old story about the devoted golfer who played all the time.

After a particularly good round, a young admirer who didn't know him well, said, "Fine round!"

"Thank you, son."

"I guess you play a lot of golf?"

"Son, I play eighteen holes every day except Sunday."

"Oh, you spend Sunday with your family?"

"On Sunday, I play thirty-six holes!"

The bulk of the calls are in now, only a few stragglers left to be fielded.

Harry picks up Bing's pad on which he had written games, bets, and bettors and eyes it carefully and quietly, the light of the desk lamp stretching them into shadows.

Harry clears his throat and then looks up.

Syd sits across the desk from them, looking his notes over as well. Feeling Harry's gaze, he lifts his head, leans forward onto the desk, laying his writings out for Harry to see and match. They both read the other silently and then return to their own.

It is critical to be accurate now. Repetition might be boring, but to be lax and miss something now would be an expense that no one needs. It is the time of the early evening where the cumulative fatigue of the week and the length of the day combined to potentially vex them and they know it. They slow themselves down.

And then Harry begins to read them off, each and every one, while Bing and Syd sit and listen, and are in a few minutes satisfied.

Harry says, "With a few left to come in, that's a handle north of 50K and

I feel good that we've got a good balance considering about a third of hits are on the Tobacco Road group. State and Wake are pretty evened out and the Duke and Carolina crowd have sucked into teats that look like love, not good sense, to me." The last part comes in good humor and with a bit of a sneer too.

This sort of regular analysis of the beginnings of the weekend handle was as close as Harry ever got to a soliloquy, a benediction of the day's offerings and receipts.

Syd chuckles and says, "Harry, don't you ever have a team you just care even a little something about. I mean, hell, you grew up in these parts. Isn't there one that caught your fancy somewhere coming down the line?"

Harry says, "Now, Syd, you ask me that from time to time and my answer ain't changed yet and ain't gonna."

Syd smiles and says, "Yeah, I know. Harry's sure got favorites. Harry is for Team Harry and even Team Syd too. Hoodamnray!"

Harry's chin bobs. And they laugh. It is almost time for a drink.

Bing nods. He wants them to be for Team Bing too. But it isn't time. He doesn't like that so much but he also knows it is so. He is a good soldier.

"Syd, you want a pop?"

"That'd be welcomed."

Harry gets up and walks into the back to return with a good bottle of brown and some Dixie cups.

"Here, y'all go. Bing, you still don't look old enough for this, but you've earned a pop too."

"Thank you, Daddy." And Harry pours for them all.

A phone rings and Harry says, "Bing, take that." And Bing does and writes it out and repeats it back and Harry neatly writes it out into the book as he does.

They quietly sip. A few more calls come in and Bing's voice is muffled into the receiver and shadowy dark of the back warehouse room.

Eight o'clock comes along and Harry pours another for himself and silently asks Syd if he wants another too.

"No, better not, I got to get on back up the mountain. Nice work today, Harry...and you too, Bing. I'll check in tomorrow at lunch and will have the pro lines hopefully by five tomorrow afternoon. I'll let myself out. Y'all have a quiet evening."

His chair scrapes and he silently heads to the front, and the door is heard opening and closing.

Harry says, "Bing, you go on home now." And Bing leaves too.

And Harry looks at his desk and as was his habit, began to scratch through the papers and work on his business, ciphering and notating as the night comes on.

Chapter Ten

Pleasure

Charlie May's family farm has about 70 acres. As you come up a steep curling rise off the old Pumptown Highway it crests and there is the main house, not fancied up, just white with green shutters and its two low stories melt into its place and sprawl about the land comfortably. There are two barns for horses and storage, equipment and hay just above it to the right and down below in a long, stretching meadow, horses graze. The expanse of it is encircled with tall trees that have been there a very long time. A circular gravel drive lies in front of the house.

There are a number of cars slotted here and there along the edge of the drive and two men, Jimmy and Harvey, stand under the back portico, back lit by the lamps that frame the doorway. They are there to help and also to cook. They have been serving drinks and hors d'oeuvres and when they had heard J.T.'s car coming up the hill, they stopped to assist the arriving company and now step forth to open all the car doors.

A gaggle of folks on the big porch overlook the rolling field that is lit up from the house. Their conversation burbles in the falling purple dusk along with the sounds of their emptying glasses. There is a low, sort of crooning music that sounds so nice, as though the world has slowly stopped here on this soft pinpoint in the countryside and that nothing else much matters.

J.T. unfolds handsomely from the wheel seat and says, "Hello, Jimmy. Nice to see you. How have you been?"

Friday Calls

Jimmy, tall with an Adam's apple of a goose neck replies, "Great, Mr. J.T. You?"

And then he adds with a respectful nod, "Good evening, ladies."

His helper Harvey says about the same and in a rustle come forth the girls, all smiles and giggles, and the party on the porch moves down the steps to greet them with many hugs and approving looks.

Jimmy and Harvey gather up the small overnight bags and cases from the trunk. The girls head to the porch to preen and flutter and continue the carryings on.

Once inside, Harvey takes the luggage to the assigned rooms as instructed by Jimmy. The bedrooms, as is true all throughout the house, were done in understated and comfortable good taste, the country house look of Sister Parrish. Jimmy heads back to the bar on the porch to refresh and renew all of their drinks. He carries the steaks and shrimp that have been picked up earlier. And as the heat of the day releases and fades, and the breezes of the cooling earth come along out of the trees, it is almost time to cook.

Kenny's head continues to swell and throb as does the bloat in his belly, but it is time to get in and go to work. PeeWee is not much better and in spite of it all, starts up the steps behind Kenny. There are a few people on the front porch, but they are just smoking and quiet. Curt Minor meets them at the door.

"Hello, boys."

"Hey, Curt."

Curt says, "PeeWee, Here's twenty bucks. I want you to run down the street and grab plenty of ice and three or four cartons of cigarettes: Winstons, Camels, Salems. Take Kenny's truck. Kenny, you go on in and help Rise with whatever she needs, plus I think Bo wants to tell you some things."

They nod and move, one in and one off. PeeWee had never bothered to get a driver's license, but then again once Kenny had gotten the old used truck, he'd let the insurance expire so PeeWee couldn't drive it legal anyway. It is the way of their world.

Kenny trudges up the stairs and on through the front room into the large, long back countered kitchen. There is Bo.

"Hey, Peak? You get my order from C.B.?" Bo's tone is challenging.

"Yeah, you know I did. It's right there under your feet. Why you be messing with me about that?"

Bo ignores him on that point and says, "I need you to later on be making some small deliveries for me, if you know what I mean. There might be a little something in it for you if you get my drift..."

"Well, you already owe me for those lawyer fees you said you and Curt said you were gonna pay and you got me Mr. Big Shot Attorney-at-Law down there across from the court house and, and..."

Kenny hesitates. This is not going well to open the bidding. His head hurts and he is foggy. But, he isn't going to start taking anything back.

"...and I just paid for y'alls order over at City B and hauled it over here so y'all owe me for that too..." His words drip down.

"Let me tell you something, you big dumb nigger," Bo shoots back. "I'll get you some money later, but right now, you be in my employ and I do not need right now to be hearing a bunch of shit-talk coming out of your big-headed mouth. Do you understand me? You work for me, right, Catty, right, Curt?"

Kenny thinks, *What the hell? I ought to kill this little son-of-a-bitch now... strangle his gnarly old ass...*He can feel the red coming up into his head and his breathing coming shorter and faster. He starts pulling his billfold out of his pocket as an exhibit to all of the straits of greater unfairness he has just been flung. It is only getting deeper. A big "damn damn damn" buzzes in his brain.

He looks up at Curt and Curt has a hard, flat stare that goes only barely over Kenny's head.

Rise looks up from behind the counter, shakes her head slightly and says, "Come on, now. Let's everybody be cool now. People are coming. Y'all don't need to be running people off before the bank starts to grow. Kenny, come round here and help me." She shifts her bulk alertly now.

Felicia looks dopey-eyed away, lost in self-adulation and used to Bo's hard, tough-talk, cruel ways that are part of the price of keeping herself in his game.

Kenny glances at Rise and she jerks her head and the big slicing knife

Friday Calls

she's using to cut tomatoes up for the sandwiches. Bo studies the rings on his fingers. Kenny knows he is going to work harder for his money tonight.

And people are coming in. There is BobCat, head Shine Master at the Hotel. He is a little guy but friendly, nice and always interested in everybody else. He works for Mr. Jigs Willis and Mr. Harry Johnson, has a black and white shine stand with chrome legs and also a mahogany shine box he works off when the barbers have someone in the green leatherette chairs. Miss Irene does their nails, he does their shoes. He can flat snap that rag. He has a lady with a pretty summer dress on with him.

"Hey, everybody—what we drinking tonight? Hot out there, ain't it? Darlin', what you want?"

Is he oblivious or just studiously ignoring the flaring geyser easily within his earshot and eyeballs?

"Hey, Cat, step right up." Bo gestures.

Here comes lumpy Donald, the hardest working Blue Bird Taxi Company cabbie wanting to wet his whistle and relax before his graveyard shift begins at midnight. Here is Helen Rater. She had been married to Daddy-Oh from the radio years before, but he had slapped her around too much so she had just moved on—and Libby Craft and Rose Hill, all of them cooks and maids for the well-to-do over in the northwest part of town. Here comes lumbering, sweet, goggle-eyed Roosevelt Truesdale and Mr. John "The Stick" Tedder and Buck Mason, yardmen and orderlies at the big hospital. And in come neighborhood folks from the city work yards and the tall office buildings and the airliner repair hangers. It is going to be a good night.

Kenny moves behind the counter with his sister. She says, "Here, get this bread good and covered up with Dukes so we can put these sandwiches together and please turn the fish in the pan. Let's just stay cool, okay?"

Kenny shrugs and grunts and does as he is told.

The weather inside has cleared.

Curt Minor stands and watches and walks to the front, head straight ahead, tight-smiled and eyes swiveling.

Chapter Eleven

The Boiling

The hulking black Ford, a no-nonsense, sturdy epitome of a company car noses down the hill onto Reynolda Road. Archer has errands too and there are going to have to be a couple of pauses along the way. As usual, he is running late.

First is the big service station down near the high school. He rolls to a stop next to one of the gasoline service islands. As he comes to a halt, two fully uniformed and be-hatted oil jockeys are next to the car, saying hello, checking tire pressures and wiping his whitewalls, cleaning the windows and filling the tank with gas.

Archer steps out and says, "Hello, boys."

They reply as mockingbirds, "Hello, Mr. Glenn!"

Archer strolls across the lot over into the office where the station manager sits at his desk. Harry Bennett is a sparrow of a man, and has been at the station for more than a quarter of a century. He chirps, "Uh-huh" more than most people seemed to blink. It was his universal language and was known well to his customer base.

"Hey, Harry."

"Archer. Uh-huh. Uh-huh?"

"Harry, could you please get the boys to whisk broom me out and dust me up a little bit? I know it needs a wash, but I haven't got time…"

"Uh-huh. Yes. Uh-huh."

He flutters out onto the pad.

"Boys. Boys. How about give that Ford of Mr. G's a good dusting. Uh-huh. Uh-huh. Good!"

"Thank you, Harry."

"Uh-huh. Uh-huh."

The sun continues its bend to the west while the station's neon garage door stripings and big yellow and red shell-shaped signs flicker into brightness.

Archer sits on a small bench just outside the office door. He lights a cigarette and watches the boys quickly broom his car's interior from every angle like locusts covering a field.

After one of them waves the ready sign, Archer goes to the car, signals the offered purchase ticket, thanks them and rolls out.

Archer drives around a long sweeping border of a city park and then turns up onto a quiet street in a still, tree-swathed neighborhood. He drives up the hill a few blocks and then eases over to the curve and parks.

He gets out, goes around the back of his car and notices the trunk is unlocked. He glances in, sees the cardboard box that had been delivered to him earlier. He cocks his head and briefly studies the case. The "C.B." written on the box does not have any sort of official look and as a matter of fact he had never seen such a marking coming out of anything he'd ever gotten from City Beverage. He feels he ought to check it as it is his gift to his host and friends for the evening's festivities. He peels the tape off the seam and opens the flaps.

Two dark, empty slots out of twelve stare back at him.

"What the hell..." Reflexively, he snap-reaches into the spaces and then pulls the ten other bottles out to look at them.

He mutters, "Damn, I've been shorted..." and also knows immediately City Beverage has not done it. Harry Davis and his boy may be sour and unpleasant, but they always counted exactly down the line. And, too, he knew that Frank from the Club hadn't done it. Frank is an honorable man and surely would not risk his job over a mere two bottles of hooch, good hooch though it might be.

It, now that he looked, was an amateur deceit and one which probably left, doing a fast equation, the culprit as whoever made the delivery from City B. to Frank. He could let them find out that he knew about their trick on him next week. He is running a little bit later and later and needs to get moving. He still has one more stop before heading to Charlie May's and once close, he knows a liquor store over that way that sold out the back door after hours so he could punch fill his box and deliver it properly.

He goes up a short walk, up a few brick steps and opens the front door. Inside the door, he briskly picks up a bag sitting there. He walks back to the car, places the bag in the trunk, gently closes the passenger door, and then is back at the wheel, moving again.

Archer turns on the radio and rolls the dial until he finds music. He wants a drink, a big drink. And he doesn't want to wait. He is off-duty, on his way to not work and he can feel himself begin to sag with the beginnings of release. It is a welcomed weariness, as though his whole body is exhaling, burning off the office and home.

Home. Home is not easy. Home is a lot of things, some good, some not so good. He turns the radio up a little louder and speaks quietly to himself, "Well, here comes the weekend..." and he smiles ever so slightly.

As he pulls away from the curb, he thinks where to go in the direction he's heading and grab that big drink along the way when it comes to him.

Archer drives back into the center of town and then past the rows and rows of warehouses and factories, the strong scent of the tobacco redolent, carried in the hot breeze in the early evening dropping sun. He lights a cigarette and eyes the corner just up ahead.

It is Leon's, a combination sandwich, drinks, beer and sports and girlie magazine shop tucked into the corner of R. J. Reynolds Building 116. Leon had been there, serving the shifts and shifty for as long as he could remember. One could get a bit more there too if one knew how to ask. Leon could help with an abortion, a bet, a gun or a good drink of whiskey.

Archer pulls into the alley to the right of the building, his car deep shadowed by tall red brick walls tight on either side. He gingerly exits and walks briskly down the way and around onto the sidewalk.

Leon is dressed in a dirty white T-shirt, is of massive bulk that starts and ends with his nose and belly. He leans in blank repose with a large white towel folded over his arms behind the long counter. In front of him are chrome stanchion red-topped circle-rimmed stools lined up like sentries. A couple of men in bib overalls smell of cured leaf and sweat sit on two of

Friday Calls

them, long-necked beer bottles and smoking ashtrays before them. A few more are sprinkled toward the back, hunched down in the few booths in the corner, past the wall racks of magazines and newspapers, beer and cigarettes in hand. It is well past the shift change from second to third at three that afternoon and as it is Friday, the usual, post-work drinkers and talkers and lingerers have slipped on toward further on out there. It is quiet save for the radio in the kitchen. Sam Cooke is crooning "Darling, you send me, honest you do, honest you do, whoa."

No one looks up. No one looks at Archer, not even a glance. Only Leon's big bug eyes swivel slowly toward the door and languidly eye the handsome gentleman in the clothes of the weekend gentry.

"Well, hello, Archer." Leon smiles. "And to what do we owe this pleasure?" Leon's arm royally and slowly swings the compass of the long room.

Archer blinks and softly asks, "You know, I'd like to get one of those fine milkshakes you make from time to time."

"Well, yes, of course. What flavor would you like?"

"Chocolate. Good and very brown. Very icy. Please."

Leon nods and says, "Let's step to the end of the counter where I make them."

They parallel step one another down the length of the counter. At the back are the booths of the few unwatching and a large rack of magazines and paperback books of what could only be called serious, adult, high-test pornography. It is known or soon known to all who came in there that only the familiar, the regulars, the discreet are allowed back there in the deep end of the place.

Leon, reaching under the counter, produces a large milkshake cup and fills it with crushed ice and then puts his hands back under the counter and in a few seconds hands Archer a large, to the top cold bourbon with a snap plastic lid on it. Archer pulls cash from his pants pocket and hands it to Leon.

"Thank you, sir." Archer heads to the door.

"You are very welcome, sir. Have a nice weekend. And by the way—football season is finally here!"

"Yes, it is. Just in time."

No one looks up.

Archer returns to his car, looks around, gets in and says, "Here we go." And pausing just a beat, "Now, we're cookin'." He takes the lid off the cup for a long pull. He pauses and sighs with the shiver of the drink rolling down into him. He backs out of the alley and heads east.

* * *

Curt Minor's place is filling up and the lights are on with the music playing. People are playing cards, shooting craps, visiting, arguing, flirting, dancing, drinking. The volume is coming up. Money and talk are moving all over the back rooms, washing in the Friday night now a part of them.

Rise has Kenny moving at her appointed tasks and he is transitioning to the long kitchen counter that is the evening's bar. He makes drinks, popping caps off beer bottles, takes money, trying to be careful with it. Kenny can see Bo eyeing him. Bo, like the Cheshire Cat, there one second, gone the next, back again as an apparition of mean cheap.

PeeWee has returned from delivering the cigarettes and change to Minor, counting it out with precision. PeeWee stands stone still before him, awaiting his further instructions. There is a pause, and then—

Minor says, "I let David Edwards go—he'd rather play than pay attention...so, PeeWee, I want you to go out back and just keep a watch out. Sit down low on the back steps. Stay in the shadows. That flood light above your head ought to give you good looks. We got a good crowd tonight. I don't want any sons-of-bitches coming through the backyard to visit the drawer. If you see anything, and I mean anything, you get your skinny ass to me faster than greased owl shit. And that means cops too. You got it?"

"Yessir." PeeWee loves being the lookout. It appeals to his sense of furtiveness and importance, both of which want to run strong in him. He is well aware he is totally of this earth in this moment and the idea of a future is beyond indistinct. The future is out in the rat-ass old scraggy backyard that dims out before him.

He moves through the kitchen and out the back, the screen slapping in that off-key, off kilter, not-quite-fitting anymore clap. He sits down on the bottom step and fingers his Zippo. He decides it is all right to grab a smoke and does, taking the cloud deeply, knowing it will be his last for a while.

Inside, Curt Minor hands the cartons of cigarettes to Rise who in turn parcels them out to Kenny. Minor watches everything flat-eyed, not beady like Bo. It is Minor's house after all and Bo is just the local flash cash man.

There is a burst of loud laughing and hooting that surges out of a group tight up at the bar. David Edwards, a line mechanic at the tobacco company, a burly man with a sweet face has come in, gotten a double, downed it quick, said hello to all about him, gotten another and is finishing a good story about Daddy-Oh and it is a true one too.

Daddy-Oh always had a high-falutin' streak and when he drank, which was all the time, he became even more convinced of his self-exalted celebrity. He had been at Triple-A for more than five years and was feeling unappreciated and underpaid. His patter was superb and his playlist of rough and tumble blues, scream and shout was hotly sought.

He felt it was time for a bigger gig so one afternoon after belting a few brown waters back, he thumbed the Yellow Pages, eyed the numbers and called the general manager over at WAIR, one of the two bubble-gum whitey AM stations in town. WAIR had been in a two-horse race with WTOB for years and had yet get close to winning any ratings contest. It was a symbiotic call. A meeting was set for in the morning. The GM was intrigued.

Mr. Oscar Alexander, aka Daddy-Oh On The Patio, pressed the up button, tugged at his tie, rolled his neck and then stepped forth and presented his zooted, hooty-tooty self to Dick Benedict at the station's studios in a tall office building in the center of the city. Benedict had heard the man for years and knew he had a following that wasn't just colored. Within thirty minutes, a one-year deal had been cut and Daddy-Oh was going to do the most important eight to midnight shift in direct combat with WTOB. And the demographic was going to change.

And it did. Daddy-Oh's following followed him. Triple-A was left with a couple of station engineers to bumble where Daddy-Oh once strutted. Young whites began to listen to the moaning growlings presented nightly and WAIR was on the move.

But like Icarus, Daddy-Oh flew too close to the sun. At Triple-A, he had but the loosest of supervision and he picked what he wanted to play and say. Such as, "Here in the atmospheric conditions of our universal solar system—it's clear as a bell and hot as—98 degrees!" This was racy stuff.

At WAIR, management was white, buttoned-down and formulaic. Daddy-Oh was allowed to play lots of his picks, but too was required to well lace the offerings with the toned down American Bandstand cookie-cutter treacle.

And, of course, his slot being the night, usually by time he got to the station, he'd had a few, was carrying some more and as the records played, sourly contemplating the tight harness he was now in. They were paying him good money, more than he before had ever made, but now he was, well, a slave. He chafed.

And so one night as the broadcast engineer read the sports pages and dozed, Daddy-Oh grandly announced he was going to take requests and the lines lit up. Daddy-Oh pushed the button and a caller asked for "The Trumpeter's Prayer." And Daddy-Oh said, "You got it!" and played "Shake a Tail Feather," the Five Du-Tones' feral, ass-shaking tribute to booty and all its enticements. And the next caller asked for "Town Without Pity" and Daddy-Oh said, "Man, you got it!" and played "Shake a Tail Feather" and it was game on and the engineer woke up and buzzed into the studio and Daddy-Oh said, "Hooty tooty we just having some fun now!" and otherwise ignored the poor schlub, save for grinning through the control booth window while he took another pull off the fifth he coated in.

And caller after caller, knowing what was going to happen, called and requested everything from "Happy Birthday" to "Mary Had A Little Lamb" to "Beethoven's 5th" and one and all got another raucous serving of the infamous, scandalous "Shake a Tail Feather." And the word went out all over town that an amazing, outlandish and very rebellious and funny thing was happening and WAIR's ratings that night went through the roof.

And from time to time, Daddy-Oh could be heard on air mumbling, "They can all go fuck their candy ass white asses…" and other variants on the theme which made it all the more titillating.

Well, I heard about the fellow
You've been dancing with
All over the neighborhood
Tell me why didn't you ask me, baby?
Or didn't you think I could?

Well I know your partner will never step aside
I've seen you do the Jerk all night.
Why didn't you ask me, baby?
I would have shown you how to do it right.
Do it right
Do it right
Do it right
Do it right
Do it right

Ahhhhhhhuhh pussy! Twist it
Shake it
Shake it
Shake it baby
Here we go loop de loop
Shake it up baby
Here we go loop de lie
Bend over and let me see you shake a tail feather
Bend over and let me see you shake your tail feather
Bend over!

Aside from its dead-on raunch, the use of the word "pussy" in such a format was the basic signal flare to hell.

And after a while, Daddy-Oh was dead drunk snoring and the phones weren't being answered. The turntable rasped in circles with its needle in a dead-end plastic crease and Mr. Benedict yelled in his bathrobe, pajamas, and slippers and others did too. The harsh, hard banging on the locked studio door all came to a crashing end as the door was smashed open with a fire ax wielded by a mystified and amused janitor. Mr. Oscar Alexander, eyes and brain at half mast, was warned sternly about the FCC's prohibitions on vulgar words and was roughly escorted downstairs to his car and summarily fired.

And so Daddy-Oh became the biggest legend in radio in the city and south, took a half-cut in pay, and crawled back to Triple-A.

The crowd howled with glee save for his ex-wife nearby who glared and said with a tight smile, "He was something and he is always an asshole."

Just before the tale and the jocularity, Edwards cheerfully announces, "Well, I did get fired by Minor a little while ago, but he said it was fine to be coming around so here I am. Hell, it's Friday night, right?"

"What happened?" he is asked.

He replies, "Minor says I'm lazy and not any damn good at keeping an eye on things. I expect he's right. It's all right. Now lemme tell y'all a good one. This just happened last night..."

And after the Daddy-Oh tale, he slow walks off into the crowd, smiling broadly with his arms waving over his head like a prize fighter who has knocked the guy out.

Kenny is hustling. Bo says, "Boy, you can be messy clumsy sometimes." Kenny thinks, *Slow down—speed up—nothing gonna suit you sorry-ass nigger.*

Kenny has about had it. He is scraping cups through the ice and pouring and trying to focus.

Kenny stands taller and says in a low voice out of the side of his mouth, "Bo, you know I paid the man at City B out of my own pocket this afternoon and I'd like to get that back this evening and you owe me for those dope deliveries from a week ago and you and Minor said you were gonna help me with the lawyer's fees for me taking the fall for you and keeping my mouth shut..."

And Bo, who has been leaning on the door jamb to the kitchen, says, "Fuck you, nigger."

Kenny steps away from the ice chest and walks around to the service side of the bar, becoming part of the crowd. He is struggling to exhale. Rise watches from the back of the kitchen.

Curt Minor also watches and listens to this. David Edwards, tight as Dick's hatband, is dancing mostly with himself and anyone else who wanders into his orbit. It is hot and crowded. Minor glides up to Edwards and quietly says, "I need the gun." Edwards is always carrying, just to show Minor he is reliable.

Edwards asks, "Why?"

Minor clips him off, "None of your goddamn business." Minor snatches the gun from the side of Edwards's pants and puts it in his belt underneath his coat drape. The music keeps coming up, tracing the talking and laughing.

Bo Diddley keeps coming to the ear.

Tombstone hard and a graveyard mine.
Just 22 and I don't mind dying.
Who do you love?
Who do you love?
I rode a lion to town, use a rattlesnake whip,
Take it easy Arlene, don't give me no lip.
Who do you love?
Who do you love?
Night was dark but the sky was blue,
Down the alley the ice wagon flew,
Heard the bump, somebody screamed.
You should have heard what I just seen.
Who do you love?
Who do you love?
Who do you love?
Who do you love?
Arlene took me by the hand,
And said OoohWeee Bo, you know I understand.
Who do you love?

Minor walks over to Kenny and opens his coat wide enough for Kenny to see. David Edwards, now suddenly alert and alarmed, stumbles over and says, "Curt, don't you be opening your coat if you don't want them to be having the gun."

"Shut up, boy."

Bo's eyes get big and he, trance-like, steps toward Curt, his ring-up'd right hand starting for the piece.

But Kenny, eyes red as the fires of hell, reaches quick for the gun and takes it tight in his big hand and holds it to his side.

Chapter Twelve

Over the Edge

Charlie May's farm smells like late summer and early fall, all the smells of green ripe and cool breeze and apples all mixed together. The dusk has gone now to dark. Besides the windows of the house and the candles on the porch tables, the only other signs of light glowed off in the distance from other houses way across the way.

The group sits about the deck that spills down toward the pastures, drinking and talking, the men showing out for the ladies, the ladies paying attention to the men. It is a trading game, no less than pelts for wampum.

Others have joined them. Madge Roberts, renowned as a local beautiful and constantly sought-after courtesan and madam with a stable of well-to-do bored housewives sits quietly, drink and cigarette in same hand, evaluating the old and the new talent before her. Countess Tommy, statuesque, blond and already half-drunk, giggles over the basic tittering of it all.

Jimmy walks across the deck to Charlie May.

"Mr. May, we've done put everything in the assigned rooms and are you ready for us to light up the grills and put it all together?"

"Well...let's see Jimmy..." He looks around the group and pauses and says, "Let's all have one more and if you and Harvey would pass those crackers and things again. Archer's not here yet so let's wait a little more so we are all complete in a little while."

"Yessir."

"Y'all know Archer. He'll be late for his own funeral."

They all laugh. It is true. For all of his business sense and personal goodness, his clock ran an easy thirty minutes behind the rest of the world.

J.T. says, "He's balancing and balancing."

Purvis chortles and adds, "Yeah, the Business and the Missus and the Misses...too...sometimes..."

Some nod. Others just refresh their drinks and keep enjoying the lovely night that has come along. Someone told the joke about "What do you do with an elephant with three balls?"

There is anticipatory giggling and Nickels says, "Okay, I'll bite. What?"

"You walk him and pitch to the rhino."

They all laugh. It is an old chestnut but a good one, just mildly provocative early in the evening.

Somewhere in the pleasant chatter comes the obligatory minister, priest and rabbi prod, something about the effectiveness of preaching to a bear. It rambles along a loose track and ends with a punch line that has the rabbi in a hospital bed beaten all to hell, telling his fellow brethren of the cloth that it is probably not such a good idea to begin his conversion pitch with the performance of the bris. They all hoot and holler and the night moves on.

The ladies glow in the candlelight and the men are stirred by them and the whiskey and themselves. The tree frogs and crickets croak and saw. There is no rush. The time and night are languid.

Someone says, "Did y'all hear about that crazy son-of-a-bitch on the radio last night?"

"No, what?"

"Seems that Daddy-Oh On The Patio guy who used to be over on Triple-A got a job at WAIR and got drunk on air last night and played "Shake a Tail Feather" about a thousand times in a row and cussed everybody out in between until they got him out of there."

"Damn. Sounds like a career suicide move."

"Those negroes will surely be cutting up from time to time."

"Yes, that is so."

And so forth.

The time moves along and Charlie finally calls for Jimmy and says, "Let's get started. He'll be along after a while and we can always have his plate ready for him when he gets here."

Someone says, "Well, hear hear!" and matters thusly proceed.

* * *

The train moves steady, rocking slightly, its cars clicking and clacking. They are coming down around a long sweeping curve of track that is enfolded in miles of hardwood trees and thickets of late summer growth. The sounds of the behemoth are sealed in the column.

Knight and Gordon lull along with their train. They are coming along toward Greensboro Center in about twenty minutes and will begin the long slowing soon. Not too fast, not too slow, just right—so the cars won't bunch and jump. No need for that.

They pull past and out of the last copses of trees and the train's headlamps and ditch lights find the track clear ahead at the Franklin Street junction, some 200 yards off.

* * *

Archer has come on through Greensboro and swung to the south to pick up the road to the old Burlington Highway. It is now all dark out in the country. Small houses and farms slip by here and there as he goes. He has finished his large cup of brown liquor and is just sucking on its ice in warm and settled silence. The radio plays. He turns it up. As he comes up the road, there is a short but steep grade. It is as though he is in a sweet cocoon. He laughs quietly and sings in his low, kind voice along with the great James Brown—

I love you, yes, I do.
I love you, yes, I do.
I'm yours my whole life through,
Since I first laid eyes on you.

He pats the seat and his right leg in time with the music and touches out beyond.

The whiskey is nice and has slowed him as he looks up to the left, beyond the uptilt grade before him and there sits Willie Dascomb's liquor store. Its pink and green neon sign blinks and buzzes and it is well after closing time, but Archer can see the florescent lights on in the back and in the parking lot and Willie's Chevy parked behind the building. He'll zip in there, make a quick back-door buy to replenish his evening's offerings and most likely take another short pull for the pleasant warmth of it all and carry a little gifting toter back to the car as well. Always good to keep the eyes on the prize.

He then looks lower, more level, first to his left and then to his right and sees a big truck moving toward him from the west on the Old Burlington Road, its very bright lights washing toward him, making him shade his brow and squint. And as he crests the sharp little rise, his headlights get swallowed momentarily by the bank of the climb just before the tracks. He is invisible and as the darkness gathers him, he hears the truck's horn; it's very loud and the interior of his car gets bright very quickly and then everything explodes into a complete black silence.

* * *

Kenny steps back just aways into the foaming, slinking crowd, sort of tucking himself into its undulating slow-motion Friday night slide and strut. It is loud in his head and then it isn't and of course, as with any action such as that which was within seconds forthcoming, everything slows way down. He hears dice rolling and tumbling like the seconds of a clock's tick. He hears a truck shifting gears, grinding them along, going up the little hilled street next to the house. All the voices around gurgle as a drowning, marbling into laps of sound.

Kenny raises the .38 and really doesn't see Bo. He does not care to see Bo, to see his nasty, mean face. That will put some personal into it and Kenny is sick and tired of the personal, the beat-downs, the mistreatment of his person. But he does see his form and he tries to find the center as he lets the hammer fall.

The form of Bo stops moving and yanks like being startled, jerking to the right, a pulling back away like un-huh, no, no you don't, and then Bo's chin comes up and down like a fast nod and then he cat-dances back to the bar counter and slumps a little bit, but stays more due north than not.

And then as if being snapped suddenly out of a trance, the hypnotist is the big black, solid blast from the gun and it rings out sharp loud and everything starts going real fast, faster than before.

Voices start hollering and screaming. And there is fast commotion everywhere around him and as all that starts up, Kenny hears two, maybe three, lighter snaps and Bo saying, "Damn. I am shot..."

There is a lot of,

"Oh, shit!"

"What in the fuck?"

"Goddamn!"

"Get down, get down goddammit!"

"Oh, my God."

And so forth.

Kenny fires again but it is high and he does not care very much, for he has been true enough on the opening bid. The smoke from the discharges begin spreading through the back room and the sour stink of cordite bites into the air.

Kenny's arm comes down slowly, halted by heavy gravity, and the gun is snatched from his hand by Curt Minor.

Rise is standing solid in the doorway, just behind and to the side of where Bo is folding up. Kenny sees her looking at him and watches her mouth silently, but she clearly says, "Go outside and wait."

Kenny turns and hot-foots it out the front door and sees Pete Miller coming out down the steps right behind him. Miller has a pistol in his hand, a baby .22. Kenny says, "Boom, what the fuck you doin' with that"? Miller just grins and says, "Nothing, just trying to help old Curt out." and zips quick into the dark.

Curt Minor has gone to the back door and hisses loud for PeeWee whose face appears at the foot of the back stairs.

"What happened?"

"No time for talking but you got to be doing now, you understand?"

PeeWee says fast, "Yessir!"

"PeeWee, take this gun and run and run some more back toward town and drop it into the biggest, darkest, deepest blackest motherfuckin' storm drain up near the tobacco washing sheds and wipe it good with your shirt just before you do. You understand?"

Friday Calls

PeeWee understands.

"And then walk back over this way here real cool and calm on this hot night and wait for me in the back vestibule of Gilmore's. And you don't know shit, right?"

"Right." And he takes the piece and slips into the dark across the back of the lot and keeps on moving. All sorts of old dogs in the dark are pulling on their chains, howling, barking as he runs past, the dancing of the broken field run.

PeeWee thinks as he moves, "Well, truth be told I don't know shit, but I expect I will soon enough."

Minor goes back into the house. Only seconds have passed and the confusion and terror and amazement is still riding the rooms.

Felicia now has Bo in her cradling arms and is moaning, "Oh Bo, oh Bo, oh Bo," crooning it, her best close up for all to see.

Women are still screaming and men are still cussing. It is like a heart monitor bouncing all over the screen, zagging and zigging and zagging again.

Curt Minor goes quick and gets his shotgun and holds it straight up to the ceiling and pulls both barrels. The crashing crack of its detonation instantly stuns and quiets the people. He yells for quiet as the smoke plums out and bits of the hole above him flutter down. "I don't think anybody really knows what happened here, but I do think everybody ought to be going now before any new visitors arrive. It is a good time to know how to leave and to know how to forget."

No one knows his words as anything but a command.

And like quail being flushed from covey, they are all quickly gone except for Felicia and Bo and a couple of fellows, David Edwards and Donald the Cabbie, who Curt has nodded to, directing them to stay. A queer boy named Johnny Iberia, a root doctor who has been there telling fortunes in trade for drinks, dope, giggles, and chances stands there real still looking at the leaking mess that slumps on the floor, rattling. Iberia is wearing a dashiki and a raggedy ass straw hat as part of his hoodoo-voodoo get up. His gaiety is now misplaced.

Iberia mumbles, "Some bad juju going down. Some bad juju..."

Curt knows it is time to keep reshuffling the deck.

He puts the shotgun in a corner and makes sure it is in plain view.

"Iberia, go the fuck on away from here now. Put a good spell on your and everybody else's ass so their memories becomes nothing but sweet dreams. You got it?"

"Oh, yes, I got it Mr. Minor." And he is gone in a swish.

Curt Minor takes all the money out of the cash box, counts and folds it fast and snaps a big rubber band on it. Rise watches him. He hands it to Rise and says, "Stick this in your tight britches. They won't search you. I've got the count. You'll get some. I'll get up with you through Ben. Got it?"

"Yes, but I need to go stand with Kenny."

"I understand."

Curt knows she is a pro.

Felicia keeps wailing and caterwauling, rocking in her very real, draining loss and soaking drama.

Bo moans and mutters something about, "Moms Catty Moms, take me to my car. I've got to be going." There is a lot of slow ooze spreading on and under him. He is going to rattle it out very soon.

Curt Minor says to the other men, "Let's go." And they do, snatching Bo from Felicia and carrying him fast out to his car at the curb and splaying him into the front passenger seat. Felicia follows and gets behind the wheel. She cranks the Caddy up and starts to pull away. They will let her play act at being the saving angel, but then Bo finishes his last fucking up by dying.

But they have gotten him out of the house and that is a start. Felicia wails.

Kenny is standing under a tree about half a block away.

Kenny knows he has fucked up bad, but his fear of Bo and his hatred of Bo have jumped up on him and taken his free will, just sucked it out of him like a vampire. He looks around for his sister. The light is sparse and flutters in and out from the tree. She comes down the stairs.

Rise sighs and says, "Well, be still now. The police will be here soon. Don't make it worse by trying to run. And don't say a word when they take you in other than your name. Tell them right off you want a lawyer. Understand?"

Kenny nods.

Rise says, "I'll be busy on that. I'll be to see you tomorrow. Now, no more dumb stuff."

The sirens are coming from downtown.

Rise says, "Didn't Bo used to pack? Didn't Bo used to carry that little piece of shit two-shot derringer? Remember that when you talk to the lawyer. You were threatened. You thought you were. Got it?"

And then she walks back up into the house and begins to clean up in the kitchen and watch Minor and the others, quietly and carefully. Felicia has come back inside too and is beginning to realize that she has a lot of blood all over her and that her sugar daddy has achieved room temperature. Her prospects have tanked.

* * *

As the big train sweeps around the long tree-lined curve, there are just a few lights glimmering out along the line sweeping past. Dark had come on. It is warm. And then H. E. Knight screams and Jenkins Gordon snaps his face to the track line in front.

Knight hollers, "Brakes! Brakes!" and pulls back on his throttle in a death grip yank, the ratchet back sounding like the lightning bolt shuffle of a deck of cards from hell. Gordon sees the disaster before them and is frantically twisting the dials to let the air brakes grab friction. The train jerks and strains to slow, to stop. The tracks are squealing a horrible wail. Conductor Kevin, in a hazy doze in the jump seat behind them starts up into a clearer consciousness and says, "What? What?" And he instantly knows as did the other two that something or someone was getting ready to be sent to Kingdom Come. It is all happening too fast.

Knight lays on the giant air horns and the ditch lights roll up on a black sedan moving onto the track. It is going to be too late. Everything seems to be going in slow motion but the sensation is a lie. The strobing Gyralites at the top of the cab micro-flash the car in and out of its brighter, then dimmer, view.

"Is he playing chicken with us? Is he trying to kill himself?" Knight and Gordon think in mute concert. Trainmen know these things, have seen these things, but this is the Friday milk run and those few beers have relaxed their minds and their hands.

The train is piling up with the cars slugging into the backs of those before them, creating an uncoiling, slamming thrust. They are certain more than a few couplers jerk lungs as they bust loose. The train shakes, rocks sideways on the track. Air hose lines pop loose. Even as the train seems to slow, it feels as if it is being shot-slung down the track, an enormous, accelerating missile, fighting against itself to no avail.

Somewhere within seconds of something after 8 p.m., Southern 1105 slams broadside into a dark sedan, carving it almost in two, the impact simply a slight jerk and a shudder inside the cab even as gashing, ripping, tearing metal, screeching louder as the huge engine's deep steel catcher has now taken hold of the car and is shoving it, carrying it, dragging it down the rails, its tires blowing up, sparks deep showering up above the windows of the engine, glass shattering until the car's nose is smashed into a stout signal pole just off the tracks. The car is flung away, set free to whirl airborne, parts and pieces of it flying, twisting in brief flight. It then rolls hard into the ground of the deep graded gulley off the tracks, rolling one last time into the weeds and trash, a trailing flame like a dying Roman candle pluming from its rear, bright flaring, sputtering, then gone.

The train keeps slowing as it passes the automobile's carcass and it keeps going, more than another thousand yards, its length steadying but looser now. The car's parts have come apart and are in pieces, moving with the lessening momentum. The train has killed and come rag doll loose and is settling into its yawing slowing and stop. Its drivers had lost its control and the fear of it all instantly floods their throats and guts in sour thick bile.

Chapter Thirteen

Deeds Done

Harry Davis has finished his paperwork and now sits quietly save for the low creaking of his chair. Only the lamp light on his desk lays out the neat stacks of notes and records, each weighted by smooth river stones gathered long ago when Harry was a boy. Harry regards them fleetingly, remembers who he was, an innocent. He had washed the white and round stones in the shallows of the river, and he had picked many of them out to use for what he did not know then. But he had kept them and now they squat on his legal and illegal affairs with their nice weight, feeling good in the hand as a baseball does. He had become a man of important affairs in a small niche of a place and was relied upon. The thought of such is laughable to him, but only a simple pleasant exhale of head-shaking cynicism blows forth from him.

He rolls his shoulders, squeezes his eyes and pinches the bridge of his nose, pulls his palms down over his face and stands up.

He thinks, *Well, this was a good day. Deliveries made. Bets taken. Cash in hand and more to come tomorrow. Time to go home.*

He turns out the light on his desk, walks to the door and thinks then as well, *There will be more news tomorrow. There always is.*

And then he empties his mind, flips the "Open" sign to "Closed" and goes out the door to his car parked in the back. As he pulls out into the street, the phone inside the office rings and continues to ring for a long time. He does not hear it.

***

Curt knows Bo is dead. He told the others to take his body out of the car and carry it up the hill past the drink house to lay it down in the graveyard next to the little wooden church. He told them that once they had done that work to each grab a couple of bottles of liquor and leave quick and to "think about all the things you will never remember again" and to go home and carefully discard their clothes far away and to bathe as if preparing for baptism, drink a good deal and go to bed.

All tasks finished, they vanish, apparitions into the night.

The sirens grow closer.

Curt grabs Felicia and walks her back up into the drink house. She is silent.

He snatches a bar of octagon soap from the kitchen sink, turns the water on very hot and then begins to roughly scrub his hands and arms.

Felicia then softly asks, "Why did you take him out of the car up to the church yard?"

"Everybody thought it was the right thing to do, get him nearer to God and all..."

"Oh. Yes." She looks off into the distance.

"I never knew him to go to services. Do you think that helped?"

Curt nods, "Yes, I hope so. Why don't you sit down over there. The police will be here soon... and Felicia, watch your mouth real good and tight. You understand?"

She glares at him. Then she nods hard and she sits down hard, arms crossed.

Curt has lied and keeps on lying. Move that body around. Make a mess of the scene. Confuse and scatter up whatever scanty witnesses and evidence might be left. Going to get Bo in tight with God down the stretch? Only the devil could make that deal and he seems to be disinterested. Curt knows Felicia will say she has seen it all, heard it all and would pin it absolutely on Kenny and only Kenny.

He gets a bucket and fills it with hot water and sloshes it across the floor and against the wall where Bo had splayed out before his abortive car ride and haul up the hill. Then he does it again and then he walks out and stands on the porch. Rise stays back in the kitchen, cleaning and straightening up, just like folks always do when the party is over.

Two black and whites pull swiftly up to the curb with quick finishing tire squeals as their sirens wind slowly from soprano to baritone to bassoon. Their dome lights rotate, swinging cherry red slices over and over again across the houses and street. Two uniformed officers get out of each, look at each other, eyeing for what might have been important.

They see Minor up on the porch.

One of them calls, "This your place?"

"Yeah. Yes it is."

"What happened here?"

They start to go toward him and then pause.

An unmarked pulls up to the curb and two plainclothesmen got out. The detectives have arrived and thus the hierarchy of the scene has been set. The first arrivals wait.

The senior men confer quietly with the uniforms and then the men in sport coats walk toward the drink house. One was named Wilkins, the other Miller. Both are middle height, middle-aged, corpulent, splay footed with pocked, pasty complexions. They move easily, with confidence, no rushing about—rather not quite a dawdle, more like an easy glide. They have worked together as a team for many years.

"Hello, there. This your place?" asks Wilkins.

"Yeah."

"Aren't you Minor? Curt Minor?"

"That's right."

"We got a call. Someone in the neighborhood called in gunshots. From here. What's the story?"

"Fellow got shot."

"You see it happen?"

"No, was in the back making food."

"Uh-huh..."

They walk toward him and up the steps.

"Mind if we come in?"

"No, help yourself."

The two step in while Minor holds the screen door for them.

The front room is dark, save for the one lamp on below the framed pictures of Dr. King, President Kennedy and Jesus.

The back room and kitchen are still lit with the many strings of red, green and blue Christmas lights and one bare bulb back in the kitchen glares too.

"How about we turn on some lights in here?"

"This is all I got."

"Party going on?"

"Sure, Friday night, good time to have one. Hot summer night. People like to have a good time."

They see Rise. They see a shotgun leaning in the corner next to her.

"Who are you? That your gun?"

"No. I'm Rise. I help cook."

They survey her enormity. She is mountainous. She evinces no threat. She is calm and polite.

"You see anything?"

"No, I was cooking and making sandwiches and the like."

"That thing loaded?"

"Not that I know of."

"What do you know of?"

"Not much."

The food and instruments of Friday night street dining are arrayed in front of her.

She is instantly credible. Wilkins and Miller side-glanced at each other. They know they have decided to let that weapon just sit there.

They turn back to Minor.

"Where is the guy that got shot?"

"Not here. Not exactly sure. Up the hill somewhere. You might ask her."

Minor nods toward Felicia, sitting slumped, head down.

"What's your name, young lady?"

"Felicia. Felicia Lineberger. Bo was my man."

"Who's Bo?"

"My man who Kenny killed."

"Who is Bo?"

"Bo Diddley. Uhm...Benjamin Winphrie."

She raises her head, a brief defiance of her ruined place and station flaring.

"Oh. Bo Diddley shot and killed?"

One detective looked at the other. They both nod. One winks.

"That's right."

"And who did it? Kenny? Who is Kenny?"

"That son-of-a-bitch Kenny Peak."

"Okay. Now where is Mr. Diddley?"

"Some mens took him up to the church up the hill."

"Okay. Now where is this Kenny Peak?"

"He ran out after he shot Bo. I saw it all. He's out there. Somewhere."

She waves an arm vaguely toward the front door.

"Okay, you stay right there."

Rise steps forward, beyond the counter.

"Sir. Mr. Detective. Kenny Peak is just down the street, standing under a tree."

"Really? So you say...how do you know that?"

"I saw him there. I told him to stay there. I don't know what happened. He is not armed. He's my brother."

"Oh. Really? Okay. You both stay right here."

Wilkins steps to the front while Miller looks around and basically notes there had been a party, there is some blood on the floor and in the poorly lit rooms, he cannot discern any signs of other physical evidence. Curt stands aside steel-eyeing Felicia. She catches his gaze, tries to look hard back and her eyes drift away.

Wilkins opens the screen door and calls for his men.

They gather in front of him.

"You, go inside and stand with those three. Nobody leaves. Be pleasant. Make nice conversation. Might find something out. Send Miller out here. You two, go up the hill to that church up there and see if you can find a body. Black male. Benjamin Franklin Winphrie. Well-known to us for a long time. Hopefully you'll find him somewhere up there. Then come back here and wait for us. And you are coming with us down the hill where I expect we'll find our shooter."

They each head toward their assigned spaces.

A young cop, Maxie, goes into the house, eyes the three with an innocent wariness and says,

"No one gets to leave. Understand?"

Minor says, "Don't worry, son, we ain't gonna cause you no trouble. Mind if I sit and grab a smoke?"

"Uhm...no, that's okay. Sure. Uhm...what happened here?"

Minor's lighter flares before his face. "You know I don't know. Didn't see anything. Rise? You?" He looks three-quarters sideways at her.

"No, I was head down cooking in the back. No, I didn't."

"What about her? You. Miss?"

Felicia looks up at the young guy and behind him sees Minor's mean eyes with smoke flaring from his nostrils like a dragon and Rise beside him, her look no more comforting. Haltingly, carefully, composing as she goes, Felicia says, "Kenny Peak shot Bo."

Softly, Maxie asks, "How do you know it was Kenny Peak that did the shooting?"

"Everybody said he did it."

"Who is everybody?"

"Uhm...lots of folks."

"Like who?"

Curt's eyes have Felicia in an iron vise.

"I, I...not sure right now...it's all...everyone was running around and yelling...and..." and she begins to weep and wail again.

Felicia is not very sure about anything now, so she stays quiet.

Wilkins and Miller walk with a skinny policeman named Logan down the cracked sidewalk, under a couple of shaded streetlights and come to a very large man standing underneath a tree.

"Evening, son."

"Evening, officers."

"How do you know we are police?"

"Been watching."

"What's your name?"

"Peak. Homer Kenny Peak, but folks just call me Kenny."

"Well, Kenny, we've just been told you just shot a fellow named Bo Diddley."

Kenny looks off across the street.

"You know anything about that?"

Kenny keeps looking off across the street, almost as if in a reverie and then it comes to him. He is spurred to be reminded.

"Bo Diddley carried a two shot small gun, what do you call it? A...derringer. He was a scary man."

"So, tell us a little more."

"And I want a lawyer. I got nothing else to say about anything."

The detectives sigh and shake their heads in off-key unison.

"You sure you don't want to talk to us a little more? Might help you out down the line." Kenny remembers his sister's stark, hard instruction.

"I want a lawyer."

"Okay, now turn around. Logan, cuff him. No cute stuff now, Kenny, right?" They all know that if this Kenny Peak wanted to cut and run, he could toss all of them away like leaves in the wind. Then they'd shoot him if they could. More damn mess.

"No trouble, officers, no trouble."

"Pat him down, check him out. Spread your legs and arms out, please."

Kenny complies and Logan goes through his pockets to come up with a fat bag of dope, a wallet with a few hundred dollars in it, a small pocket knife and a few small pieces of paper with various numbers scrawled on them.

"No gun."

"Not surprised."

"Okay, Mr. Kenny Peak, at the current time we are soon going to be charging you with felony possession of marijuana with intent to distribute and sell. That's a right good-sized amount there, isn't it?"

Not expecting any response, Wilkins goes on.

"I'm going to now read your Miranda rights to you. Please listen carefully."

Kenny nods.

"You are being placed under arrest. You have the right to remain silent. Anything you say can and will be used against you in a court of law. You have the right to representation by counsel, a lawyer. If you cannot afford a lawyer, one will be appointed for you. These are your constitutional rights.

Have you heard and understood them?"

"Yessir."

"Well, Miller and Logan, why don't you take this strapping young man down to the magistrate's office for processing and booking and then on to the jail. I'm going back up the hill to see what the others might have found."

Wilkins begins his walk back up the hill, but first, stops back in the drink house.

"Maxie, get everyone's full names, see their IDs and get their dates of birth. Y'all stay here until I get back."

They all nod.

Wilkins thinks to himself as he keeps moving, *Is this gonna be a long night? Hell, I got a 'maybe' shooter, no gun, a big bag of dope, a bunch of nobody knows anything except some maybe not so bright, hopped up whore child and not even a body yet. But he's gotta be up this way somewhere. There was more than a little blood on the floor back there. Somebody got popped. Bo Diddley. Damn. Bo Diddley. Bo Diddley, where are you?*

He eyes the little church as he comes up on it. A block and a half up from the drink house, it sits on a slant made of old bowed out nail popped wood, just a long hall with small double doors and a small, cross-topped belfry, all of it leaning slightly back down the hill as though a long time ago it had been slugged and staggered and never quite recovered. On its whitewashed side is a large ragged cross and smiling beneath the cross crawls the even bigger words, JESUS SAVES. There is a porch light on over the doors and they are opened. He walks in and sees the flashlight beams of the two officers in the dim light, swinging here and there, looking and moving.

He says, "Boys, y'all been up here a while. Found anything?"

One of them says, "No, sir."

He walks back to the inside wall of the shallow vestibule, shines his flashlight and finds the light switches. He clicks them on for the interior lights up. Pews, an altar, colored glass window lights, a few statues and many more pictures of Jesus, all standard issue for the work of saving souls. He walks the place up and back knowing all the while there is no body to found in the sanctuary.

"Gentlemen, let's go outside and start at the top side of things."

And they do.

Chapter Fourteen

Lost and Found

Conductor A.P. Kevin's stomach has gone steel explosion. He wants to shit, but knows if he did, he would fall apart. He mentally strangles, grips, and squeezes his frozen entrails back into stasis. As conductor, the next act is all his.

The train has stopped, steaming and metal screech creaking and its dissipating energy hovering shakes up and down its broken spine. There are no other sounds, not a cricket, a dog, a human save for the engine's bells clanging down in a dying metronome. Knight says, "Mr. Kevin, as the conductor on this now very fucked-up ride, you need to grab a couple of lanterns and go to it. You, sir, are in charge. Gordon and I will secure the cabin. And here, start chewing this gum and do not spit it out. Go now! We will be back there soon." Knight hands him two pieces of Dentyne. Gordon stands to the side. He stands very still.

An unsteady Kevin steels himself. He knows to some degree or another what he is going to find. Kevin takes two large lanterns and climbs down the ladder from the side of the train from which the car, now an easy thousand feet back down the rails, has been flung, speared, and crumpled in a sudden mechanical rictus.

They watch Kevin lower himself, rise back up and with a startled jerk, ask, "What's our story? What about Green's?"

Knight says, "There is no story except some idiot made a bad decision. Green's did not happen, understand? Forget that part. Got it?"

Kevin nods and heads down again and they hear his feet land in the gravel bed and then his slow, then faster, footsteps moving off toward the back of the train. Gordon looks sideways at Knight in the dome bile yellow emergency light of the cab and murmurs, "What in the hell happened?"

"Some damn fool either tried to chicken us across or just never saw us or was drunk or...fuck. Fuck! Fuck! I don't know..." Knight's voice rose in anger and fear and then slips off to a softer place.

"First, let's check this place out and make sure any 'evidence' or some such goes away very quickly. And, here, gum for you." He shoves it toward Gordon. It is no offering.

They both quickly unwrap the little pieces of gum and begin to chew them hard while picking up beer bottles and sandwich wrappings. It isn't so much that more than one person has to take it away, and Gordon takes it all and hustles off the train into the deep thickets of brambles and briars to the deeper side of the tracks. He stuffs everything randomly into the trash pit of bottles, cans, broken glass, bald tires, the detritus that is the ever-evolving archeology of a place that hadn't been trimmed down in months and would not be for months more.

The sirens are coming.

Gordon clambers back up. Knight has secured the controls and throttles all the way back to "full off," making sure all ditch lights and headlights are "full on" and that the bells keep ringing. He tells Gordon, "Let's go back there." They take more lanterns and go fast. They want to get to whatever the disaster is before the law does. They run.

* * *

They all had a lovely dinner at Charlie May's. The night was perfect, the lights twinkled, the food was sublime and the drinks copious and the conversation was just right for the pre-assignation exertions to come. They had even danced a bit, slow swaying to syrupy music floating in the evening's cooling. There was a universal ignoring of anyone not at the gathering. It had happened before and surely would happen again. Folks get caught up with work or the backflow of domestic maneuverings or simple weariness or apathy. The boys cleared the plates and offered coffee and dessert and passed silver dishes of mints and cigarettes and lit those with lovely Tiffany table lighters.

One of the boys asks Charlie if they should make a plate for Mr. Glenn and keep it in the warming box. Charlie nods, says, "Yes, that'll be nice. Make sure you set aside some rolls and pie for him too. He'll know where the whiskey is should he be so inclined." Charlie winks.

Slowly, as the candles taper down and the fire sputters, in silent twos, they slip away quietly, down hallways and up and down small staircases to private places. There is by some of the men some last desultory low conversation about the game in Chapel Hill tomorrow, some prognosticating, some inquiring as to the logistics of transport and who has the tickets and who they might see at the pre-game tailgates and fraternity houses, which boxes they would be in, what the weather looked to be. This was the male marking of the event, the ladies standing mute with but blank appreciations of the mild posturings.

The ladies are not going to the game. Some wish they could go, to see the spectacle, the players and the hitting, feel the excitement, hear the crowd of thousands scream and curse and yell. But they all know they are not going. It is not their place, their station. They are going home in the morning, by then having already provided many matchless pre-game high kicks and stunning exertions, leaving their fans in awed and happy admirations. They are Friday night's majorettes and drill team and they are very good.

* * *

As they run, Gordon stops, bends over and vomits, his career roaring out of his gut. Knight comes up behind him and exhorts him to spit his mouth clean while shoving more gum into his hand. They keep going. It is a longer way than they imagined and running in the large gravel and on the cross beams and in the dark is something difficult and tiring. They do not yet see any sign of anything, of Kevin or the car.

They go to the back of the train, the caboose's red back light flashing. They can see one of the lanterns Kevin has taken hanging from the back coupling chains. Knight adds another so there is greater opportunity for the train to be seen if another came up upon it. The sounds of the sirens grow louder. They look around and then realize they have much farther to go up the line. They continue and up in the distance, see two Sheriff's Department cars diagonally crawl up onto the track at the intersection of the crash, all lights and flashers on. Knight, seizing any initiative he can, calls to the men getting out of the cars. No response. He yells then, as loud as he can. Now he can see their heads turn and focus.

"Hey! Hey! Down this way!"

He looks to his left, peering for Kevin, a wrecked car, anything. He sees nothing. Just underbrush and trash and dark.

He says quietly to Gordon, "Let me take the lead here. It'll be all right. Chew the hell out of that gum. You sure you got rid of all that trash?"

Gordon nods glumly and then nods again.

"Hey, you guys, hey, we're down here."

They can see flashlights coming toward them, beams jerking up and down. Two deputies come up to them, all out of breath and wheezing, bending over.

"What the hell happened out here? We got a call. Said a train had hit a car. On the grade crossing back there. Trucker radioed it in."

They stand in the staggered illumination of train lanterns and long-beamed flashlights. Knight says, "That's right. Some son-of-a-bitch just pulled up right in front of us. We hit the brakes and horns, tried to hard reverse. No way. Too late. Too late. We hammered the car. It flew off over this way somewhere. Our conductor is out here looking for it."

"Where is he?"

"Dunno, but over here this way somewhere.

Knight yells, "Kevin! Kevin! Where are you?"

Nothing comes back.

Knight yells louder, "Kevin! Dammit! Kevin! Where in the hell are you?"

"I'm over here, I can see your lamps, can you see mine?"

"No—hold it higher. Swing it. Come toward us."

They all turn toward Kevin's voice and begin to move in that direction, all holding their lights high.

It is uneven, tilted ground, covered in tearing scrub, briars, saplings, and trash.

They spread out.

"Kevin? You find the car?"

Closer, louder now, "No, not yet."

"Damn."

Then Kevin comes up to them, sweating, dirty, torn at. He looks haggard, spent. Knight says, "What do you think?"

A deputy says, "Why don't we all spread out about ten yards apart and work our way back toward the crossing. That gives us a good four- to five-yard fan."

Knight replies, "Sounds good to me. What the hell. It's out here somewhere and I can promise you it ain't going nowhere."

They part and begin the halting, stumbling search, swinging their lights back and forth. Gordon sees it first. A chrome bumper twisted and buckled, blown tires sagging burst above it. He is twenty yards from the rear of the car.

The smell of gasoline and antifreeze is heavy in the air.

"It's here, over here," he says flat and loud. The others come to him.

They all stand together, all their lights playing over the car. In the inconsistent illumination, it is easy to see the car had been carved and caved in, totally crushed and ripped, upside down as though it had been exploded into the ground.

The trainmen are wary and still. It is quiet where they are, as though they are encased in a bubble.

One of the deputies says, "This probably isn't going to be pretty. I'll take the look."

The rest step back as he works his way up to the driver's side, gets down on his knees and guides his flashlight in. There is a pause.

The deputy then says, "Well, I've never seen worse..." and he gets up off the ground and comes back to them. His face is steady, but very pale.

"Whoever that is, and it looks like a man, has been taken apart and is spread out in there, spread out everywhere..." His voice trails off. Then he says, "You fellas go back down to the engine and radio your people so they can get folks out here to help with your train and just wait for us. We'll need to get your statements. We have to see if we can find some kind of ID and we need to get some help out here too and we need the coroner and an ambulance and a big pull wrecker and..." He is thinking, ticking off the list of cleaning the mess up.

Knight says, "Okay. I'm Knight, the engineer, this is Gordon, the fireman, and this is Kevin the conductor. We'll go on back and be waiting for you." He wants to get away from there as quickly as possible. Both deputies nod.

The deputy shines his light on the car's license tag, pulls out his pad and pencil, tilts his neck to see it and writes it down.

"North Carolina Business...B-25910."

The other deputy says, "What about a registration?"

"As you can see, the car was hit dead on in the passenger's side. It's a God-awful mess in there and I don't think either of us needs to be fishing around in there right now for a small piece of paper that is soaked down in whatever it is. This is a good start on the ID. Let's go call it in."

The trainmen start to walk back to the locomotive. The deputies head to their squad cars. As they move, other sirens are heard on their way.

* * *

As Wilkins and the two uniforms walk further up the hill to get above the church and then work their way back down, Wilkins asks, "Boys, what are your names?"

The two are both following him, about the same size and build, squatty and wide, double-chinned with that go-to-the-gym-and-lift-lots-of-weights look, each appearing to be in their late twenties, their crepe-soled police issue shoes squeaking on the pavement.

One answers, "I'm Essick and he's Preston."

Preston grunts an affirming, "Uh-huh."

"Y'all ever worked one like this?"

Essick, clearly more of a talker than Preston, says, "Not as I can recall. So, we are supposed to find a fellow shot up here somewhere, a body?"

"That's the general idea, but damned if I know..."

They crest the hill and turn and look down at the church, now about a hundred yards from them.

Wilkins says, "Okay, now, let's spread out and take our time. Each of you take a side and I'll take the middle and we're going to be real careful looking as we go down to the building. Got it?"

"Yessir. Yessir," they reply in staggered unison.

The sweep down the hill reveals nothing and as they get to the rustled old bent up side of the building, Essick says, "Now what?"

"We're going to go to the back now and work to the fence and then swing back on down the way back toward the drink house."

They do so, the scrubby grass crunching under their measured footsteps, their flashlights sweeping and again, nothing is found. They reassemble at the edge of the church and look at the small, unkempt cemetery, raggedly drifting down the hill before them easily holding more than a few gravestones, markers and mounded earth. Many of the markers have plastic flowers long faded; it is both promising and problematic as they walk through.

Wilkins says, "Let's cut it in thirds and look it hard."

Preston unexpectedly says, "Well, graveyards be for bodies."

The search continues and in a few minutes, Essick, who is working the side farthest away from the street and its lights says, "Sir, I think I've found him."

Essick's light is beamed straight down and holding in one spot and as Wilkins and Preston move up to it, there is a man, very small, folded into a slot between two burial mounds, his large hat centered on his side. He is obviously dead. His fancy clothing is greatly stained in drying blood and his face is stone-still in anger and surprise. A distinct cross in blood has been marked across his forehead.

Preston inhales a low whistle.

Wilkins says, "Well, well, Bo Diddley, Bo Diddley, how the mighty have fallen." And he pauses. "Preston, you are right. Graveyards be for bodies and here is Exhibit 'A'. This is our man. Essick, go call this in. We'll need the coroner and an ambulance—oh, yeah, tell them to bring a good sturdy body bag, and we'll need a department photographer, lots of yellow tape. Tell them to hustle. It's getting late and I don't think we need to stay out here all night."

"Preston, you go down to the drink house and stand with Maxie, tell all of them there we have found in the church's graveyard the body of a gentleman who fits the description of one Benjamin Winphrie, aka Bo Diddley, and that it is obvious that he is dead and say nothing more. Just watch carefully for their reactions. I'm going to stay here until the photog and the coroner get here. Then I'll be down to help get some statements, only one of which may be helpful but what in the hell do I know...Jesus, these people..." His voice tails off.

"Yes, sir."

As the uniforms start down the way, Essick says, "That cross on his face? What do you think...?"

There is a long pause, one of those loud silences and then Wilkins chuckles and says, "I expect that whoever hauled him up here knew he was surely headed to hell so they gave him a little Christian forgiveness on his way out...and used his own rotten juice to do it with too...that's rich... now, let's get on with it."

"He was that bad a guy?"

"He was a sorry piece of shit. End of story."

Both officers do as they are instructed and in quick time, an ambulance wails up the street and the police cameraman, an old grumpy guy named Anthony, and the coroner, Mr. Freunde, arrive. Everyone knows the drill. Flashes pop as the subject is peeled by the coroner, rolling Bo Diddley over and straightening him out. It appears from the tears in his clothes he has been shot multiple times.

Anthony is asked by Wilkins, "You got enough here?"

"Yeah, sure."

"Okay, how 'bout go down to the drink house and get the pictures you need. I'll be back down there in a few minutes."

"Okay," and Anthony heads down there.

The ambulance driver and his attendant are standing off to the side, their stretcher gurney and folded canvas bag at the ready.

Freunde says to them, "We're done here now. Boys, bag him and take him over to the hospital. They'll put him in the cooler until the autopsy can get done. Tell them we'd like Podgorny to do it when he can get around to it."

And they take Bo Diddley and bag him up and zipper him into a further closed darkness and take him away.

Chapter Fifteen

Trails

"Tag is NC Business 25910, right?" The dispatcher at Highway Patrol Headquarters in Raleigh reads it back to the Guilford County's Deputy Sheriff who has called it in for identification.

"Yeah, that's it. What you got?"

"Hang on. We're running it. What kind of deal y'all got over there Greensboro way?"

"Train hit a car. Someone in the car got splattered all over hell and half of creation."

"Know that's a mess."

"Yeah." The deputy's stomach did a few more quick flips.

"Hang on. Okay. We got it. You got a pencil?"

"Yeah."

"The car is a Ford sedan, Tag Number NC Business 25910, registered owner is Quality Textile Company of Winston-Salem, North Carolina. Burntwood Avenue."

"Okay. Got it. Will call WSPD and see if they can run somebody down. Thanks for your help."

"Anytime. Good luck with that mop job. Over and out."

The deputy does not feel like saying anything more.

The radio crackles off.

The deputy sits there quiet for a minute, trying to sort of what he had seen in the car. He sighs and picks his microphone back up and calls into

Central Dispatch in Greensboro.

Static, then clearer. "This is Guilford County Central Dispatch."

"This is Sheriff's Deputy Sooner, badge number 918. We are working a train car crash out off of the Old Burlington Road. We need four or five more units out here to secure the area and keep the track and investigation site clear. And can you patch me through to the Winston-Salem PD? We've ID'd the subject's vehicle as belonging to a company in Winston-Salem."

"Will do and I'll get your assistance on the way right away."

The line is quiet, just the radio line waiting.

After Sooner gives all the necessary details to Corporal Roberts at WSPD, he asks, "He make it?"

"Negative. Very negative."

"Okay. What's the company? Even though it's the middle of the night, I'll call over there. Might get a recording or a night watchman. If that doesn't work, we'll send a black and white out."

"It's Quality Textile Company. Burntwood Avenue. Winston-Salem"

"Yeah, I know it. Ride past it all the time. You got a number?"

"Negative on that."

"It's okay. I'll look it up. No reason for you to stay on the line. If we get a contact or a hit, I'll call GC Central back."

"Thanks. Appreciate it." Sooner clicks off the line.

Corporal Roberts opens a drawer and pulls out the Winston-Salem phone book and begins to thumb through the Yellow Pages until he got to the Q's. Finger scanning down the page, he finds the number and dials it. It rings and rings some more. There is no answer. He reopens his central radio line and says, "Need a car in the vicinity of Burntwood and Silas Creek. Respond. Over."

In a minute, the reply is, "This is Dawkins, Car 117, what you got?"

"Go to Quality Textile Company at 1920 Burntwood and see if you can find a contact or a call number. One of their vehicles has been hit by a train over in Guilford County and there's a fatality. We need to get in touch with them."

"On it. Will report."

"Thanks. Will stand by."

Roberts stands down and pulls his log out to make the entries as to what he has been told and what his responses are. A few minutes pass. Then Dawkins is back on line.

"Hey. Went to place. All locked up and dark. But on both front entry door and a back door too, there is a sign that says, 'In Event of Emergency, please call 47873.' You know this is the Glenn business?"

"Say again? Glenn business?"

"You know. The big textile Glenns. Big deal Buena Vista people. Them and the Taylors and the Williamses are the biggest cotton and fabric outfit in this part of the state. They are big operators. Hell, how many of their mills and factories you see all over town? Not sure you wanna just be calling that number and telling 'em there's a dead guy in one of their company vehicles without maybe getting some directions from higher up the line. Don't want to have bad manners or get cussed out on a deal like that...Anyway, I don't think..." The voice tails off.

Roberts pauses and then says, "You're right. I'll check it in with the night desk sergeant before I do anything. Thanks. Resume regular patrol. Over and out."

He rolls his chair back and then sits there for a minute and thinks, *Yes, the smart thing to do is to kick this on up the department line. No good reason for me not to. A dead person, probably a guy, blown all to bits in a rich company car out on the other side of Greensboro—in the country at this time of night. Doesn't sound like no "employee" to me; sounds like someone higher up.*

His resolve set, having been satisfied by his logic and also the cautioned warning he'd been given, he stands up, askes his back-up in the dispatch office—the fellow is snoozing off to the side—to wake up and take the radio chair while he goes back to talk with the night desk sergeant.

Roberts walks down the linoleum-floored hall, the fluorescent lights need replacing, and they are blinking, tossing multiple shadows of him across the cinder block walls.

He turns the corner into the older part of headquarters, where there's nicer, wood paneled walls, wooden floors, with old green covered lamps above in the ceiling, all the bulbs lit up. At the end of that walk stands a high wooden altar, just like in church, looming over the room. Above it hangs an old brass light fixture that shines down on the altar and the floor below it. On either edge of its top level there are black sculpted stanchions, sculpted in the shape of the blindfolded goddess of justice and atop these supports sit large round milk glass shades surrounding very bright lights that glare. They are simply lettered, "Police."

And between the lamps on that desk are the broad shoulders and impassive pie face of the desk sergeant, the King Buddha of that night. Before him stands a short line of patrol and beat officers and their prisoners whose next locations will soon be determined by the man in control. Roberts falls in line, thinking about the man in the car.

Sergeant White asks pleasantly of the first couple, "What you got?"

"Drunk and Disorderly... Fighting with his old lady...again."

White looked down disdainfully at the detainee and says offhandedly, "Mr. Wilson, why do you try our patience so?"

Wilson looks away and slurs, "Shit, I ain't done nothin'. It's Friday night. I had a few and she starts bitchin' on me. She come at me like she always does. So I did defended myself."

White says, "Wilson, same shit, different day. Put him in the drunk tank. She'll be down here in the morning to haul his ass home for her punishments."

The two, one cuffed and the other steering, head off.

"Next. And...?"

The officer says, "Mary Jane and switchblade and wad of cash. He was doing trade down in the street off Patterson Park. We watched him 'til we were sure."

"What's your name, son?"

It slowly comes forth. "Jackson. Romulus Jackson. I don't want to talk about this."

"Fine. Have I seen you before? Yes, I think I have. Yes, we have a problem. Take him next door and book him. Get the evidence weighed, measured and secured in the property room. Pull a sheet on him and put him the holding cell until we figure out whether we can lace a felony or two up here."

Jackson hisses, "Shit, shit, shit." to no one in particular. He is led away. Roberts is getting impatient, but it wouldn't be long now.

Between a suit and a uniform stands a large man, easily wider than the two that flank him. Sergeant White nods and says, "Good evening, Detective Miller. How are you? Well, I trust. Been a while."

Miller replies, "Hey, White. Fine. How are you, your family?"

"They're all still speaking to me, so that's a start."

They smile at each other.

Then White asks, "Now, who is this young officer with you? Son, I've not seen you before, I don't think."

Logan, not wanting to be reticent, says, "I'm Logan, sir. Just getting started on the force."

White winks at Logan with a big eye and asks, "Miller, on-the-job training?"

"Exactly."

"Okay, what have you brought me to ponder? Who is this subject of your interest this dark evening?"

Miller says, "White, this is Homer Kenny Peak. It is said that tonight he shot and killed one well-known to us all as Benjamin 'Bo Diddley' Winphrie in Curt Minor's drink house over on 14th Street. When we took him into custody, we recovered no weapon but it appears we have a number of witnesses to the shooting. He also had a good amount of marijuana on his person. He gave us no trouble."

Peak says firmly, "Bo had carried a derringer all the time. I was afraid. I want a lawyer." Again he says in a louder voice, "He carried a derringer. I was afraid. I thought he was pulling it on me. I want to talk to a lawyer."

White looks down upon them all. "All right, Mr. Peak. All right. We all hear loud and clear your exposition of innocence, but you seem to have put yourself in a most difficult place which we, as the well-sworn law enforcement of this great city, have to look at and divine the roses from the thorns. Right now, you have the look of a very large thorn and thus, these fine gardeners here, are going to begin the process of pruning the bed."

White is amusing himself. Miller enjoys it. The rookie cop furrows his brow and Homer Kenny Peak stares at White and beyond him thinking, *What the fuck is that old fat honky sayin'?*

White says, "Miller, you and your nice helper, please take Mr. Peak here over to the Magistrate's office. Put him in the holding cell while the proper paperwork is prepared for service upon him and his bond will be set or not set, and he will thus be delivered into our court system. It's nice to see you all, gentlemen. Have a good evening."

The three walk down the hall.

White looks down at some random paperwork on his desk and Roberts steps forward.

"Sir, I'm Roberts from radio dispatch."

"Yes. What may I do for you?"

"Sir, we just got a call about half an hour ago from the Guilford County Sheriff's Department. They've just had a train car crash out in the county, east of Greensboro. Appears there is a bad fatality; they think it's a male." Roberts pauses, gathering his thoughts.

White leaned a few inches forward. "Yes, go on."

"Well, sir, they called Raleigh and the HP office down there ran the tag and the car came back registered to a Winston-Salem company. So I sent a black and white out to see if there was anyone at that address who we could let know what has happened."

White repeats, "Go on."

"There wasn't anyone there but there were signs on the doors that said in event of an emergency, call such and such a number."

White pulls some glasses from his tunic pocket, pushes them down his nose and looks at Roberts.

"What company would this be? Where is it located?"

Roberts had a sense that he has done the right thing by going up the line.

"The car is registered to Quality Textile Company. They've got offices out on Burntwood. They're the big cotton folks."

White leaned back just a ways, and says, "Yes, I know them well. Can you get any ID on the person in the car?"

"All they said was they thought it was a fellow. I guess they're still looking."

White is very still, thinking it through. He has been around a long time. He pieces a worst case scenario together quickly. "What was the number?"

"Uh, I'll go get it."

"Yes, please do."

White sits motionless until Roberts returns with the number. He hands the slip to White.

White says, "Go on back to your station. I'll be down to speak with you in a few minutes. Thank you for bringing this to my attention."

Roberts nods and walks back to the radio room, wondering. White picks up his desk phone, dials, listens and then speaks.

"Chief, this is White on the night desk at the station." He pauses to listen.

Then quickly he says, "Justice, I am very sorry to awaken you. I think this is something that might need your attention. Our radioman just came to me with a report from Guilford County Sheriff Department of a train striking a car in eastern Guilford County earlier this evening .The vehicle is registered to Quality Textile Company out on Burntwood. It appears quite certain that a male occupant of the car has been violently killed. We sent a car out to the company to see if we could locate someone on duty. No one was found but there is an emergency contact number on the door."

Chief Justice Tucker asks, "You got the number?"

"Yes, it's 47873."

The Chief repeats it and then says, "Oh, shit, that's Joe Glenn's number." A pause and then he says, "Okay, I'll take it from here. I'll be back in touch."

"Yessir."

The line goes silent.

White stands up, walks down from the desk to the radio room.

"Roberts, thank you for bringing that information to my attention. That was the correct thing to do. The matter is being dealt with now."

Roberts, still wondering, nods and says, "Thank you, sir."

White leaves.

* * *

The three trainmen sit in the cab. The adrenalin is burning off quickly and as it does, the space between them grows tighter. They are encroaching on each other. They are uncomfortable, can't get comfortable. An involuntary restlessness takes hold of them. There is the mingled stench of scared sweat and chewed-out gum and sinking weariness washing over and striking them down. And there is the smell of guts and blood and a body exploded and metal shredded and electricity and scorched rubber that has gotten into their clothes and nostrils and it is all foul.

No one speaks for a few minutes. They are in a torpor of stupor, sucking deeper into their minds' eyes.

Knight says, "Kevin, you've got to call this in."

Kevin looks at him, face blank and gray. He is there and not there.

Kevin says in a low, flattened voice, "I can't do it. You know I can't..." His voice straggles off.

Knight says, "I know. I'll do it. I'll tell them you're still out at the scene."

Gordon looks at Knight and nods.

The lights of many cars flash and beam in the distance, all moving toward them. Their shadows are backlit, then dim, then backlit again.

Knight says, "Buck it up, boys. The cops will be back down here in a few minutes." Knight reaches up, switches the microphone on and makes the call to Richmond.

When a train hits a car or derails or smashes into another train or a boiler explodes or a planned suicide steps out in front of the engine, or pick just about anything else that can get things sideways, it is always just one great big mess.

It's worse when it's a passenger train because a lot more people are involved that can get hurt, get killed, get tossed about, put out and always get inconvenienced.

There are those moments just before the bad thing is going to happen when usually the train starts to shudder as its operators try impossibly to slow it down. The wheels screech against the tracks. The horns blow and wail, the bells ring furiously, usually always to no avail and then the smash of crash or leap from the tracks starts and it's all in a perverse sort of slow motion except everything is moving way faster than usual. A temporary disorientation comes over everyone. And then there is an impact or a jolt or smash and baggage and people get launched or tilted and thrown in every direction never envisioned.

Then, when gravity and physics bring a skewed stasis, it is all still and there is a brief silence as though all have been struck deaf.

Until the shouts and cries start and dust and detritus mysteriously appear and drape everything as fog lies out. And the smells of torn metal, burning brake line, all the accompaniments of modern day, industrial trauma unfold and envelop.

This train wreck was no different. In fact it was a classic, a textbook model.

Friday Calls

Train rolling along, car quick climbs the grade crossing, getting into the engine's crosshairs perfectly, car gets blasted, train slows and grinds to a stop on down the line, well away from point of impact.

And it was a passenger train. There were going to be hurt people, maybe worse and their belongings all over the place. Many of the cars had busted loose from one another, tearing brake and electrical connections up.

Radio calls had gone to Company Headquarters Richmond, Raleigh Central, Greensboro Central, Atlanta Main. There were quick calls that there had been an incident, along with the location, the known and probable results. Details and reasons would be addressed later. Of course, there was going to be an investigation. Liability people, insurance people, lawyers. Right away, routes had to be changed, relief trains sent for those able and willing to go on, track and train inspectors and repair crews and rolling cranes and other repair equipment requisitioned and sent out.

And already the place was a growing, glowing anthill, lit up in strobes of red and blue and white and yellow. Flares smoked and sirens, lots of sirens. Squad cars, fire trucks, ambulances, utility vehicles, rubberneckers parking and thrashing through the brush from the highway parallel.

Lots of people wandering off the train, lots of people running to the train, lots of calling and yelling and crying out, lots of confusion. And thus the great putting together of the great coming apart began in the dark of a Carolina night that was pumping like a big heart under the stadium lights that had been badly strained. It is but hours before dawn.

Deputy Spooner sits in his squad car perched up on the grade crossing and stares down the tracks to the west. It is a wrinkled line of Christmas tree of lights and shadows and silhouettes, all moving. Behind him, just back down the track to the east, in his rear and sideview mirrors, he can see men setting up large smudge pots and bright yellow and orange barricades, closing down all access to the crossing from any direction. He goes back to his radio and asks the dispatch if he should resume his assigned patrol duty as everybody else in the known world has now descended on the scene and there is next to nothing that he could lend to the efforts before him. He is told to get back on the road. He rolls down his window and calls to the men behind him. There is no response. They can't hear him. He gets out of the car to approach them.

"Hey, there, can y'all pull that barricade back just for a minute? I've got to go back on patrol."

"Yeah, why sure. You one of the first ones here?"

"Yeah."

"You see it? I mean, what happened?"

"Yeah. I don't think y'all might want to see it."

"That bad?"

"Worse."

They all nod to one another in the glow of the lights and flames and the men move the barricades to the side and Spooner gets back in his car, backs down then up and goes off and away.

The coroner, who calls himself Dr. Jimson, though he is no doctor, arrives and walks off into the scrub and brambles to the wrecked car. The uniformed officer is accompanied by two ambulance attendants whose professional garb make them look to be like lost dentists. They drag and bump a folding stretcher along with them. There is a sense that this would be not be a very useful addition to the project of corpus mortis extraction.

The coroner is portly and older and he moves stiffly. He is dressed, even at that hour of the night in a three-piece wool suit. His paunch leads him like a sextant. He has a cigarette in his hand which he pulls at one more time and then tosses away. This is his jurisdiction and his job to see and direct. He is not enthusiastic.

The driver's side door has been pried open and flashlight beams shine into the exploded interior. The coroner slowly gets down on his hands and knees, hesitantly pushes forward and cranes his head into the door's opening.

"Oh, Jesus," he murmurs. "Hell, we're gonna have to take whoever that is out of here with a spoon. Goddamn, boys, glove up and lend a hand."

He pulls back out, reaches into his jacket pockets for long, heavy, yellow rubber gloves, the kind used to lube up horses asses at the big animal vet when they needed to go deep inside to see what was wrong. The attendants do the same. They are all gloved. The officer steps back, the putrid stink slapping at him. The officer turns away.

The coroner, now more limber, warming to the task, shoves himself into the car's interior and reaches out for the remnants of the shattered

Friday Calls

body. One of the attendants has edged himself into a small space left beside Jimson and he grasps forward too.

They pull the broken thing off the dashboard and wheel. It appears to be a white male in nice, now blood-soaked clothes. Parts of him are jellied, parts are holding together, the face a placid, contorted, eyes-wide-open flat pan. His extremities are either missing or askew. He has obviously been killed instantly.

The other attendant unfolds the stretcher and unzips a body bag. Gingerly, the remains are set in the rubber cowling it and are covered quickly with a fast-reddening sheet. They might as well have been slow juggling tomato aspic.

They are loading the bag into the back of the ambulance when an officer walks up and says to Jimson, "Evening."

"Evening."

"Take the body to Hanes Lineberger in Greensboro. It'll be picked up there."

Jimson eyes the man.

"No autopsy?"

"No. From what I hear, you don't have much more than a coffee cup of anything left to fool with, do you?"

"That's true."

"And by the way, what's the point anyway? That's blunt force trauma. Isn't it?"

"That's true too."

"We square?"

"Yes. Boys, close the door. Let's go."

Jimson does not need convincing. He's been ordered. It makes his life easier.

Spooner drives north, away from the lights and up into the dark. He rolls his window down and lets the air blow over him. His stomach is screwed tight and beneath his shirt, he can feel the vomit surging and then slowing. He can taste the bile in his throat and he clinches his esophagus by lowering his chin and concentrating. Slowly, the wave subsides.

He knows he is on duty, but he also knows he needs a drink and a cigarette. He steers back toward Green's.

He pulls into the gravel lot, to the back of the building and kills the engine. The big neon sign is off and only a few cars sit still in the parking lot. Low light filters through the drawn shades of the front bar.

He can see Bozo's shape moving in and out of view, flickering. Bozo's stamina is legendary. He does not sleep. He is always gliding. Always kind and happy. Spooner needs to see him.

Spooner gets out of the car. The stink of where he had just come from is soaked into his clothes and skin. It is the same as having been in a place that has just burned. It is in his hair. He is breathing through his mouth to keep it somehow out of his head. He crunches across the parking lot and knuckles softly on the door.

Only a few seconds pass before the slot peep at the door's eye level slides open. Bozo says, "Oh, hey, lemme get this thing open."

There is a click, a snap and a key turning a lock and then last, the slide of a cross bar rod.

"Spooner. Hey. Come on in. Late for you. What may I do you for...?" Bozo chuckles.

"Well, Bozo, if you don't mind, I'd like to sit for a few minutes, get a good, stiff drink of brown water and smoke a cigarette." The sentence wanders and steams away into nowhere.

"Why, sure. What's your pleasure? Always happy to be watering you good folks who tend to us." Bozo smiles, then pauses. "Spooner? You okay? What's going on?"

Spooner inhales big, blows it out like a little wind and sits down.

"Bozo, there's been a terrible awful wreck. Train hit a car. Down toward the Burlington Road. The man, I think it was a man, driving the car is so torn to pieces dead." He lights a cigarette. "It was some kind of company car, from Winston-Salem best we can tell so far, businessman best I can figure. I got to see it, had to see it. Part of my job but just too close for comfort. It was awful. I need to steady a moment."

In the dim light of the front bar he is sweeping, Bozo's grip on his broom tightens and his eyes open just a tiny bit wider as he does the calculus in his mind. It is a quick computation, too easy, too precise.

Friday Calls

"Oh my, that's awful. I'm sorry to hear this. Poor fellow. Hope he didn't know what hit him. What may I get for you?"

"Bourbon, please."

Bozo puts an ashtray down on the counter and walks behind the bar and pulls a bottle.

"Ice?"

"No, no thanks, just good-sized straight, please."

"You got it."

Bozo takes an Old Fashioned glass and flows it good. He hands it over. Spooner holds it, regards it and takes it in two swallows. He thought of what the old Southern fellow had said long ago, "Whiskey is serious business. You just gotta take it."

He can feel it burn and it feels good. He pulls hard on his cigarette, its tip glowing orange. He sits still. Bozo watches him. It is very quiet. The only sounds are cars passing out on the highway and Spooner's breathing, more sighing than anything else.

Spooner arches his back up, rolls his shoulders forward and stands.

"Thank you, Bozo. I've got to get back to work."

Bozo asks, "Did that help? I hope it did."

"Yes, thank you. I'll let myself out. Thanks again."

Spooner walks to the door, opens it and quietly the door is pulled shut behind him. Bozo stands at a half-blinded window, watches the squad car's lights come on and then the vehicle makes a large sweeping turn through and out of the parking lot and onto the highway, gunning it as it touches the blacktop. Its red lights eye smaller and smaller until they were gone.

Bozo stands just a minute longer, then locks and bars the door. He walks back around the bar, past the office and into the kitchen. Old Rowdy, tiny and knotty, scrubs down the serving counter between pulls of his usual rotgut.

Rowdy says, "Hey, Boz, whatcha doin'?"

Bozo says, "I gotta run an errand. Won't be gone long. Come over here and lock up this door behind me."

"Okay, where you going?"

"Never you mind on that. Just lock the door and keep cleaning and don't let nobody in here. You understand? I'll be back directly."

"Okay."

Bozo, his affable smile tighter, more drawn now, eases his big frame sideways quick out the back door, stands to listen for the bar and the lock, is satisfied it is done and heads to his car. It is an old but beautiful Chevy, gleaming black like a panther. He cranks it up.

He thinks, *Damn, how long am I gonna be gone? I gots to hustle.*

Chapter Sixteen

Deliveries

Chief Justice Tucker pulls into the circular brick drive up to the front door. There are no lights on inside, no outside porch lamp on. Tucker has put his uniform pants and jacket on over his pajamas and holds his hat in his hand. He pushes the button and hears a buzzer sound inside the house. He waits and pushes again. A light, dim and yellow flares up, out of sight, back within the house.

"Who is it? Who is it?" a man's sleep crackling voice calls.

"Joe." Louder. "Joe! It's Tucker. We need to talk."

Joe Glenn comes around the corner from a back hallway. He holds a 410 shotgun at the low, ready. He switches on another light in the front hall. He has his pajamas on and is in his bare feet.

"Tucker? Damn, Tucker! What's going on? Oh, hell, let me put this damn thing down. You've startled us." Glenn looks at Tucker, quizzically, the sleep gone from his face now. "Justice, what's wrong?"

Then appears Joe's wife, flowing in a floral nightgown, slippers on, hair tossed back, planting her glasses over her nose.

"Justice, why are you here, what has happened? It's not about Daddy, is it?" She quivers ever so slightly and turns her body sideways, ready to ward off a blow.

"Good evening, Rose. I'm sorry to disturb y'all like this. No, Rose, it's not about your daddy." *It's your brother-in-law*, he wanted to say.

He turns to Joe Glenn.

"Joe, we are not exactly sure what's going on, but there has been an accident."

Joe Glenn keeps looking at Tucker, very straightforward, not moving.

"Joe, the accident was over east of Greensboro. It appears to be a company car owned by Quality Textiles. A black Ford sedan."

"What happened? Keep going."

Tucker clears his throat.

"A man has been killed. Do you know who might have been in that company car?"

Tucker looks away as he asks the question.

Glenn nods grimly, looks at his wife and exhales the name, "Archer, it had to be Archer..."

Rose shudders, stiffens and then releases, "What in the world...are you sure, Justice, are you sure?"

Relieved to have someone else to talk to, even for a moment, Tucker looks at her and says, "I believe Joe has filled in the missing information. I'm sorry. I'm so sorry..."

Joe Glenn runs both his hands up through his gray hair and then drags his palms all the way down across his face until they land on his chest. He starts to lightly tap, rhythmically. His face is sad and he is thinking too.

"Justice, please call Greensboro and get his body taken over to the funeral people over there, Hanes Lineberger, I think it is. Let them know the family does not, repeat, does not want any autopsy or testing. Get him in a coffin and lock it and have them called Freunde's here and have them send S.D. over to pick it all up as soon as possible, and tell S.D. to put it in a back room and lock it up. We've got to go tell Louise. We've got to get everyone together and go tell Louise right away before she sees it in the newspaper or anything like that."

He pauses. Then thinking it all through as best he can, he continues.

"Rose, do you have any way to get in touch with Mamie and Retha?"

"Yes, I have their numbers. You don't think it was Jimmy, do you?"

"No, it wasn't Jimmy. It was Archer. Have Mamie and Retha meet us in the driveway over there. The girls are going to need some steadying."

"I understand. Yes. How can you be sure?"

"I'm sure. Let's leave it at that. We need to get dressed. Justice, thank you for coming. Can you get those wheels turning like I asked?"

"Yes, I will get them turned. I'll go now."

Tucker leaves, pulling the door behind him. They can hear his car engine start and roll away.

Rose says, "Oh, Joe, oh Joe, I'm so sorry!" She begins to weep.

Joe's face is a mask of sorrow and he hugs his wife, pats her back and says, "I know. I know. This is all very sad. But before we get too sad, we need to get to this unhappy job. We need to button this up good and then we all can be very sad."

He pauses.

"Oh, I think we need to get Henry and his bag over there, don't you? No telling what kind of shape Louise is in, much less how this poison is going to be received. A hypodermic may be in order..."

Rose pushes her sadness away, understanding it is a thing to be pushed away for now. She understands that something horrible has happened, that its circumstances, whatever they might end up being, were not of the proper and well-to-do unfortunate type and that calls and contacts and arrangements needed to be made to start cleaning up the back end of whatever parade had just gone to hell in a handbag. They all needed each other's help.

"Yes, Joe, you're right. I'll go make the calls and let's get dressed and get going."

Joe says, "I'll call Jimmy and Martha Ann once you're done. I'll go get on a suit first." And he holds her hand and kisses the top of her head and murmurs, "Thank you." He looks into the hall light and he might as well have been flying in outer space.

* * *

The ambulance slowly backs up to the loading dock at the big Baptist hospital. Two attendants, smoking and chatting, stand out in the warm night waiting to receive the body of Bo Diddley.

The hum of the hospital's electrical transformers stationed to one side of the dock sound the chords of the energy pulsing into the buildings. The flapping double-door entrance to the Emergency Room on the other side waits in red-signed, white-blue fluorescent anticipation for its next arrivals.

There had already been more than a few that Friday night, cuttings and crashes not being the exclusive traumas of the coloreds.

If Bo had only been wounded, even gravely or critically, he would have been taken to the blacks (only) hospital—Katie B it was regularly referred to—named for Katherine, the good-doing wife of the city's tobacco giant. But as Bo was now graveyard dead, his shriveled, punctured corpus was delivered to the big whites (only) hospital where all autopsies were done and as there was more than ample evidence that his death was "not from natural causes" (though there would be those who, considering his social milieu and environment, would argue that point), an autopsy was mandated by state law. It appeared that a gun crime had been committed and thus the evidence of that violence had to be recorded and memorialized for the inspection of the District Attorney's Office.

The driver of the ambulance slowly gets out and stretch-ambles to the back and wearily opens its back swinging door. It has been a slow run as there is no emergency now. Only the red running lights are blinking as the big Cadillac engine idles. There has been no need for the siren and the driver is in no rush. He is just killing time until his rented out shift ends at 7. The dome light comes on and therein lays the lumpy sack on a gurney.

The two attendants step forward, take hold of the gurney, slide it out and up, its braced legs snapping into place. Its wheels jiggle, then settle. Two straps are wrapped and snugged around the bag.

"Paperwork?" asks one attendant.

"Of course," responds the driver and holds his clipboard and a pen out for the required officialdom of it all.

As one of the receivers takes the proffer, the driver says, as he always does, in a cheerful sing-song, "Press hard—three copies." It is nothing more than a transaction at the bank or the post office. The Meat Wagon has come and is soon going.

The attendant hands the manifest back to the driver who briskly puts his pen back into his driver's smock breast pocket, holds the clipboard and razors the hospital's yellow copy for Bo Diddley's forthcoming forensic travels.

"Thank you, gentlemen. Always a pleasure. Y'all have a nice evening, well, rest of the evening."

"Thanks, same to you."

The gurney rattles into and down a long, hospital green tiled hallway to an elevator station where it boards to the eighth floor.

One of the men reads the paper he had been given as bells indicate the passing floors.

The other says, "Well, who is it?"

"Black male. Benjamin Franklin Winphrie."

"Hmmmm...never heard of him. Now, Benjamin Franklin I have heard of."

"Yeah, wasn't he that guy from up north who flew kites or something...?"

"Yeah, that's it...I think. Guess this guy didn't get this way flying a kite." They laugh as the doors slide open.

"Yeah, I think you're on to something."

They roll down the same green hall, through the double doors over which read, "Department of Pathology, Forensic Pathology." And beneath that, "Where Death Delights."

A fellow in a chair sits behind a small desk. It has all the appearance of "take a number" at the DMV.

"What y'all got?" He stands up and stubs his cigarette out in a butt-crowded ashtray.

"Black male, multiple gunshot wounds. Here's the manifest."

"Ummm-huh. Friday night's biting again. Lemme see." He takes the one sheet and looks at another on his desk which had many squares, some marked and named, some blank, the big bingo game of who lands where, all in black and cold.

"Put him in 14. Please."

"Right."

They go to a wall of stainless steel doors, scan the numbers and find the assigned freezing tunnel to open it and slide the counter out. They hoist Bo's bag of mortality onto it, stretch out the rubbered canvas, making sure nothing falls over the edges to get snagged, and close it all in. The door shuts loudly and firmly with the snap of a good German car.

The room attendant comes over with a handwritten label and slots it in a holder on the door's face.

"Benjamin Franklin Winphrie. Black male. DOB undetermined. Multiple gunshot wounds.

Probable homicide."

"That's some name, ain't it?"

"Yeah, we were talking about that on the way up."

"That Benjamin Franklin. Wasn't he an inventor or something?"

"Something like that...well, this one sure didn't invent anything 'cept getting plugged a few times."

"Hey, shit happens..."

They all nodded to each other and the two leave the one to light a cigarette and wait for the next.

And thus did Bo Diddley begins to come to his final, examined, scalpeled, measured, enumerated and refrigerated encounter with the courts of justice.

* * *

All the family are telephoned with the grim news and all the help is summoned—the two maids are not yet told, but they both know instantly something awful was afoot—and the family physician is informed and asked to come equipped to help them deal with a most probable eruption. It is agreed that it is best to meet on Virginia Road a few houses down from the Glenns where Louise slept the sleep of the night's earlier slow, steady gulping of most of a bottle of good bourbon. The little girls just slept.

It is probable that their gathering would disturb the house, but they needed to be assembled all together and go in together. Dawn is a few hours away. Soon six cars are in a line and all are standing in a tight clot off the curb.

Mamie and Retha are quickly told that Mr. Archer is dead, that he has been killed in a car wreck and they are greatly needed to help with the girls and Miss Louise. They gasp and hold each other and they know they must be steady.

The Joe Glenns and the Jimmy Glenns and the Bill Butlers all hug each other and some tears are briefly shed, but all know what is getting ready to happen and the searing, sad and fearful anticipation of it welds them. There is some quiet discussion as to maybe they should wait until morning, but Dr. Henry Valk, tall, handsome, brilliant and measured, softly notes that he thinks it best to get it over with now as the coming of the day will bring possible newspaper articles, probably many telephone calls and maybe even well-meaning and curious visitors and, too, many other difficult tasks to be confronted and dealt with.

The group nods their assent. The men take one last pull on their cigarettes and drop them to the ground, grinding the embers out with their shoes. The women all clutch their purses and squeeze their eyes shut for a moment. The world is spinning faster for all of them. Handkerchiefs are put at the ready.

It is decided that the three siblings—Joe, Jimmy and Martha Ann—will go upstairs to Louise's room and that Rose, Sarah, and Bill will stay downstairs in the front hall. Mamie and Retha will go upstairs, down the hall, and stand at the ready at the girls' door.

Dr. Valk will be just outside on the landing.

There is a collective hesitant pause, the herd tentative, agitated and then Joe Glenn says, "We've got to do this. Maime, Retha, may I have the house key, please."

Chapter Seventeen

Cleaning Up

PeeWee has done exactly as he has been told. He still holds the gun in his pocket, keeping it from flopping by his pressing hand. He has through the east neighborhoods, through some projects, down under the big highway leading into the tobacco factory complex, ducking behind trees or in the bushes or behind wherever there is to hide whenever a set of car lights appeared. There aren't many, two or three, just a few.

He wishes he had taken the bullets out before he started running, but he could not stop or slow now. He is careful to keep the pistol still.

The night has gone quiet. There are few police patrols in that part of town. There are a few night watchmen, but they just stroll the fronts of the factories, smoking and visiting with each other. All the buildings have high-set windows and locked and chained doors.

No third shifts run on Friday nights. He knows there are many large leaf washing sheds the size of bus depots attached to the backs of the stolid, red brick buildings whose sluices constantly and forcefully run the dirty water into large storm drains. Those drains then pipe the detritus out into the river that runs on the south side of town. There is a constant roar from the discharge.

The factories make an endless, silent squat line of fortresses that are full of brightleaf tobacco and rolling machines and conveyor belts. The rush of the waters is the only noise, save for the buzzing and humming of hundreds of utility lines above.

Friday Calls

PeeWee slows to a walk, gets away from any streetlights and finds a dark, dead spot in the back of the fourth factory down the line. He pulls the gun from his pocket and carefully breaks it open. He drops the remaining bullets into the palm of his hand and puts the gun down on the ground. He rubs each bullet with his shirttail and gently tosses them one by one into the gushing waters foaming with farm dirt, stems, and leaves too far gone or not good enough to be turned into cigarettes.

He then picks up the gun, puts it back in his pocket and carefully, watchfully, walks two more factories down to where its torrent is. PeeWee takes off his shirt to wipe the gun down with it. He almost drops it into the current when a thought comes to him. He lays his shirt on the ground and gently nudges the gun with his foot onto its flat sheet. He then takes the shirttails and the sleeves and makes a good four-cornered bundle and ties it all together.

He picks the bundle up and rolls it around in his hands. It is steady. He shakes the bundle. He shakes it some more, harder this time. It is secure.

Confidently, PeeWee reaches down and places his assigned cargo into the rushing flow, letting its force take it out of his hands as he watches it carry down and away.

He turns and runs away from the factories and once he gets clear of them, he trots to a walk, almost a saunter. He knows that if he gets stopped, there is nothing unusual about a little Negro kid with only shorts and sneakers on, walking the street late at night in the hot quiet.

He goes down and back under the big highway, walks up the long hill and comes onto Patterson Avenue. "Patty," as it is called by those in that part of town, is the main artery of colored town. Gas stations, movie theatres, hair salons, clothing stores, grocery markets, clubs and cribs, churches and dope dens, barber shops, all usually busy places, lined up it and down for about ten blocks in either direction. It was the epicenter of the Eastside.

And Gilmore's Funeral Service was there right in the center. Run now by the third generation of Gilmores, it was upper crust gentrified old-school oleaginous pants creased white gloved service. Mr. Robert "Buck" Gilmore was the current chieftain, a big man who ran a big service. The long, low brown brick building with the chapel-colored glass is landscaped and immaculate, and it is no mistake that the fleet of white Cadillac stretch limos and hearses are displayed prominently for all to see at its towered entrance.

Mr. Buck is often known to say with a knowing nod, "In the end, everyone in this part of town comes to and through Gilmore's." Mr. Buck well knew and understood, as did all his family before him, that it is the tri-legged stool of the Baby Jesus, the Dying and the Planting that nourishes many colored souls with little else to cleave unto; and, oh yes, Gilmore's also sells, for but pennies a month, burial insurance so that the last ride out is guaranteed to be plush, stylish and the talk of the neighbors until the next parade of death is occasioned. Folks up and down the street often say as a mantra of belonging, "You bank at Wachovia, you smoke Reynolds, you die with Gilmore's."

Behind the show row of crowd and coffin carriers is a long covered carport where the machines are always washed, polished, and buffed before each procession, and inside the now dark back of the structure is a long bench where the attendants sit, smoke, and yack between jobs. The only light is a mild lamp over the steps on the side of the mortuary entrance and some slight glow from streetlights well away. There is a blinking yellow traffic light down the way that peeks in and out.

PeeWee figures it is certainly not a good thing to sit on the front steps of Mr. Buck's, and pausing at the side stoop to await Minor's next summons makes him uncomfortable too.

Now he is out in public and he has no shirt and that makes any explaining more uncomfortable than he wishes. He goes to the back of the carport, sits on the bench, quickly lights a cigarette, cups it from view and waits. He knows Minor will find him and he knows that Minor will be cautious when he does. It will happen in due time and before first light.

* * *

Bozo drives faster than he ordinarily does, but not so fast as to draw attention. It is not a good time to be halted by the law in the middle of the night driving around in the country. The radio is on, but he switches it off. Its music and patter is but noise now, empty and distracting. He is glad he has not had time to have his customary late-night highball. The glass for that regular, small pleasure sits empty on the corner back at the club, its partner bottle of brown having surprise-served the deputy.

Friday Calls

It also is not a good thing to get stopped with liquor on his breath.

He needs to think. He tries to think but the scope of it is trapped and narrow, running into a box canyon in his mind. In a quarter of an hour or so, he turns in past some nice gates and goes up a graveled drive. He turns the engine and lights off, exhales long, gets out and goes to the door and knocks loud, harder than he imagines he would. It does sound so loud.

Within a few seconds, a light comes on inside. The front porch light comes on and the door opens and Mr. Charlie May, resplendent in a red and blue silk robe, still tying his belt and at the same time, smoothing his hair, calmly says, "Well. Bozo. This is a bit of a surprise. What brings you out this late at night? I think it's been a while since you visited."

"Good evening, Mr. May. Please excuse me for coming now, this late I mean." Bozo's eternally affable face was tight and tense. He could feel his smooth, sweet voice stammering.

May nods and watches.

Affirmed, Bozo continues.

"Mr. May, I don't presume to be sure but am I correct in thinking Mr. J.T. Barnes is here?" May's eyes narrows and his brow furrows.

Slowly he says, "Yes. That's right. Bozo...what is this about?" May is alert, consciously avoiding asking, "What is wrong?"

"Mr. May, I need to speak with Mr. Barnes. I will tell you both as soon as you can get him for me."

"Yes. Let me go get him."

May turns and walks into the dark of the house. There is muffled knocking, voices and soon, J. T. Barnes strides into the front hall with Charlie May.

With a forced jocularity, Barnes says, "Bozo, this is a pleasant surprise. To see you twice in one night..." He trails off.

There are seconds elapsing, an enormous wave of time that make it all go fast and make it all go slow.

They all have always been friendly and kind to one another. That has spanned many years.

"Bozo?"

And then there is no more stutter, just a plume.

"A man has been killed. He was hit by a train. I expect he was headed this way to be with y'all. One of the deputies that had been where the crash happened, a guy I know, one of the guys that helps us out from time to time, came by the club. He was shook up. He wanted a big drink and I gave him one. He told me enough for me to put the two and two together. He said it was a black Ford business car from a company in Winston-Salem. He said the man in it was killed, terrible killed and he had nice clothes on. Oh, I hope I'm wrong..."

J.T. Barnes and Charlie May look at each other quickly, a glance and a look away and May says in a low, calm voice, "Bozo. Thank you for coming by. I'm sure we'll all see you soon. Drive home safely. Have a good night." And he holds the door open for Bozo who understands the audience was over.

Bozo gets back in his car, turns around, drives away and knows he is right, knows he has done the right thing.

Inside the house, May looks at J.T. grimly and says, "Let's get them all up. Tell the Winston women nothing. You take them back now. I'll speak with the others and they'll be along soon." Nothing else is said.

And now, they are all going to be not only friendly, but friends as well, lashed together by a choking cord of fact.

* * *

Detective Wilkins watches them yellow tape the house and Bo's car. They station a man in a black and white up next to the church to watch where Bo's body had been found and also to be able to look down the hill at all the rest of it. It will only be a few hours until first light and a few hours after that when a full complement of the forensic team can get on scene and shake it down. Worthwhile? He doesn't think so.

He ducks under the tape and goes up into the house again. Minor is standing back in the kitchen still as stone, a sphinx. Wilkins knows he knew plenty and knows he isn't going to give any of it up. Minor is a polished professional in this ragged ass game. He really isn't a suspect and there is no way to hitch him up to being an accessory after the fact and even if they could, the D.A. would decline to take it to the Grand Jury.

Damn. Really is a waste of time, but still it's a crime, he thinks as he watches Minor.

Killing just a little bit more time, he pauses and looks around, trying to make sure he has not missed anything in his first scan.

He looks up at the ceiling and says, hoping for a hit and expecting a miss, "That's an interesting hole up in your ceiling." Torn shredded sheet rock splays black and gray and dangles precariously at its edges.

Minor says, "Yes, it is interesting."

"From that 16 gauge there in the corner?"

"Uh-huh."

"Fresh?"

"Not really."

Wilkins knew that whatever Bo's killshot wound or wounds had been, they had not been caused by any shotgun pattern. It is an "aha" and "so what" moment, all at the same time, a juxtaposition that happens all the time. It is an interesting blast hole, but it does not really have anything to do with the explaining of the dead man's journey. Wilkins reflexively shrugs his shoulders.

Minor says, "I see you've taped the house. You got anything else for me? I like to be going on now." He could see the tired in Wilkins. It lay on him like a jacket.

"Don't you live here?" It is a lame last rattle of a try.

"No."

"Own it?" Wilkins cocks his head a little bit, a slight smile flickering across his face.

"I guess."

"I presume you're not leaving town, are you?"

"No plans to."

Wilkins has nothing else and just stands there.

"Well, I'll be going on now," and Minor walks past Wilkins and out of the house and down the wrinkled sidewalk toward "Patty."

Wilkins waits a few minutes, takes the shotgun up anyway in with a handkerchief for prints and heads back to headquarters to start the damn paperwork. He sees the black and white up the hill with its lights on. That is about as much as they can do for now.

He has no idea what he is going to do with the damn thing. It won't be returned and it won't be asked for either. So they brush it for prints. So what? Nothing that would lead to anything.

As he turns from 14th onto Patterson, he sees Minor walking, comfortable and steady. As he passes him, he honks once quick, just for the hell of it, just to see if Minor will start or jump or look around.

Minor does nothing of the sort and as Wilkins rolls by Minor simply jerk-waves a quarter-length right arm back from the shadows and keeps on moving.

They understand each other.

* * *

Miller and the rookie slow-shuffle down the hall with Kenny, there being no speed to the travel as Kenny is a big, wide young man. He has wide hips and displaced space and the shackles that had been snapped onto his ankles have no drag, no slack between the cuffs. His stride is truncated unto mincing steps.

Kenny walks woodenly, stiff-legged, silently except when he repeats his mantra, "Bo had a derringer, I'm sure he had a derringer," something he does twice on the way to the Magistrate's Office. Each time he speaks, Miller stares straight ahead and only nods and notes that it is the fourth time in his presence that the defendant has so quietly declaimed.

Miller thinks, *He may look dumb, but he's trying to give himself some space down the line.*

The rookie just looks and tries to think it through. It is a lot for a kid to take in. Wilkins walks up the hall and tells Miller they have found the body in the church graveyard just up the hill from the drink house and that it is being taken for post-mortem examination.

Miller says, "Hmmmm...nice touch. Who put him up there?"

Wilkins replies, "Anyone of about ten people as best I can tell. They ain't gonna tell us shit. You know that. You know when they check out and dust that Caddy, not only are they gonna find plenty of blood but enough fingerprints to keep everyone busy for days if they want to try...a complete waste of time. You know that too."

"Yes, I do."

"Tomorrow morning we need to go over there and tighten this up and move it along."

"Yes, I agree."

"It ain't like someone shot the Mayor…"

"I'm with you."

"I'll see you in the morning."

"K."

They understood that this is not a high priority case and that it would behoove them and the system to herd it along efficiently without nit-picking it along the way.

Wilkins turns and walks away. Miller is hungry.

Kenny has listened and is pleased. His people are not going to roll on him. There will be someone who will try—there always is—but not his people.

They come to a metal door. All the doors are metal with big chicken-wired shatterproof square windows. There is another door just like it ten feet beyond. In this rat's maze it is all like that. Once you get fed into the place, slot by slot, it is harder and harder to even imagine getting away. Kenny isn't going to try. He just likes thinking about it.

Miller takes his service revolver and places it in a drawer next to the door and nods to the rookie to do the same.

The drawer swallows the weapons.

Miller speaks into an intercom and a loud buzzer sounds and the door clanks and rumbles open. They lock-step into the compartment and the door closes behind them. They buzz out of the second door and repeat the drill again to stand in a large, too brightly lit room that has all sorts of people in it: cops, drunks, bail bondsmen, prisoners, family, friends, lawyers, highway patrolmen. There is a lot of noise.

Everything is cinder block beige.

Kenny has been here before. He knows he is going to get stood on a lot harder this time in the barrel. He sighs, readying himself for the push down.

Miller guides him to one of the magistrates standing behind the counter.

"Evening, no, morning, everyone. Hey, Miller. Hey, son." The magistrate tilts his head briefly toward the rookie. "What do we have and what do we suggest?"

Miller starts, "This is Homer Kenny Peak. He has been here before on less serious charges. His previous booking and arrest information is in your file system. We have brought him in as the prime suspect on what appears to be an intentional killing of one Benjamin Franklin 'Bo Diddley' Winphrie. We have a credible eyewitness who says she saw Mr. Peak here pull a pistol in a house on 14th Street and shoot Mr. Winphrie. We have no information that indicates this was a spur of the moment thing. This appeared to be willful."

Kenny thinks, *Ain't this some shit...*

"The man's dead I take it..." says the magistrate.

"When I departed the scene to bring Peak down here, they were still looking for the body which we believed to be in nearby vicinity. My partner Detective Wilkins who was just here has now informed me that the victim's body has been found and transported for autopsy."

The language is a minuet, formful and repetitious.

The magistrate already understands that the detectives want Kenny Peak held close to the bosom of justice and thus he should be afforded only the strictest limitations now.

Miller says, "Also, Mr. Peak was in possession of a large amount of what appears to be marijuana and there is no doubt that rises to the level of a felony."

Kenny knows this one was coming. *They are always going to toss some drugs, any drugs onto the fire. All these fellows need a few hits to calm their asses down.*

"Y'all find a weapon?" The magistrate is just curious. He doesn't give a damn. He was going to freeze Peak up as soon as the paperwork was done. Miller, on the other hand, is annoyed.

Miller thinks, *Why does this eyeshade want to mess with this now? It was a good thing there isn't a worth a damn lawyer standing there pulling an oar for this big goon. Damn, I want some pie.* Miller smiles tightly and says, "Not yet, but we have the eyewitness as I said who saw Peak shoot and kill Winphrie... with a pistol."

"Okay, you are asking for an intentional killing with forethought? Murder One?"

"Yes."

"And felony possession of marijuana with intent to sell or distribute?"

"Yes."

"Well, since you are willing to stand to it and swear to and sign the affidavits, we'll get about doing the paperwork and have Mr. Peak here placed in the Sheriff's custody soon. I hope a $500,000 bond will be satisfactory to you."

Miller nods, and the trio stilts Kenny over to another holding cell.

As they get that door opened, Miller says, "Peak, you don't know me and I don't know you but it appears we are joined at the hip for a while now. You understand these are serious, very serious charges. They are a real threat to you. You know that. I don't want to be mean-spirited. I am presuming your family and friends don't have enough money to get you out for now."

He pauses. Kenny's face is a mask. Miller is still dancing the minuet.

Miller continues, "How about sit down with me and Detective Wilkins early next week and let's talk about what happened and see if we can't find a way to help these big problems get smaller."

Kenny looks up at the ceiling of the holding cell.

Miller crouches down and in a calculated act of institutionally required kindness unlocks and releases and pulls away the shackles from Kenny's ankles.

Miller concludes his homily. "Peak. Homer Kenny Peak. We'd like to help you. We want to help you. Come on now. What do you say?"

Kenny looks at Miller and says, "It sure is bright in here. Anyway y'all can get these lights down low so I can get some sleep?"

Miller unlocks Kenny's handcuffs and Kenny ambles into the cell.

The rookie goes back down the hall, then to the Toddle House to have some pie.

Chapter Eighteen

Finishings

It is still dark. Very little traffic goes by out on Patty. Every now and then, PeeWee hears the quiet whoosh of a car passing or the grind of a truck. It is very quiet. He does not wear a watch but the clock in his head tells him it is a few hours from dawn. He sits quietly. Long ago, he had learned the patience that comes with having nothing. You just had to wait to get much of anything. Wait at the Laundromat. Wait at the pawn shop. Wait to get some money. Wait to get noticed. Wait for better times to come.

Being poor does it. Being colored sinks it in lower. He knows it. It does not hurt or bother him. It is just the way things were. Civil rights? He's heard folks talk about that. It carries no weight with him. He is not going to protest anything. He likes being invisible. If he can't score some scratch or some dope or some pussy off it, it is not on the vague menu of opportunities that floats in his head. Civil rights. What is that? Sort of like going down to the water and waiting for freedom to come in on the boat. Don't wait too long, suckers.

And he waits on Minor by the funeral home. This is different. He has been trusted to do something important. He wonders if anything else is next. He wants there to be. He is not sure what the penalty is but he knows, well, pretty much knows, that the pistol has been part of a shooting that is not for sport and that he has disposed of that weapon. He knows all of that added up to a felony, some serious shit. It punches his ticket. He is alert.

He closes his eyes. His lids shade almost down but not completely. It is though he has the two lids of a cat. He has been told that before.

He does not drift. He calms himself.

He has a few cigarettes left and knows he has to conserve them. He slowly rubs his lighter. He does not flip its top back and forth as he usually would because it makes loud metallic clicks in the quiet night. He needs a shirt.

He hears a low bird-like whistle. Then he hears it again. He sits up straight and opens his eyes. The third time he heard it, it's closer. He low-asks the dark, "Minor?"

And then Curt Minor stands over him. He really could not see him but it is him. It is his tight shape as shadow.

"Hey, PeeWee. You do like I told you to do?"

"Yeah."

"Exactly?"

"Uh-huh," he nods.

"Good. Uh, where's your shirt?"

"I wrapped the gun in it so the washing waters behind the tobacco factories would take it easier."

"Good. Good." Minor almost purrs in approval.

"Anybody see you?"

"No." PeeWee feels he needs to be definitive. He really does not know, but he has to cement his reliability with Minor.

PeeWee's eyes are adjusting from his short watch sleep. Minor is taking his shirt off and handing it to him. He has a very white T-shirt on underneath.

"Take this. You need it. You got a little more work to do. Stay here."

PeeWee puts the shirt on. Minor is a much bigger man than him and the shirt flaps down to his thighs. PeeWee sits still and Minor moves down the bench to a work sink and fishes around under it.

Minor brings two plastic buckets back, one larger than the other. Minor pours something out of the bigger one into the smaller one and hands it to PeeWee. It isn't much. He tosses a couple of car cleaning rags into the container. He then counts out and gives PeeWee a hundred dollars in fives and tens and a few twenties. PeeWee folds the money and shoves it deep into his pocket.

He talks softly and clearly with PeeWee as he does these things and then he gives PeeWee a long look in the dark and asks, "You got it?"

"Yeah."

"Exactly?"

"Yeah."

"Wait a few minutes and then go. Be cool. Take care of this right. I'll be in touch."

"Okay."

Minor walks down the length of the car shed and steps into the funeral home's shadows, headed for the street. Then he is gone.

PeeWee leans down and ties his shoelaces good and tight and sits until he calculates a few minutes have passed and then, carrying the bucket, eases out into the back of the place, finds the back alley and keeps moving.

* * *

The lanterns bracketing the front door are not turned on. The screen door does not creak as it's opened. The heavy oak door takes the key lightly, its polished brass knob rolling easy as the house is opened. The house smells of old leather and silver polish and hardwood smoke and deep wool and lilies of the valley. It smells of long, old success.

A small bouillotte lamp glows beneath its filigreed shade on the front hall table. The light is a serene silver yellow. It bodes quiet.

Dr. Valk holds his small bag in one hand and the door for them all with his other as they file in, filling the front hall. Valk steps in behind and gently pulls the front door to them. They are all soft stepping, almost tiptoeing. They are as silent as a grave. There are some watering eyes. They look around, waiting for the time to make a horrible thing more horrible.

Joe Glenn nods, starting up the stairs and the others follow and go to their places. There is no sense in waiting. Just go ahead and get it done. There will be no "get it over with." Dread cloaks them as does a distant queasiness. They know they are the executioners. They will deliver the death message and complete the circuit. For a few seconds more, Archer still lived in that house, is a vital, lively part of its grace and comfort and after a few seconds more, he will be dead, violently killed.

Joe, Jimmy, and Martha Ann gather at the bedroom door. Henry Valk stands a few feet below, his bag now opened. A syringe is dimly cupped in his hand and he looks up toward the three. Joe inhales deeply, then exhales and opens the bedroom door.

Beneath a bedside table lamp still lit, Louise sleeps deeply on her side on top of the still-made bed, ragged snores rising from her open mouth. A mostly empty bottle of bourbon and an empty glass sit with a cigarette butt-loaded silver ashtray. She wears her day clothes poorly now and her makeup is smeared, her hair strangled. There is no subtlety.

The three walk to her bedside and study her. They peer at her. They analyze her. She is motionless, giving no sign that she is aware that they are there.

They frown and grimace and sigh.

Joe reaches down and softly shakes her shoulder and says low, "Louise." Nothing.

He touches her more firmly and again calls her name. Nothing.

He looks at the others. Jimmy holds his hands palms up and shakes them, the universal gesture for, "I have no damn idea." Martha Ann, tiny and severe, steps back a step, her lips pursed, her brow arching deeply inward. She nods at Joe, sending the "go on" ahead signal.

Joe, now louder, "Louise. Louise. It's Joe and Jimmy and Martha Ann. We need to talk to you."

Louise's eyes flutter and she rustles and then she sits quickly up on the edge of the bed.

They step back. The film of oblivion on her now-opened eyes drops away. She looks at them and then speaks hard, "What do you want? Can't you see I am trying to sleep!"

"Louise, we need to talk to you."

"It'll have to wait. Dammit. I am sleeping." Her voice is obscure, clouded but she speaks sharply with flat, precise anger. She looks far beyond them. She speaks to the desk, the wall, the inanimates across the room. She lies back down, curls up and turns her back to them.

They wait, glancing at one another. Their task is a swelling wound, a bad toxin brought by them to intentionally infect. The bedroom door behind them cracks open and Henry Valk eyes them quizzically through the narrow slit. A tall man, his eye is searching from well above them. Jimmy waves randomly back and then points at Louise and shrugs his shoulders again.

"Louise. Louise. Please wake up." Joe's voice is disturbingly loud.

Louise Glenn speaks quietly and clearly, "What is it? What's wrong?" Her tone is knowing.

She sits up again and flattens her skirt and then looks up.

"What's happened?"

Henry Valk steps into the room's shadows.

Joe Glenn speaks quickly, looking at her now lifted, fearful eyes that flit to each of them.

"Louise, this is very bad. There has been an accident. Archer was in the accident...a wreck. It was a bad wreck. Archer is dead. He has been killed." They all lean down toward her.

After a few seconds, she softly murmurs, "Oh. Oh."

And then she is very still.

"Louise, do you understand? Do you understand what we've just told you?"

A sudden tortured moan escapes from her nodding face, loud enough to be clearly heard by Mamie and Retha well down the hall. As if on cue, they slip into the girls' room. The cry soars louder again and then it freezes.

They step forward to comfort her, to hold her hand, to squeeze her shoulder, to try to do all the inadequate things that do not help at all when such a bomb has been exploded in the mind of the recipient. And as they do, they realize that she is rigid. She has become a dead-eyed statue. She is no longer there.

Henry Valk steps in between them, looked intently at Louise and then bellows, "Louise! Louise!" And getting no response, he pulls his long right arm out well above him and without hesitation slaps Louise hard.

"She's catatonic. Louise?"

And she jerks and slumps forward and begins to cry and wail and Valk says, "Hold her."

And they do and he slides the needle in quickly to her white forearm and steadily presses the plunger and in seconds, she is out and her breathing is labored and they lay her back out on the bed and cover her with a blanket.

Dawn is an hour away.

Friday Calls

* * *

Moving quietly, picking his way past tumbled fences, back gates, clothesline poles, old junked cars, scarred backyards and piles of trash, PeeWee keeps heading back up and into the projects and beyond. His pace is regular. He is calm. He moves in and out of the dimmed random lights of the backsides of ratty old houses and apartments.

Every now and then a dog barks. He hears it yank and rattle its chain.

PeeWee crosses a low ditch, walks under some trees and pauses behind the drink house, now double wrapped loosely with distinct "Police Line-Do Not Cross" yellow tape. He ducks under the ribbons and goes up under the place, crawl-squatting in between the piers and their connecting struts. It is all old pine wood, long ago dry cured by time. Pregnant with resin, it is cracked and brittle.

He quick lights and closes his lighter and spies the kitchen plumbing connections and the exterior base of the gas line feeding a small hot water heater. He takes the soaked rags out of the bucket, lays them neatly on the struts nearest those hookups. He pats them flat. His Zippo lights again and he touches the flame to the rags. They glow blue and then the blue jumps down the line to yellow and the flames lift and the first crackle of that early morning snaps out. It is going to burn good and burn fast.

PeeWee shoves the Zippo into his pocket, tosses the plastic bucket underneath the house and backs out from underneath and briskly, but with no show of hurrying, heads back the way he came. He has gone on through a couple of hundred yards and is beside another old house leaning down the hill when he hears the blast and roar. The gas heater has blown. The place will now cave in on itself and burn completely unto ashes. Now he hears sirens. They make no difference now. The sun is sliding up over to the east.

Chapter Nineteen

New News and Old

Equipment sent over from Greensboro has jacked and lifted the train and it has been reset upon the tracks. Its airbrakes and couplings have been checked and re-hooked and tested. The passengers transferred to other trains that have come over from Raleigh and out of Greensboro to make the pickups. Some of the injured are just shaken and banged up. A few are taken to local hospitals. Railroad company investigators are en route to inspect the scene and interview the crew who had been taken all together to a hotel in Greensboro.

A substitute crew is also on its way to take the train on. The crumpled Ford has been chained and pulled out of the gulley and hauled to an impound lot for holding.

The driver's body has been quietly taken to a local funeral home and quickly picked up by another funeral home and whisked into embalming for whatever services lie ahead.

The scene is quiet now with only a few deputies there. The intersection crossing has been reopened. Another hot day is starting to rise above it all.

Two deputies are walking the length of the track, just taking a last look. The train will sit in place until the investigators and new crew get down to take it over.

"Helluva mess, ain't it?" one deputy muses.

"Yeah. It was," replies the other.

They walk along. They've been there all night and now it is day and they are tired and hungry.

And one says, "What's that over there?"

"Where?"

"Over there." He gestures first with his head and then points in the direction of the sun, away from the tracks.

The deputies peer and begin to walk that way. After twenty yards or so, they stop and look down.

There is a body, not much of it left, shoved up into the dirt and weeds. It is a young woman, legs and arms splayed and torn and all mottled blood-dried. Her head is partially caved in. A rag doll tossed. She has hit the ground hard. It is easy to tell she had been a pretty young thing.

"Who is she? Where'd she come from?"

"Offhand, I don't know but I'll bet a dime to a doughnut that she came out of that Ford that got hauled away from here."

"Uhm...any ID?"

"Don't see any from here and we better not touch her until the coroner gets back. You stay with her. Don't touch her. I'll go back to the car and make the call."

"Jesus, Joseph and Mary. What a mess."

There are flies buzzing about. The heat is rising up. The rot is too.

* * *

Kenny sits Buddha-like on his bunk, his legs crossed up under him. He has been here before. He knows the drill and mostly the drill is be quiet, be patient, and listen out. It is Saturday morning and the sun is hot. There is another guy in the cell with him who is small. He won't cause any trouble or try to mess with him. They just nodded to each other when Kenny was escorted in. Kenny said, "Kenny," and nodded toward him. He answered with a nod of his own and said, "Jerome." He had been sleeping and had awakened as Kenny entered.

They would talk later about some things but never about what their crime stories were. You never knew who the rat was, but there was always a rat just waiting to sift some words and make a problem a bigger problem. Kenny is grateful. He knows immediately that Jerome is not a talker, not a loud mouth like some of the ever-present yapping clowns a few cells down. They are always hollering for cigarettes, cursing and prancing about and always laughing fake, too loud, bragging, and making jackasses of themselves. "All hat and no cattle," Kenny thinks.

Soon after Kenny was celled, they brought him the ratty, plastic tub. It was the standard issue—a Swiss cheese blanket, a scratchy sheet, a long-dead pillow, too-small towel, flip-flops and county jail jumpsuit. A little bar of soap and a toothbrush with a little tube of toothpaste and the last of the niceties, a thin washcloth.

Jerome had soon turned back over, pulled his blanket up over his head and gone back to sleep. Kenny fixed his bunk and put the other items under it.

As he sits there, he thinks about shooting Bo. He knows he had done it and he knows that's why he is sitting where he is sitting. But it doesn't bother him too much. Bo had treated him like dog shit and finally the business end of the dog had shit on Bo. Fine. He wonders if he just does not care. He wonders if he hated Bo. But these are matters of philosophy that are straining to Kenny and he consciously chooses to let them float away. Were he to ponder such things, he will become uncomfortable and that would interfere with his patience, his ability to wait effectively.

He knows he's in some serious trouble but he also knows it's a messy situation which does not hurt matters one bit. Lots of drinking and doping and noise and crowding and confusion had been going on. That was good. He puts on his issued jumpsuit. It's bright orange and reads across the back in big, fresh, black letters, "INMATE—FORSYTH COUNTY JAIL." He had put his arrest papers in its deep pockets and he feels for them and fishes them out. . The one about the dope doesn't bother him not at all. It is at worst nothing and at best, a trading card. It is the Murder in the First Degree that's the nasty one, the nub of the matter. "...with malice aforethought...did intend to kill..." and so forth.

Kenny looks at the long, pink paper carbon copy and slowly, for that was his only way to try to read, looks at it word by word, piecing it together, softly mouthing what he feels the word and next words sound like and then processes them into a cohesive meaning. It is fair to say that Kenny had done poorly or not at all in school and had departed those dull, narrow environs for good after the fourth grade. He was a manual laborer, a fine lifter and hauler, but he was diligent and strong and had an all-day all-night

Friday Calls

constitution, but his skill set in totality was badly marginalized by the work available to him in this ever-increasingly modern world, his weak mind and his race. These are things he gives no specific thought to; he just knows his limitations and does not lament them.

As he marches along with the words, the cell door opens and the jailer says, "Come on, Peak. You have a visitor. We're going downstairs to the interview rooms. Bring your papers."

Kenny asks, "Who?"

"Lawyer. Says he represents you. Is that so?"

"Yes, bound to be, I hope," and waits for the cuffs to be reapplied to his wrists. They walk to the elevator which stinks of sweat and long ago embedded in the paint food odors. They descend one floor and he is un-cuffed and is sent into a room.

There's a scratched-up table, two scratched-up chairs and a younger man, tall enough, broad with a full head of hair and owlish, round lens glasses. He has energy. He wears a pressed, dark suit and blue necktie and looks like he had just fallen out of the window of a fine men's clothing store. His tie is bright and his shoes are shined and he has a crisp white handkerchief in his breast pocket, folded and pointing just right up. He sticks out his hand as the door closes and says, "Hello, Kenny. I'm Eddie Terrell. I have come down here to help you if that's all right with you."

Kenny looks at him and speaks. "Rise?"

"Yes, Rise."

"Okay."

They both sit down. Eddie Terrell looks at Kenny quietly for a few moments, and studies him. He has a briefcase and from it he pulls out a long, yellow legal pad, a gold Cross pen, a pack of Camel cigarettes and a gold Ronson lighter.

"Kenny, as you have already figured out, your sister Rise has gotten me down here. She called me this morning. You may know I have helped her in the past. Considering all things, we did pretty good...." He takes a cigarette out of the pack and asks, "Smoke? You mind if I smoke?" He also offers Kenny a cigarette.

"Yeah, sure, thanks." Kenny takes it and Terrell lights them and they are soon quiet exhaling.

Kenny asks, "You not court-appointed?"

"Nope."

"You not a rookie? You helped Rise before, right?"

"Nope and yeah, that's right."

"How you gettin' paid?"

"That's been taken care of...in full. You don't need to be worrying about that."

Kenny let out a flat, "Hmmmm..."

He hands Kenny a couple of his cards. Kenny reads one.

"Edward F. V. Terrell, Attorney and Counselor at Law."

"How long you been doing this?"

"Long enough to know my way around and long enough to know that you have some pretty big trouble out there on your radar. Kenny, did you bring your papers with you?"

"Yessir."

"May I please see them?"

He holds his hand out and Kenny lays the folded sheets in it.

Terrell sits back, cigarette in his lips and reads them, up and down, up and down.

"Kenny, we need to talk. Now remember, anything you and I talk about, that's just between us and nobody gets to know about any of it. I know you've had some difficulties before and had had lawyers help you before. Do you remember them telling you about the attorney-client privilege?"

"Yeah, I think so."

"Okay, you understand what the two of us talk about is secret between us, got it? But if you tell a cellmate or a jailer anything or you're just talking to yourself and someone hears you, all that's fair game and I can promise you the cops and the prosecutors will use it against you if they get hold of it. So watch yourself. You understand?"

"Yessir." Terrell's face is kind but his eyes narrow down and he is now coiled.

"Now, I need to find out all about you and I need to find out who all was there last night and I need you to tell me what you saw and heard and thought. I'll start here in just a minute asking you questions. I'll be careful with those questions, the way I word them and say them and I want you to think hard and concentrate as you answer them and I want you to be honest and careful with your answers. But, and this is a big but, I do not want to know whether you did anything that you might be guilty of last night. Do you understand that? It's real important."

"So I can't tell you about some things about last night? Why?"

"Here's the deal. I'm going to learn things along the way. I'm going to learn a lot along the way. I am starting, right now, thinking about how I think your case ought to be prepared, how it ought to be set up for a trial in front of a jury. One of the many things I've got to think about is whether or not during that trial—which would be some months from now—whether or not I want to put you up on the witness stand to testify under oath. If you were to tell me things now that pointed toward your guilt and then you were to get on the witness stand and say you didn't do such and such and I knew you had done such and such, I would be enabling a witness to lie under oath before the Court. I cannot do that. We'd both get in a lot of trouble and neither of us needs anymore of that. Do you understand?"

"Yeah, but don't that happen all the time? I mean, shit, don't lawyers want to know what happened and ask their guy and the guy says, 'Yeah, I did whatever,' and then the lawyer helps them lie it around as it goes once they find it out?"

"I'll grant you that is probably so, but there's more than one way to put the whole story together and so let me do my job. Hell, one day I may ask you flat out about it all but that may or may not happen. So, please listen to me carefully when I ask you questions and let's take our time, okay? We're going to be visiting more than a little bit as this thing goes forward."

Kenny nods.

"Now, I'm going to jump around a little here, you with me?"

"Yeah. Okay."

"Did you know the fellow who got shot?"

"Yeah."

"How?"

"I known him for a while. I ran errands and did stuff for him."

"He pay you?"

"Sometimes."

"Were you working for him last night?"

"Yes, some, but I was also working in his and Curt Minor's drink house."

"On 14th Street?" Terrell is looking at the warrants, smoke pluming out his nose and rising above his head.

"Did you get paid for last night?"

"No, Bo...Ben Winphrie owed me money from some earlier jobs."

"How much did he owe you? How many jobs?"

"Couple of hundred. There were at least three pickups and deliveries."

"How long had he owed you?"

"Couple of weeks plus he owed my lawyer I had before on some earlier charges that I'd gotten. He said he was gonna take care of that lawyer, big fat tall guy with greasy hair, and I was gonna keep my mouth shut about where the stuff came from. I did and I have, but he ain't paid the guy and the lawyer ain't doing nothing for me now. He says, I mean he said he never said he's doing that but he did."

"What's that lawyer's name?"

"Rodenburger, Harry Rodenburger. You know him?"

"Yeah, I do."

"They told me he was a bigshot, that he does the works for the drink house and drug peoples."

"Is that what Ben Winphrie was? A drink house and drug guy?"

"Yeah, for sure."

"Hmmmm...what are these other charges about? Are they still out there?"

"Yeah, they's a couple of misdemeanor possessions and one felony with intent to sell and deliver near a school."

"Okay, I'll go see Rodenburger and see what's going on there. That okay with you?"

"Sure. I don't think that stuff just gonna disappear."

"No, I think you're right there."

Terrell is thinking about how to leverage with those charges, another running track moving in his mind's tunnels. He had never learned to play chess or cards. But here, he could move the variables in an algorithm like the best three-card monte guy you'd ever see.

"Did you and Ben Winphrie get along?"

"No. No, he wouldn't pay me on time hardly ever and he talked shit about me to me and in front of other people all the time."

"That make you unhappy?"

"Yeah, made me mad. I needed my money. I didn't like getting talked shit to. I was doing his works for him and..." Kenny's voice tails off.

"You didn't like him?"

"No, and he didn't like me. He carries a derringer all the time. Used to show it to me flashy. Make me understand he was a badass and he would use it on me. He was mean. Always actin' high and mighty. I ..."

Terrell is sensing something more coming than he wanted to hear right now, so he holds up his hand and Kenny stops.

"Good. Glad to see you are paying attention. Now, who all was there? Who all may have seen things that would be of interest to us?"

"Uhm...Curt Minor was there, my sister Rise was there, lots of people. It was Friday night, crowded. Bo's crib bitch Felicia was there."

"Who might have seen whatever happened?"

"Hmmmm...maybe a few. It was hot and crowded."

"Who do you think? Minor ever treat you bad, want to score on you?"

"No, always treated me fair. Never much of a talker but always treated me fair."

Kenny was trying hard just to answer the questions and not add anything else. Of course, there was a lot to add.

"Okay. Your sister I don't think gonna have much to say about all this, do you think?"

"Naw, she's cool."

"Now, this Felicia girl—she's Bo's girlfriend? Is that right?"

"Yeah. They beens together a while now."

"Tell me about her." Terrell is smelling a trail.

"She young, don't weigh a hundred pounds soaking wet. Put on airs just like Bo. Don't work that I knows of. Has a kid but I don't think Bo's the baby daddy. She walks the line Bo tells her to."

"She kind of mirrored Bo, acted like he did?"

"Yeah, if Bo felt one way, she was gonna feel that way too."

"So...fair to say, if Bo didn't like you, then she didn't either."

"Yeah."

Terrell knows where the blow is going to come from.

"Kenny, where was she when all this happened?"

"I don't know. Maybe in there, in the room...I don't know. I don't really know. Maybe Rise can tell you."

"Okay, how is this drink house laid out?"

"Quiet front room. Bigger room in back where the party was and a kitchen bathroom behind that."

"How many people in there last night?"

"Plenty. Like I said, it was crowded. Maybe twenty-five, maybe more."

"What all was going on? What were those people doing?"

"Everything you does on Friday night. Blow off steam. Drink, dance, dope, gamble, cut up. It was a regular Friday night."

"Where the alcohol come from?"

"Well, it's a drink house. Cut liquor. Watered. Some beer but mostly liquor."

"What about the dope?"

"Always plenty of dope. Guess from Bo. Never saw anything different."

"Any cocaine?"

"Naw, never seen that."

"Who owns the drink house?"

"Bo always acted like he did. I don't know."

Terrell thought there now was a trip to the deed vault in the offing to verify ownership. Lord, he hated that place. When he had first started, his first client was buying a piece of cheap property, a rundown rent house over in the same part of town. He was hired for $90 to search the title to it, to make sure the buyer could get a clean title. So he went to the deed vault and began pulling down these huge leather-bound land transaction books and peering at the hieroglyphs that were the old deeds and their trails. It was awful. He did not have any idea what he was doing and even if he did, he did not think this kind of lawyering was going to work out for him. It was quiet, boring and had a negligible human element save for watching other men in shirtsleeves looking down and smoking while they silently scratched out notes. Alarmed, Terrell went outside to smoke a cigarette and ponder what was looking like a bleak Sisyphean future. While on the sidewalk outside the courthouse, his partner lumbered toward him from across a parking lot in an obvious state of agitation. At this time, they were but baby lawyers, having tossed in together after a night of post-bar exam study and significant drinking.

His partner, Tommy Rumpler, was carrying their little office's only other file, a court-appointed case involving a recidivist, teenage shoplifter waif by the name of Angel Monique whom a wearied and sick and tired of seeing her ass in his courtroom, Judge Abner Alexander, more affectionately known as Big Ab, had tossed into the county jail to await yet another useless trial on her multiple counts of pilfery. Tommy was thus marked to be her lawyer and after visiting the jail to interview her and, like Terrell, had no idea what he was doing and even if he did, he did not like it one bit.

Upon Terrell's inquiry, Tommy noted that the jail was nasty, it smelled bad, the people were rough and cussed and hooted at him and there were a bunch of fat, mean-assed cops and sheriff's deputies all over the place. There was a sense of imminent and dismal violence about the place and that the client was a bored, semi-literate child of apathy who had no appreciation of her difficulties. This he later learned was the Really Don't Give A Shit Approach which deflected many a problem.

Tommy then asked Terrell what his tasks were like and upon accurate exposition, Tommy and Terrell decided (no one remembered who initiated the move) to switch files and start anew.

Tommy went to the deed vault and loved its order and lack of olfactory offense. Tommy had been a good law student and had already learned to think like a lawyer. Terrell, a desultory and often deficient law student, but a great lover of the movies and television, went to the jail and loved its theatrics and perpetual motion. And thus, happy new paths were opened for them which endured.

Terrell snatches himself out of his memory and asks, "Kenny, do you own a gun?"

"No."

"Well, on the night all this happened did you have a gun?"

"Uhm...you want me to answer that one?"

Terrell knew that he was hunting close to the heart of it.

Nodding slowly, he said, "Yes."

"I did for a little bit. Yes."

"After whatever that little bit was, what happened to the gun?"

"Someone took it away from me real fast. I don't know who. There was a lot of confusion."

"Before whatever happened happened, did you and Bo have any discussion, do any talking about the money he owed you?"

"Yeah, earlier on."

"How'd that go?"

"He told me pretty much to go fuck myself."

"Did that make you angry?"

"Yeah."

"Was that gun a pistol?"

"Yeah."

"Do you know what caliber it was?"

"No."

"Do you know where that pistol is now?"

"No. No idea."

"Kenny, do you know much of anything about guns?"

"No, not really."

"Have you ever owned a gun, had one registered in your name?"

"No, never. The kind of business I do, it wouldn't do to have one."

"Never been charged with anything having to do with a gun?"

"No."

"Kenny, what did it sound like in there when all this happened?"

"I don't know. It was a lot of yelling and screaming. I didn't hear much of anything. Everything was going real fast."

Terrell is quiet now. He sits and thinks. Kenny watches him.

Terrell knows now that the chances are slim and none—and slim has already gotten up and left the room—that he will put Kenny on the witness stand, which considering all things, he is glad to get have that deduction out of the way sooner rather than later.

Kenny asks, "What do you think?"

"I think we have some things going for us and some things going against us. This is enough for now. You did fine with me and I appreciate it. I have got to go talk to a lot of people and take a look at some places. I'll be back in a few days. The first person I'm going to get up with is your sister. I know she'll be here to see you soon. Do not, do not, do not talk to her or any other family about last night. There ain't no privilege with them—just and only me. Keep your mouth shut. Oh, and don't write anything down. Nothing.

I'm going to explain all that as soon as I can to her though I expect she already knows it, understands it. Do you understand me?"

Terrell buzzes for the guard to come take him downstairs.

"Yes. Thank you for coming, Mr. Terrell."

Terrell starts to reply along the lines of "just call me Eddie" but he catches himself. There is no reason to shorten the distance between them. Formality, not familiarity is going to be needed. They are not equals and they aren't going to be. This is going to be a tough one and he needs to have respect on his side when the time comes.

"You are welcome, Kenny. I hope I can help you. I am going to try. Please be patient."

The door clangs open and Terrell exits with the deputy. As he leaves, he nods to Kenny who nods back but does not invite Terrell to call him Mr. Peak. It is never going to happen.

* * *

J.T. Barnes and four women, all looking tired and worse for the wear from their hurried and hasty departure have driven back to Winston-Salem in a sour and ominous silence. They have all been rousted and told they are all leaving now. There is no repartee or giddy laughter in the flat-given order to move quickly. No one sends them happily off as they had been so welcomed but hours earlier. No cocktails are served. Cigarette smoke is the perfume of the hour. It fogs the car's interior despite the windows being cracked. The ladies are no longer the sought-afters. They have been rapidly demoted to the get-rid-of's and they know it. Barnes is preoccupied and keeps running his hand through his hair which now lacks its Vitalis sleek. The ladies are rumpled and sullen.

They all know something had happened, something that is not good, but no one is telling and no one is asking.

As they draw near the outskirts of the city, Barnes pulls the car over into the gravel lot of an innocuous farm and tractor supplier. The only sound is the tires' harsh, grabbing crunch on the rocks. The sun is coming up. He puts the car into park, stares straight ahead for a few seconds and turns and looks flatly at each one of the females. He has not spoken to them during the ride until now. His face is drawn and gray. There is a brief, involuntary shiver to his head as he stretches his right arm across the top of the bench seat and clears his throat just a little too loudly. He hack-coughs. He looks at them but they might as well have not been there. The twinkle in his eyes of just a little while ago has burnt down to a black cinder.

"Uhhh...well, I'm sorry, we're real sorry about all of this, but it had to be done. Wish it had all turned out differently but it didn't. I'm going to drop each of you off in just a few minutes. Whatever has happened has happened and it won't be long before y'all learn about it. I tell each of you now, tell you as directly as I can that each of you would be well-advised to remember that you were not where you might have been earlier. Do you understand?"

He then focuses slowly on each one, his strained gaze meant to elicit their acknowledgment of their complete understanding of their disappearance. They know they were being summarily dismissed and there is no respect for them at these departures. They each nod resentfully. They resent him and all of them.

J.T. spins his wheels and goes on the way to the empty, tainted goodbyes.

Chapter Twenty

Comings and Goings

Eddie Terrell comes out of the jail and walks back down street and up the hill to their offices on Cherry Street. It is an old house some good success had helped them buy. It is comfortable and handsome and it lends itself to their feeling like "real" lawyers. Since he had never set out to be one, much less a guy going to court all the time, there is still a surreal feeling to it all. He says, "Hey" to the girls bent over their humming typewriters and sits down at his desk, picks up the phone, looks at a corner of his file and dials the number found there.

"Rise? Hey. Eddie. Gotta make this quick. Want to get stuff done while it's fresh. Met with Kenny. Got a lot of info…yeah, some good, some not so good. He knows to keep his mouth shut and when you go see him, remind him again. Tell me this. Where was this Felicia gal when whatever went down went down?…uh-huh. uh-huh…yeah? You pretty sure about that? Okay, good. Thanks. I will want to meet with you early next week… right… tell Big Ben I said, 'Hey'… later… oh yeah, I appreciate the business and feel free to send all you got."

Eddie Terrell puts the receiver down and thinks, *You know, I could almost try this case tomorrow if I had to.*

They don't teach any of this good stuff in law school. You either got it or you didn't. Eddie got it.

* * *

Dozing PeeWee rocks along with the wheezing bus, its shock absorbers and tires trampolining across the macadam of state highways long in need of do-overs. The bus interior smells like a long gone to ashes auntie whose house had been closed up for years, musty and sour with the dead and gone. Its seat covers are worn to greasy, slick nylon patches barely covering the heads of thrusting springs. There is a sprinkling of passengers, here and there, sprawled across two open seats or sitting up looking out decrepit windows long since stained opaque by the sun. The bussie's head bobbles in the front, lighting up and then fading as traffic passes going the other way as if an apparition in the fun house.

It is a local, not an express, and a late night early morning derelict at best. They will stop every half-hour or so, sometimes at crossroads under single blinking yellow and red traffic lights, sometimes in a little, soon to be dead-on-arrival towns with blank storefronts and used car lots. This is not a Greyhound Sky Cruiser. This is hollowed-out steerage. Sometimes someone gets off or on. Sometimes nothing happens. The café doors creak open, hot exhaust quickly surges in and, after a few minutes of scheduled wait, the doors whines shut and the bus gasps a sclerotic compressed air burst and the gears grind and catch and it rolls off.

Having completed his tasks for Curt, PeeWee had low-key-loped to the Union Bus Depot in the center of town. Don't run hard. Someone will remember you sweating a lot. The terminal is always lit up with all sorts of people wandering in and out, rumbling buses coming and going. He had bought his ticket to Baltimore, round trip please, sir—no sense in giving the Fuzz, if they came around asking questions, some idea that anyone was going for good—nothing unusual in that kind of behavior. There was an all-night cafeteria and café hooked on the place. He was hungry but nixed the idea of going down the line where many folks could see him. So he sat on one of the long wooden benches under the center of the vaulted ceiling. He could be hungry for a while longer—nothing tough about that. He knew how to do that. And he wanted to marshal his money. He figured he'd be able to earn once he got to Maryland, but was penurious, just in case it took a while to get hooked up. So he went to the end of a bench where it began to slide into shadows down where the tall bus lockers were and waited for the loud speaker call for his trip out.

Friday Calls

He mumbled to himself, "Wonder what the train ride to up there would be like? Maybe I ought to find out one day." He looked at the chalked-in schedule board hanging over the ticket windows. It wouldn't be long.

He caught himself speaking albeit quietly and then was quiet again. In about twenty minutes, a tinned out flat voice intoned, "Lewisville Lines, Local to Ballymore, number 461, now arriving on Gate Six, ticketed passengers please report to Gate Six." It was repeated. And again.

PeeWee went on first call to Gate Six and was punched aboard. He sat toward the back and watched the door with attention. Soon there was last call and the bus pulled away from the curb and headed north in fits and starts.

PeeWee is guardedly pleased with himself. He has done his jobs with skill and accomplished all that was asked of him. He's been given responsibility and a good sum of money. But he wonders. Is Curt Minor satisfied with his work? He isn't going to get any feedback for a long time. He has been given a taste of the big-time. He wants more. He curls up in his seat and can do no more.

* * *

The daylight pulses over the earth as the sun rises. J. T. Barnes had deposited the women quickly and silently. He then found a newspaper rack box and stuffed the change in and quick-snatched a copy. He gets back in the car and unfolds its pages, peering intently at the newsprint, scanning up and down, side to side. He is trying not to go too fast and miss something and so he looks again and finds he has not missed anything as there was nothing to miss. He drives onto Old Town Club and sits in the parking lot toward the back near the "Colored Only Help" sign and door. He is frozen in his thoughts which keep running away from him. He has done nothing wrong. Yet someone, a dear friend, is dead and he could feel his hands deep in it. And it will not be over soon. The whispering and glancing and shunning and shutting off will be part of it. An entire stable of luscious and willing fillies have been cut loose and run off. Any further assemblage of such scope and quality is not remote. It is impossible. There has been great ease and comfort in their shared evasions, the dispersion of guilt by the cover and comedy of the herd. The herd is now culled, each bull now cowering, awaiting the tight clamp of the *burdizzo*.

There will be angry questions at a lot of nice homes from their elite spouses. The ensuing inquiries, accusations, towering silences, tears and thundering findings of their certain guilt will be white-hot pokers, well and smartly placed to evoke maximum discomfort. And they will be permanently and contritely handcuffed and chained to narrower, colder lives. The starter's pistol, once the signal to go hard, is now leveled at them and there are no blanks in the chamber. Misery now appended to the failed and they are helpful to avail.

J.T. waits and soon enough Frank Cuthrell's gleaming two-tone Chevrolet crosses his vague view. Cuthrell immediately recognizes Barnes and looks quizzically at him. He isn't supposed to be here. He is supposed to be away and going to a football game in Chapel Hill. Cuthrell parks and walked over to Barnes' car. J. T. slowly hoists himself out to stand before Cuthrell. There is no energy in him; he's only flat, gray, and sallow.

Cuthrell sees it right away and J.T. knows he does. Cuthrell knows there is a problem, that bad news is near.

"Hello, Mr. Barnes." Frank, always deferential, but this time curious, too.

"Hello, Frank." The formality of it always preserved.

"I thought y'all were all going to the game."

Barnes nods, looks down, looks up. "Frank, something real bad has happened. Mr. Archer Glenn got killed last night."

Frank's eyes widen. His head jerks an inch backward.

"Mr. Archer? How? What happened? Oh, me, what happened?"

"His car got hit by a train...outside Greensboro. I felt I should come tell you, not have y'all just hear it."

Frank nods. He liked Mr. Archer. He would miss him. He likes Mr. Barnes. Hell, he likes almost all of them. They are polite and well-mannered. They always passed the hat to help out when one of his crew needed help. They all gave nicely to the Easter and Fourth of July and Christmas Funds. They treat them all with respect. They are funny and fun to be with. They are bawdy and bad. And lively. They tip well and they let him, no, expect him to and look to him to run his rooms his way. They know their places just as he and his staff know theirs. They all trust one another.

And the sadness of it is not lost on him. Things will change. There will be a greater distance between them all now. There will be greater reserve. The room will be quieter, more subdued. A great shrinking is on the horizon.

Frank gently shakes his head. "Well, that's kind of you. I appreciate it. I'll let the boys know so everyone acts right. I guess you don't know when the services are. I'd like to bring some of my long-timers to pay our respects."

"That would be nice. I know the family will appreciate that. It just happened last night. I don't think anything has been arranged yet."

"Right, of course."

"Well, I need to go on. Maybe I'll see y'all tomorrow. Maybe I'll know a little more then."

Frank says, "I hope so. Thank you for coming by."

Barnes nods and Frank turns and walks into the back entrance of the club.

Barnes slowly gets back in his car. He has no place to go except home. He does not want to go there.

Frank Cuthrell punches in on the clock and sits down on a bench in the locker room. He is the only one there. Bratcher and Blaylock and Big James and Robert will soon be there. They need to know because tread soft time has come.

* * *

Saturday morning, Harry Davis has let himself in the back at City Beverage. He moves slowly in the decrepit fashion of a man twenty years older. He always had the gait of a tortoise and had never moved quickly. His walk is deliberate as though his feet are his antennae, sensing his next footfall. He gingerly makes his circuitous way around the crates and boxes to his desk and sits down heavily with a matching sigh. He will open up at ten and awaits Syd's return. Bing will be in by eleven. With the weather being warm, plenty of juice and jug will cross the counter in addition to the backroom business. Today will be some more college action and the professional football lines are now available so that would start as well. Harry and Syd's clients know that the window closed on Sunday's games at 6 p.m. sharp and no one picks up a phone for a play on Sunday.

Harry turns his gooseneck lamp on and cranes it over the detritus of the desk, an organized mind surveying a sea of mess. He looked over his notes and yesterday's and last week's sales receipts, makes some more notes and scratchings and as he gets up to get a Coca-Cola from the flat slide cooler, his desk phone rings. He picks it up.

"City Bev-rage."

"Is this Mr. Davis?"

"Yes, Frank? Is that you?"

"Yessir, it's me. Sorry to bother you at the start of the morning. I need..."

Davis genially interrupted, anticipating another order says, "Frank, let me find a pencil so I can write it down right."

"Uh, Mr. Davis. It's not an order. It's...well, Mr. Archer Glenn has been killed. Got hit by a train. I felt like you ought to know."

"Frank, what happened? When did it happen?"

"Happened last night, Mr. Davis, over some place outside Greensboro. That's all I know. Mr. Barnes came to the club and told me."

"And he's dead? You sure?"

"Yessir, Mr. Archer was supposed to be with Mr. Barnes and a few others. They were going to the game today."

"Okay, Frank, let me ask you something."

"Yessir?" There is a wary question in that affirmative.

"Are you worried about anything?"

"Well, maybe...you knows we got the liquor from you for him. I don't guess it would it have made it through a train wreck. I just worry that someone might find something and start working it backwards."

Davis pauses, does the probabilities in his head.

"Frank, I think the odds on that are pretty long. I appreciate the call. I'm sorry for Mr. Glenn and his family. I really am. Let's just sit tight on all of this. I don't think anything will come of that. Let's just be quiet. Don't you think that's the best way?"

It really wasn't a request or even a suggestion. Cuthrell knew it was an instruction to be honored.

"Frank, too, it was all a cash business, right?" Davis explores.

"Yessir, all cash on both ends."

"Good, let's let it be a mouse. You don't know anything. I don't know anything. Let's keep it that way, okay?"

"Yessir. You know you can trust me."

"Yes, I do. Let's let that sleeping dog lie."

"Yessir."

"Frank, if anyone comes around asking anything, please let me know."

"Yessir, I will. Is there anything else you think we need to talk about?"

"No, but I appreciate your asking. If something comes to mind, please call me."

"Yessir, I will."

Davis signs off. Just everyone needed to keep their mouths shut. He and Frank Cuthrell had done a lot of business over the years and there was no reason to spook him out of more down the line. Being gentle is the best way. Bing comes in, nods to his daddy and heads to the front.

A few minutes later, Syd Siddon is announced by Bing and strides in to find his chair.

"Morning, Harry."

"Syd."

"What do you think about today?"

"Well, today will come right along, but right now I'm thinking about something else."

"Yeah?"

"Yeah. One of my, one of our, bigger players died last night."

"Yeah? Who? What happened?"

"Archer Glenn. Hit by a train outside Greensboro."

"Glenn. That's too bad. Always hate to lose a whale. He on the books for this weekend, isn't he?"

"Yes. I expect, considering the circumstance, we need to mark it a null."

"Fair enough. Big bet?"

"Big enough." He pulled the ledger from the night before and showed it to Siddon.

"Yup, big enough. But, we'll survive."

"True enough. True enough." And that is enough of that as they begin the preparation for today's work.

* * *

The train crew had with many a nod and wink been secured, sheltered, fed and given a chance to clean up by railroad personnel. And only then were they interviewed by railroad investigators. It was the constants of off-the-book procedures. The watch commander for the Sheriff's Department on that side of the county knew full well of the relationships between Green's Supper Club and his personnel and knew too that this was of interest to important others outside his jurisdiction and it was always a good thing to help one's neighbors as one day they would help them.

This was simply a matter of a damn fool and his cutie pie company riding up in front of a huge train and getting blasted into kingdom come. There is no reason to make it more complicated and try to juice it up. The watch commander knew to just treat it routinely, help get the mess cleaned up and do the paperwork and move on efficiently. Let the railroad handle its people as they saw fit. Law enforcement had a "train hits car" end of story, file closed.

Knight and Gordon sang the song of truth incomplete though it was, that there was nothing they could have done; they came around the bend, the car pulled in front of them, and they crashed into it. They brought the train to a halt on down the track and all immediately went to see if there was anything that could have been done to help. They could not have stopped in time to avoid the collision.

They had called it in right away. They had followed the rules.

Kevin, the conductor, said pretty much the same thing though his recitation of events was prefaced by his having not seen it, he just knew what had happened and had joined in the search after the crash. He wept and sniffled and cried during the questions and the railroad dicks wanted to be done with him quickly.

Only perfunctory questions were asked about alcohol and sleep and their answers were perfunctory too and all understood that plausible denial was the watchword of the day and that any lawsuit—if indeed there were any—against the railroad would get run into a box canyon very quickly and snuff out from the lack of the oxygen of fact.

The three were then put on a maintenance train back to Richmond where they would go on paid leave for a month or so while investigators would go through the innocuous motions of looking at the law enforcement files and visiting the scene again, taking photographs of the scene and the shattered car and interviewing a few folks who did not know anything about anything. And then a report would go into a file and it would be impossible for any pin to be pulled out of any grenade. And the three would then go back on station.

The compartmentalization and sanitation are adroitly done. There really is nothing to see here. Move along.

* * *

Wilkins and Miller learn of the drink house fire at 14th Street early that morning and head immediately back to the scene. But there is no scene left. Just smoldering, collapsed, caved in ruins, charred black and still hot to the touch. As the sun rises, the hot air shimmers over the remains like a blacktop to nowhere in the desert. The officer up on the hill assigned to watch it all had called it in when he saw it, but there were questions as to when he saw it. Those questions weren't going to be asked. This was an old rickety house with shaky, sparking wiring, struts and supports and flooring made of highly flammable heart of pine where the resin and sap would burn white hot once it was sufficiently heated. This was a nigra-on-nigra drink house shooting. The parameters of what was going to be done were thusly tightly circumscribed.

The two detectives walk from their car to the smoking pile. Some hanging and fragile sticks and boards of the wooden skeleton are propped and lay as pick up sticks, remnants of less than nothing. There is no question this is an arson well-done, but the main question is who did it and why was it done. They are going to toss the place calmly and good in the light of the day after last night's excitement. That was a lost cause now. *Curt Minor?* thinks Wilkins and then quickly dismisses it. While a little bit of time has elapsed from when he had seen him walking down the street to the time of the fire call-in gave him opportunity, it is a certainty that he probably didn't do this and if he had, he had an airtight alibi.

Why was it done? Spite? Rivalry between the Bucket of Blood operators? Burn up the evidence? What evidence? They had a big guy in jail under a heavy bond who wouldn't talk to them, an eyewitness who swore up and down she saw it happen and it was intentional. She is a waif angry whore of a girl whose reliability didn't exactly call to mind lux et veritas; a bunch of satellite folks who were there, most drunk or high or both and none of whom are going to, out of the goodness of their hearts, gag up the magic clues. And the place where it happened is now a forensic wasteland.

There is a lone fire investigator on the perimeter of the scene with a long rake, pulling away at the cooling edges, playing shuffleboard with meaningless cinders. They show him the badges and nod.

"Anything?" is asked.

The fellow shakes his head. "No, and I expect y'all already have figured that it's a real long shot to think that I'm going to make a diving catch in centerfield to help y'all pull anything meaningful out of this..." The man is sweating like a whore in church, face heat reddened and wears his demeanor of resignation like a soaked beach towel.

The two suits nod. "Well, if you get something, let us know."

"Yeah. Of course."

They watch a while longer and then without further conversation, they return to the car. They are sweating now.

Wilkins stuffs in behind the wheel and says, "Let's go find our star witness and see what she looks like this morning."

They had her address at the DOA Winphrie's lodgings, a rundown housing complex of trash-blown apartments over on North Liberty. The clotheslines flap with tattered clothes, there are broken up toys scattered about, the garbage cans flare with stink. There are more red clay patches than grass, the screen door is open and its top and bottom screens are torn. Broken glass lies everywhere along with dog turds and used diapers. A desolate, stripped-out place.

Wilkins and Miller had, over the years, been here many times. You just breathed through your mouth and got through it.

They knock the door sill and a squeaky voice says, "Who's that?"

"The detectives from last night. Can we come in for a minute and just go over what you told us last night?"

There is a silence and then an obliging, "Okay."

They walk in and Miss Felicia sits on a plastic-covered couch. She is drawn up as high as she can get to and she has smeared dignity across her face.

"You mind if we sit down?"

"No."

They pull two kitchen chairs from a plastic covered table. There are the obligatory pictures of Dr. King and Jesus and some too of Felicia holding a baby and of Bo and Felicia standing close, all decked out in weekend finery. There are matching lamps at either end of the couch, a nice television set in the small corner. The place is clean and neat and orderly.

"That's a nice picture there of the little girl. Is that your baby?"

"Yes, that's me and my baby." She corrects. She is clipped and guarded. She has been weeping and little wadded up balls of Kleenex sit on the table in front of her red eyes.

"Ah, well now...that's a nice picture. Uhm, can you tell us again about last night? We know you are in a hard place and we don't want to stay long. We don't want to bother you, but we need to make sure we got it right. We hope you understand. So, if you would, please go over it again."

"Yes," Felicia recites woodenly. "I was standing there next to Bo. Kenny pulled out a gun and shot and killed him, just past where the counter ran out toward the kitchen. He killed Bo."

"Are you sure you have identified the shooter, Kenny Peak?"

"Yes, I am sure it was Kenny Peak." She is beginning to shake, the cracking of her shell becoming visible.

"Do you need to see any photos of Mr. Peak to make sure that it was Kenny Peak?"

Her eyes narrow and her voice lowers. "No. I've known him for a long time. Him and his fat bitch sister."

Wilkins and Miller glance at each other.

"Did Peak and Mr. Winphrie know each other?"

"Oh, yes, for a long time."

"Did they get along all right?"

"Yes, Kenny would run errands for Bo sometimes. Everyone knew their place."

"Uhm...what's that mean, 'knew their place,' please."

"You know, Kenny worked for Bo. Bo didn't work for Kenny. Simple as that. What else y'alls want?"

"Did you know what kind of gun Peak used?"

"No, just a pistol."

"Did Mr. Winphrie ever carry a weapon?"

"No, why would he do that?"

"Well, we heard that he might carry a small pistol, a derringer, from time to time so we needed to ask."

"I don't know nothing about no derringer gun."

Silence for a beat.

"Well, we'll be going. Thank you. We'll need to stay in contact with you. Do you have any plans to go away, travel?"

"No, where would I go? No, I'll be right here. I want to see justice done. Bo was my man."

Her eyes are leaking.

"All right. Thank you. Thank you for your time and help. We'll be in touch. We'll see ourselves out."

The seeing of themselves out is about five feet.

Back in the car, Miller looks at Wilkins and asks, "Whaddaya think?"

"Well, we got a dead guy. We got a hard ID on the shooter. It sounds planned. We got the place where it happened. We can put the shooter in the place, even though the place is gone. Wish we had the weapon. Maybe it'll turn up in that burned down train wreck over there. But we got a pretty solid eyewitness and if she holds up, we get to the jury on the high charge. Yeah, there may be a deal later but still a heavy deal. What does the shooter have? The 'he had a derringer maybe' defense. None found and if it were in the house last night—that's pretty much gone—so that cuts both ways—and it sure wasn't found on him at the scene. There isn't the second shooter on the grassy knoll out there. I don't see the 'I didn't do it defense' out there and even though Bo Diddley was scum, I don't see the 'the son-of-a-bitch needed to die' defense. Ballistics we'll need but it wasn't little Red Riding Hood that killed him. Jury gonna disapprove of all this drunk/drugs stuff. Peak is a really big guy, not exactly your basic lovable teddy bear. Felicia Lineberger gonna need some work but she seems steady enough. The place burning up? Can't blame old dead Bo for that so D.A. can play it as being on Kenny's behalf. Smells bad. I think we're in the game."

Miller nods. Wilkins puts the car in gear and they drive away.

Felicia Lineberger watches them go. Now she must protect fallen Bo's honor. She has begun her noble quest last night and her fortitude has held well. She is the keeper of his flame. She will defend his legacy.

* * *

Eddie Terrell sits in his office. It is 7:30 Monday morning and he is having a third cup of black coffee while he chainsmoked yet another one of RJ Reynolds' finest Camels. The coffee and cigarette diet started the morning with a burst that held and sustained him the length of the day. He flips through the North Carolina General Statutes. He thinks about Kenny's case, the charges against him, what he had learned so far. He also thinks about what he needs to learn next and what he needs to get done. He wants to see the lawyer representing Kenny on the drug charges. He needs to sit down with Rise. He needs to go to the scene. He needs to take a look at where the decedent had lived. He needs to find and if possible talk with the Felicia girl. He needs to talk to the forensic pathologist. He needs to visit with the officers assigned to the investigation. He needs to find out which assistant district attorney was to be assigned to the case. He needs to make an immediate motion for a reduction of bond hearing and a preliminary hearing to see how much probable cause they really had. He can be fairly confident that since this was a bad part of town garden-variety shooting, there will be no rush on the part of the District Attorney's office to hustle for a presentment for indictment before the Grand Jury.

He needs to get a tighter feel for it all. And since Kenny's case is the brightest new silver dollar in his bulging purse of small and large change and some were dogs—you know, if you opened the file drawer, those would howl at you like a miserable, ugly cur dogs—and too there are the many others worthy of pursuit: fees, court, deals, defense, and trials and they shine and beckon. They purr as the goodness of the trial lawyer's work is bestowed upon them. And he loves them so and lavishes his attention and energy on them. All of these items are worthy of close care and some are more worthy than others. It is simply the way of the world.

And all that does not include the growing number of tort cases, personal injury cases, medical malpractice cases, slip and falls, car wrecks, big wrecks, little wrecks, people getting hurt, workmen's compensation.

He has climbed on the big horse and hasn't fallen off. He is earning his spurs.

Early on, he had cut his teeth on little this's and that's, court appointed cases, misdemeanors he would pick up trolling about the halls of the court house. You always always always hung out in the courthouse when the work was scarce. You made yourself visible. You walked tall and erect and sat the same way. You carried files and legal pads comfortably and with athletic ease. You never lumbered with them, wheezing upstairs with your shirttail out. You were immaculately dressed in a suit, white shirt, gorgeous, colorful, eye-catching neckties perfectly knotted. There were only to be lace-up shoes in your uniform closet. Shoes were high-sheen shined by the great and garrulous and usually half drunk or all-in high, BobCat, who spit shined and snapped his rag in time and riffed with the black music of the day. Your hair was always well and properly cut in the chair of the high pitched cornponing Grady Venable whose green leather throne with chrome loomed protectively over BobCat's dance floor. You smelled good. You were always ruddy—face scrubbed and bathed. You wore a creased white handkerchief in your breast pocket and carried its twin squared on your hip in case of the need for the offering of tear drying gallantry. You carried at least two hundred dollars in crisp clean low denomination bills in case there was the need to make change in a hallway off away from the center lobbies and waiting areas in a breast pocket wallet of obviously fine leather. You carried a sleeve of high-quality, raised print engraved cards that were never smudged and hard to bend, much less tear. You had briefcases of varying sizes, all of impeccable manufacture. Your nails and cuticles were never dirty or ragged. You carried two gold Cross pens (fountain pens were just too risky and it would not do to be Scripto ink stained in the courthouse). You were always in good humor, attentive and alert countenance, leaning in empathetic ready to deal without hesitation. You were a Matador, a Knight, an Ace. You made yourself by thoughtful practice and acquisition a Prince on his way to the seat as one of the Kings of the Courthouse. You made yourself a lawyer, a trial lawyer. A daredevil, an orator, a defender of the Constitution, a scientist, an engineer, a human factors expert, a doctor of whatever needed scrutiny and study.

Eddie Terrell was pleased with himself. But it is time to prioritize. Leave the reveries behind. He is also always running scared. He always recalled when he drifted into deep self-congratulations and the swamp of unbridled ego the ancient cautionary tale of the victorious Roman general riding into Rome on gilded chariots as their troops marched thunderously before them. In the last chariot with the commander there was a slave who placed a garland of ivy on the head of the officer and as he did, whispered in the man's ear, "All fame is fleeting. All fame is fleeting."

So Eddie Terrell needs to live in his case with another rule he had fortuitously run across years before.

"If you want peace, prepare for war."

He likes that. It is Roman Empire-centric too.

He summons his secretary Patty, a chainsmoking-cussing-like-a-sailor-get-it-done-in-the-flash-of-an-eye-assistant and asks her to get a motion for Prelim Hearing and Bond Reduction ready to go to the clerk's office ASAP.

He calls and sets up an appointment with Rise and Ben for that afternoon.

He calls Rodenburger and sets up a meet after he talks with Rise and Ben.

First he gets in his car and drives to the crime scene on 14th Street. He brings his camera with him. Upon arriving and seeing that the place is nothing but a pile of burnt ash, it takes only a few seconds for this visual to please him.

His guy couldn't have done it. He was in the cooler. The victim couldn't have done it. He was in a cooler too. So, someone else did it. On behalf of whom? Was this part of the Kenny Peak-Bo Diddley bullet club meeting or was this a separate storyline? It strikes him that whatever it was, it was beneficial to his client. Kenny didn't have a pot to pee in, much less a window to throw it out of. Bo Diddley, on the other hand, was at the very least running a drink house for serious cash profit so the place's burning up lodged in the dead man's negative column. Someone was trying to cover up something big on Bo and it is to be one of the bricks in the wall Terrell is little by little mortaring up.

There is no one there, just a pile of charcoal on an ill-defined, hard scrabble lot. Curled remnants of the yellow scene tape lie on the ground. It is getting hotter. Big high thunderclouds are building to the west. He walks around the ruin, taking lots of photos. Most will be useless and redundant but there'll be one or two which emphasizes the arson at a best angle. After that, he walks around the scene, looking carefully to see if there is anything to be seen beside debris. He shuffles the toe of his shoe here and there about the perimeter. It is too hot to explore further in. Here and there, there is a bent fork, a broken glass, roasted liquor bottles and beer cans, scraps of clothing, warped 45s and 33s, their vinyl disfigured and warped by the heat.

But there is nothing that says this is a connect, this is a hook. He can smell the rain coming in the heavy breeze that is picking up. He wants to get into the center of it and needs a good summer frog strangler to drench it and cool it down.

It will be dirty in the guts of it and he isn't about to ruin good clothes on what looks like not much. But he has to look.

He'll go home and get some jeans after his other meetings and come back and hopefully be able to grub through it.

Terrell heads to Rodenburger's office in a tall building downtown. Rodenburger, known within the bar as Rodehard, is well known as a successful guy and a shady dealster. His word is often worthless and is often made up out of whole cloth. He chronically lies and exaggerates blusters and bullshits. However, he is a smart, good lawyer, oleaginous and sometimes even servile.

They talk. Terrell learns that Rodehard hadn't done much with Kenny's charges as he hadn't been paid except by a small retainer by Bo. When Rodehard learned that Bo was gone, he said, "Now you got Kenny and I ain't gonna get paid ever and so how about helping by the taking of this worthless cup from my lips."

They agree that Terrell would. Rode says he will sit still and make no motion to be relieved as counsel of record until asked to. It is a quick meeting. They shake hands, a basically empty gesture, but Terrell knows he wants Rode in it till the end. Better to work with the devil you know as opposed to the devil you don't.

Terrell goes home, changes into jeans, a work shirt, and work boots and heads back to the office to meet with Rise and Ben.

As he drives back, the big storm breaks and cracks and firehoses over the city, moving fast and windy. It takes the storm drains a while to swallow the runoff down.

Friday Calls

Ben and Rise are sitting in the waiting room for him and they go into his office and he shuts the door.

Rise looks him over, laughs and notes, "Well, well, this is a new look for you. Working man. Get your hands dirty for once. It won't suit you. You like it cleaned and pressed."

Terrell and Rise laugh together and cigarettes are offered and are lit all around. Even a thin smile passes Ben's mouth. He is a man of less than a few words and is almost always implacably poker-faced. They lean in and talk earnestly. Rise says the cops have come to see her but that she said she was just there cooking and that's all she had to say. She pointed out to them that Kenny Peak was her brother and they ought to respect that.

She then describes in detail to Terrell what she has indeed seen. Ben just nods from time to time. It is helpful information. Terrell asks her to go see Kenny regularly and emphasize to him the necessity of staying quiet, never discussing any aspect of the case with anyone except him and if any cops or D.A.s came around, he is to say, "I want my lawyer here." He also tells her to tell Kenny that he'll be back to see him in a few weeks to catch him up. He thanks them for their confidence in him and they leave.

Patty comes in with the prepared motion. He reviews and signs and she goes to get it filed on record.

He drives back to 14th. The storm is gone and has done its job. The lot is now muddy, soggy and the remains are good to touch. He begins to move about in the scarred bones of the house's twisted skeleton. As he burrows deeper in, he finds blackened refrigerators and the stove and the exploded water heater, gashed open by the pressure and heat of the fire. Its base is partially melted. He surmises that it is from somewhere beneath the heater that the fire rose up. It is improbable that it came from above or the sides. He digs down carefully, clearing and spreading out the wood and ashes and scorched things. He finds a super-charred patch, not black but very white. It is the ignition point and in that calcified, cracked target, there lies the twisted and too discernible metal handle of a bucket, its wooden carry handle seared off into oblivion. But there was no bucket at the crime scene.

He takes more pictures, puts things more or less back into their confused places and wriggles and backs out of the ruin.

He does not consider it to be a working crime scene. There is no fresh tape or new notices. But if anyone came back to investigate under the color of law, there is no sense in courting a tampering charge, empty though it might be.

As he stands there musing over the scene, he becomes aware of a man standing just off to the side of him.

He turns and sees an older man, neatly dressed and of respectful mien.

"Oh, hello."

"Un-huh, who are you?"

"I'm Eddie Terrell."

"What's your interest here?" the gentleman asks pleasantly.

"Well, I'm a lawyer, trying to help out some of the folks that got caught up in this."

"Like who?"

"Well, to be honest, I'm Kenny Peak's lawyer."

"The big fella? He the one charged with shooting Bo D? Kenny seemed to be a nice young man."

"Yessir. I know some of his family. I think they're good people. I'm trying to help." He shrugs his shoulders and presses his lips together to generate the "aw shucks" look.

"You know Bo Diddley was a rotten son-of-a-bitch?"

Terrell waits for a little more.

"You know he treated a lot of people like cow shit?"

"Yessir. I'm beginning to get that picture. Uhm, you ever come in here... when it was still running?"

"Oh yeah, yes, from time to time. It was a good spot, even with strutting Bo around. Good group of folks always came around." He nods. "You know I can't live on the Lord all the time." He smiles gently.

"Were you here when it all happened Friday night?"

"No. I'd just be gone. Was at home down the street. Kinda sorry I missed it all."

"Do you know the girl, Felicia? Felicia Lineberger. Who was Bo's girlfriend?"

"Knew who she was. Knew she thought she was a princess. Saw her with him."

"You know where I can find her?"

"Well, she lived with Bo so I expect that's where she'll be. I don't think she'll be running off this soon. I heard that Bo lived up off North Liberty. I don't think she worked, save for getting Bo to keep her up."

"Thank you for your time, sir."

"Nice talking to you, son. Good luck on your hunting about. Bo wasn't much. Hope the boy can get shed of his troubles."

"Me too. Thank you again. May I please give you my card in case you come across anything you think interesting about all this? And, excuse me. May I please ask what your name is?"

The man takes the card and looks it over. "Nice. Good stock. Very nice." He looks up and says,

"My name is Roosevelt Truesdale. Like the president. I'll keep it in mind."

He extends his hand and they shake. It is gold compared to Rodeburger's dross.

The next morning Terrell heads to the courthouse as soon as it opens. There are two things he hopes to accomplish. First, is a visit to the criminal side of the clerk's offices. He asks an assistant clerk if she has listings on one Benjamin F. Winphrie. She goes to her indexes, returns and says, "Yes, Plenty. What you need?"

"Can I get a copy of what you've got so I can go look at some of his shucks? And, anything pending?"

Shucks are the essential guts of criminal cases. Traffic, misdemeanors, felonies all carried in the manila envelope with the cellophane face that displayed The State of North Carolina versus Fill In The Blank and the year and CR and file number. Warrants, motions, bond set, date tracks of activity, assignments, dispositions—all the basic cradle to grave documentation and only that upon which were the decorations of fact and law hung as a case proceeded through its steps. There were thousands and thousands of them date and time stamped, stuffed and crammed into all sorts of places. Older ones in file cabinets, even older and disposed ones in boxes on rows of shelves surrounding the large room and current ones in large open trays spread out on tables. It was the Dewey Decimal System of Bad Acts.

The case numbers of each shuck started with handwritten, and then typed records, that were maintained in large binders by the defendant's name, charges, date of receipt. Each time there was activity in a case, it was duly recoded by the various courtroom clerks and passed onto the central office. It was the fail-safe system of keeping track, backup on backup. The room is eye-wincingly lit from above. There is always one clerk of court and often two at high desks with enfilading sight lines on all four sides of the room.

The room opened at nine sharp and closed at five sharp with no exceptions. It was a vault.

Cameras had recently been installed in each of the ceiling corners.

Some lawyers and their faithful staffers would from time to time surreptitiously help their client's shucks to disappear, to just go away. Such expedient pilferage created a void in the tracking system and all the backup writing in the world meant little when always harried folks would fill the boxes for the various courtrooms each day and as the various D.A.s went through them one after another, and rarely would anyone notice. Of course, this was illegal, unethical and too highly effective if the brazenness and money for the snatch worked its magic without detection. Driving Under The Influence case shucks, which included breathalyzer results, were especially high value targets.

"Nothing pending but looks like there are four or five from a few years ago. Nothing too serious but you can tell he is no stranger to this side of the courthouse. I'll make you a copy but I gotta charge you a nickel for it. The county, you know..."

"No problem with that and thank you."

The assistant clerk goes into a back room and he can hear the copier top slap and the machine purr a piece of paper out. She returns. He trades the little buffalo for the information and goes to a chair, sits down and carefully studies the documents.

Winphrie had charges of solicitation of prostitution, a couple of misdemeanor possessions of marijuana, public drunkenness and a contributing to the delinquency of a minor. All had been resolved, the last charge having come about a year and a half ago. He had paid fines and received light suspended sentences except did he do thirty in county on the last one.

Terrell thinks, *That Felicia?*

He pulls each envelope. They all list Bo Diddley's address when charged as being Apartment 8B in the Cleveland Avenue Homes project just off North Liberty.

Terrell drives out into East Winston, finds the place and knocks. There is no answer. A few passersby look at him with more than one glance, his bespoke tailoring signaling his being an alien. He is used to this kind of response. He has been taught to always go to where whatever happened, and you had to go with confidence; otherwise you wouldn't get shit.

After knocking again and getting but silence, he turns to a lady hanging wash.

"Ma'am, excuse me. I'm Eddie Terrell. I'm a lawyer. I'm looking for a lady named Felicia Lineberger. She hasn't done anything wrong (except probably lie her brains out to fuck Kenny Peak over...). I just want to see what she might know about something. Here's my card, ma'am."

The lady in her weary fifties looks him over slowly, looks at the card that she has reflexively taken, looks him over again and clears her throat.

"Lawyer, you say? Well, you does dress the part. Lookin' for who now?"

He knows she heard him the first time. It is her small test of his resolve and his manners.

"Yessum. A lady by the name of Felicia Lineberger. I was told she stays here some."

There is the inevitable, measuring pause and then she snorts.

"Lady?! She be's around here all the time with that slick snake Bo Diddley but she ain't no lady! Child bride trashy street walking smart mouthed kid bitch is what she is. Let's him pimp her all over, right here in this neighborhood, too. And proud of it too! She's trash what she is. What do you want to know from her? Hell, she'd cross the street and climb a tree to tell a lie she could as easy tell standing on the sidewalk..."

Her eruption subsides, and she asks again, "What you wanna know, son?"

"Ma'am, may I ask you your name, please? And I'm happy to tell you what's going on. I just need to talk to her."

"Craft, Elizabeth Craft. Most just calls me Libby."

"Thank you, Libby. May I call you Libby?"

"Sure. You look nice enough to do that." She grins a toothy gold speckled grin.

"Okay. Libby. Mr. Bo Diddley is dead. He was shot and killed at a drink house not too far from here on 14th Street about ten thirty or eleven o'clock last Friday night. Felicia Lineberger was, is, a witness to what happened I've been told. I'd really like to find her and see what she has to say."

"Damn! Dead you say? How 'bout that? He was trash too. Birds of a feather. Well, good. Maybe that'll keep her scrawny ass away from here..."

"I've knocked a couple of times and no one answered..."

"Yeah, I knows it. I watched you. I got eyes in the back of this old head," she sniggers. "Who you working for? The guy that shot him?"

"Yes, ma'am."

"You think your fella is guilty?"

"Uhm, Libby. I can't really talk to you about it. You know, lawyer rules and all..."

"Yeah, I gots it. Perry Mason and all. Well, I'm glad the fool is gone. God rest his sorry soul.

You might have some luck if you go up to the AFDC on Patterson. She got a little baby. Don't know if it's Bo's or not. She don't bring it around here but a few times. I've been told she hangs around up there a lot. Good luck. Come back around and tell me how it all ends sometime. A good mystery, like TV, ain't it?" She is engrossed and curious, nice as could be.

"Yes, ma'am. I will. Thank you for your time. Take care."

She has turned back to her laundry and he goes on. He thinks, *You don't know unless you ask and you don't get to ask if you don't even show up. Righteous!*

He goes on to the AFDC offices on Patterson. The place is crowded—lots of little children and their mothers with much gibberish and crying going on. The place smells like sour formula, sweat and diapers that needed changing more than a little while ago. The noise is a low then rising then low again cacophony, a Tower of Babel. The Aid for Families with Dependent Children was part of yet another safety net, always well-intentioned but in truth, trapped these people in poverty and subservience, made the black community almost totally Mommy-centric as the baby daddies rarely gave a damn once the fun ride was over and helped more criminal motivations for petty theft, fraud and complicity creep over the desolate lives like kudzu. The socio-cultural observations were mostly abstract to Terrell. The last of them he liked, understood and was another easy make-work fountain for him to drink from.

There were four intake windows manned by four disinterested, equally

Friday Calls

obese women either staring off into a long distance or surveying their straggled cuticles. These were women who spent more on their weekly piled up hairdos and glittering nails each week than was doled out monthly to take a number of girls and their waifs in the rows of plastic chairs in the big room.

Terrell decides for no real reason to go to the third window in the line. Sometimes you can end-run the need to be bureaucratically official if you go off the directional arrows.

He shoots his cuffs, smiles sweetly and murmurs, almost cooing through the round hole in the separating glass. "Hello, there. I'm Ed Terrell. Would you please be able to tell me if Miss Felicia Lineberger is here today? I would really appreciate it."

The woman looks up and says, "Who are you and what do you want?"

"Oh, yes. I'm Ed Terrell. I'm a lawyer here in town. I'm here to help Miss Lineberger."

Which is theoretically true as he might be able to truncate her inconvenience and exposure when she is on the verge of being fed into the maw of the state's criminal justice system with probable fantasy and perjury in her heart.

The women at the other windows turn and look at him and her, their supersonic hearing collectively picking up immediately the possibilities of something beyond the humdrum of calling names, the endless march-ups and backs and the same desultory, brief Q and A sessions with poor women, poorly if at all educated, who are now part of the great swaths of barnacles that are slathered on the ass of the great ship of state.

The lady says, "I'm Miss Treva Brown, Senior Assistant Aid Manager here on Patterson. Mr. Terrell, Terrell, is it?" A brief pause as Mr. Terrell nods obsequiously. She hands him her card and asks, "Do you have a card I may have?"

It is a remnant reminder of the old cotillion tea dance card days, so long now vanished when the young ladies would favor the fawning young gentlemen with the privilege of signing for a waltz or a box step. It was the most passive kind of aggression, signaling that compliance would come with connection, albeit so brief.

"Why, yes, of course. Here you go."

She takes the stiff vellum and strokes its strength with her razor-nailed thumb.

One of her compadres interjects, "Is there a problem?"

"No, ma'am, as I've just told Miss Brown here, I'm a lawyer, duly sworn and licensed by the State of North Carolina and I'm here to see if I can find Miss Lineberger and speak with her.

There has been a personal loss within her family and I'm here to offer help to her but it is very important that I speak with her so I can do so."

He bows his head toward all of them and looks back up imploringly. He is in their debt and they will serve him. He is a polished and attractive sycophant who has paid fealty to them in a vapid and empty way and they have eaten it up with a big spoon. He has brought sartorial mercy into their depressing wasteland and he is to be rewarded. It works almost all of the time. He could also play the rube.

Miss Brown quickly glanced at her colleagues and receiving their blessing says, "See there on the third row, toward the back, that skinny girl in the yellow sundress with the pink clips in her hair with the child in her arms?" He looks and nods. "That's her. Lord, she needs to have a sandwich with plenty of may-o-naise on it, a lot of it and a lot of them." She stretched the word "mayonnaise" out to emphasize the strength of her observation. "Well, that's her. Fair to say, she's a pretty surly one. I don't guess you can tell us what happened?"

"I wish I could but I hope y'all understand that it's a private matter."

They all nod.

He moves away from them, genuflecting his head as he turns. He weaves his way along the rows, dodging rug rats and ratty toys and pacifiers as he steps gingerly to the right and left, avoiding the disaster of hot footing one of them. He gets down to the end and there is his prey. As he sits down next to her so as to shield both their faces from neck-craning officialdom, he speaks to her quietly and quickly and clearly. He has long since learned that a combination of the spoken word and physical space invading movement has a freezing effect on its target.

"Miss Lineberger, I'm Ed Terrell. I'm a lawyer. I'm here to see if I can't help you."

She quarter-jerks toward him so that the sleeping infant in her arms vibrates, but she just stares for a few seconds. She looks into his eyes. Her eyes narrow with suspicion.

She hisses, "Lawyer? Help me? How the hell you gonna help me?"

"Miss Lineberger. I've been asked by a number of people (which was literally true) to talk with anyone that might have any knowledge about the sad and terrible events of a few nights ago. I am very sorry for your loss (which was true—it had ginned up some good work for him). I'm an officer of the court (true). I have no friends to reward (mostly true—he was friendly toward his clients, but didn't drink with them). I have no enemies to punish (was true—the D.A.'s office was simply an adversary, not an enemy). I just need information (true). I am not here to hurt or harm you (true)."

She looks at him. She says, "You know about Benjamin...about Bo?"

"Yes, ma'am."

"Why you coming around here and talk to me? How did you know where to come?" He can now see she is tired and that all the lights on her control panels were not coming on and were not going to come on.

She is basically not smart, which is only one notch above stupid, in way over her head, and not prepared to do anything save stick to whatever story she gave the night of the shooting.

So let's get the door to that opened up.

"Yes, ma'am. As an Officer of the Court, I'll be meeting with the investigating officers whom I believe you have already spoken with... I went by your apartment up off North Liberty and a lady told me you might be here."

"Bet it was one of those snooping bitches," she briefly flares, then subsiding, she says, "I did. I did that. Met with them twice...so far, I guess."

"Yes, ma'am." She was now beginning to go down the slot. "I'll be meeting with them in a few days. I'll be meeting with the District Attorney's office. As an Officer of the Court (he said this all the time, thus painting himself as, well, an Officer of the Court, draped and dripping with and immersed in Justice). I'll be interviewing any and all witnesses I can locate. I'll be talking with the doctor at the medical school who will perform a proper autopsy on Mr. Winphrie. That sure is a cute baby. A little girl?"

He short-circuits her with the last polished swipe.

She replies raising her chin in maternal defiance, "She's Bo's only child and I'm gonna raise her the way he'd want her to be raised." She is softening and ripening nicely. Her guard is now down.

"Of course. I'm sure you will. I am well aware of Mr. Winphrie's status in your community. I know how visible he was. I know how important he was to you and your baby. What's the little girl's name? She is a cutie."

More grease, subtly slathered. "Takisha, but I calls her Baby Moms."

"That's a nice name, a nice name....and Miss Lineberger, all I'm trying to do is gather as much information as I can so I can put it together and present it as accurately as I can to the Court and since you were an eyewitness, a key and critical eyewitness to this terrible event, I wanted to start, if at all possible, with you."

She nods, grasping her importance, the gravity of her knowledge.

She says, "That dog shit son-of-a-bitch Kenny Peak murdered my Bo." It comes out of her mouth harshly and loud. People turn and look.

He nods back at her and whisper-suggests as he leans in intimately, "I know. I know this is very hard, very emotional for you. I know how important he was to you and your little girl. How about we can go someplace where you can talk with me, tell me the story, your story without people trying to listen in?"

After understanding his suggestion and seeing all the faces looking, leering at her, she is amenable to a change of scenery. Terrell nods a "thank you" to the front desk windows and they go out to his car in the parking lot.

He holds the door for her and the child. She likes that.

"Ooooh, this is nice. What kind of car is this? This is a nice ride." Her sorrow has turned instantly to a kid's wondrous, shallow curiosity of anything that is shiny. He knows he has read her as right as the answers in the back of the book.

He, with an effective "gee whiz, aw shucks" false modesty replies, "Oh, why, thank you. Well, it's a Mercedes Benz."

"These leather seats?"

"I think that's right." He pauses. "Miss Lineberger, please tell me what happened the other night. What did you see? What did you hear?"

And she does. He dares not take a note, not one jot, not one tittle of it. He has become her gallant, rich, trusted friend, her colleague and he must not disturb the working deceit he has enthroned her upon. They sit there in his car with the air conditioner cooling the heat and she talks a straight line and he listens focused and carefully.

And when she finishes, she says, "And that's exactly what happened. Kenny Peak killed Bo."

Friday Calls

He says, "Thank you. That must have been real hard for you. When you talked to the detectives, did you tell them that same, that same, exact story?" He speaks that welding question softly, gently. She nods. "Miss Lineberger, is that a yes?"

She says, "Yes. Yes. Yes." She is tired and edging toward exasperation.

"Thank you. Now, here is my card. Please be in touch with me with anything you think of about all this. May I give y'all a ride home? It's hot out there."

"That'd be fine. You know where to go?"

"Yes, remember I went by your apartment first."

"Oh, yeah."

She fingers his card steadily.

He says, "How about we go by where all this happened and then go by my office real quickly? Then I'll get you home." Terrell wants to give her a chance to jog her memory and he wants her to be impressed by his offices. He is working her head.

"Okay," she says.

She is smelling some money out there somewhere. It is indistinct, but she can sense it. They drive to the ruins, get out, and look quietly and get back in the car.

He says, "Anything?"

She shakes her head.

They drive to his office. He opens the door for her, asks her if she would like a Co-Cola or something.

"No," she replies. Terrell asks if she remembers anything else.

She is looking around at all the books and brass chandeliers and fine furnishings and thick rugs. Her mind is not on the killing.

She says vacuously, "No, not really. Can I go home now?"

"Of course."

It is a silent short ride. When they pull up to the curb, he comes around and opens the door for her. She likes that too.

As she gets out, she asks, "Say, would you have any spare monies to help me out with? You, know, I've just helped you and now, you can help me. You know, it ain't for my talking. It's to help...us. Times gonna be tough now. A hundred?"

Ah, now avarice makes its appearance. It was the old truth, the New York City taxi driver's rule. "When they say it's not about the money, you can damn well be sure it is about the money."

He looks at her with pained, feigned regret.

"Oh, Miss Lineberger, I wish I could. I wish I could. But as an Officer of the Court I am not allowed to have any financial dealings of any sort with anybody involved in any matter such as this. I am prohibited. I'm very sorry. I hope you understand."

She purses her lips, eyes narrow. "So, that's it? Hell, I helped you..." She tails off, having no leverage.

"I'm very sorry. I wish I could."

And with a "humph," she glares and turns and walks briskly down the cracked sidewalk. She wonders if she has been played. He wonders how fast he can now get away.

Chapter Twenty-One

Plantings

After a few crisp telephone calls, Archer Glenn's torn, tortured body had been quickly carried in a shining black hearse from the Greensboro funeral home to the high status church of Winston-Salem's mortuary science, the venerable and venerated Freunde's Funeral Service.

The Freundes had come out of the north German provinces to the New World with many others in the mid-1700s, and had been religiously persecuted for their nascent, tough, work-ethic spring sprout of Lutheranism. They were master craftsmen and the doers of all things difficult, many unpleasant. This included undertaking. Their faith-based community of Salem had over the years naturally grafted onto its across-the-creek neighbor of Winston with its growing, rowdy capitalism of tobacco and textiles and banking and in turn, the booming industrial city had welcomed the dignity and elegant straightforwardness of these smart and creative Aryans.

The Freundes were the perfect amalgam for families whose loved ones had achieved room temperature. They were empathetic without being oleaginous, serious in mien but appropriately affable, subtle but not distant, and professional without being pompous.

It was said by many, many citizens of the city, "You smoke Reynolds, you bank at Wachovia and when you're done, Freunde's plants you."

Mr. William "Bobby" Freunde Sr. is in the driveway in the back of the building waiting for the Greensboro delivery. He is joined by his son, Bobby, or rather S.D. which stood for "Shovel Dirt," but only at the club or in the late-night haunts of the town. The elder Freunde is just about perfect, the scion not quite so. But he does know the business and as this needed to be an "efficient" effort, it is to the benefit of all concerned that the pace of the preparations be quickened.

A few hours before Archer Glenn's arrival, Joe Glenn called Freunde's and spoke with Bobby Sr.

"Bobby, this is Joe."

"Hello, Joe. How are you and what can I do that is helpful?"

"Bobby, Archer's been killed…in a bad train wreck…over in Guilford County. We need y'all's help."

"Oh, Joe, I am so sorry to hear this. I am really am so sorry. He was a good man. How is Louise?"

"Thank you, Bobby. I appreciate it. We all do. Louise is pretty torn up, pretty shaky."

"Understandably."

Bobby…the circumstances of what has happened are going to stir up a lot of talking and gossip. It'll end up in the papers soon enough and you'll see what I mean. You won't have to read between the lines too hard, if you get my drift. Archer's body is on its way to you now. It's coming from Hanes Lineberger in Greensboro. On behalf of the family, we'd ask that you cremate Archer as soon as you can. Put the remains in a nice urn. We'll line up the service at home pretty quickly and then have him taken down to the Glenn plot at the cemetery. Can y'all please help us with that?"

"Yes, Joe. I understand. We will get it done. I promise."

"Thanks, Bobby. I'll get with you in a little while with the details. We will need cars, I think two will do plus a small hearse. Please make sure I get all the billings, too."

"Joe. We'll tend to everything as you want."

The phones click off. This isn't the first time Bobby Freunde has been cryptically asked to get things incognito and then to get incognito in the ground fast. He is surely curious as to what had happened, but he also knows to set the curious aside for later. The Glenns are good customers and they all went to the same churches and clubs. They are friends. So he summons his son and tells him what is to be done.

Bobby Sr. goes into S.D.'s office. There is the vague redolent odor of cigarette butts and stale beer coming off of S.D.. Senior grimaces. "Son, we're getting a delivery in just a bit. I want the remains cremated as soon as can be done." He pauses and then goes on, "Damn good thing we deal in dead people 'cause if they were able to smell you, they'd go somewhere else."

S.D. takes the spear and does not flinch. It isn't the first time he's heard it and it won't be the last. He just imagines it disappearing in mid-flight and it does.

"Yessir. Will do. Who is it? We know 'em?"

"Yes. It's Archer Glenn. Hit and killed by a train last night."

"Jesus!" S.D. starts. "What?"

"Yes, Mr. Archer B. Glenn. Very sad. Joe Glenn just called me. They'd like to get this done quickly. I told him we would."

"Where did it happen?"

"Guilford County some place."

S.D. muses with a mild grin creasing his lips. "That old dog. I'll bet he was out chasing some poon with a bunch of the guys from the club and got clocked. I'd heard there was a gathering last night out at Charlie May's place before they all went to Chapel Hill today for the game. How about that...that's too bad but a juicy too bad...hell, it'll be all over town faster than lightning."

Senior listens with a façade of disinterest and an internal processing that is rigorously calculating the matching of the job with the news that indiscreetly gushed from his boy.

"Son, I don't know anything about any of that." But now he does. There is nothing new under the sun. They are in the omega business. How the client gets to the finish line is of but mild interest to him. "So, come with me and let's go meet the car and then go get Mr. Wilbur to fire up the crematorium and let's get this done."

And they do, S.D. low whistling the scandal of it as he follows his daddy out onto the hot driveway.

* * *

Joe Glenn calls the family minister, the florist, the club (for food), and his office. He calls Sue Simpson, his secretary, and tells her what has happened.

"Oh my God! Joe! What in the hell? What in the hell happened? This is awful…"

She lights a cigarette and offers "uh-huhs" in a rhythmic cadence every sentence or two. He asks her to keep it quiet and to herself until he and his brother Jimmy could talk to the employees. He asks her to line up a meeting of all their people for 9 a.m. sharp Monday. He notes that by then, it surely will be in the morning paper, maybe even in Sunday's and that there is going to be a small private service at the home Monday afternoon and then internment at The Lord's Acre immediately following. He asks her to come to the service at the house and at the graveyard.

She says, "Of course I will. Thank you. This is very sad. How are you doing? Are you all right?"

"Not really, but it lays to me and Jimmy to get this done and done."

What he does not tell her right then is it appeared there had been someone else in the car with Archer. He had only about thirty minutes ago gotten another call from Justice who had just gotten a call from the Guilford County Watch Commander alerting him to the discovery of a mangled, young female found in close proximity to the final resting place of Archer and his company car. There is now an unavoidable weld of trouble here, not just family trouble but money and business trouble, too. It flashes across his mind instantly, the great searing eye on the pyramids of the dollar bills calling for an accounting. This is a sixty-mile-an-hour fastball that Archer had lobbed up for someone else to smash out of the park. He needs to talk with Jimmy and with their long-time lawyer, Bobby Stockman. They need a plan, a map that will lift them out of the growing thicket. He wants to tell Sue now but it's not the right time. She is their mother hen. She herd and organizes them. They have fine business minds and know how to make deals and do business, but she is the gatekeeper. The problem here is there is no gate left to keep.

He hangs up with Sue and calls his brother's number.

Jimmy picks up quickly. It is as though they are all hovering over the phone, waiting for other shoes to drop.

"Jimmy, hey."

"Hey, Joe," Jimmy's voice sounds tired. "You been able to get some things done? What can I do?"

"I'm okay, brother. Thank you. We need to get together. Can you meet me at the office?"

"Sure. When? What's going on?"

"I just got another call from Justice Tucker. They've found the body of a girl at the crash site. It's pretty obvious that she was in the car with Archer."

"Oh, shit."

"Oh, shit is right."

"Who is she? Who was she?"

"Dunno, but we'll know soon enough."

"I'll be there in twenty minutes."

"Good. I'm gonna call Bobby and see if he can be with us."

"Okay."

"Jimmy, we need to tell Louise after we get through at the office. This is going to be in tomorrow's paper for sure. We need to beat the presses. How about you call Dr. Valk and get him on standby. Expect she'll need another needle. Jesus, this is a damn, well…a damn train wreck."

"Sure as shit is. Christ," the voices tail off.

"Jimmy, I'm gonna call Sue and get her there too. I think she can be some help. What say you?"

"I agree."

And so the calls are made and the wheel turns some more.

The Glenn boys met at the Quality Textile offices and are joined in a few minutes by the family consigliere, Bobby Stockman. He is shown in to the back offices by Sue Simpson.

Stockman is a handsome man, all facial right angles and soft curves, a leonine head on top of a square solid figure, always immaculate in dress and thoughtful and considered in demeanor. He is a tax and business lawyer of the highest rank and he handles every numerical aspect of Quality's many businesses as would a slow motion juggler, never frantic, never stressed, always in control. His advice and counsel are valued and treasured. When he smokes a Camel, everyone else wishes they could smoke a Camel too. He is always all business with perfect, sincere, gracious Southern empathy and courtliness. No one can ever remember hearing him raise his voice save for a lovely deep laugh every now and then.

Sue gets them all Coca-Colas and the men all sit in deep leather chairs around a coffee table in an alcove off the side of a long conference table stacked with files and papers. Sue pulls up a straight back chair just a bit back from them and produces a steno pad which she presses to her lap as she watchfully purses her lips.

These are no clanging metal desk and roller skating chair offices. These are "title on the door, Bigelow on the floor" quiet sanctuaries of money and movement.

Joe Glenn says, "Sue, I don't think you'll need to take notes today. Bobby, thank you for coming. We've got a situation."

A brief pause. Stockman looks steadily at Joe. Jimmy looks at the floor. Sue looks at them all and braces—something is coming and it isn't an all-expense paid trip to Bermuda.

Joe clears his throat and continues. "Bobby, Archer was hit and killed by a train last night, over in Guilford County."

Bobby almost imperceptibly blinks and says, "Oh, I'm very sorry to hear this. This is some terrible news for all of you, for all of your family. I'm so sorry." And he is instantly and truly saddened by the news, but he knew he had not been summoned to simply learn of a client's untimely and most probably gruesome death. There are obviously very concerning attendant circumstances lurking here so he waits for the real floodgate to burst open. And it does.

"Bobby, there was another passenger in the car, a young lady who used to work here in the steno pool. She was killed too. She was about half Archer's age."

Sue Simpson leans forward and involuntarily exhales a low, "Well, I'll be damned..."

Joe Glenn says, "Obviously, this is a pretty rough time for all of us but we feel like we need to get you thinking about this right away. Our best guess is the girl's family can sue us and well, it could prove to be very embarrassing to a lot of people, if you get my drift."

"Yes, yes, I see and I understand your concerns."

Jimmy asks, "Bobby, off the top of your head, what do you think...about all this?"

Stockman sits still for a bit and thinks. He does the problems in his head and then speaks. "As a large sense of your concern seems to be as to the company, I am presuming he was in a company vehicle when this happened."

They nod.

"So first, I have to presume that as I saw nothing about this in this morning's paper, this will be in the press tomorrow. I suggest Archer's obituary be efficiently assembled and provided as soon as possible to the local press. I further suggest that his funeral service be held privately at home and that his burial be private and unannounced as well."

Joe Glenn looks at Sue Simpson and says, "I've already been in touch with Big Bobby Freunde. They should have Archer's remains by now. He is to be cremated right away. Sue, can you get a simple obit together? Freunde's will handle its placement."

"Yes, certainly."

Stockman simply says, "Good." And continues.

"I do not see any criminal charges being lodged against Archer no matter what happened or how it happened—you can't charge, much less try, a person who is deceased—but on the civil liability side, I think you are correct. The company and Archer's estate and thus his family are exposed to the claim and it may well may be the rail line is too. Do you have any factual information as to how the event happened, what the car did, what the train did that would be an indicator of fault?"

"No, not yet."

"Well, yes, we will know that soon enough. Let us set the railroad aside for the time being.

There are still completely viable claims against both Archer's estate and this company. The female victim was a passenger and no matter how contributory to the ultimate outcome her acquiescence or conduct might have been, there are no witnesses one way or another. So I see no worthy defenses to the claims unless something very unusual pops up. So there is one and probably a second liability policy involved, the company's master general liability policy and Archer's homeowner's and I presume Archer has an umbrella policy too. Do you know about that, the latter?"

Jimmy volunteers, "Sue would know, wouldn't you, Sue?"

Sue looks up, closes her eyes and says, "Yes, there are all three. Everything written through the Whaling Agency, Tommy Whaling. I don't have the exact amounts of coverage but they are pretty good sized."

Stockman says, "Sue, do you have access to all the policies? I'd like to know what their reporting requirements as to prospective claims are and of course the available coverages."

Sue says, "Yes, or I can get them. I think I have all the policies for everyone and the company, of course, in my files."

Stockman says, "Good. Please do." He looks at all of them and continues. "Y'all need to think about these things. If you report these claims to your insurance companies, they, of course, will begin their own investigations and thusly, setting aside reserves and doing other administrative things and indeed there will be big claims and much coverage to address those claims. And the whole matter and its potential resolution will slow down considerably. I'm sure it is not lost on you all that insurance companies, like y'all, are in the business of making money and they like to use what they have on hand, so they are not fast to pay it out.

"And the family of this deceased young lady is under no requirement to formalize these claims until the statute of limitations for a wrongful death claim approaches and here that would be two years. And I have to think that delay on their part inures to their benefit as to potential amounts recoverable. And I must note as well that a matter like this if it goes into litigation would be followed intently by the local court house reporter. It is, unfortunately and as you already seem to understand, a matter of some sensationalism, even salaciously so."

Stockman pauses. "Now, there may be another way to approach this. Reach out to the family with an honest apology and real willingness to discuss the payment of significant money to end the matter much more quickly. Now I am, as you all know, well aware of the company's cash and other fairly liquid assets and y'all are well positioned to discuss this kind of thing with them, if they want to listen. They need a good lawyer to advise them, I think, and I think they should be told that. And there would have to be a full, complete, and total confidentiality agreement that prohibited any disclosure as to any resolution as to anyone. The downside is once this particular road is taken, if the matter is not timely reported to your carriers they will be under no obligation to defend you or otherwise represent your rights if litigation ensues. If such happens, and it will if you choose this approach, you will have to hire and pay lawyers to defend, to provide what your insurance carriers would have provided."

Joe Glenn asks, "How long is 'timely reported'?"

"As touched on earlier, we want to see the language of the policy and I also will take a look at what North Carolina case law is on 'timely reporting of claims.' And as to any and all of it, you know I am ready to help with it as y'all like and so instruct me. Y'all need to think on it all and I ask that you do so after your minds can come away from Archer's services and burial."

"Bobby, do you have advice as to which way we ought to go on this?"

"I need to pull down some good, hard law and I need to see what the policies say, but at this point, I think we may well be able to get two bites at the apple, but we'll need to move quickly. I suggest you try a rapid, expedited and private settlement and if that does not work, report quickly to all carriers. Do y'all feel like you've got a pretty feel for what I'm thinking?"

They all nod their assent and understanding.

Bobby Stockman tells Sue Simpson he will look to hear from her as soon as she can get back to him early next week. They all thank each other and Bobby Stockman tells them all again how sorry he was about all of it and he begins to show himself out when he turns at the door and pauses.

"You all know, there's going to be a lot of talk about this and it'll spread quick. Sue, pardon my presumption and no offense intended but...the fire will start in the newspaper and much of it will then be first spread by the wives of Archer's friends and then carried further by those ladies' friends and acquaintances. I think it would be helpful, not curative but helpful, to go ahead right now and set some backfires to damp down or at least try to neutralize a lot of it. So I'll now ask something I was at first not going to ask earlier. Do y'all know where Archer was going when this happened?"

Joe and Jimmy nod.

Bobby asks, "Was it on the up and up?"

Joe and Jimmy grimace in unison and tilt their heads into their shoulders, little boys complicit in cradle robbing and with thumbs in the pie.

Joe says hopefully with thin conviction, "Well, I absolutely know he was going to the Georgia game in Chapel Hill tomorrow."

Jimmy followed with a solidifying, "That's right."

"Okay, I am thinking this would be something to do. How about start at the club and have the help pass the word that they heard Mr. Archer was taking the gal just to be dropped off somewhere and then was headed on over to Chapel Hill to stay with...who are friends he has down there?"

Jimmy says, "Oh, I get it. Ted Barnes, J.T.'s son."

"Can one of you get hold of Ted Barnes and just share that information with him? And can one of you go to the club and get the information started there?"

"Jimmy, you call Ted and I'll head to the club and see Frank. He'll handle it."

"Good. Very good. Let's turn the story a bit if we can. Also, if you know anyone who might have been joining in whatever the activities were to be, how about pass it on to them as well and do so promptly, please. Sue, would you please pass the word to the employees in this regard? It would be helpful, I think."

Sue Simpson cannot repress a small ironic smile and nods her head.

Men, she thinks, *They are such a sorry-ass lot, but too, oh so much fun...as long as somebody's not getting killed.*

Stockman leaves and the rest go back into their mourning with a great deal of money riding herd on their sadness and their appointed tasks.

The pretty, mangled girl found near the crash site is found to be one Mary Sue Martin. Her petite clutch had been jackknifed and shot into her lap skirt belt at an impact with the force of a steel stamping press and even as she exploded out the car window in a launched, tattering ball, the momentum of the blow had held it to her. When they were able to unfold her for the obligatory ride in a body bag, it offered her driver's license. And thus more paths were marked for exploration.

Phone calls were made in similar chains as before and the Glenn family received the news of the newly discovery passenger with eye-rolling dismay.

The word was quickly passed along that Archer was just giving the young girl a ride to visit with nearby friends and its lie was received with relief and uniform assignation. At least there was a fig leaf, albeit miniscule. Nice people were not to talk about this anyway, at least not out in the open.

Friday Calls

Not only was this a faux-pas of intense family embarrassment, it also would necessitate another painful, awkward visit to tell Louise of this further mortification. Joe and Jimmy called Dr. Valk and their sister and all again assemble at Virginia Road later that morning.

Louise is aware there are people coming into the house again. She has been roused from her fitful sleep repeatedly as the day moved on by the telephone ringing and ringing again. Finally, that rhythm stopped as the help took the receiver off and put it in a kitchen drawer where it muffle buzzed all the next few days.

Louise is sitting in the den, blankly smoking, a half-filled glass of bourbon on the table next to her. When Mamie shows the group in, Louise eyes them with a basic black malevolence. She understands that they are bringing her nothing more than more pain.

Louise goes downstairs to meet whomever it was. Mamie and Retha simply watch from the dining room. Louise sees them and knows again there is more bad news coming. She prepares to parry the blow.

She does not take the news well, but rather than so pitifully withdrawing as she did the night before, now in her slurred and wounded state, she is quickly belligerent and built quickly to lashing out at them all, sparing no invective and cussing them all unto hell for inflicting such horrible pain upon her that rose off all of them in a shimmering stink of hesitant decay, the remains beginning to rot.

They are responsible for her husband's gruesome death. They are responsible for her sorrow. They are responsible for the trashy whore strumpet who had "cuckolded" her. They have never cared about her. They have always treated her like a simpleton. They have done it all and more and now they will just walk away.

They have no choice but to receive the whipping in a twisting silence and let the storm blow out. In a few minutes it does and Louise haughtily wraps her silk robe tightly about her shaking body, tosses her rumpled mane back and marches resolutely back upstairs, defiantly calling for her servants, her bourbon, and her cigarettes.

Dr. Valk calls, "Lousie, Louise, will you talk with me for a little bit please, please?"

"No. Not now. Go. Get out. All of you!"

And her bedroom door slamming shakes the house. An antique plate on the front hall table leaps from its stand and shatters on the floor.

The news of the disaster was in the Sunday morning newspaper replete with a front page photograph of the crushed-in car. The article was short and the grainy black and white was fuzzy, but it was raw and dramatic and frightening, too. Its brevity did not prevent the simple, eternal joinder of the two deaths. It begged the puzzle. It was simply scandalous.

That Sunday afternoon on Virginia Road the family, the help, and Dr. Valk looked at their shoes and then glanced at Louise and then looked down again as the ashes were prayed over at home and then they were quickly dirted over on Monday mid-morning at the family plot. The fine minister of the Methodist Gothic rock pile came to the house and brought his friend, the Episcopal Bishop Frazier. It was a fine idea and one that Dr. Depp had arrived at unilaterally once he had been alerted as to the mess that he was asked to officiate over in a hurry. To have a Protestant funeral on a Sunday was not anywhere close to the norm, but considering the circumstances, Depp reached outside his professional piety of comfort and knew with some harsh reality that this was a planting that needed to be done as rapidly as possible.

He also knew that Louise Glenn was surely cocked and primed with fulminant venom and hurt and a good dosing of good bourbon and some combination of drugs as well and as such, was tailing a short fuse just looking for a hot match for her chemistry. Archer Glenn was a casual Methodist at best and Louise was no more than a wandering Episcopalian, so core matters of faith were not critical to them. New Testament solace and resurrection meant about as much to them as would preaching to three dogs be an effective connector with the Trinity. Thus such reliance on any hopefully messaged homily would be basically spitting into the wind.

But Depp also knew that the trappings of high station were very important to these people and they wrapped themselves in such at every opportunity. They liked the ermine wherever it could be had or bestowed. And he knew that Louise Glenn, in whatever state of resentful haze she found herself, would just not walk across the lines of propriety if her congregational mitered bishop loomed benignly over her. So Depp called Lyons Frazier, explained his assignment, made his request and the good bishop gladly signed on.

Thus was Louise neutered enough to get through it all without exploding, breaking things, cussing people out, and generally embarrassing everyone terribly.

Both before and after the quick service in the living room with the copper urn of Archer sitting roundly in mute mystery before them on the coffee table, Frazier dressed in the most impressive robe and regalia spoke gently and soothingly in sotto voice to only Louise, taking her hand and leaning into her as he did. It was intimate and practiced and it was just enough benediction and balm. Oil had been spread albeit temporarily on the roiled waters.

The next morning is desultory and anti-climactic. Louise is exhausted as are the rest. Freunde's has the cars and a squadron of head-bowed-hands-clasped-at-the-crotch men in black suits and ties at the house at 8:45 as the heat rises with the day. Big Bobby Freunde is their trail boss. It is the same weather, breathless and wearying. The participants silently heave into the cars, Louise being last in with Jimmy and Joe by her side and Dr. Depp following. The little girls stay home.

By 9:30 the short black parade of four gleaming stretch limousines roll off with two city motorcycle cops leading and herding the way through stoplights and intersections.

In twenty minutes they are winding their way down into the verdantly lovely cemetery. As the solid thuds of the big Cadillac doors being closed sound, they all gather at the small, opened plot under furls of dogwood and magnolia. It is but a small incision in the ground which require only a bit of the fake, putt-putt green to cover the bore of the shovel and auger's pilings. The urn is ready. Across the way, a few people can be seen clipping and trimming and watering their plots. There is a green funeral tent being erected up the slope behind them.

Dr. Depp softly reads the liturgy in a soothing, rhythmic sing-song that lulls. It is over quickly. They low the "Lord's Prayer" and an "Ashes to Ashes" and an amen. Depp hugs Louise and hands her the service Bible. The sun broils above. The party begins their slow-dragged down way back to the cars. Louise, leaking tears, and sweating the mean stink of used up bourbon and ground down cigarette butts, stands, sways, stays, leans down and picks up a red clay clod and fingers it until it crumbles away. She looks away and down and then walks back to the waiting car.

They go back to Virginia Road. Dr. Depp speaks one last time to them all. Louise goes upstairs compliantly with Dr. Valk to her room. He asks her, "Would you like me to give you something?" She nods.

He then came back downstairs in a few minutes, and says, "She's quiet. She's resting," and joins the others for a quiet early lunch. Mamie and Retha have made chicken salad and buttered toast points and cut fresh fruit and deviled eggs for them all. It helps. Later, they take Mrs. Glenn a tray. She silently waves them away, then tells them to bring her whiskey, cigarettes, a glass and an ice bucket. She is going to wash away her pain.

* * *

Terrell has gone by the hospital to see if he can cold-catch the Medical Examiner to see where things stood with the unravelings and underpinnings of Bo's corpse. He soft-shoes into the front of the M.E.'s office, gleamingly introduces himself to the young lady at the desk, asks if Dr. Podgorny was in and if he would be so kind as to spare a few minutes for him.

She, pleased to be in the glare of Terrell's solar gaze, says dreamily, "Sure, why sure. I'll go ask him for you. Would you please tell me what it's about? He'll ask me that I'm sure." She titters and Terrell titters with her.

"Of course. I'd like to see where things stand with a fellow brought in a few nights ago. One Mr. Benjamin F. Winphrie. I believe we are talking multiple gunshot wounds. Does that help? Oh, and I'm the lawyer representing the man who is supposed to have done the shooting but about that... well...we will see..." He smiles, the minuet of propriety and sales box-stepping with guns and death playing behind his eyes.

"Oh, yes. I'll be right back. Please have a seat and I'll be back in a jiffy."

"Okay. Thanks." He does not sit but stands and waits, looking out the long windows at the tall buildings and squat factories to the east.

She is back quickly. "He'll be glad to see you but just for a few minutes. I hope that's okay?"

She just wants to please him.

"Of course," and she takes him back into the tomb of stainless steel doors, slabs, sinks, hoses, instruments and huge overhead goose necked lamps. Podgorny is a forensic iconoclast, a findings and facts driven man from the Baltic, short, squat with a friendly face, low forehead and a moustache exquisitely waxed to the finest of points, which wings over his lips, barely moving when he speaks. He loves the research of death in all its forms, how his "patients" can never be difficult or non-compliant, how they receive his care and attention without a whimper or complaint. He speaks clearly with a Freudian-Jungian lilt which lends great weight to his mostly monotone and deliberate speech. He is not anti-social, but he, as a grower of orchids, is indeed attuned to the solitary relationships that he cultivates with each cadaver. He is dispassionate and always welcomes inquiry.

Podgorny greets Terrell, asks his name again, explores his interest in the matter and notes his time is short, but that all he has at the present time is basic exterior findings. He is gowned and gloved. He switches on two large lights above, adjusts their aim and slides Bo from the drawer and undrapes him. Bo is a dusty pallid shade with blued lips. He is not reposed in the peace of death; his face is locked in an unhappy rictus. At the moment of his achieving room temperature, he has obviously been irritated.

With a nod, Podgorny begins.

"Mr. Terrell, obviously this gentleman has been shot a number of times, by my initial count four times. All wounds appear to have been made by bullets fired from a pistol or pistols, I should say. Two bullets have been recovered or at least located. One, a .45 caliber, was found distorted from impact and tucked in the decedent's clothing, resting in the folds of the front of his coat. We also know from radiographic scanning of the body that there is a second bullet, appearing to be a .22 caliber, lodged in the subcutaneous tissue of his posterior right hip.

"Our scans have revealed no other bullets. As you can see, there are four entry wounds, all in the anterior trunk, and three exit wounds." He gestures, moving his hand above the body as though divining the communications of a Ouija board. "Two of the three exit wounds are to be found on him at the front of his thoracic and abdominal areas. The other exit wound is to be found posteriorly..." He gently lifts Bo's shoulder with one strong hand and with the other, displaying the opening. "My preliminary conclusion is that this gentleman's death was caused by a gunshot wound or wounds. Until we open the body and look at the results in each area of entry and path of travel, I am sorry but I do not have anything else for you at this time. Of course, I will share my information with all sides of the matter as I am required to do by law and standard practice. I do appreciate your taking the time to come visit with me. The full autopsy results should be ready, including microscopic readings, in about three to four weeks. May we call your office when all is ready?"

"Oh, yes, thank you." Terrell understands that his interview is concluded and he knows enough not to do anything else except be efficiently well-mannered. "And thank you for your time. I appreciate it very much. I will show myself out."

Podgorny replies, "Please leave your card and contact information with our receptionist, Miss Jepson, whom you met when you first came in." It is all so formally Old World. A quick, short bow and he turns away, stripping the gloves off, preparing to scrub for the next still entrant in the march of the Grim Reaper.

Terrell is glad to visit with Miss Jepson. She is cute.

"Miss Jepson, Dr. Podgorny wanted me to leave my contact information with you. He says he'll be in touch with me in the next few weeks." He extends his card. She takes it, issuing a slow approving hum as she appraises it.

"Very nice. Very nice"." she says as she slips it into her top drawer. "Please call me Lee Ann."

"Oh, yes. Lee Ann. Thank you...Lee Ann." He smiles and she does too, right back at him. A tribute to sparkling orthodonture glittered between them in mutual coupling.

She continues, "And remember to let the family of the deceased know that once the autopsy is completed, they have ninety days to claim the remains for services. If they don't, on day ninety-one, the body will be cremated and the ashes will be taken to the county field." She speaks with deliberate authority as someone reading sonorously from a flight safety card.

It quickly occurs to him that she has already forgotten or misplaced his role in the play.

"Ah, well, thank you for that information."

She adjusts her skirt as she re-crosses her pretty long legs. He watches and she knows he did. She lightly touches and twists a falling strand of light brown hair that plays along her cheek.

"You are very welcome, Mr. Terrell. I hope you have a real nice day."

"Yes, I am and I will." He takes his leave.

As he waits for the elevator, he thinks, *Good girl, Lee Ann. Hard not to like a girl who shares.* The elevator bell goes "ding."

Over the next few days, Terrell talks with the arresting officers at police headquarters and the District Attorneys assigned to prosecute the case at their offices in the Hall of Justice Building. The former are phlegmatic and desultory. The latter are adamant and obdurate. It is always this way.

There is one thing, one big thing that all cops, from beat walkers to homicide detectives carry in common once they had become seasoned. They all became part of a never-ending, always rolling Human Misbehavior Assembly and Inspection Line. A deed, large or small, is done. The deed is then introduced to the law and in they come to assess and process. They sort the wheat from the chaff, the big from the little, the flawed from the fine, shuttle them all down chutes of varying degrees of importance and move on, always sifting and weighing and measuring. And because there is an abundance of human frailty, they are never at a pause. No one ever hears a cop say, "Gee, things are really slow right now. We need a couple of good killings to rev up the day." Their motto is basically, "Next." And as it works like this, they become part of a routine that is not without its sameness and boredoms. They speak in quick efficient bursts most of the time unless someone tells a joke, usually poorly. They by trade and construct are not personable save for the techniques of effective interview and certainly they are not socially entertaining; it will never do to say too much. Just ask the poor schlub who early on in his career stumble-walks too far out on a limb during a cross examination by the defense counsel and has his nuts sawed off. They are guarded in speech and habit and always crossing one case off and adding another. They are the back of the house, the assembly line that rattles on.

The prosecutors are the larger, well-lit decorated store-front windows where the wares for presentation are buffed and polished and put up for public display and scrutiny. The District Attorney's office is full of young prosecutors with promising careers as trial prosecutors and more than a few senior men who are old pros, experienced and savvy.

Their processes are also repetitive but carry a variety and stimulus not seen by the originating level. By the time cases get to them, there is an assembled file that allows broad scrutiny and selection for dismissal, plea, or trial. Misdemeanors go downstairs to the District Courts on the third floor where they are assigned a single assistant D.A., depending on who is rotating where—into Criminal, Traffic or Family Courts (The latter being more accurately labeled "Fucking and Fighting Court"). Felonies go upstairs to the fifth and sixth floors and are always assigned at least two prosecutors, one from the District Court level so experience with larger fishing can be gained and one from the Superior Court level who already carries trophy status. Prosecutors are fine communicators comfortable with speaking and arguing in public and are generally fervent and righteous. If they are not, they washed out quickly and go into private practice where they advertise in the Yellow Pages as being "an Experienced Former District Attorney," a nice come-on to an unwitting public.

With both Wilkins and Miller and with the D.A.s, it is, "Hey, guys, I'm Eddie Terrell. I'm representing a guy named Kenny Peak y'all have for Murder One. What you got?"

The cops, sitting at cluttered face-to-face desks just like in the movies summarize that they have a solid eyewitness, they have motive, forensics aren't back yet, but they have recovered one weapon, a shotgun, and it was a Friday Night Run Of The Mill Drink House Special—one piece of trash shooting another piece of trash in the shittiest part of town and is all cut and dried and a jury won't have any trouble getting the right answer. They may as well have pleasantly yawned and nodded through the recitation.

The assigned prosecutors, one young, eager Paul Weinman, and the been-there-forever, Charles "Buzzy" Cole are alert, also pleasant, suited and have not yet received the investigators' file. Terrell knew this was going to be the case and was simply there on a courtesy, to say hello, please remember me call. It is all perfunctory with but one slightly aggressive note tossed in at the end of the quick session by the more serious Weinman. He cautions with melodramatic finality, "Remember, this is a Murder in the First Degree case and is going to be prosecuted very, very seriously."

Terrell responds with deference. "Of course. Of course it will. I appreciate that."

Cole gives Terrell the shrug, "Kids. Whattaya gonna do with 'em..." and adds, "We know and we appreciate that too. Thanks for coming by."

Chapter Twenty-Two

Lawyering

Mary Sue Martin had been a good-looking girl, brunette and shapely with the double smile of a country girl come to the city, innocent and predatory, one layered-up over the other.

She had grown up about thirty miles west of Winston-Salem, well past the big, always muddy river, in an area known broadly as Davis Bottom. Her people were many generations of farmers. The Bottom was good growing land, rich black dirt, but sometimes flooded so some years were better than others. Her parents were ass-busters when it came to work, but also grim and narrow and mean, humorless, deep church people who disapproved of anything that approximated fun. They were very judgmental. She had younger siblings who she considered to be at best adopted, loafers and lay-abouts. She wanted less than little to do with them. She hid her happiness inside her, tucked it away to protect it from the pumice stone grinding of her parents. They had a black and white television set and a table radio which her father controlled with jaw-tightened efficiency and the calculus of a prison warden. Still, hints and signals of a life beyond this agrarian heaven could be found from time to time if you watched for and listened for the ads and jingles and waited to cheat-watch when the adults drove off to the feed- or hardware store for some riveting and exciting items like rope and millet. The house was drab, the tasks were hard and boring, the prospects more so.

Mary Sue calculated that in order to be able to leave, she needed to have skills, and she studied her arithmetic and typing and English with both aptitude and steady attention. She began this quest when she was fourteen and never wavered. She worked part-time jobs after school and always contributed some to her rack bosses and secreted the rest in an old boot in her closet. She graduated from high school. Then one early morning soon thereafter, without telling her family, she packed a few things and bought a bus ticket from the ice cream shop at the crossroads and made the hour-long trip into the city.

Adaptable, agreeable, and very pretty, she quickly approached nice-looking strangers and asked where she might find a nice boarding house in a nicer part of the city. She landed in one near the downtown area, paid down a month's rent in advance. It was within walking distance of many shops and businesses. She promptly began her door-to-door solicitations and within a few days was the new receptionist doing light typing and pulling a regular check every two weeks at Home Real Estate on West Fifth Street. Home was just a few blocks away from the big banks, the tobacco companies and their headquarters, the large textile company offices and all of the feeder businesses and bars and restaurants and retail stores that spread like piglets from the great sows' teats of money. She was competent eye candy, knew it, liked it and began to build herself in ways pleasing both to her and to all around her. She found that she made friends easily and enjoyed their company and their connections and took advantage of all, always in the nicest of ways. She found that both the company of men and women were agreeable to her as was the taste of whiskey from time to time.

Over the span of just a few years, she moved from the little real estate company to become the Senior Assistant Manager of a large loan and finance company that serviced the short term needs of the city's large populace of mill and factory workers. It was just next to the biggest bank in town and after the week's checks had been cashed and banked, portions of those people and their money would come around to address accounts and establish credit. Many a salacious dream was sparked by her sweet look, long legs and mild perfume as she patiently gave guidance, made offers and signed them up. She was always busy, required herself to be pretty every day, and husbanded her money while keeping a sharp eye out for a satisfactory match.

And along the way to the loan company, she spent more than a year in the stenography pool at the local textile firm, Quality Textiles. She made many friends there.

She never really reconnected with her family over those years after she left the farm. She had promptly let them know where she was in the beginning, and she would call them every week or so, too, and every three or four months or so drive over to visit, but it was all perfunctory, obligatory, stiff, and repetitive. She now was a glossy mystery to them. And to her they were as flat cut-outs in a store window, thin and faded by the semi-tropical Southern sun. But on the basis of those mutual understandings, they all maintained a pleasant and vapid truce.

The news and detailed facts of her violent death reached the family. There was the initial surprise and shock. Then came the far broader and deeper, though obviously more unspoken, sentiment of "I told you so," the sour hindsight of the abandoned, those who had never flown too close to the sun but will with pernicious lips tell you all about it. True, there was sadness but it was mild and finite and yet its role must be played and displayed and it was. There were the rumors of whoring about and drinking and painted hussies and cheating married men and the orgies of the well-to-do, all from Sodom and Gomorrah, but the family ignored it all, held up and teared up nicely at a hastily put together graveside service. The small crowd dispersed and the Martins went home.

Mr. Martin takes off his coat, sits down in his chair, picks up his Bible, thumbs its pages, stops and then reads to his wife.

"From Ezekiel Chapter 22, Verse 13. 'Behold then I smite my hand at your dishonest gain which you have acquired and at the bloodshed which is among you'." He reads it loud, hell fire and brimstone loud.

He looks up and there is no trace of sadness on his face, only the pleasure of a profitable vengeance.

"Missus, ain't no sense in acting through it. We done lost our girl three times. First, when she was here, then when she left and lastly just now. But you and I both know she was not of us. Now she is gone and it's time to gain. That fella she was with was rich and this is all his fault and he was married and we gonna get some of his now. And right soon. You agree?"

Mrs. Martin nods and goes to the kitchen.

He speaks to her back. "In the next few days here, I'm going to town to find a good lawyer."

* * *

Terrell had gone to see Kenny, get him caught up and then made a pass through the courthouse just to see what was going on, who was there, what was interesting, who was screwing something up. Peeking in the doorway, Courtroom 3-C holds the theater of hulking Judge Big Ab Alexander grumping audibly from the bench as always, while white-suited Harold Wilson pontificates away, a red clay Alcibiades with a jet black wig, sunglasses and a high, squeaking lilt as his female client looks on mystified. She is not convinced, but Wilson is, eternally is.

Across the hall, in 3-D, Judge Kason Keiger stares off into space as a sloppily dressed young man wearing an "I'm With Stupid" T-shirt and unlaced tennis shoes spews forth with "The Dog Ate My Homework" excuses for not paying months off past due traffic fines. The kid senses that he is taking a long run off a short dock but persists. Judge Keiger finally focuses on the defendant, pauses and then says sharply, "Son, has it not occurred to you that I have heard all of this about...maybe...a hundred thousand times before, so listen to me real good now. We have a long docket here today and you are putting my train boarding behind schedule. You have until two o'clock to get the money or go to jail. Be back here at two. I need a cigarette. Well, I need more than that. We are in recess until 10:45."

The bailiff recites "All Rise." And the kid comes out the door past Terrell mumbling something about how he is being fucked, fuck them all, fuck, fuck, fuck. It is one of a hundred behavior templates always in use, though how would he know?

Shaking his head, Terrell walks upstairs to the fourth floor where Domestic Court, also known as Fucking and Fighting Court, is in session. Judge Gary Tash watches over a tennis match of shouting erupting between an angry man and an angry woman over child support payments. Tash is known to let their hot tempers burn out as long as the language doesn't get too bad. It all amuses him as he sits placidly poker-faced.

Terrell loves it all so much. It is the great colloidal rhythm of Blind Lady

Justice's buffet of wrongs to be addressed.

He walks back down the stairs into the large central lobby of the third floor on his way back to his office. A man approaches him and asks, "You're a lawyer, ain't you?"

Smoothly he nods toward the man, "Yes. Yes, I am. How may I help you?"

The fellow, rough and worn, but dressed respectable-country says, "Can we go over there and talk?"

"Yes. Of course. I'm Ed Terrell." He extends his hand to shake hands and to also slip his card forth. No matter whether the fish were biting or not, it never hurts to keep bait nearby in case the hook needed dressing. They always kept his card.

The man says, "Yeah, I know. I been askin' 'round about you."

They walk to a quieter edge of the big room and sit on a bench with its back to a large window which lets abundant sunshine heat the room. If someone looks straight at them, they are but black silhouettes.

The man says, rushing, "Look here, Mr. Terrell. I got, me and my wife got, a problem and we need help. I've asked around and done been told you are good at what you do. Oh, I'm Johnny Martin. Sorry." He quiets quickly.

Terrell looks at him and says, "All right, Mr. Martin. If I can help, I'd be glad to. Tell me what the problem is." Terrell is willing to bet it isn't a trademark fight or a corporate contract dispute. Those things bored him, too buttoned down. Martin does not present that kind of neatly creased profile. Too, Terrell is hoping it isn't a small claims wrestle over bad tires or a piss-ant loan that went to shit. He is hoping for something with meat on the bone. He watches Martin with benign expectation. Never be anxious. Never start giving away before you first get.

Martin speaks, low and flat. His eyes look directly into Terrell's. In them burn red hot hate, resentment and anger.

"Mr. Terrell. My baby girl, our daughter, Mary Sue. Got killed. She was riding in a rich man's car. Car got hit by a train. He was sneaking off with her. I think the rich man was married. He was twice her age. He killed her just like he used a gun. I want him to pay. Me and my wife want that. Will you help?"

The sun has heated up the window and in the stillness, little particles of dust float everywhere.

Terrell thinks, *Motherlode. It was in the papers. I know this one.*

Terrell pauses, nods slowly and says, "Mr. Martin. I'm so sorry for your loss. That's a terrible thing to have happened to y'all. I am so, so sorry." And he pauses and bows his head unctuously and after a few seconds he looks back up at Martin and realizes that Martin isn't the least bit interested in Holy Assistance; he wants some kick-ass lawyer boots on the ground now, right away, hell, yesterday and thus, he adds, "And, yessir, I would be glad to try to help y'all."

Martin says, "Okay. Good. What do we need to do?" Well, there is surely not going to be any foreplay here.

"Mr. Martin, first I'm going to need to get some basic information about all of you and I need to get some things together for y'all. Could I come out to wherever y'all live and visit with both you and your wife and go over everything? I think you already understand this is not a simple matter."

Terrell clicks his briefcase open and pulls out a legal pad.

"Yeah. Sure. When do you want to come?"

"This afternoon if that would suit."

"It would. My address is Sourtown Mountain Road, Number 1, in the Jerusalem Community. Our phone number is 765-5417. My wife's name is Precious but everybody calls her 'Pray,' as in you better damn well pray she don't come after you." Martin smiles a strained and ragged yellow keyboard. He has amused himself. Terrell is amused too but he is also wary and so he asks, "Mr. Martin, you ever dealt with lawyers, sir?"

Martin wrinkles his nose and raises and flares his nostrils pig-like snorting, "A few times. Land stuff. Equipment stuff. Crop loans getting called. Nothing like this. But that don't mean nothin'. I understand y'all are mostly whores which don't bother me none." He smiles thinly.

Martin is so pleasantly affable in his brief recitation of his interactions with counsel that Terrell just nods and decides not to come to any defense of the mores of his profession. No reason to toss anything akin to preachifying high and mighty into the gravy bowl.

"Well, I'm sorry if those matters were difficult for you. I have never done those kinds of cases. I've always worked with people and families. That's what I do. It's all I do."

Martin says, "I asked around for a shark. I asked around for someone who would be willing to cut the nuts off a prize bull. Your name kept coming up. That suits me. When you coming?"

"When you want me?"

"Say, two o'clock. I'll get the Missus to knowin' what we have to do. Dress like you're dressed now. You understand?"

"Yessir."

"And, oh, I'm guessin' you know a little something about this already? It's been in the papers you know. That fair to say?"

"Yessir, I've read of it."

"Good, gets you dug deeper in a little tighter, right? By the way, how long this gonna take, you think?"

"I got a lot of homework to do, but do you want a quick hit for big or a slower hit for bigger?" Any pretense of professional rectitude has now fled screaming down the street.

Old Man Martin looks at him for a bit and Terrell waits and is both pleased with his forthrightness and anxious that he has maybe whored too hard. He needn't have worried.

"Oh, we been right poor all the time so a good lick of quicker money is worth shortening the days. Don't you think? Would be nice to have something other than dust in our pockets for once."

Terrell says, "Y'all are my boss. Whatever you'd like me to try to do, I'll go to it."

"Good." Martin stands, shakes Terrell's hand and began to walk toward the stairs. "See you in a little while."

"Yessir." Terrell processes his good fortune and this time, he tries to slow things down. Terrell sits and lets it all sink in. He has just landed a whale, a fucking Monster Whale at his feet, ready to eat, no mess, nothing but money and a lot of it.

He thinks, *My God! Holy Mother of God! Holy shit! Jonah's gonna eat the whale this time around!*

And he looks around at the milling, mostly lost, mostly poorly-dressed people and all the poor lawyers flitting about and hovering and moving in and out of them like hummingbirds with neckties and file folders and he softly exhales, shoots his cuffs, stands, and with great calm and dignity and professional purpose heads to his office.

Terrell has Patty put together the intake file and as an added touch of stardust he tells Patty he wants her to ride with him and play Della Street to his Perry Mason. Clients always liked it when you brought a bona fide legal secretary/assistant/Girl Friday who took a lot of notes, nodded a lot to create an emphasized sense of "We have our people on this."

Patty is a pro, exudes competence and toughness, and knows her stuff. She can type faster than most folks talk, knows everyone at the courthouse, half the cops, too, and is fearless. The office is his. She is the moat and the garrison.

They ride out of town toward Jerusalem. Patty had gotten the directions from a county deputy she knew. It takes a half hour. They make small talk, office talk about clients, case files, witnesses, cops, doctors. Some are great, others are assholes, some fall into the unreadable, not sure gray areas. Terrell prods her to talk and she is not shy about weighing in once out of the office. They always circle back to the old line, "Opinions are like assholes. Everybody's got one." Patty smokes like a chimney and keeps the window half open. She opines, inhales, turns, blows out the window, and then resumes her soliloquies. Terrell likes this. It is the taking of the office pulse and she is funny as she spits forth her observations and thinks on anything that jumps to mind. He thinks as he often did she would make a damn fine lawyer. *Should I send her to law school? And as always, the answer was no, don't go there. Why lose a crackerjack assistant to gain an ultimate rival to share or split with? Not a good idea.*

They pull up in the more rutted dirt than gravel drive. It is all bucolic in a rundown, worn out way. Fences in poor shape, two small barns that are lopsided. Various pieces of older equipment, some workable, some rusting in tall grass. Chickens wandering around. Old pickup truck under a tree. Martin's house is the old exemplar: too poor to paint, too proud to whitewash. These people are the invisibles, just hanging on waiting to either die or get lucky.

Terrell and Patty go up on the porch and knock on the rattling screen door. They can see inside, see Old Man Martin coming to get them, see his wife stand up from a wooden chair and smooth down the front of her dress. She is a handsome woman gone down into early old. She is obviously weary.

Old Man Martin says, "Right on time. Come on in," and holds the door open. Terrell shakes his hand, shakes Mrs. Martin's hand, introduces Patty. Martin shepherds them all in a country fussy sort of way to a small kitchen table. He is anxiously efficient. They sit. Martin says, "Okay, what do we need to do? We're ready."

And so Terrell gets going. After repeating the "I'm so sorry" mantra as a prelude to starting the money machine, he asks them lots of questions about their daughter, their family, their lives, what they knew about what had happened. Patty takes it all down in a slashing shorthand. He explains his approach to cases in general, his proposed approach to their case. He explains everything that could go wrong. He evokes their expectations and concerns. He soothes them without being unctuous. He explains and explains in professional earnest. The old man nods along rhythmically, his wife paying attention but blank-eyed. They get signatures on the contingent fee contract, medical authorizations for release of reports and records, forms to open a probate estate for the late Mary Sue Martin.

They are given some glossy brochures and information sheets about Terrell, his ever-growing and glittering biography and his firm. They are given a list of client do's and don't's, i.e., pleasant enough instructions to keep your mouths shut, talk to no one about any of this unless cleared by Patty or Terrell and to always call them or make appointments to discuss anything and everything on their minds about all this. They are warned not to compare apples to oranges, not to try to fit a template of "I heard so and so got this so we should get this" as to outcome. They answer a few taciturn questions. He assures them they will get started right away and they will be alerted to every step taken and copied with all paperwork. It all dwindles down into dry silence and a last, "Anything else?" No. They all stand, chairs scraping back signaling their meeting is over. More condolences are doled out. They leave to drive back to town.

Terrell asks Patty, "What do you think?"

She lights a cigarette and replies in her facile staccato, "Well...I've read the file. These people are pigeons. This high cotton crowd is a fat sitting duck with a neon sign that flashes 'Hit Me' on its forehead. I'd bet you a damn dime to a fucking doughnut they're waiting to get quickly, quietly and privately rolled and make this damn disaster go to ground. It's a no-brainer. I presume we're going to make one stop before we go back to the office?"

"You think?"

"Shit, I know and you do too."

He grins. "Just making sure. Into the breach we go, just huntin' a little dough," he sing-songs.

Patty adds, "Damn good thing you got me along..."

"I agree."

"No, dumbass, you need me as a witness in case they want to try to fuck you over by saying you were unethical and then burn you and the money down."

"Ah yes, of course, I knew that too." He rocks his head back and forth like a giddy kid. And so as good Southern folks so often do, they went a callin' to witness for each other and their common good.

They park in the wide lot laid out next to Quality Textile's headquarters and look it all over. There is the main building tastefully landscaped, a fellow with a lawnmower meticulously swinging through amidst the dogwoods and azaleas and boxwoods. The tall double glass doors gleam. Their brass handles shine. Down the long wing that falls off to the back are fuel oil pumps for delivery trucks, a sizeable fleet of all sorts of utility vehicles and a long line up of identical eighteen wheelers swollen behemoths that deliver the goods. There are rows of open bay doors for mechanics and repair and maintenance, neat stacks of tires and fuel tanks. There is a construction building. There are towering storage buildings. Everything is painted with the high, sleek gloss enamel of Quality Textiles' signature red and blue. It is expansive and orderly.

It does not take a Woodrow Wilson Fellow to understand that the scene pronounces Money.

They look at each other and are pleased and excited. There is no need to discuss or evaluate what they are looking at.

Terrell says, "Let's go."

At the reception desk, Terrell beams at the young lady with the headset and blinking switchboard before her.

"Hello, there. I'm Mr. Terrell. This is Miss Cherry. We're here to see Mr. Glenn."

The girl is puzzled. Softly she asks, "Uhm...do you have an appointment? And also, which Mr. Glenn?" And too it is not lost on her that the number of

Glenns available for a visit has recently been winnowed down.

Terrell is not befuddled. He replies and as he does, he hands her his card. "No, we don't have an appointment, but I am quite sure any one of them will be happy to meet with us."

The girl punches a button and speaks very softly into her microphone, "Miss Simpson. Miss Simpson. Would you please come to reception." And then looks up at them and says, "Please have a seat over there." Politely they begin to comply when Miss Sue Simpson bundles around the corner, eyes them carefully and quickly, and introduces herself. Terrell hands her a card. She looks at it. Its import was not lost on her.

"Please come with me."

She leads them down a long linoleum hall with many offices on either side, all the doors open, showing men in shirtsleeves and neckties bending to their work. The three of them are not noticed.

Those men, washed in bright fluorescent light, wreathed in cigarette smoke, are talking on telephones, clicking their calculators, flipping through pages of numbers, penciling notes, surging through the capitalism of it all.

Another heavy glass door is pushed open and now the floor is deep carpet, the light is from soft lamps, and the furniture is leather and aged. The walls are maple panel. The sanctum smells of linseed oil and candy in dishes.

They are ushered into a small conference room in an alcove.

"Please have a seat. Would you like something to drink?"

"No, thank you. We're fine. Thank you."

"Well, all right. I'll be right back."

They sit comfortably in silence.

In a few minutes, she returns to the room, stands aside for two men to enter and starts to leave.

"No, no, Sue. You stay with us all. Might be good to take a note or two." Joe Glenn looks at his brother Jimmy and Jimmy nods.

Eddie Terrell says quietly and pleasantly, "We'll get to introductions in just a second. I think y'all know why we are here. How about if none of us take any notes? Really no reason to. I promise we will keep this very short."

His tone is almost kind, like the soothing dentist who, just before the extraction, purrs, "Now this will only hurt a little bit."

Friday Calls

Joe and Jimmy understand. Understand the ask is imminent. Understood the ask is really not really an ask maybe save for some wiggling adjustment which will have to be done quickly. They understand that this proceeding is in the realm of no insurance, no reporting, no waving the bloody shirt, just all into the world of disappearing confidentiality, the entirety of it all shuttled away to the eternal solitary confinement of silence. As suddenly and furiously as it has all struck, it can now all be ended. All reduced to a number, nothing more significant than that.

The Glenns are captive, ripe, cocked and primed to spring at the bait. Not only do they need to grasp it, they want to. It is just going to boil down to the number.

Quickly, all are introduced to one another. Sue Simpson stands in a corner and out of deference, Patty Cherry leaves her seat and stands a few feet away from her. Where the two women stand, they can see the men's faces but not their hands. The three men lean in. Terrell pulls one of his cards out, turns it over and writes on the back and then holds it in his palm for the other two to see.

Joe and Jimmy Glenn are not rubes who have just fallen off the turnip truck yesterday. Terrell knows that and respects it. Hell, these men haven't put this kind of operation together over the years by shooting blind craps in the dark. They are handsome, attractive, dressed impeccably, and have sharp, intelligent eyes.

Joe Glenn reaches for a pad on a side table, pulls out his fountain pen and writes on it and shows it to his brother. Jimmy gives a slight nod and Joe then shows it to Terrell. Of course there is a difference in the numbers but it isn't a chasm. It is obvious to the men that none of them are playing this stupid. A pig gets fat and a hog gets slaughtered. You want to eat, not choke.

Terrell speaks. "Split it." It isn't a question but not a declaration either.

Joe and Jimmy nod. Joe crumples the piece of paper and pushes it into his suit pocket.

Joe speaks. "Ends it all for everyone, correct? The company, the estate, the widow and children."

"Yes."

Patty and Sue look at each other with quick question marks in their eyes. Jimmy speaks, "How soon you looking to take receipt of this?"

Terrell answers, "Not too soon. How about ninety days?"

Jimmy says, "That'll be fine. I do think we need to pay, say, ten percent, as a good faith deposit to insure the deal."

"Okay. That works. It can be held in trust. Settlement documents? Confidentiality agreements? I presume y'all have your lawyers."

"Bobby Stockman at Hudson Petree will handle our end. You'll of course review. We will all jointly approve. And, please give me another of your cards. Bobby will be in touch with you in a few days."

"I'll handle probate on our end. Presume Mr. Stockman will on y'all's end?"

"Right. Yes."

There is no air of bonhomie in the room. But there is the pleasant efficiency of business, a deal being struck professionally.

Terrell says calmly, "I think we're all on the same page?" He looks around. Five poker faces look at each other, ten eyes barely flickering. "Yes, I think we are." He stands up. "Thank you, gentlemen." He says it with respect. They shake hands.

Jimmy laughs a small laugh, sort of a snorted, muted chuckle and says, "Well, usually we say something like 'Thanks for stopping by' but I'm not sure that fits the bill today."

Terrell says, "How about thanks to all of us for getting it done?"

Joe says, "Yeah, that works."

They all nod and crisply move away from each other.

The whole thing has taken less than ten minutes.

Once Terrell and Patty have left, Joe and Jimmy sit in Jimmy's office. Sue still stands.

"Sue, what do you think? I felt, I think we both felt that it's better to just get this damn mess cleaned up and put into the dark. Poor Archer. Poor Louise. Poor kids. Poor dead girl. Poor all to hell. But we gotta run this business and we've lost one of our legs." Jimmy vacantly studies his shoes, head a bit hangdog as he speaks.

"First, what's the number? Hell, boys, I know it's your show and y'all know what you can put into the pot, but gee whiz, I'd sure like to know so we can frame it right for the accounting department people and all the tax stuff that goes with it." She smiles a wan clown smile and arched her eyebrows.

Joe pulls the paper out of his pocket, smooths it on the coffee table and shows it to Sue Simpson. Jimmy looks out the window.

"This less 250."

"Well, y'all paying a premium but the value is there on both sides. That's not as bad as I thought it might be. That boy could have probably gotten more but still, that we can...I mean, y'all can handle. Y'all know if I'd felt there was craziness in that room, I'd put the brakes on. I must say no one showed their ass in there and there were plenty of chances for some serious cheek flapping and I am sure as not talking about the ones attached to the gums..."

Joe says, "That's true. That's true." He lights a cigarette. "I have a thought. Whaddayall think of this? Once we get all the paperwork done, I'm thinking it wouldn't be a bad thing to put that Terrell fellow on a nice, long retainer. He's smart, gets to the point, got manners, seems to understand what sub rosa is... Let's hold him real close...we'll owe him and he'll owe us..."

Jimmy says, "Yes, I like it. Sue?"

"I'm good with it. Get Bobby to make the approach. Now y'all understand that young man is getting a big chunk of change in ninety days, a big chunk courtesy of good old Quality Textile Company, served up hot, fast and delicious. Might be looking at a fat head in three months..."

Jimmy says, "Let's watch him. Bobby can do that for us too."

Joe says to no one in particular, "Damn, I'm tired. A big buster wouldn't hurt. Jimmy, let's go to the club, want to? Let's go have one."

Sue Simpson says, "Yes, y'all go on, get out of here. There'll be plenty to do in the morning." Joe burns the piece of paper in an ashtray.

As long as the number was not spoken, it might as well have been monopoly money—the strike price for the death of a pretty young girl and the secreting of their brother Archer's what...? indiscretions, stupidity, naiveté, libido, carelessness, innocence...hell, who knows? They just knew they would really never know and really did not want to know. The bombs had dropped. Everything had blown up. The crater was being filled in, the details left to others. The thing was becoming silent forever.

They doff their hats and leave. As they walk to the parking lot, Jimmy says, "We know Bobby's got judges that can keep this graveyard. Think that young man does too?"

Joe says, "Oh yeah, no doubt. I think this is going to be a run silent, run deep and that's the way it has to be. I expect young Mr. Terrell and Bobby will wrap this up around midnight one evening in a selected His Honor's kitchen table and the papers will all be dark boxed in a blink."

Jimmy nods. "Joe, you given any thought to what happened, how all this happened? I'm trying to get my head around it and right now, just not doing a real good job of it. Maybe later on we could ask some of the fellows who were out at May's?"

Joe sighs. "Jimmy, I have thought about it a little bit, but same here, just too much flying around. And, I'm glad you brought that up. I do not think it is a good idea to ask anyone about anything. Let's let sleeping dogs lie. Let's just let it be a mouse. We go turning over rocks...there's just no telling what might be under one...or two."

Terrell and Patty drive away without speaking, without so much as a nudge and a wink, without so much as a flash glance. When they pull into the office lot, Patty asks, "Curious...why'd you say ninety days...expect they could get it done next week, don't you think?"

"Oh, sure. I'll tell you why...couple of reasons...I liked those men. I liked that lady Simpson with them. They were cool. No handwringing, no oh woe is us. Just let's get to it. Money talks, nobody walks. Their lawyer Bobby Stockman is as big time as it gets. I want to let this cure in, settle in, give everyone a chance to see that our word and our actions are twenty-four karat solid gold. No slam bam, thank you, ma'am. This is marketing opportunity that few get. I want them to come to like us and want them to come to think of us as helpful. I will make myself available to Stockman. When he whistles, I'll come running and if he says, 'Shit,' I'll say, 'How high and what color'.

"And second, we need a little time to build our file, earn our fee. Sure, Old Man Martin pretty much said he'll take a good lick sooner rather than later but we get it for them too quick, the odds of a rare back go up. So we'll be putting together an activity list that will show them how hard we've worked after this. And this is a no kidding big lick. I want to keep dividing it by three, right? I want you and me to go see the Martins once a week until this is done so mark the calendar."

"Okay. Sounds good. And gotta ask. How many commas?

"Two."

"Nice. Nice. Very nice. Aren't you glad you know what a comma is? Good thing you went to school... would that fall under grammar or law?" She laughs, finally laughs. She is pleased. She knows there will be nice good green sprinkles on her ice cream in a few months.

"How about filthy lucre?" he grins and they go in. Patty just shakes her head. Happy whores they are.

Chapter Twenty-Three

Court Room

A month and a day after Bo is rendered graveyard dead, Kenny Peak's Motion for Preliminary Hearing to Show Probable Cause and for Reduction of Bond is heard. Here is the transcript of the proceedings.

STATE OF NORTH CAROLINA FORSYTH COUNTY	IN THE GENERAL COURT OF JUSTICE DISTRICT COURT DIVISION 83CR-19367
STATE OF NORTH CAROLINA,	
VS.	PRELIMINARY HEARING
HOMER PEAK,	
Defendant	

This was a criminal matter heard before the Honorable James A. Harrill, Jr., Judge presiding, in Courtroom 3C, Forsyth County Hall of Justice, Winston-Salem, North Carolina, beginning at 10:56 o'clock a.m. on Thursday, May 19, 19XX.

Judge Jimmy as he is affectionately known, is smart, easy going and easily amused. He always knew and never forgot how incredibly ridiculous and humanly stupid so much of what passed before him was. There is never any reason to get riled up in front of him because a) he does not like such behavior and b) such conduct in all its righteous, malignant forms always played against the angry, strident and loud perpetrator no matter what kind of clothes they had on.

APPEARANCES

FOR THE STATE OF NORTH CAROLINA:
Paul Weinman, Assistant District Attorney

Weinman is a good guy, but sometimes drank too much Kool-Aid. Terrell is delighted to see him assigned this day. He is of medium height, broad shouldered with a great big head and mop of reddish blond hair that he never gets properly cut. It always flops over his forehead and eyes which always get him to quick-blowing it and pushing it out of the way not once but many times. These are futile acts, especially when he is caught up in drinking too much Kool-Aid. Such acts add to the ever-present impression that he is frantic, nervous and pressing which make many people such as judges uncomfortable and thus often move the needle of judicial neutrality against him. It does not help or hurt, depending in what chairs one sat, that he sweats a lot, adding to a general sense of discomfiture.

FOR THE DEFENDANT:
    Edward F. V. Terrell, Esq.
    231 West Fifth Street
    WinstonSalem, North Carolina 27101

INDEX
PROCEEDING: 3
EVIDENCE FOR THE STATE

Witness	Examination By	Page
Felicia D. Lineberger	Direct – Weinman	3
	Cross – Terrell	6
Felicia D. Lineberger	Direct – Weinman	3
	Cross – Terrell	6

EVIDENCE FOR THE DEFENDANT

Witness	Examination By	Page
Mattie Cane	Direct – Terrell	43
	Cross – Weinman	44

COURT FINDING   47
ADJOURNMENT: 47
REPORTER CERTIFICATION   48

PROCEEDING
(10:56 o'clock a.m.)

THE COURT: He does wish a hearing, is that right, Mr. Terrell?
MR. TERRELL: Yes, I do, Your Honor. We've got a court reporter here as well to transcribe everything.
MR. WEINMAN: Your Honor, I am preparing an order asking for a copy of this transcript.
THE COURT: Let the witnesses be sworn, please.
(All witnesses were sworn.)
THE COURT: Yes, ma'am. Around back here.
WHEREUPON, the witness, FELICIA DIANE LINEBERGER, upon being first duly sworn, testified on her oath as follows:

DIRECT EXAMINATION
BY MR. WEINMAN TO FELICIA DIANE LINEBERGER

Q. State your name for the Court, please.

A. My name is Felicia Diane Lineberger.

Q. How old are you, Felicia?

A. Eighteen.

Q. Ms. Lineberger, did you have occasion to be in the area of the 1500 block of East 15th Street on the night of April 21st of this year?

A. Yes.

Q. Did you know a gentleman named Benjamin Winphrie?

A. Yes.

Q. And did you see him in that area that night?

A. Yes.

Q. And did you also see the defendant?

A. Yes.

Q. Would you please describe for His Honor what happened between the two of them?

A. Well, I was sitting up at the bar, and Benjamin Franklin was behind—I was there at Curt Minor Drink House.

THE COURT: I'm sorry. Where did she say she was?

THE WITNESS: At Curt Minor Drink House.

THE COURT: Oh, a drink house—Curt Minor.

A. (By the Witness) I was sitting up at the bar, and Benjamin Franklin was behind the bar, and the music was going real loud and everything.

Q. (By Mr. Weinman) By Benjamin Franklin, you're referring to Benjamin Franklin Winphrie?

A. Yes.

MR. TERRELL: Your Honor, may I ask her to speak up a little bit?

THE COURT: Yes, ma'am, I know you're probably a little nervous, but if you would, just slow down and keep your voice up a little bit.

THE WITNESS: Okay.

A. (By the Witness) I was sitting at the bar, and Benjamin Franklin was behind the bar kind of at the end—kind of. And Kenneth Peak came up to the bar.

Q. (By Mr. Weinman) Are you referring to the defendant sitting over here?

A. Yeah.

Q. Go ahead, please.

A. And he came up to the bar, and he come, and he stood kind of this way at the bar and stood—because Benjamin Franklin was—where he was standing was kind of at the end of the bar—Kenneth Peak. And Benjamin Franklin was right there. (Witness indicating.)

THE COURT: Turn around so the court reporter can hear you, too. You may stand up if you wish.

A. (By the Witness) And he stood and held the gun out and started shooting him; he didn't say nothing. And then he walked away.

Q. (By Mr. Weinman) The defendant here fired shots at Benjamin Franklin—

A. Uh-huh (yes). I seen him.

Q. —Winphrie? How far apart were they?

A. Well, like I say, he was at the end—he was standing—Kenneth—he was standing at the end of the bar. He came like—just say the bar's right here, and at the end of the bar right here, and he stood. (Witness indicating.) And Benjamin Franklin was behind the bar, so he just came up and just started shooting.

Q. How many shots were fired?

A. I heard about four.

MR. WEINMAN: May I approach the witness, Your Honor? You may have a seat.

Q. (By Mr. Weinman) Can you identify the gentleman in that photograph?

A. Benjamin Franklin.

Q. That's Mr. Winphrie?

A. Uh-huh (yes).

MR. WEINMAN: Your Honor, I'd move to introduce this at this time.

THE COURT: All right.

MR. WEINMAN: No further questions.

CROSS EXAMINATION
BY MR. TERRELL TO FELICIA LINEBERGER:

Miss Lineberger is very nervous to open the proceedings and will not look at Mr. Terrell. When Terrell begins his examination of her, an obvious cloud of agitated malevolence drapes over her. Her eyes slitted as she responds to Terrell's questions. Judge Jimmy is both curious and amused by her drama.

Q. Ms. Lineberger, how old are you?

A. I am eighteen years old.

Q. Are you in school?

A. No, I am not.

Q. When was the last time you attended school?

A. Well, it was back about the ninth. Well, I've done forgotten because I got a baby. I forgot. I ain't even been keeping count.

Q. It was in the ninth grade?

A. About the ninth or the tenth; I've done forgot.

Q. How old were you then?

A. About sixteen.

Q. About sixteen and in the ninth grade. What is your present address, please?

A. Ten fourteen Todd Street.

Q. And where is that in relationship to the 1500 block of East 15th Street where the shooting occurred that you were talking about?

A. What do you mean relationship?

Q. How close it is to there?

A. Well, from my house until there?

Q. Yes.

A. It's a long ways.

Q. How far is a long ways?

A. I don't know how long, but you've got to ride on the highway to get to my house.

Q. Ten minutes...twenty minutes?

A. I don't know.

Q. Who do you live with?

A. My mother.

Q. And your baby?

A. Takisha, my baby— we live with my momma at home.

MR. TERRELL: I'm sorry, Your Honor. I can't hear her answers.

A (By the Witness) I stay with my mother—me and my baby and my brother. We are our family.

Q. (By Mr. Terrell) Do you work?

A. No...I get AFDC.

Q. How long have you gotten AFDC?

A. Ever since I was sixteen when I first had my baby.

Q. I see. On this day of April 22, 19XX, what time was it when this shooting occurred?

A. Well, I know happy hour was from nine to ten, and it was after that—after happy hours. I would say close to ten-thirty—something like that. I'm just giving a time because I didn't have no watch on.

Q. I see. Well, you wear a watch, don't you?

A. I just got this watch.

Q. Was that a gift from somebody?

A. Don't worry about it.

THE COURT: I'm sorry; I didn't hear you.

THE WITNESS: That's for me to know.

THE COURT: I'm ordering you to answer the question, please.

Q. (By Mr. Terrell) Where did you get that watch?

A. What? Where did I get it?

Q. Yes.

A. I bought it.

Q. Does your mother work?

MR. WEINMAN: Object.

THE COURT: I'll sustain.

MR. TERRELL: I'll move on, Your Honor.

Q. (By Mr. Terrell) Let me ask you, Ms. Lineberger, how long had you been at—this was a drink house, wasn't it?

A. I said I was at Curt Minor Drinking House.

Q. Does Curt Minor own that property?

A. I guess so. It's in his name.

Q. And does he live there?

A. I don't know all that. All I know I come there.

Q. You do what?

A. I be there.

Q. And how long has that been Curt Minor's Drink House?

MR. WEINMAN: Objection.

THE COURT: Sustained.

Q. (By Mr. Terrell) Do you know how long it has been a drink house?

MR. WEINMAN: Objection.

THE COURT: Sustained.

Q. (By Mr. Terrell) Do you drink?

MR. WEINMAN: Object. Well, I'll withdraw the objection.

THE COURT: Overruled.

MR. TERRELL: Thank you.

Q. (By Mr. Terrell) Do you drink?

MR. TERRELL: Your Honor, I'd ask you to instruct her to answer the question.

THE COURT: I'm sorry—

A. (By the Witness) Yes, I drink beer.

Q. (By Mr. Terrell) You drink beer?

A. That's right.

Q. Had you been drinking beer on the evening in question?

A. I had one.

Q. You had one beer?

A. That's all.

Q. How long had you been at the drink house?

A. Ever since happy hours started.

Q. And what time did happy hour start?

A. Nine to ten.

Q. You had gotten there around nine o'clock?

A. Yes.

Q. And so you had been there about an hour and a half, is that right?

A. Ever since happy hour started.

Q. Now, how many people were in the house?

A. A houseful.

Q. It was crowded, wasn't it?

A. You had to step on people's foot to get by.

Q. And how long had it been crowded?

A. Ever since happy hour started from nine to ten.

Q. Was there music playing?

A. Yes.

Q. And had it been playing ever since happy hour started?

A. Uh-huh (yes).

Q. How was the house lighted?

A. Well, it was red lights, but up at the bar, they have lights like Stroh lights and stuff like that.

Q. Strobe lights?

A. You know, like lights like people has in drink house—Stroh lights and Miller lights like this.

Q. Do you mean like Stroh like Stroh beer?

A. Yes.

Q. Like S-t-r-o-h?

A. Um-hum (yes).

Q. Do they have strobe lights...lights that flash?

A. No. Like a light there, a little light there.

Q. And they also had red lights in there, didn't they?

A. Sure did.

Q. Now, your nickname is Moms, isn't it?

A. Moms.

Q. Moms?

A. Moms.

Q. How do you spell that?

A. Mom.

Q. Like your momma?

A. Momma.

MR. WEINMAN: Objection.

THE COURT: Sustained.

Q. (By Mr. Terrell) What was your relationship to Benjamin Franklin Winphrie?

A. Do it matter?

Q. Yes, it does. Answer the question, please.

A. A friend.

Q. You were his girlfriend, weren't you?

A. Why do you want to know that?

THE COURT: Wait a minute, ma'am. Answer the question, please.

MR. WEINMAN: Answer the question.

A. (By the Witness) No.

THE COURT: The answer is no.

Q. (By Mr. Terrell) Ms. Lineberger, you have spoken to me before, haven't you?

A. Let me tell you because you came over there to the welfare place where I was.

THE COURT: Ma'am, wait just a minute. I want you to listen to the question, please, and answer the question. Repeat your question, please.

Q. (By Mr. Terrell) Ms. Lineberger, you have spoken to me before, haven't you?

A. I sure did because you was messing with me...that's why.

Q. And I came over to the welfare place?

A. The social service place.

Q. The social service place to see you?

A. Uh-huh (yes), and I was wondering what it was about.

Q. And I asked you if you would go to my office with me, didn't I?

A. You told me to take a ride with you, and I told you that I had to go home to my baby. Then you come asking me all these old dumb questions—don't even concern the case.

Q. And you did come to my office, didn't you?

A. Yeah, because I was in your car. You took me; you tricked me. That's what you did.

Q. And did you talk to me?

A. You questioned me, didn't you?

Q. Yes, and did you answer my questions?

A. I answered in a nasty way.

Q. And then did you ask me to give you a ride back to social services—?

A. I told you that I was—don't tell no lie like that. No, I did not; I told you to take me home.

Q. And did I take you home?

A. —because I was ready to go.

Q. Did I take you home?

A. You sure did, and you let me out because I was ready to get out.

Q. And did you show me the drink house where this happened?

A. You seen it.

Q. Did you show me where it was?

A. I sure did, but that ain't got nothing to do with this murder.

Q. Did you show me where they found Ben Franklin's body?

A. (No response)

Q. Did you?

A. I sure did, but that ain't got nothing to do with the shooting.

THE COURT: Wait a minute, ma'am. That's why I'm here—to determine whether it has anything to do with it. Now you answer his questions, please.

MR. TERRELL: Thank you.

Q. (By Mr. Terrell) Who were you talking to when you were sitting at the bar?

A. A friend, Sam Roberts, and Benjamin.

Q. And Benjamin?

A. That's right. That's what I said.

Q. Did you see where the gun came from that you said my client shot Ben Franklin with?

Friday Calls

A. I seen him with the gun in his hand. That's good enough.

Q. Did you see where it came from?

A. It came from him. I seen him with the gun. I don't care where it came from, but I seen him shoot Benjamin Franklin; sure did.

Q. Did you see where the gun came from?

A. I did not, but he had it.

Q. You did not see David Edwards at the drink house?

A. No, I seen him in the drink house. Yeah, he was there.

Q. He was there?

A. He sure was.

Q. Did you see David Edwards bring the gun to Ben Franklin?

A. No.

Q. You didn't?

A. No.

Q. Was Ben Franklin your boyfriend?

MR. WEINMAN: Objection.

THE COURT: I believe she's already answered that. Sustained.

Q. (By Mr. Terrell) Did you see Pete Miller that night?

A. I sure did.

Q. And did you see Pete Miller with a gun?

A. After it occurred.

Q. What kind of gun did you see Pete Miller with?

A. It looked like a twenty-two to me.

Q. What kind of gun did you see Kenny Peak with?

A. It looked like a thirty-eight.

Q. Do you know what these things—do you know what these guns look like?

A. I've seen a thirty-eight gun before.

Q. Now did Ben Franklin wear jewelry?

A. Yes.

Q. What kind of jewelry did he wear?

A. He had a watch.

Q. Did he have some rings?

A. He sure did.

Q. Who is wearing his rings now?

A. I don't know.

Q. Didn't you tell me Curt Minor had his rings?

A. (No response)

Q. Didn't you?

A. Yes, I did, but that don't matter about the killing.

Q. Now Ben Franklin carried a lot of money, didn't he?

A. Every man will have some money not unless they wouldn't be—if they ain't have no money; ain't nobody going to walk around broke no more.

Q. Ben Franklin carried around a lot of money with him—four or five hundred dollars at a time, didn't he?

A. I don't know; you tell me.

Q. Didn't you tell me that?

A. This is what I told you. I told you ain't no man going to be in no drink house if they ain't got no money because ladies do be wanting drinks.

Q. And so Ben was one of these people that carried money, wasn't he?

A. He wasn't broke.

Q. Do you know what happened to his money when they found his body?

A. I guess it was gone.

Q. Do you guess or do you know?

A. When they—what you talking—make yourself clear on that.

Q. Did Ben Franklin have money with him that night?

A. He sure did. I told you ain't no man going to be broke in no drink house.

Q. Did you see his money?

A. I ain't got to see it to know. This come from my mind. I know.

Q. He spent it on you, didn't he?

A. No, he did not.

Q. He didn't spend it on you?

A. Not that night. Why you worrying about all that now?

Q. Did Ben Franklin ever use drugs?

A. Not that I know of.

MR. WEINMAN: Object.

THE COURT: Sustained as to that question.

Q. (By Mr. Terrell) Do you use drugs?

A. No, I do not.

MR. WEINMAN: Object.

THE COURT: Sustained to a general question—

Q. (By Mr. Terrell) On the night in question had you used any drugs?

A. No.

Q. Now you saw Kenny Peak—did Kenny Peak remove the gun from his person?

A. Say that again.

Q. Did he, before he shot Ben Franklin, remove—take the gun out of his pants or his pocket or what?

A. What you talking about? Before he shot Bo?

Q. Yes.

A. I already told you I seen him with the gun, and I seen him shoot the man. That's what I'm talking about.

THE COURT: But the question was, ma'am, did you see him pull a gun out of his pocket or under his pants or—

THE WITNESS: Huh-uh (no). I just seen him with it in his hand.

Q. (By Mr. Terrell) Did you see Kenny Peak before you saw him start to shoot?

A. Yes, because I was talking to Homer.

Q. Is Homer and Kenny the same person?

A. He is Kenneth Peak—Homer—to me.

Q. And had you been talking to him before he started shooting?

A. Yeah. A friendly conversation like always.

Q. What had you been talking about?

A. Huh?

Q. What had you been talking about?

A. I don't do nothing but jive with him.

Q. Well, what were you talking about?

A. I done forgot. This has been last month some time.

Q. It was what?

A. I done forgot what I have said to him just like I'm talking to you.

Q. So how long had you seen—how long had Kenneth Peak or Homer Peak been there before he shot—

A. He was there early during the day. Him, Curt, Pete Miller—all those, because when I seen them, I walked over to them and asked them had they seen Bo.

Q. And so what time was that?

A. That was early in the daytime.

Q. Was the light...the sun still shining?

A. The sun was out.

Q. So you were there when the sun was out?

A. I had came up there, and I left because I moves around.

Q. How long had you been there earlier?

A. I just came up there and left.

Q. How long were you there?

A. Not about five minutes—not even that long.

Q. What time of the day was that?

A. I just told you.

Q. What time? I'm sorry; I didn't catch the time.

A. About four-thirty or five; it was in the evening time.

Q. Four-thirty or five-thirty?

A. Somewhere in there because I told you I didn't have no watch on. I don't give you—

Q. Do you have a car?

A. No.

Q. How did you get there?

A. On my legs, on my feet...I walked.

Q. Did you walk from your home where you live with your mother?

A. No.

Q. Where did you walk from?

A. I was already in the neighborhood around there at the soda bar getting me something to eat.

Q. Had you been to Sam's Liquor House before you went up there the first time?

A. Why do it—do it really matter?

Q. Had you been to Sam's Liquor House before you went there the first time?

A. What you talking—when I first went?

Q. Yes.

A. I went through there because I travels—I was walking—doing a little stroll to lose weight.

Q. So now you've told me you've been to Curt Minor's Liquor House at least on two occasions on this day, is that right?

A. I go—I leaves and then I comes back, and then I leave again and come back.

Q. Well, where did you go?

A. Huh?

Q. Where did you go?

A. About my business.

Q. Well, where did you go?

A. Hunh? What you mean? Where did I go? I be going everywhere. So you—

Q. Well, tell me some of the places you went.

MR. WEINMAN: Objection.

THE COURT: Sustained. You'll have to be more specific as to the time.

Q. (By Mr. Terrell) Now were Bo and Kenny Peak arguing that night?

A. No.

Q. They weren't?

A. They sure wasn't.

Q. Were they mad about something?

A. No, they was smiling and grinning. He was grinning—his face.

Q. Everybody was happy, weren't they?

A. That's right. Seemed that way to me.

Q. And you weren't impaired in any way?

A. What you mean?

Q. You weren't drunk, were you?

A. I sure wasn't. My head was on straight.

Q. And you had not been using drugs, had you?

MR. WEINMAN: Objection.

A. (By the Witness) I sure had not.

THE COURT: Well, she says no.

Q. (By Mr. Terrell) All right. And did you—so you could remember everything real clearly?

A. That's right.

Q. And weren't Kenny Peak and Bo Franklin really good friends?

A. It seemed that way because he was smiling and grinning with him all the time.

Q. But now you've known Bo Franklin for a long time, haven't you?

A. Why? I sure did.

Q. And you've known Kenny Peak for a long time, too, haven't you?

A. No.

Q. How long have you known Kenny Peak?

A. Ever since I got my apartment on that trashy place on 18th Street.

THE COURT: We don't know when that was, ma'am.

A. (By the Witness) It was about November.

Q. (By Mr. Terrell) Have you still got that apartment?

A. No. I told you I was staying home with my momma—me and my baby.

Q. Were you on AFDC when you got that apartment?

MR. WEINMAN: Objection.

THE COURT: Sustained.

Q. (By Mr. Terrell) Was Ben Franklin arguing with anybody about anything?

A. No.

Q. He was very happy, wasn't he?

A. He was real happy.

Q. Now what kind of work did Ben Franklin do? Did he have a job?

A. I don't know.

Q. You have known him a long time?

A. Just because you know somebody, you don't have to know everything they do and how they do it—where their money come from and all that, because, see, that ain't my concern. You see what I'm talking about?

THE COURT: Would you repeat your question? I don't know whether she answered it.

MR. TERRELL: She didn't, Your Honor, but I'm not going to repeat it.

THE COURT: You asked her if he had a job.

MR. TERRELL: That's all right.

Q. (By Mr. Terrell) Do you know these people sitting out here?

A. Who? These people?

Q. On the front row.

MR. WEINMAN: Objection.

THE COURT: Sustained.

Q. (By Mr. Terrell) Did you come to court with some of these people?

MR. WEINMAN: Objection.

THE COURT: All right. Sustained.

Q. (By Mr. Terrell) Do you know the lady in the green jacket?

MR. WEINMAN: Objection.

THE COURT: Sustained.

Q. (By Mr. Terrell) Who is Deana?

MR. WEINMAN: Objection.

THE COURT: Sustained to form.

Q. (By Mr. Terrell) Do you know someone named Deana who was at the drink house that night?

MR. WEINMAN: Objection.

THE COURT: Overruled.

MR. TERRELL: You may answer.

THE COURT: Do you know someone named Deana—

A. (By the Witness) I don't know her; I know of her. I know her name just like I know your name.

Q. (By Mr. Terrell) Was she at the drink house the night of the shooting?

A. Yes, she was.

Q. Was David Edwards at the drink house the night of the shooting?

A. I don't know him. I might know his face, but I don't know him. Do you have him here?

Q. Do you know Pete Miller?

A. Yes, I do.

Q. Was he at the drink house the night of the shooting?

A. Sure was.

Q. Was Dell—somebody named Dell at the drink house the night of the shooting?

A. I don't know him.

Q. What's Curt Minor's wife's name?

MR. WEINMAN: Objection.

THE COURT: Sustained.

Q. (By Mr. Terrell) She was there, wasn't she?

MR. WEINMAN: Objection.

THE COURT: Sustained.

Q. (By Mr. Terrell) Was Curt Minor's wife present at the drink house when the shooting took place?

A. She sure was.

Q. Who else saw the shooting besides you?

A. My cousin.

MR. WEINMAN: Object.

THE COURT: I'll sustain as to what someone saw.

Q. (By Mr. Terrell) Did you have a cousin that was there at the drink house the night of the shooting?

MR. WEINMAN: Objection.

THE COURT: Overruled.

MR. TERRELL: You may answer.

A. (By the Witness) Yes.

Q. What is her name?

A. Melody Lewis.

Q. Melody Lewis...Melanie Lewis?

A. Sure.

Q. Is she your first cousin?

MR. WEINMAN: Objection.

THE COURT: Overruled.

Q. (By Mr. Terrell) Is she your first cousin?

A. No. Does it matter?

Q. What is her address, please?

A. I do not know all of that.

MR. WEINMAN: Objection.

THE COURT: Sustained.

Q. (By Mr. Terrell) How long did you see—did Kenny Peak talk to Ben Franklin before he shot him?

MR. WEINMAN: Objection. She said that about three times.

MR. TERRELL: Your Honor, she hasn't. She just said she saw him stand up—

THE COURT: Overruled. All right. One more time I'll let you ask the question.

Q. (By Mr. Terrell) Did Kenny Peak talk to Ben Winphrie before he started shooting?

A. A friendly conversation. Like I told you, everybody was talking friendly.

MR. TERRELL: Your Honor, may I approach the witness, please?

THE COURT: Yes, sir.

Q. (By Mr. Terrell) Now, Ms. Lineberger, how close—I am standing how far away from you now?

A. I don't know. We close. You can see me.

Q. About four or five feet?

A. I don't know all of that; I don't know about feet and all—inches.

Q. Was Kenny Peak as close to Ben Franklin as I am to you now?

A. He was close enough.

Q. Was he this close? I've stepped forward.

A. Wait a minute. We ain't got no bar here, but he was...go back some just a little bit. He was close enough.

Q. Was this about the distance between them?

A. Okay. I'm Kenneth Peak. I'm behind at the bar.

Q. Yes, ma'am.

A. You turn this way.

Q. Okay.

A. You look out that way.

Q. All right.

A. Say like you at the bar...you behind the bar.

Q. All right. Am I back here a little bit?

A. No. I told you to come up here.

Q. You put me right where you want me.

A. Right there. And say you're behind the bar. You can see people out there.

Q. Here's the bar, and I'm Ben Franklin?

A. Right. That's right. And I'm Kenneth Peak.

Q. All right. Are you as far away from me as he was to him that night?

A. What? See, I'm directly—say I'm right here. I'm right there in front of Benjamin Franklin.

Q. Were you sitting right here across the bar?

A. I'm directly—say I'm right here—I'm right there in front of your face.

Q. Okay. So, Ben Franklin—

A. Uh-huh (yes). And I'm right there. Just pretend I'm there, and I'm Kenneth Peak. Okay. This chair is in my way. I am Kenneth Peak, and I'm right there, and this is the end of the bar. I'm standing right here and that is the distance. And then he started firing. See what I'm saying?

Q. When he started firing, he stopped at some point, didn't he?

A. He shot, and he looked around, and he kept on shooting. And Ben was going down.

Q. Did you hear—were you watching him shoot?

A. I sure was. I was right there.

Q. And while he was—he would fire a shot, right?

A. He was firing his gun—that thirty-eight.

Q. And he fired how many shots the first time?

A. Well, I heard a shot, and he was doing some cool—you see what I'm saying? (Witness indicating.)

Q. Did he pull off four shots in a row?

A. No.

Q. Did he pull off just one shot and then look around?

A. All I know he shot Bo. Bo went back. He shot him and some way Bo went back. He seen him go back, and then he kept shooting like he was a dog or something. You see what I'm saying?

Q. And he looked around, didn't he?

A. He sure did. He looked around and kept on firing like he was crazy and intoxicated.

Q. Did he fire a shot and then look around, or did he fire two shots and then look around?

A. I'm going to tell you...like I told you, I wasn't keeping count of the shots. You see what I'm saying? But I know he shot that man. You see what I'm saying?

Q. Now, you answered one of Mr. Weinman's questions earlier. You said he shot about four times?

A. He sure did. I heard four gunshots. I don't know if all of them was his or what.

Q. Did you hear—now, you were watching Kenny Peak while he was shooting, weren't you?

A. I sure was. He was at the end of the bar, and Bo was right there; when he shot him in the neck, he went back. He didn't have to shoot the man no more because he seen the man was going down then. And he kept on and on and kept on. Do you see what I'm saying?

Q. Did you see Kenny Peak shoot Bo Franklin in the neck?

A. Yes, he did.

Q. And did you see him shoot him in the side?

A. He shot the man. I wasn't keeping—the man had on the leather coat. How do I know all of this? I know he shot him.

Q. Did you see him shoot him in the side?

A. He shot the man.

Q. You said you saw him shoot him in the neck, right?

A. I seen—yes, he don't—he shot the man, and the man went back. He didn't have to do no more. He kept on shooting like he was crazy, like he was—

Q. Crazy?

A. That's right.

Q. Was he crazy?

MR. WEINMAN: Objection.

THE COURT: Sustained.

MR. WEINMAN: I don't see any need for him to be up there.

MR. TERRELL: Your Honor, I think it is absolutely critical. She testified earlier.

THE COURT: I think you can go back to—

MR. TERRELL: All right.

Q. (By Mr. Terrell) You said earlier in your response to the District Attorney's question that he shot him four times, is that right?

A. I told him that I heard four gunshots.

Q. Did you see four gunshots?

A. I heard them. That's good enough for me.

Q. Did you see four gunshots?

A. He shot the man. Did I see the gun...the bullets coming out of the gun?

Q. Did you see the gun go off four times?

A. I sure did.

Q. You saw it go off four times?

A. I sure did.

Q. Did you not hear any other gunshots?

A. It sounded like something else was going on, but I was...I had my mind on him because he was shooting Bo.

Q. And it sounded to you at some point, didn't it, like some other gun was being fired, too, didn't it?

A. Sure did. But let me tell you this—

MR. TERRELL: Now wait just a minute. Your Honor, I'm going to ask her to be responsive here.

THE COURT: All right.

MR. WEINMAN: I think she's trying to explain her answer.

THE WITNESS: That's what I'm doing. I'm telling you what I saw and what I heard, and I can't tell you no more now. And I can't add nothing. I'm not fixing to change nothing around, so you know—

MR. TERRELL: I understand.

Q. (By Mr. Terrell) You looked at Kenny Peak while he was shooting, didn't you?

A. I sure did. I seen the man.

Q. And you saw the gun going off, didn't you?

A. Uh-huh (yes) You could see the fire coming from the gun. See what I'm talking about.

Q. And you saw that happen four times?

A. I heard...yes, I did, and I'm not going to change it. Yes. The gun—

Q. You're not going to change it no matter what, are you?

A. I don't care if hell comes—

MR. WEINMAN: Objection.

THE COURT: Sustained.

Q. (By Mr. Terrell) When the gun was not being fired that Kenny Peak had in his hand, you heard other gunshots, didn't you?

A. I told you...let me tell you something, man.

THE COURT: You may sit down, ma'am.

THE WITNESS: Okay.

A. (By the Witness) I saw him shoot Bo, and that's all I got to say.

THE COURT: Would you repeat your question? Listen to the question, ma'am.

Q. (By Mr. Terrell) Please listen to me carefully, Ms. Lineberger. You have testified that you saw Kenny Peak shoot Bo Winphrie?

A. Yeah, he did.

Q. You saw it with your eyes?

A. I saw it with my eyes and I heard it with my ears.

Q. And you saw the flames jumping out of the gun?

A. That's what I said, yes.

Q. And you saw him shoot how many times?

A. About four times.

Q. Is about four—is that four times?

A. Four times.

MR. WEINMAN: Objection.

THE COURT: Sustained.

Q. (By Mr. Terrell) You also testified that you saw Ben Franklin fall?

A. He was going down; he was going down, but he was shooting him like he was a dog. That was too cold for me.

Q. You also said in response to one of my questions that there was something else going on, didn't you?

A. Everybody was...the music was playing, and then it stopped. And everybody was getting out of the way. You know what I'm talking about?

Q. And what was the something else that was going on?

A. Something else?

Q. Didn't you hear another gun being fired? Didn't you tell me, Ms. Lineberger...

A. It sounded like two guns going off at the same time, but I seen him shoot the man four times with my eyes.

Q. After the shooting what did you do?

A. Huh? What did I do?

Q. Yes, ma'am.

A. I was still sitting there on the stool scared to move, and then Ben told—Bo said, "Mom." And I got up and went around and I kind of just—he was—like he was trying to get up or something. And he was trying to tell me something. What he was trying to tell me, I don't know.

Q. So Ben Franklin called for you, didn't he?

A. Yes, he did because he heard me— (Witness indicating.)

Q. You were crying?

A. He heard me; I sure was.

Q. And did you go to him?

A. I went to see what he wanted; he called to me.

Q. What did he say to you?

A. "Mom."

Q. Did he say anything else?

A. He didn't get a chance.

Q. And then what did you do?

A. What did I do? I got out of the way; when they told me to get out the way, I got out of the way.

Q. Who told you to get out of the way?

A. Curt Minor.

Q. And what did Curt Minor do? Did he then go to Mr. Franklin—Mr. Winphrie's side?

A. Huh?

Q. What did Mr. Minor do?

A. What did he tell me?

Q. What did Mr. Minor do?

A. I guess he was trying to get him out of the house.

Q. Did Ben Franklin then get up?

A. He was trying to help me at first, but somebody told me, "Bitch, get the fuck out of the way." Curt told me, "Bitch, get the fuck out of the way." I didn't know what I was doing so I got out of the way.

Q. And did they help Ben Franklin to his feet?

A. They got him out.

Q. Did they help Ben Franklin get up?

A. Yeah.

Q. And did Ben Franklin then walk?

A. I ain't seen all that because I was going crazy then.

Q. You were very excited at that point?

A. I was mad.

Q. From the time that gun started shooting, you had gotten very upset, hadn't you?

A. I was still mad and I was looking too.

Q. You were what?

A. I was looking. I was mad, but I couldn't do nothing.

Q. Did you talk to Mr. Weinman today before you took the stand?

A. Who is Mr. Weinman?

Q. This man right here.

A. I think I've seen him. How you doing?

Q. And you have talked to other people at the District Attorney's office, too, haven't you?

A. Like who?

Q. Mr. Walker.

A. I know Miller, and where's Wilkins—right there—the good guys.

Q. Had you been over here—they're the good guys?

A. They are the good guys.

Q. Have you been over here to this—was Bo Franklin a good guy?

MR. WEINMAN: Objection.

THE COURT: Sustained. Do you have any other questions, Mr. Terrell?

MR. TERRELL: Yes, I do, Your Honor.

Q. (By Mr. Terrell) What did you do—did you see where Ben Franklin went after he had been shot?

A. Okay. Afterwards—after he got shot and everything, I went on out the door crying and going on and screaming. And then I seen him laying in the church yard up on this hill kind of.

Q. How long after that did you see him?

A. The policewoman came. Where she at? It was the blond-headed lady came.

Q. Blond-headed police lady?

A. Yeah, lady.

Q. Did you know her name?

A. Huh uh (no) because I forgot. I was upset.

Q. And did you see Ben Franklin fall out there in the church yard?

A. I didn't see all that because I was still in the house screaming and crying and going on. And somebody came there and got me and brought me outside.

Q. And then you saw that Ben Franklin—

A. I seen him.

Q. And did you later go on down to Sam's Liquor House?

MR. WEINMAN: Objection to what she did—

THE COURT: Well, sustained.

Q. (By Mr. Terrell) Did you see Pete Miller later that night?

A. Yes.

Q. And where did you see him?

A. Down at Sam's in the basement.

Q. In Sam's Liquor House, didn't you?

A. Yes.

Q. And did he have a gun with him?

A. Yes.

Q. What kind of gun was it?

A. Looked like a twenty-two in his right back pocket.

Q. And didn't somebody want you to come outside?

A. Uh-huh (yes).

Q. And what happened then?

MR. WEINMAN: Objection.

THE COURT: Sustained.

Q. (By Mr. Terrell) Now you say Homer Peak had a thirty-eight, didn't you?

A. He sure did.

Q. Has anyone threatened you about testifying in this court?

A. Ain't nobody here.

Q. Haven't you told me that some people had made some threats on you?

A. Yes, but it didn't get next to me though.

Q. It didn't bother you?

A. (Nodded head no.)

Q. What did they say to you?

MR. WEINMAN: Objection.

THE COURT: Sustained.

Q. (By Mr. Terrell) Were you frightened?

MR. WEINMAN: Objection.

THE COURT: Sustained. She said it didn't get to her.

Q. (By Mr. Terrell) How many times have you been threatened?

MR. WEINMAN: Objection.

THE COURT: Sustained.

MR. TERRELL: Just a minute, please, Your Honor.

Q. (By Mr. Terrell) After Mr. Peak fired the shots at Mr. Winphrie—let me ask you this: have there been any fires at this place or this house where the shooting took place?

MR. WEINMAN: Objection.

THE COURT: Sustained. You don't have to answer that.

Q. (By Mr. Terrell) Since this shooting have there been any fires?

MR. WEINMAN: Objection.

THE COURT: Sustained.

MR. TERRELL: Thank you. I don't have any further questions.

THE COURT: Thank you, ma'am. You may come down.

MR. TERRELL: One last question, please.

Q. (By Mr. Terrell) Are you crying?

MR. WEINMAN: Objection.

THE COURT: Sustained.

A. (By the Witness) What does it look like, punk?

THE COURT: All right, Mr. Terrell. Is he out on bond?

MR. TERRELL: No, Your Honor, and I'd like to put one witness—is that all you're going to put on?

MR. WEINMAN: Yes.

MR. TERRELL: I'd like to put one witness on, Your Honor.

THE COURT: For what purpose?

MR. TERRELL: To talk about this twenty-two, Your Honor. She testified that she thought she heard other shots going on.

THE COURT: Well, now that—

MR. TERRELL: It won't take long, Your Honor.

THE COURT: If you don't get into any jury matters.

MR. TERRELL: We're not, Your Honor. You need to be sworn.

WHEREUPON, the witness, MATTIE CANE, upon being first duly sworn, testified on her oath as follows:

DIRECT EXAMINATION
BY MR. TERRELL TO MATTIE CANE:

Q. Ms. Cane, would you give us your name and address, please, ma'am?

A. Mattie Cane, 2809 Piedmont Circle.

Q. Is it 2009?

A. It's 2809 Piedmont Circle.

Q. And how long have you been a resident of Winston-Salem?

A. Ever since '60.

Q. You know who Pete Miller is, don't you?

A. Yes, I do.

Q. Did you have some twenty-two caliber bullets that you gave to Pete Miller?

A. I had twenty-two shots.

Q. Yes, ma'am. Did you give those to Pete Miller?

A. I give Pete Miller some bullets—January.

Q. In January?

A. Yes, sir.

Q. And did you see him from time to time?

A. Yes, sir.

Q. Did you know that he still had your bullets?

A. No. I didn't ask him.

Q. When is the last time you saw Pete Miller?

Q. Was the last you knew about these twenty-two caliber bullets you gave Pete Miller in January, correct?

A. Yes, sir.

THE COURT: Thank you, ma'am. You can come down.

MR. TERRELL: Thank you, ma'am.

THE COURT: Has a bond been set?

MR. TERRELL: Your Honor, he's under a $500,000 bond. And I'd like to be heard very quickly.

    He has had a prior record although nothing serious. He has had some traffic matters; he's had some misdemeanor—marijuana; he's had some trespassing. There is no propensity of violence anywhere in his past history. I knew his mother; I knew members of his family, including his sister. He has—it would be

Friday Calls

very helpful to me, Your Honor, if he would be able to have an attainable bond. He has no employment right now, although, he does have an opportunity for employment.

This happened over in a part of Winston-Salem that Your Honor is well familiar with from having sat on the bench in this jurisdiction for a period of time. It is difficult to locate witnesses; it is especially difficult for a white lawyer to locate witnesses. It would be very helpful to have access to Mr. Peak and his locale.

I would be certainly willing to stipulate to the Court that any conditions in order to secure his presence—his family is of limited financial means. Most of them have turned their backs on him during the course of this trial—the situation he is confronted with. He has a sister and, in essence, a family friend who will provide him small sums of money. I am privately retained. This is not your typical Murder One case. I think the State's got problems with the way their proof is going to come in and the places that it's going to come from. And I would ask Your Honor's help in terms of setting a bond that is reasonable under the standards that we apply.

THE COURT: I don't know if this is important or not, but this is the man that shot Bo Diddley.

MR. TERRELL: And Your Honor knows Bo Diddley. I wasn't going to go into that. Ben Franklin Winphrie a/k/a Bo Diddley was one of the real players in this courthouse for a long time.

THE COURT: I think for his own protection—anyway, does the State want to be heard?

MR. WEINMAN: The man has a record, and I don't think the pretrial release conditions are set so the lawyer can prepare his case. He doesn't seem to have any problem locating this witness.

THE COURT: I understand there's a hold on him for Superior Court?

MR. TERRELL: It is involving—he was supposed to comply to one hundred ninety-three dollar fine, Your Honor, and he's been in jail. Ever since he's been arrested on this he's been in jail.

MR. WEINMAN: I think if you'll look at his record and see why he's being held, he's not very good at meeting his obligations.

THE COURT: All right. Order for arrest, Order for arrest. I'll tell you what; I'll lower his bond to $250,000.

MR. TERRELL: Thank you, Your Honor.

MR. WEINMAN: Your Honor, may I approach the bench with this order?

MR. TERRELL: Your Honor, may Mr. Weinman and I both approach the bench?

THE COURT: Yes.

(Bench conference.)

MR. TERRELL: That's all we have, Your Honor.

THE COURT: Thank you.

WHEREUPON, at 11:40 o'clock a.m., the hearing in the above-styled cause was adjourned.

CERTIFICATION
STATE OF NORTH CAROLINA
COUNTY OF FORSYTH

I, Clarice Einstein, Notary Public and Court Reporter in and for the County of Forsyth, State of North Carolina, do hereby certify:

That on the 19th day of May, 19XX, there appeared before me the foregoing witnesses in the above-entitled cause;

That the said probable cause hearing was then taken at the time and place herein mentioned, commencing at 10:56 o'clock a.m. on Thursday, May 19, 19XX;

That the testimony was taken by me and recorded by Stenomask and thereafter transcribed by me, and the foregoing 47 pages are a complete and accurate record of all the testimony given;

That the undersigned, Clarice Einstein, is not of kin or in any way associated with any of the parties to said cause of action or their counsel, and that I am not interested in the event thereof.

IN WITNESS WHEREOF, I have hereunto set my hand and seal this the 2nd day of June, 19XX.

/s/ Clarice Einstein
Clarice Einstein
Court Reporter
My Commission Expires:
July 30, 19XX

Chapter Twenty-Four

On Go

Terrell had learned to keep a number of clocks in his brain. The "when to wake up clock," "the when to shut up clock," "the time he might just be able to find a witness clock," "the best time to schmooze a judge or a cop clock," and "the every bit as important when does really important evidence disappear clock." His office had gotten a call some weeks ago that Bo's autopsy was done. The "90-day come get him or he's gone clock" is now activated.

Three months and a week later, Terrell goes back to see Podgorny. When he arrives again with no appointment, Lee Ann Jepson recognizes him quickly and with animated interest and accommodation.

"Well, hello stranger. Where have you been keeping yourself? We called you a while back about that fellow, Thomas Jefferson or George Washington...I thought you'd be right over." A silvery giggle and pretty batting eyes completed the welcoming trifecta.

Terrell gathers the lovely bait and replies with a smile, "Well, hello, stranger yourself. For your information, Miss Lee Ann, Lee Ann, isn't it? I've been busy standing for Lady Justice and moving quickly as I do. Besides, a watched pot never boils, right...?"

She nods, just for assent and surely not for comprehension and smiles back, her eyes rising as her chin rises from her chair. She rolls back from her cubby. Terrell looks at her long legs. She knows he looked. She smooths her skirt and stands.

He says, "Miss Lee Ann. Do you know why a smart fellow keeps moving?"

"Why?" She is amused.

"So they can never get a clean shot at you."

She cocks an eye and asks, "Do you ever slow down? Just a little bit...?"

"Sometimes," he says and the words tail off. Hold the mood. Move the mood. Mind the mood.

She clears her throat and shifts back to officialdom.

"I suppose you are here to see Dr. Podgorny?"

"Yes, hoping to get filled in on the final autopsy results for the late, great Benjamin Winphrie."

"Right. That's it. Benjamin Franklin. I do recall it was a history-like name. Well, I will let Dr. P. know you are here. I am sure he will be able to spend a little time with you."

He bows slightly and speaks a sincere, firm, "Thank you" and then says, "Before you go back, would you please check to see if the dead man's remains are still here?" He pauses. "It's important."

She understands that, pulls a fat, black notebook open, flips the pages, fingers scanning the lined entries, mumbling to herself and then looking up quizzically. "He's gone. Is that good?"

"Well, yes, yes it is."

"Then good. I'll go get Dr. P."

As she moves through the swinging double doors to the back, Terrell watches her carefully. She is of fine proportion and stock. Terrell notes he is glad he still has a pulse. He reminds himself too that in the ever-lurking jangling jar of libido, pheromones can instantly strike a man blind. He exhales long with intent, clears his head and waits.

Soon the doors swing back open, the old-world gentleman holding them open for Lee Ann's entry. He holds a slim file in his hand.

"Mr. Terrell. How nice to see you again. Let us go into this small room next door and we can talk for a bit."

"Thank you, sir."

And they do. It isn't too long a visit and Terrell is careful to pay close attention without taking notes. He keeps is eyes on Podgorny, letting the doctor talk in narrative, not interrupting with questions. As they conclude, Podgorny hands him a copy of the file.

"Here. As you well know, this is the same copy I will give the authorities.

If you have further questions, please get back to me."

"Thank you, Doctor. I wish it were under different circumstances, but I guess I will see you in court when the time comes."

"Oh, do not fret. It is a shared occupational hazard. We got into professions that call for us to all go into the ring together from time to time. Some days I kill the bull. Some days the bull kills me. Right!?" He laughs, jovially claps Terrell on the back and says, "I must go back to my quiet patients now. Miss Jepson will help see you out."

As Terrell goes out the entry doors, he turns and looks at Jepson. "Buy you a drink sometime?"

"Yes, that would be nice. Please come back and see me and we can make a little plan. Okay?"

"Yes, I will. Thank you."

She says, "Good luck with whatever all that is all about. I hope it turns out good for you."

"Thank you. Let us see said the blind man. Maybe I can tell you all about it one of these days when it is all said and done."

"Oh, that would be interesting, I bet."

He nods and is on his way again.

Terrell knows a trial setting is imminent. He drives back to the office.

"Patty, come on. Let's walk down to the courthouse and have a visit with the D.A.'s office about Kenny Peak."

"You want me to come? How come? Happy to, but how come?"

"As you well know, I usually do this old soft shoe by myself but on this one, I'd like you there. Need a second set of eyes and ears. Want to make sure as to what we hear and see. Fair enough?"

"Fair enough."

They go down the hill to the building and take the elevator up to the clerk's office to check the trial roster. Kenny was up first in two weeks. Time to tighten up the game plan and see if a deal could be worked.

Terrell and Patty arrive on the 5th floor and ask if Richard Lyle is in. He is and they are taken into a tired conference room, its walls ringed with numbered and dated file boxes, piled on one another so that their tops are caving in and their corners sagged. There is a scratched-up Formica-topped table and a gaggle of mismatched, ratty chairs. They sit and wait.

Friday Calls

"Classy, huh?" says Terrell to no one in particular.

Patty replies, "This place has never been anything but a dump."

Through the open door emerges Richard Lyle, followed by Paul Weinman.

"So, you don't find the inner chambers of our Palace of Justice to be worthy of Lady Justice's blind beauty." Lyle smiles thinly.

"Damn good thing she's blindfolded so she doesn't have to see this rat's nest." Terrell returns Lyle's flat amusement in kind.

Terrell says, "Y'all remember Patty Cherry here my long-suffering secretary, legal assistant, and Girl Friday..." Plenty of nods and handshakes all around. They all sit.

Lyle is a fine prosecutor, a veteran. Short, broad built, he can rough and tumble with the best of them. He smiles constantly, but the smile is a combination of the Cheshire Cat and a set of poorly fitted dentures that hurt with any movement. He is cocky, pugnacious, direct and overworked, a *Reader's Digest* of an Assistant District Attorney. A true believer, he is a left side of the courtroom lifer.

They all look at each other for a few seconds and then Lyle says, "Mr. Paul Weinman here thinks you've come to visit on the onerous matter of the premeditated killing Mr. Benjamin Winphrie by your client, Homer Kenny Peak. Would that be correct?"

"Yes," says Terrell. "May we talk plea bargain?"

"Maybe. But I caution you now, don't get greedy."

"What do you think we're looking for?"

"Ah, now, why don't you tell me what you're looking for and we'll go from there. You damn well know I'm not going to go bidding against myself."

Weinman nods, lending an unnecessary assent to a scripted dialogue sculpted decades ago. Richard Lyle's sidecar, he is being trained for the move upstairs from District Court to Superior in due time.

Terrell says, "Okay, let's start with this. We all know this is no more a Murder One case than I'm able to leap over tall buildings in a single bound."

"Not so fast, my friend. This surely is. Now, I'm not hunting the death penalty here and that's one hell of a concession in your favor, a big one and your boy ought to be grateful for that."

Terrell wanted to retort, Oh, bullshit, you were never going after the gas chamber on this one and you know it and so you've made no gift here, just typical hot air. But he didn't because it will just rile the little bull up and Terrell is there to see if he could make some headway.

"Well, Richard, we appreciate that, but I think the charge is still way over the top."

"Look, Eddie, here's the big picture. That big, threatening black buck took a pistol with malice aforethought and did intentionally shot and kill Mr. Winphrie. And at short, killing range. We've got a solid on the ground but a few feet away eyewitness. We know Peak was Winphrie's errand boy and we know that Peak was unhappy that Winphrie owed him money for tasks done. No matter what those atmospherics may be, that is Murder One."

"Richard, y'all don't even have the weapon."

"No matter. I've got the gun in his hand and Winphrie dead. Now, tell me what y'all are looking for." Lyle sits back, obdurate, arms folded across his banty rooster chest. Weinman parrots, following suit.

There will be little else coming from Lyle so Terrell decides to bottom fish, just to get Lyle going and to see if he can narrow the distance between life and less.

"Okay, Richard. You know there's a self-defense play in here on our side of it. Peak was just trying to protect himself. He was sure Winphrie was going to try and shoot him. He just acted in a split second. How about a max out on Involuntary Man with no credit for time served and you can box car the two Mary Jane beefs on top and that's getting Peak damn close to a solid three years.

Lyle waits for dramatic effect, his eyes lit up and he splutters, "Oh, for God's sake, do you really think I've gone over the bend already? Jesus Christ, Eddie! That's such a crock. No way! No! No way. No fucking way!! Are you gonna get serious real quick 'cause I already am and we're deep into time wasting time now. And sorry about the language, miss, but I expect it ain't the first time such has passed your ears... "

Patty laughs and nods. It was all a good show.

"Richard, really, how about you think about it? Really, I think we could get close to something if you'd get off the Big Red One."

"So, you're looking for some Two, right?"

"Not necessarily."

"But maybe...?"

Friday Calls

"Not necessarily..."

"Jesus Christ. No way he's going to dive into the pool of Voluntary Man. Not from this office."

"Not necessarily..."

"Okay, you're driving me nuts with the 'not necessarily' shit. I'm calling impasse here. You go talk to your client and if y'all can get reasonable, come back and see me. This one ain't exactly hard to try, you know."

"Well, I guess that cuts both ways. If you have further thoughts on the great strength of your prosecution, give me a call. I'll come running with baited breath."

"You ain't ever gonna change, are you, Eddie? You're always hunting soft landings. Sometimes, we gotta lock this kind of shit up."

Just for fun, Terrell deadpans, "Not necessarily..." and Lyle laughs. Weinman is a beat slow on the uptick, but does manage to fake a lame chuckle out.

They all stand, all smiles, all shake hands, all take their leave.

Terrell and Patty are starting back up the hill to the office. Patty asks, "So...?"

"I know how I'm gonna try this case. Lyle's right. We got a dead man and a fervent eyewitness. But, we got some stuff too. I think we can ultimately get into Murder Two range, but we're gonna have to try it to get there. Never can be sure but this Murder One charge looks soft to me. I'm gonna need to get Kenny's permission."

"Oh, okay...let's get it ready...make me a list."

"Sure. Yes. And I need to talk with Rise and Ben too. How about get them in tomorrow first thing. They've got a little work to do. And by the way, ain't no way Kenny is getting on the witness stand. He ain't sharp enough to head off Lyle. We'll talk about it. I think he'll understand. Like all of us, a man needs to know his limitations."

Patty laughs. "And when will that knowledge be coming to you?"

Rise and Ben sit in Terrell's office. Terrell had shut the doors. Terrell says, "How's business?"

Ben grins. "Now, you know we ain't gonna tell you 'bout none of our business but it would be fair to say business is good."

Terrell nods, pleased, has his fingers steepled.

"Good. Now, a few things. Three to be exact." He pauses to make sure they are paying close attention. "First, I need Rise to go see her brother and tell him that the prosecutor assigned to the case is a real ball buster and a real good one at that. I need him to become, shall we say, a bit fearful about this upcoming trial. Kenny has gotten a little slack sitting in the can, getting three squares a day without having to take a lot of shit from guys like Bo and each time I've been down to see him, he's been almost, well, almost boastful about how he's gonna tell everyone when the time comes about what a little punk shitass Bo was and that Bo was gonna try to kill him, but he beat him to the draw. And, boys and girls, that ain't gonna play. So, Rise, I need you to put some fear of God into him. You've been in the system. It ain't fairyland to you. You know. Heart-to-heart time, right?"

Rise nods, solemn.

"And, Rise, another thing. The prosecutor ain't gonna chase the death penalty here but he's still shooting for life in prison. We went over and had a talk with him and he's got a stick up his ass about this."

Ben says, "Ain't that some shit..."

Terrell replies, "...and more. We gotta play this careful. We are going to have to try this thing to get them to move, maybe move to something not so...uhm...harsh in terms of sentence. Go see him later today while all this is fresh in your head and then come back over here and let me know. Then, I'll go see him. And Rise, scare him good. The prosecutor will talk circles around him. He'll twist Kenny like a hog's tail. Kenny won't be able to keep up with him. There is real risk here."

Rise says, "What can you do? I know Kenny ain't smart. He ain't a good talker. He ain't quick."

Terrell says, "We are not gonna put Kenny on the witness stand. That just wouldn't work. You don't need to tell him that exactly. I will later, once he thinks it's his idea. Just get his attention real good so it'll soak into his big ol' sweet head."

Ben chuckles, "That's so. Boy's got a melon on his neck."

Rise shoots Ben a look and then leans forward toward Terrell. "I got it. What else?"

"Tell Kenny to keep on keeping his mouth shut. Don't say nothing about nothing to nobody. We don't need anyone down in that jug to find out that we have any worries."

Ben says, "Mr. Terrell, you got a plan?"

"Yes, it's coming together in my head. Not really sure what it looks like yet, but it's in there cooking along. When the time comes, it'll be there. And there is one other thing. Y'all know I bust my ass for y'all, right?"

They nod, strongly.

"Now, I have an idea. Y'all have paid me a nice retainer to help Kenny out. But we all agree, don't we, that it's nowhere close to what a normal, fair and square retainer would be for a murder case."

Rise says, "Yes."

"So I was thinking, it might be good business for us all if y'all were to start referring folks to me—you know, crimes, big, little crimes, car wrecks, people falling down in stores, anything and everything...do you see what I'm saying? And then, if the case came from y'all, there'll be finder's fees."

Ben says brightly, "Like kickbacks!"

"No. No. No. Nothing like that. We'd always call it business development and never anything but that. Do you understand?"

They both say, "Yes."

"And nobody else should ever know about this except the three of us, right? Y'all down with that? Y'all like that plan?"

They both say, "Yes."

"So we are agreed? Yes?"

"Yes."

"Good! Now, Rise, please get on over to the jail and help Kenny understand things and then let me know soon as you can."

"Right." And they are out the front door.

Patty comes in. "How'd it go?"

Terrell grins. "You know, Patty, if I didn't fly too close to the sun, I'd probably never get shit done."

Patty flat stares at him and laughs. "Just don't tell me. Thank God I have transferable skills. Damn, there just ain't no telling..."

Terrell said, "No, you are right. There ain't gonna be no telling."

Terrell sits at his desk reading Kenny's case file, ruminating on the large roll of the dice that is beginning to swell and bulge in his brain. He knows he has some margin for error, but the rails are pressing close, chaffing him. It is the rough caress of a lover who is going to take him hard and if he succumbs, the taking will not be gentle. But it also holds the promise of an exhaustive, beyond satisfying climax. He keeps pushing it away, trying to think of alternative ways to set the case up and for a good long time, he will succeed in making the distance and then it will come high-assed stalking and strutting back in, leggy and hot. He keeps thinking, *A pig gets fat and a hog gets slaughtered. A pig gets fat and a hog gets slaughtered...* And he keeps distilling it.

A wise old lawyer told him long ago, "Son, a case headed to trial is like a big funnel. You pour all the facts and law and people and maybes and prospects and mistakes and top cards in and it all swirls around and around and around as it heads toward the ever-thinning neck and when you do it enough and think about it enough, your case is going to spit its essence out at the tip. It may be a lot, it may be a few drops, but there's your case."

And that was staying in his mind too.

A car horn sounds sharp from the parking lot just beyond his window. He turns and Ben's big winged gleaming bronze like-a-kid's-baseball-trophy Caddy is idling just over the sprawling boxwoods that surround the place. The car's window eases down and Ben's big black hammer paw gives him the high sign. Terrell stands up and sees Rise just beyond Ben. She is giving a thumbs up. Terrell waves a quick salute at them and they drive away. He thinks, *They really are a pretty damn neat couple.*

And then, he sits down and doodles desultorily on a long, yellow legal pad, standard lawyer issue. And as he crosshatches and circles into more circles and writes his name over and over again and studies the art of it in the thick fountain pen ink. The beauty of it as it is his name, the name he owns. His mind settled, he opens the door and asks the stalking strumpet of risk to come in and sit and visit with him. He knows when she does they will soon be in the assembly of a fierce congress. If you want peace, prepare for war.

He walks out to Patty's office and says "Well, fuck it, the case is almost ready in my head. Let us say our prayers. I'm going to the jail. Not sure how long I'll be gone. Not too long I think..."

His voice tails off and empty-handed, he goes out the front door.

Patty calls, "Don't you want the file? A pad? Something?"

He shakes his head and walks down the hill, heads down as he thinks and thinks some more.

He walks in the jail, signs the log and is taken up to an interview room on the third floor.

Shortly, a deputy brings Kenny in. The deputy leaves and locks the door. Terrell gets up to check that the call intercom is off and locked. Terrell gestures for Kenny to sit down facing him. He speaks softly, leaning forward to Kenny.

"How you doing? We're getting close you know...?

"I'm okay. Getting a little scared, I guess. Rise came to see me. Told me that the D.A.'s office don't want to much deal, that they assigned a mean cocksucker to the case..."

Terrell silently thanks Rise for her imbedding vaccinating. He just looks at Kenny, saying nothing, face flat, expressionless.

"Mr. Eddie Terrell, what we gonna do? I'm worried about getting there and talking my story and then having that guy coming after me from lots of different directions...so what we gonna do...this first degree murder charge is bullshit but if they get me, they get me good." Kenny's face is knitted in apprehension.

Terrell leans even closer and says, "Kenny, here's what we are gonna do..."

Chapter Twenty-Five

Showtime

They are no longer in the on-deck circle. They are walking to the plate, a big bat of fact and bluff held to their side. Showtime in the Superior Court of Forsyth County, North Carolina, is here. The courtroom is full. People lean forward when Sweet Kenny, Kenny Maybe A Killer, Hulking Kenny is brought out by the bailiffs.

Kenny looks pretty good. Terrell and Patty have done a credible job of getting his sizes down close enough and had gone out to Belk's to gather up a blue blazer, a couple of white and blue shirts, some striped neckties, khaki pants, a belt, and brown lace-up shoes.

There are just two problems with his look. For all of his prepped-out crispness, a black now bespoked son of the Carolina underclass, he is still an enormous anomaly. One of the bailiffs quietly snort-taunts Terrell.

"Hell, Fast Eddie, you think that jury gonna buy let's play dress up? You can put all the lipstick you want on a pig but it's still a damn pig. Oink oink." Terrell has heard it before.

He grins and leans over.

"Deputy, it ain't lipstick. It's performance art. I ain't trying to turn him into Harry Belafonte. I'm just shading him to a more likeable tone. You know what the old Chinese proverb says?"

The deputy looks blank.

Terrell says, "Oh, never mind. I'm just looking to get one of two of them let their limbic eyes override their conscious brains."

Terrell says, "Oh, never mind. I'm just looking to get one of two of them let their limbic eyes override their conscious brains."

"Huh?"

"Sir, we will continue this later but I gotta go to work now." Terrell's eyes swivel.

"ALL RISE," thunders across the great room and there was the great shuffle-ruffle that happens when a hundred people lurch up from the benches in the unison of damn close to church.

The Honorable Douglas A. Albright is up on the bench. He is a big, powerful man, too, and his black robes unfurl like a well-packed 82nd Airborne parachute, something Albright well knew. He'd played football at Duke, then gone to Duke Law, then to Fort Bragg and Vietnam, come back, became an assistant and then Chief D.A. of the next county over. He was known to be relentless, a bulldog, and also a fair and smart one. He had the judicial "it." He did not suffer fools lightly. He suffered them not at all. A cracking pointed voice and a matinee idol handsome face gave him command of all arrayed before him.

Terrell loved trying cases before him.

Albright had a sly sense of subtle humor, possessed semaphore signal flashing eyes, was downright funny in chambers and looked after all lawyers in front of him as long as they respected their work and did it earnestly and well.

He was one of the reasons the law was a jealous mistress.

Albright, like the fine sky jumper he had been, swoops and swings like a huge, feathering bird of prey into his throne-like, high backed chair and cranes his head forward to survey the courtroom in fractions. First, the overlook to the large gallery beyond the bar, onlookers, spectators, gawkers, idle but interested lawyers, the flotsam and jetsam of a Tuesday morning.

The bailiff calls, "All rise! Oyez, oyez, oyez! This Honorable Court is now sitting here in Forsyth County, North Carolina, for the dispatch of the State's business. All who have business and proceedings with this court now draw near. The Honorable Douglas Albright of Guilford County presiding. God Bless this court and the state of North Carolina. Be seated. No talking!"

The eloquence of the presentation is but little weakened by the first grade admonition as to "no talking." Terrell silently laughs in his head, "At least he left out the no chewing gum part..." All seat themselves in the loud, precipitous rustle of a mass of bottoms and backs settling into the hard-backed benches.

Then Albright quick-scans the perimeter where court personnel and sheriff's deputies are sitting and standing, arrayed as living pieces on the chess board of Lady Justice's next game that will soon begin. Below and next to him are the witness stand, the court reporter, and the county clerk and his clerk.

Lastly, he brings his tight gaze to the fore, before the bar where the prosecutors, defense counsel, defendant and other witnesses and assisting staff gather in separate clutches at their large gleaming counsel tables. The board is properly and completely laid out.

Albright notes to no one in particular, "Well, good morning, gentlemen. Good morning, Mr. Defendant." He looks down at his papers. "Excuse me, Mr. Peak. Mr. Kenneth Peak. Good Morning, Mr. Peak."

Kenny beams.

"Gentlemen, I heard Motions and Pleas yesterday, heard them all day long until the sun was setting. As I recall, I heard nothing from any of you as to Motions and/or Pleas regarding the case styled as The State of North Carolina versus Kenneth Peak, a matter of first degree murder. Is that correct, gentlemen?

The lawyers stand, shuffle, nod. "That's correct, Your Honor."

"Further, I understand the State is not seeking the Ultimate Penalty, the Death Penalty. Is that correct?"

"It is, Your Honor."

"And there have been no recent discussions as to resolving the controversies at hand?"

"No, there have not been any such further discussions, Your Honor," says the prosecutor straight ahead.

Albright sees Terrell purse his lips and tilt his head into a flickering tremor of grimacing shake.

"Mr. Terrell?"

"Frustrating, Your Honor."

"Well. Well. Gentlemen, let's go to my chambers for a few minutes."

And they follow his billowing black robes out of the courtroom.

Friday Calls

"Okay, gentlemen, what's the story here?" Terrell begins to speak, but Albright's upraised palm seals him. "Prosecution first. Who speaks for the State? Richard or Buzz?"

Richard Lyle recites the State's position, the facts as he felt them to be.

"Plea discussions?" asks the judge.

Lyle says Terrell is greedy, that he is willing to go to a 2nd degree plea, but Terrell kept fishing for Involuntary, that that was not acceptable to the State.

Albright turns to Terrell, "Okay, Eddie, are you being greedy?" He smiles. He has been the interested moderator in these high-low principled quasi-debates for as long as he can remember.

Terrell lays out his side of it and notes that he feels like Peak was being badly overcharged, considering the evidence and that while he was willing to compromise, neither he nor his client were willing to take a three-mile walk off a one-mile dock.

Terrell then does something calculated. He quietly says, "Your Honor, this is just ridiculous." "Ridiculous" came out close to being a harsh spit.

It works. Richard Lyle's face began to redden. Lyle says, "It is not. Your Honor, you see, we have nothing further to talk about. Can we just get about trying our case?"

Albright looks them over, spends an extra second ask-looking Terrell, "Why'd you do that?" and then says, "Well, gentlemen, let's get to it. Back into the fires and we will see what we will see."

He holds the door to his chambers open for their file out, climbs the steps to his bench, rubs his hand together vigorously and calls, "All right now, bring us the panel of jurors."

Jury selection was efficient. The lawyers questioned the panel closely, trying to feed little bits of their case strengths into the dialogue.

"Now, if the evidence should show..."

"Would you be willing to consider..."

And of course, always, always the presumption of innocence.

To the epitome of the well-to-do little old white lady with her church clothes on and her purse clutching tight in her lap with the proper Chrysler in the garage, Terrell asks, "Now, Mrs. Bascomb. Yes, ma'am. Please follow me closely here. This is the most important, most important part of what we all here stand for, the foundation of this house of justice. Do you understand that my client, Mr. Kenny Homer Peak, is presumed completely and totally innocent as he sits here with us and will be for the duration of these important proceedings?" Terrell gestures at Kenny, moves his hands New Testament open with his eyes looking straight at her, then one by one to each person sitting on the panel.

Mrs. Bascomb nods, tentatively.

"Mrs. Bascomb. Is that a 'Yes'?"

"Yes," and then a little stronger, "Yes."

"Mrs. Bascomb, is it fair to say that even though you understand that Mr. Peak is charged with taking another man's life, that oftentimes in this life, in our lives there are circumstances, real circumstances that happen in the flash of an eye that provide an explanation as to why such a thing would come to pass. Do you understand that? Do you agree with that?"

"Why, yes, yes I do." With a firm commitment now. Terrell is inoculating them now. And there is nothing the District Attorney's office could object to. Terrell is wrapping them all in the flag, the Constitution, the Fourth of July Picnic and the Baby Jesus. It is his courtroom, he owns it and Judge Albright is going to help him when the claim is soon to come for his property.

"Mrs. Bascomb, does Mr. Peak frighten you? He's a big man. He's had a rough life. You'll hear all that soon enough. Are you in fear being here near him? Does he worry you?"

Judge Albright leans back in his high backed chair, rocks and watches.

"Well, yes, at first now I was a little worried. He is a very big man. We know he's charged with something real serious. But not so much now. He looks nice. I'm fine."

Terrell makes a mental note to send Mrs. Bascomb roses.

The give and take of the voir dire, the to speak, to see, continues back and forth, each side trying to mentally wrestle individual members of the panel into some comfort with one side of it or the other.

The prosecution dismisses any black person on the panel with the thinnest of reasons. The rationale of course is that the races hang together. There is no prohibition in doing such. It just smells to high heaven.

The prosecution also lose a few men and one woman who are adamant that they couldn't sit in judgment of such a thing, one nigra shooting another nigra in a nigra drink house in the middle of the night in nigra town while lots of other nigras were dancing and drinking and carousing as nigras will always do on pay day. Their shared dismissive vehemence as to the idea of nigra innocence and circumstances are so blatant that Judge Albright dismisses them for cause. They cannot exercise thoughtful and independent judgment. They are poisonous and are shown the door.

The prosecutors think, Why couldn't they have just kept their mouths shut. Instead they fed off one another...

And as always, the process winds down, the prosecution jettisons those they feel are going to align with the large, black man. The defense tosses overboard the conservatives, the law and order lookers, the suit and ties. And what is left was a bland, unknown clot of white people, an amorphous knot...of what? Truth be told, no one knew. Mrs. Bascom made it. She was so sweetly fair, for the prosecution to ditch her would make them look expansively unfair. But Terrell is no fool. He holds no hopes that Mrs. Bascom can guide or captain the Not Guilty boat—she is too nice.

And thus a jury is efficiently seated. Terrell has held all of his cards back. And even as he did, he draws more. Cut the cards, split the deck, I'll take my chances.

Terrell loves courthouses, especially the dull hallways and small meeting rooms off those dull hallways that connected to courtrooms where live-fire trials happened. Those spaces are always lined and often filled with milling disparate herds of people, all of whom either smoked or smelled of something or other. The ceiling tiles had long since gone nasty yellow-gray and the silver haze of a hundred burning cigarettes gleamed beneath the fluorescent lights, waves in an ocean of babble. The halls are full of uniforms, plain clothes, lawyers, clerks, assistants, runners, social workers, probation and parole officers, witnesses, pass through types, the lost, the curious, the sneaks, the bums, the thrill-seekers, the weirdos, the observers and so many more. It is a menagerie of types, louts to lords.

There is no security. Anyone can get back in there and often everyone did. Terrell has been taught early on to get to the courthouse early and watch the dynamics, the interactions between people. Listen. Listen all the time. Filter out the chit-chat from the meat on the bone. Watch and watch a little more. Terrell is so happy in these corridors.

Terrell had come early and is happy this particular day too, yet he is apprehensive. It is beginning.

"Ladies and gentlemen of the jury," says Judge Albright. "You have been sworn in and empaneled. Our proceedings will now commence. Please give your full attention to the lawyers. District Attorney Lyle will give the opening statement for the State. Mr. Edward Terrell will then give the opening statement on behalf of his client, Mr. Kenneth Peak. Opening statements are not facts. Rather, they are the laying out of the positions of each side, a roadmap, if you will, as to what course the trial of this case may take. We will then begin to hear from witnesses. Gentlemen, please proceed."

Lyle walks briskly before the jury, squares his shoulders and explains the act and the charges. He is simple, straightforward. Anyone can tell he is angry, in a feisty mood. He closes by pointing at Kenny Peak saying, "We will show you this man, this Kenny Peak, is manifestly guilty of the first degree murder of Benjamin Winphrie." He whirls and sits down. He spoke for less than five minutes.

Slowly, almost languidly, Terrell rises, stands behind counsel table and his client, steeples his hands as if in prayer and then puts one each on Kenny's broad shoulders. He speaks softly, in a kindly fashion.

"Folks, Mr. Lyle is a fine prosecutor. But he has left a lot out of his story, the story he has just told you. So we will soon begin to show you all sorts of things that will show you Kenny Peak is not guilty of something so awful, so ghastly as first degree murder. And we will do so quickly and efficiently. Thank you."

And Terrell sits down and Judge Albright says, "Call your first witness."

The State calls Detective Samuel Wilkins to the stand to be sworn in.

And Terrell thinks, If we're gonna pull this rabbit out of the hat, we gotta do it fast.

Lyle walks Wilkins through who he was, his job description, when he got the call, who Miller, his junior partner was, when they arrived, what did they see, who did they talk to, what statements did they take, when and where did they take Peak into custody, how he was processed, what their follow-up was, what the basis of the charges were and everything else Lyle felt is necessary to get the elements of premeditated homicide nailed to the courtroom wall.

Then Lyle says brusquely, "Your witness."

"Thank you, Mr. Lyle. Mr. Wilkins, where this happened is called a drink house, right?" asks Terrell.

"Yes," Wilkins says tersely.

"A drink house is an illegal establishment, it sells alcohol illegally? Lots of drugs too, right?"

"Well, yes, well, sometimes."

"Mr. Wilkins, let's set this straight for this jury. Drink houses exist for one purpose: to sell alcohol illegally and to sell illegal drugs, marijuana, cocaine, heroin; all on a cash, no taxes paid, basis. Isn't that right?"

"Well, yes," Wilkins grudges.

"There are how many drink houses in this city?"

"I'm not sure."

"Mr. Wilkins, you and your partner Mr. Miller have routinely and regularly patrolled and worked these areas for many, many years now? Right?"

"Yes."

"Are there more than ten of them in East Winston? More than twenty?"

"Uh...yes."

"More than thirty?"

"Probably."

"You can identify each and every one of them by sight, can't you?"

"Well. Yes."

"In all your and Mr. Miller's time on the police force, have you ever pressed criminal charges to have any of them, just one of them, closed down?"

Lyle pipes up, "Objection!"

"Overruled. Please proceed, Mr. Terrell," says Judge Albright.

Lyle sits down, grumpy. Miller is restless on the bench behind him.

"Have you?"

"Uhm, well, no."

"So, you on behalf of the citizens of Winston-Salem and Forsyth County, allow these places of drug dealing and illegal alcohol and taxes avoided to just go on and on, right?"

"Well, they don't cause a lot of trouble."

"Answer my question, please. You let them operate illegally and let them do so on the taxpayer's dime, right?"

He mutters a resigned, "Yes."

"Now, in this drink house where this incident is supposed to have happened, you know that the decedent Ben Winphrie was better known to you in law enforcement as Bo Diddley, isn't that right?"

"Yes."

"And old Bo Diddley was very well known to y'all as a fellow with a long and busy criminal record, that he was often antagonistic, that he often carried a weapon, that he was a dealer of drugs and other illegal things, right?"

Lyle shouts, "Objection!"

"Overruled." Lyle sits, slumping a bit now. Miller is looking down, picking at his cuticles.

"And y'all knew that old Bo Diddley was a well-known criminal presence here in Winston-Salem, right?"

"Yes."

"And y'all knew that he was part-owner, part manager of this particular drink house, right?"

"Well, yes, we think that's right."

"You think? Don't you know for sure?"

"Well, we're pretty sure."

"So we have a fellow, Bo Diddley, with an extensive, often violent criminal past, running an illegal drug and drink house? Right?"

"Yes," Wilkins says flatly.

"Now, my client Kenny Peak over here does not have an extensive record like Bo Diddley did, right?"

"Right, just a couple a misdemeanor marijuana charges."

"Nothing violent?"

"No."

"Kenny Peak is charged with premeditated intent in the killing of Bo Diddley, right?"

"Yes."

"Have you identified any witness, any person, any human being who will come before us today and will tell us of Mr. Peak's stated intent to so act?"

"No."

"You know Bo Diddley regularly carried a small pistol, a derringer on his person and often threatened others with it? Right?"

"Well, I've heard that..."

Lyle and Miller are shaking their heads. Weinman is staring a hole in the wall across from him.

"Your only eyewitness, Miss Felicia Lineberger, was Bo Diddley's girlfriend and cribmate, right?

"Objection!"

"Sustained as to cribmate." Albright smiles and says, "Come on, Mr. Terrell, you can do better than that."

The jury chuckles, Terrell smiles and nods. "Yes, Your Honor. May I please continue?"

"Proceed on."

The prosecution table was taking on the visage of Mount Rushmore, etched into a grimacing stone.

"What was the age difference between Bo Diddley and his girlfriend Felicia, and by the way, she's here in the courtroom today, isn't she?"

"Uh, yes she is. I recall the age difference is a little more than twenty some-odd years."

"And she was seventeen when this happened, right?"

"Uh, I think that is right, close enough."

"And you and your partner interviewed her again earlier this morning for what, the fourth time since this happened, right?"

"Yes." It was beginning to dawn on Wilkins that he wasn't going to be allowed to spit the bit; that he was just going to have to take the beating.

"Now, she told you that Bo owed Kenny money and that Bo often referred to Kenny as a, please excuse me, a 'dumb nigger' right?"

"Well, yes, we knew that."

"She says she saw four shots, four flashes come from the .38 caliber pistol that she says Mr. Peak was carrying, right? You've read the transcript of the preliminary hearing that was earlier held in this matter where Felicia so testified under oath. That those four shots came at virtually point blank range?"

"Yes."

"Was that .38 caliber weapon recovered?"

"No."

"Were any weapons recovered at the scene?"

"Well, there was a shotgun..."

"Was Bo Diddley wounded by a shotgun blast?"

"No?"

"So the shotgun recovered has absolutely nothing to do with this case."

"Well, that's true."

"And no weapons of any other type were recovered, right?"

"That's right."

"Now, Bo Diddley's body was carried by a number of individuals a couple of hundred yards up the hill to a church where it was placed between two gravesites, isn't that right?"

"Yes."

"Did you ever identify who any of those folks were that did the carrying?"

"No. Nobody knows anything."

"You knew that Bo Diddley always carried a large roll of cash with him, right?"

"Yes."

"Yet when y'all finally found Bo Diddley's body, you didn't find that cash, did you?"

"No."

"And you didn't recover his derringer pistol either, did you?"

"No, we didn't."

"Fair to think that some person or persons liberated those items from Mr. Bo Diddley's person while he traveled from the drink house to the graveyard?"

"Well, it's possible..." Wilkins voice is beginning to trail off and begins to look around. He asks for a drink of water. Terrell gets it for him.

"Now, you found no weapon on Kenny Peak when you took him into custody, right?"

"Well, he had a pocket knife on him and a bag of marijuana too." Wilkins is trying to be gratuitous.

"Let's see, the pocket knife has nothing to with this, right?"

"True."

"And neither does the marijuana, right?"

"True."

"Now, Felicia Lineberger has consistently told you that Kenny Peak shot four shots at Bo Diddley, right?"

"And that they all came from the .38 caliber pistol he had, right?"

"Yes."

"Have you or your partner Mr. Miller ever interviewed a Mr. Pete Miller or a Mr. David Edwards about what went on at the drink house that night?"

"Uhm, no, we haven't."

"You learned that they were both present that night and that they both were said to have weapons on their persons that night."

"Yes."

"Were Kenny Peak's hands and clothing ever tested for gunpowder residue?"

"No."

"Why not?"

"We didn't think it was necessary."

A couple of the jurors have started looking about quizzically. A couple are shaking their heads.

"Oh, by the way, this drink house was burned completely to the ground by a probable arsonist within hours of this incident we are here in court about. Is that right?"

"Yes."

"That happened while Kenny Peak was in your custody, right? So he could not have burned it down, right?"

"That's true."

"Why do you think the drink house was torched? Who would have the motive to do that?"

"I don't know."

"Well, what do you think?"

"We just don't know..."

Terrell gives one of those gentle "y'all don't know much of anything" looks.

"Now, who is Dr. George Podgorny?"

"He is the Chief Medical Examiner at the Department of Forensic Pathology at the Wake Forest Medical School at Baptist Hospital."

"He is the man who did the full and complete autopsy of Bo Diddley, right?"

"Yes."

"He is highly respected by your department and has been for years, correct?"

"Yes."

"Have you interviewed him about this?"

"No, my partner Miller went by and saw him."

"When was that? Before or after he had completed his autopsy?"

"Uhm, it was early on, so I recall it was before he had completed it. But we did get his report."

"Have you reviewed the report with Dr. Podgorny?"

"No, but I did review it with others in the D.A.'s office."

"When is the last time you reviewed it?"

"Oh, a couple of weeks ago."

"Did it tell you that four .38 caliber slugs were found in Bo Diddley's body?"

"Uhm, no."

"Did it tell you that Bo Diddley's death was caused by a sole .38 caliber bullet?"

Terrell is now peering at the report over the top of his glasses. The prosecutors are all looking at their copy, heads together. Miller is picking his cuticles more vigorously now.

"Uhm, not exactly."

"What does mean Mr. Wilkins? Not exactly? Mr. Wilkins, they never recovered any .38 caliber bullet, did they?"

"Objection."

"Sustained. One question at a time Mr. Terrell. Proceed."

"Yes, Your Honor. They never found a .38 caliber slug or bullet did they?" asks Terrell.

"No. But there was a wound that seemed to have the configuration of a .38."

"Yes, that's the wound that was a flesh would; it entered his upper right arm above the bicep and exited through his upper right shoulder. It was found to have nicked the very upper portion of Bo Diddley's right lung lobe. Isn't that right?"

"Yes, I recall that it is."

"And Mr. Wilkins, Dr. Podgorny never told you or Mr. Miller or wrote in his complete autopsy report that that wound was the killing wound, did he?"

"Well, no, he didn't." The jury is now restive, shifting about, leaning forward.

"Now, how many other wounds did Dr. Podgorny report?"

"Uhm...three..." Wilkins looks around, looks at Judge Albright. Albright looks away.

"There was a .45 caliber wound in Bo Diddley's mid sternum, his breastbone that tore through his large central artery, transversed his right lung's full length and rested in his right kidney, having torn its kidney capsule. Isn't that right? "

"Yes."

"That according to Dr. Podgorny's official report is the most likely killing wound, isn't it?"

"Yes," Wilkins responds low and slow.

"And that's not all, is it?"

"No."

"There were two other wounds weren't there, both of which could have been killing wounds, both of which according to Dr. Podgorny were surely contributory in Bo Diddley's death. These were both .22 caliber bullets, Saturday Night Specials y'all call them, right?"

"Yes."

"One went through his left kidney and his mesentery intestines, where they are attached to his abdominal cavity wall. The other went through his right hip and through his right kidney. Isn't that right?"

"Yes."

"So on the evening in question, Bo Diddley was shot four times with maybe a .38, surely a .45 and two .22s, right?"

"Yes."

"And the killing shots, the killing wounds came from the .45 and the .22s, right?"

"Yes, it looks that way."

"And the four angles of entry are from all different directions, not just straight on as Miss Lineberger has earlier testified to."

"Yes."

"Your one and only eyewitness, Miss Felicia Lineberger sitting over there in the back of the courtroom, has never told anyone that Mr. Kenny Peak used multiple weapons in blazing away at Bo Diddley, has she?"

"No."

Now, time for the "can't lose" question, thinks Terrell. No matter how he answers it, Wilkins will take on more water below the hull line and he can't bail fast enough to save his hide.

"Now, Mr. Wilkins, does it occur to you after we've been through all this that maybe, just maybe you've got the wrong guy?"

Wilkins looks up at the ceiling and takes it for the team.

"We've got the right guy." The jury shakes its collective head.

Terrell steps behind counsel table and shuffles some papers. Then courtroom is quiet. Judge Albright says, "Mr. Terrell, do you have anything more for this witness?"

"Yes, I do, Your Honor."

"Proceed."

The prosecution table is glum. Kenny Peak sits stone still.

"Mr. Wilkins. You and your partner Mr. Miller were standing in the back hall this morning,

smoking cigarettes and talking. Do you remember doing that?"

Warily, Wilkins looks at Miller. "Yes, yes I do."

"Do you remember talking about Mr. Bo Diddley?"

"Well, yes."

"Do you recall that I was standing just across from you?"

"No."

"Would it help your memory if I told you I was reading the newspaper, had it open so it covered my face?"

Wilkins nods slowly. "If you say so."

"I do say so. Now, tell the jury what you said about Bo Diddley's death."

"I don't recall."

"Well again, let me see if I can help you refresh your memory. Did you not say that Mr. Bo Diddley was a worthless piece of shit and that Kenny Peak performed a public service for the citizens of Winston-Salem and Forsyth County by blowing his sorry criminal ass away."

"Uhm…"

"Do you deny saying that?"

"No."

Judge Albright is crimson glaring at Wilkins. The prosecution table is stricken. Kenny Peak's eyebrows are knitted up.

Terrell says, "That's all I have for this witness unless further new subjects are elicited by the D.A.'s office on any re-direct."

Lyles stands, "Nothing further, Your Honor. May the witness please be excused, Your Honor?"

Judge Albright stands abruptly.

"No, he is to stay here. In this courtroom with his partner. We are in recess. I want all the lawyers in my chambers now."

Judge Albright is livid.

"Richard Lyles, that's the sloppiest thing I have ever seen. What's your offer now?"

"Well, Your Honor, we think…"

Albright cuts him off. "No, I think your thinking is that there should be a plea to Involuntary Man, max of five years, three of which suspended, credit for time served, both marijuana charges dropped, fine and fees waived."

Albright turns quickly on Terrell. "Now don't get cocky. Your man obviously had a gun and did some shooting in there along with God knows who else. Yes, I'm throwing the ridiculous Murder One charge out, but would charge the rest and if the jury did something weird, I'd have to pop him with a bunch more than what I've laid out here. Richard, you're a fine prosecutor, one the best, but every now and then, a turd shows up in the punchbowl of life. I think the deal I have proposed is fair."

"You?"

"Yes Your Honor."

"Terrell, nice work, but you got real lucky. Go out there and sell the deal to your man. Remember what they say…"

"Yes, Your Honor, A pig gets fat and a hog gets slaughtered."

And within minutes, the deal is done.

Judge Albright takes Kenny Peak's plea, Kenny is walked back to the holding cell after hugging Terrell and Patty and smiling broadly at anyone within his orbit. Terrell and Patty head back to the office. There is work waiting.

Epilogue

Mary Sue Martin's parents moved to Charlotte. Mr. Martin took a job selling used cars.

Quality Textiles kept going and growing.

Georgia beat North Carolina 27-13 in their football game.

Louise eventually steadied herself somewhat and lived with her pain in a hazy, occasionally good-natured dignity.

Terrell bought Lee Ann a drink, and then another. Patty tried with minimal success to minimize his distractions.

Kenny got out in due time and ended up with a little lawn service operation. His regular customers included Terrell's grandmother.

Rise and Ben stayed busy.

Curt Minor stayed in business.

PeeWee remained in Baltimore working with some serious dealers.

And Harry Davis sat in his chair, waiting for the phone to ring.

Author's Note

For years, people have been telling me to write a book. So I did.

This is predominantly a work of fiction which surrounds a couple of very large truths. Some of these folks in here are real. Some are not. If you ask me, maybe I'll tell you about some of it and some of them.

And, if you have come this far, it should be interesting to note that Freedom of Information Act inquiries of the Guilford County Sheriff's Department, the North Carolina Highway Patrol, and the Greensboro Police Department involved in "the automobile matter," were replied to with "We have nothing." The same response was received from the history archives of Norfolk and Southern Railroad. There are also no records as to any of this at the Forsyth County Courthouse. It seems back in those days, a carcass could be picked and bleached almost totally clean. "Curiouser and curiouser" indeed!

CPSIA information can be obtained
at www.ICGtesting.com
Printed in the USA
LVHW041210260720
661543LV00006B/66/J